Acclaim for Monique Charlesworth's

The Children's War

"Gutsy. . . . Charlesworth's novel holds its own in [a] distinguished crowd [of literature on World War II], in part because the characters are drawn with such precision. . . . Without describing a single battle, it captures the essence of the war and the wrecked lives of so many who survived it. . . . Beautiful and heartbreaking."
—*Fort Worth Star-Telegram*

"A five-star read from start to finish, Charlesworth's book ranks with the best of illustrious historical writers." —*Edge* (Boston)

"Charlesworth explores the lives of ordinary people and young children caught in a war they may or may not have believed in—a war from which they were powerless to escape for it followed and found them no matter where they tried to hide." —*Milwaukee Journal Sentinel*

"*The Children's War* is that rare fiction that has the feel of actual life. Once I became engaged by the child Ilse's perilous journey through the Nazi occupation, I was compelled to escort her to safety. This is a beautifully composed book of past terror that calls to us during our present international peril." —Laura Shaine Cunningham,
author of *Sleeping Arrangements* and *Dreams of Rescue*

"[An] impeccably researched novel. . . . Charlesworth describes [the war] with singular power and imaginative reach. . . . This suspenseful and beautifully written work about the Second World War will inevitably give rise to reflections not only about the story it ostensibly recounts, but also about today's children of war."
—*The Globe and Mail* (Toronto)

MONIQUE CHARLESWORTH

The Children's War

Monique Charlesworth was born in Birkenhead, England, and has lived in France and Germany. She began writing fiction while living in Hong Kong and is the author of three previous novels. She has worked as a journalist and as a screenwriter for both film and television. She lives with her husband and two children in London.

The
Children's War

The Children's War

MONIQUE CHARLESWORTH

ANCHOR BOOKS

A Division of Random House, Inc.

New York

FIRST ANCHOR BOOKS EDITION, SEPTEMBER 2005

The Library of Congress has cataloged the Knopf edition as follows:
Charlesworth, Monique, [date]
The children's war / Monique Charlesworth. —1st American ed.
p. cm.
1. World War, 1939–1945—Children—Fiction. 2. World War, 1939–1945—France—Paris—
Fiction. 3. World War, 1939–1945—Germany—Hamburg—Fiction. 4. Hamburg
(Germany)—Fiction. 5. Paris (France)—Fiction. 6. Jewish girls—Fiction. 7. Boys—Fiction.
I. Title.
PR6053.H37218C47   2004
823'.914—dc22
2004040815

Anchor ISBN: 1-4000-3207-5

Book design by Soonyoung Kwon

www.anchorbooks.com

Printed in the United States of America
10 9 8 7 6 5 4 3 2

For Alex, Sophie and Jonathan

The
Children's War

ONE

Marseilles, March 1939

Ilse held her suitcase safe between her knees. There was a continuous loud crackle of announcements, which she could not understand. After an hour she moved to the corner seat beside the frosted glass window, for this gave an angled view of the Gare St. Charles. There she watched the constant flickering of single and multiple blurs against the yellow advertisement for Amer Picon. Any one of those blurs might open the door from the huge vault of the station and solidify into the person collecting her. This was distracting. Each time the door opened and it was not for her, she could not settle. In the guidebook, the tour of Marseilles occupied twelve pages, whereas Paris took up thirty-three. Marseilles was a mighty port, the oldest of the cities of France. Ilse shut her eyes and conjured up the map of the harbour which, facing west, was defended by its two great forts, Saint-Jean, to the north, and Saint-Nicolas, to the south. How happy her mother had been to find a guide-book in French in the tiny foreign-language section of the Wuppertal public library.

Greeks from Asia Minor had landed here twenty-six centuries ago, dark men in galleys with long oars. Centuries passed. Another hour went by. The city of enthusiasms welcomed the revolution, sent five hundred volunteers to Paris. The soldiers from Marseilles electrified the crowd with their rendition of a new marching song. It became the hymn of the revolution and was renamed in their honour. The guidebook had printed all the verses. She sang them in her head: the day of glory has arrived. People came and were collected and were replaced. Yawning, she feared to sleep. Marseilles, she recited to herself, is the great western emporium for trade with the Levant, importer of grains, sugar, peanuts, copra and Indian corn. How hungry she was. The big boy with the scuffed shoes unwrapped and ate his picnic, shovelling bread into his mouth. The woman with two small children went away to the café and then returned with chocolate bars. But Ilse did not move. What if the Red Cross woman came and did not find her there? Her legs felt funny, tingling with pins and needles but also very soft. Anxiety blurred the din, sharpened the ceaseless turning and returning of the same thoughts. Her head jerked up as once more the door opened abruptly, letting in a swell of noise.

It was a short woman with dark hair dyed blond. "Du bist Ilse,"* she said. She was not German. Ilse stood, a little wobbly. Certainty, which should have brought relief, was worrying. How had she recognised her? The Red Cross woman beckoned to Ilse to come nearer. She smelt of sweat, her pink face thickly powdered. With a pencil, she trailed down her typed list and crossed off Ilse's name, scoring it deeply. "Come! Hurry you along!" she said in an odd mixture of German and French.

They hurried through to daylight and dust and wind. A huge flight of steps led past massive statues down to a boulevard. There was a hotel opposite and the sprawling city below, a patch of green to one side. Ilse noticed some young children playing and paused just for an instant but the woman (red woman, cross woman) hurried her on. They were to take a taxi. As she opened the door, the woman told the driver to go straight to the ship's offices and to take the most direct way. She was disinclined to talk, which seemed to Ilse a great pity and an opportunity missed. Wriggling forward in the seat, the woman took off her jacket and eased her feet out of her shoes, as though she was on her own. How

*"You are Ilse."

busy she must be, to need this moment so badly. Her feet were swollen with angry-looking bunions, the blouse ringed with sweat stains under the arms. She studied the list, which was typed on both sides of the piece of paper, as she bit at ragged cuticles. Her hands looked raw and used. Perhaps she went back and forth all day, shuttling unknown children on and off boats, to and from stations. Ilse hoped so. She badly wanted a companion.

Jolted against the acrid odour of sweat and perfume on the turns, Ilse looked in vain for traces of the great trading city. There was no sight of the world-famous Canebière ("broad boulevard at the heart of Marseilles where those touring Provence must choose to stay; site, in more turbulent times, of a permanent guillotine"). She saw unremarkable streets full of people and trolley cars and trees whipped by the wind. She tried to see the street names, for the French loved liberty, equality and fraternity. Every town in France boasted a street named after deputy Mirabeau, a Jean Jaurès or a Garibaldi. Her mother had explained that France honoured great men who fought for freedom, even the foreign ones. There could never be a Hitlerplatz here. This was why everyone loved France. Hard as she tried, squinting against the light, the streets reeled by much too fast for her to read the names. But for the dirt and the names of the shops, it might have been Düsseldorf. They turned into smaller and darker streets. There was still no sign of the sea but she had smelt it in the sharpness of the wind; she felt its nearness in the way the streets all hurried down towards the water.

She cleared her throat and spoke in her careful French. "Can we go to Notre-Dame-de-la-Garde? From the peak, one can admire the view of the town and the Mediterranean."

"What?"

"A church. It is called Notre-Dame-de-la-Garde."

"You want a church?" said the woman, giving her a curious, sidelong look.

"There is a lovely panorama over the sea," persisted Ilse. The steeple, with its gilded ten-metre-high Virgin, rose fifty metres above the hill. The guidebook said that it was the Virgin who kept the city safe.

"Ah no, there is no time. It's the opposite way," she said.

Ilse had the timetable of her long journey firmly fixed in her head. She knew that she had hours to spare. She looked at the woman and the way her fingers ripped at each other, and her turned-away face.

They turned into a square and then the taxi drew up at a big cream building. The woman told the driver to wait. A queue spilled onto the street. The woman forced her way inside in the face of protests, tugging Ilse behind her. She cast one look at the room, which was packed with people, and pushed Ilse on, one hand in the small of her back, not unkindly but firmly.

"These people are waiting for the boat to Oran. You'll go from La Joliette. That's the new port. You can walk to the dock from here. Go with the others. You understand?"

Ilse nodded.

She watched the short figure stumping out to disappear into the haze, the last link in the human chain that had moved her to this place. She knew that the woman was supposed to see her onto the boat. Sitting on the suitcase, Ilse was level with the legs shuffling towards the ticket office. She had been wrong to mind the smell of sweat. The Red Cross woman was the sort of person whose kindness was all used up in her work, leaving nothing over for conversation, no space into which other people might intrude. She would probably never talk to the children she took from place to place. Ilse thought with regret that she had had her opportunity to see Marseilles and she had sat in the station and not taken it. From Strasbourg to here, she had crossed the whole of France without even drinking a cup of the prized French coffee: for this she had nobody but her stupid self to blame. It was nearly three o'clock. French people took two or three hours for lunch. The tables at the charming seafront restaurants would still be full. Her mother had told her how to order food in a proper restaurant and had recommended the bouillabaisse. She would have undertaken any of the excursions her mother and she had planned, had they been offered. But Ilse was incapable of leaving this room, where she had been told to remain, to go to an unknown café, however near.

Weeks ago, her mother had bought a berth in a four-person cabin in a cruiser, a white ship which would set sail from the harbour built by the Romans as the sun set. Big though the ship would be, it hardly seemed possible that all these people could get cabins. They looked hard-pressed and too poor for a luxury cruise. The woman at the guichet was bad-tempered and snapped at anyone who showed the slightest impatience with her. Every berth was taken. There was space on deck. She shrugged her shoulders. If they didn't want this boat, then they could take the next. For you to choose, she said. But it would be just as crowded if not more so. One or two went away. Most just bought tickets.

Her stomach rumbled. There would be dinner on the boat, perhaps at the captain's table. Because it was such an expensive journey all the meals were included. Conversation would be animated and pleasant, and the captain would salute his guests in champagne, making toasts to every one of them. "A votre santé, Monsieur le Capitaine." "Et à la vôtre!"

The people waiting did not look as if they were the kind who dressed for dinner and she felt embarrassed in advance for them, for the awkwardness when they found out. Her good dress was at the top of the case, and she hoped it was not too crushed.

At six o'clock a man in a blue official-looking jacket opened the double doors at the back of the room. The crowd pushed forward. A short walk from the back of the building lay the sea, which was not blue at all but nearly black. The wind blew hard and she held her coat together to keep warm. From the quay she saw that despite the pretty name, the *Belle de France* was not a cruise ship but a ferryboat. Streaks of rust lay down the funnels. There could be no sun loungers on this deck, no pursers in white uniforms. There was no first class. She had been told to find a steward who would have a passenger list and tell her where to go, but no such person seemed to exist.

The decks were already full of people who had no berths, who lay or squatted on the floor and should have been unhappy, but had a kind of ease. Men in long gowns with dark faces and sandals were smoking strong-smelling cigarettes. These were probably Berbers, natives of Morocco. One man gave her a welcoming smile. Coffee-coloured, he was beautiful with eyes of a miraculous, deep blue. She was not to smile back. Her mother had been very clear about whom to talk to (almost nobody) and when (only when essential).

It was stuffy down below, where a long snail of passengers trailed down corridors all carrying luggage and looking for their cabins. Ilse held her suitcase in her arms as a buffer before her and followed the others. People argued. Nobody knew where to go. The names of the passengers were handwritten on slips of paper pasted outside the cabin doors, so each door created another obstacle in this already crowded place. Ilse reminded herself that those like her, shuffling from corridor to corridor, sidestepping and stumbling with their luggage and fighting to see the scraps of paper, were the lucky ones. They would have a bed to sleep on. Mademoiselle Blumenthal's berth was at the very end of the corridor a further floor down; there seemed no way that fresh air could penetrate these depths. She read a French name and two more German-sounding ones, a Madame Ginsberg and a Mademoiselle Tischler. The door was open: a nun sat on a bunk reading. A fat middle-aged lady wearing a lace blouse sat on the other side with suitcases piled beside her, with eyes closed. When Ilse knocked, she gave a start.

"Bonjour, Mesdames," she said quietly. A lucky chance had allocated her the top bunk. She lifted up her suitcase and heaved it up, then scrambled up after it. She had not had a space of her own for days. There was a little net on the side, which would be a good place to put her book, her own light switch and a hook for her coat. The blanket was folded in a neat way and perhaps the sheet was clean. She hung up her coat and lay down, and through her trembling legs and the heaviness of her head, which was now aching quite hard, she felt deep relief at being in the precise place which her mother had selected for her. With her eyes closed, she could almost see her mother's face.

"Are you Mademoiselle Blumenthal?" The fat German lady stood in the middle of the cabin, beaming and looking at her.

Ilse said that she was.

"Miriam Ginsberg, very pleased to meet you."

She stared too hard. Ilse wondered if she had a smut on her nose. She rubbed it, unobtrusively, checked that her hands were clean.

"My dear. You won't fall down, will you?"

Ilse said that she was fine. She opened the case, took out *Winnetou* and hid behind it.

"What are you reading?"

She held up the book politely.

"Isn't that a book for boys?"

She shook her head, concentrated and read on. A tall, thin woman came in and the fat lady whispered something and then introduced her as her sister, Fräulein Tischler. The sister, who had a sweet smile, held out her hand. Ilse climbed down, did her curtsy, offered her hand and climbed back up again. The thin one whispered through one cupped hand to the fat one, something that Ilse had been taught was extremely rude and quite unnecessary when a person was not even looking in their direction. She turned on one side and read on, facing the wall. If she remained that way round and kept her head down, she could avoid seeing them.

Old Shatterhand, feigning timidity, said he could not swim and asked how deep the water was. The Indians despised this. When kicked into it by Intshu-tshuna, he threw up his hands and dropped into the water with a show of terror. Once in the element he knew so well, everything changed. Like an otter he swam under the cold water, holding his breath, surfacing at the overhang on the opposite bank where there was just room for a man to lift up his face and breathe, and the chance that he would not be seen. It was a daring and a courageous plan.

"Would you like to come and sit with us? It's much more comfortable down here."

"No, thank you."

The Indians had believed his show of fear, despising him, and now they stood, amazed, scanning the waters and wondering where he had gone. With lungs full, Old Shatterhand slid down into the water again and swam with powerful strokes on to the distant bank. The water eddied and flowed, and the Indians stared. By now, surely, he was dead.

"Are you hungry?"

Ilse turned round. Miriam Ginsberg's eyes were big and brown, her hair done in plaits coiled about her head, lipstick disappearing into the furrows round her mouth.

"I'm going to eat in the restaurant later, Frau Ginsberg," she said.

"The restaurant! I don't think you'll find one on this old tub." The face withdrew.

Ilse forced herself to read every word of passages she knew by heart. Anticipation, especially this kind, was so much more interesting than surprise. Most surprises, at any rate those she had experienced, had nothing pleasant in them at all. The scraping sound was the suitcase being pushed from side to side, the clicking was the sisters opening it. A rich smell arose. Ilse cast a sideways look. There was a Camembert and a packet of butter wrapped in several layers of newspaper and greaseproof paper, which rustled. Her mouth was watering. There was a good slab of pumpernickel and a knife and napkins. The dragging sound was Frau Ginsberg pulling a big leather bag out into the centre of the cabin to use as a table. She inserted a knife, prised apart slices of the dark bread and buttered them. The rich smell of cheese filled the cabin.

The thin sister caught her looking and fluttered her hands in an anxious way. "Please, sit with us. We'd so like the company," said Fräulein Tischler. "We really would."

Ilse put the book into the net and scrambled down. The sisters offered food to the nun, who gravely shook her head. Ilse tried not to eat too fast. The cheese was wonderful. Frau Ginsberg levered open a jar of gherkins, saying she had preserved them herself.

The suitcase was full of food: tins of meat and anchovies, two bags of coffee beans, a thick packet of cakes and preserves. Perched on top was a box of sticky delicacies, which Frau Ginsberg appraised and then closed again.

"These pastries and tarts are from the best pâtissier in Marseilles. On the Canebière. He'll miss us, even if nobody else does. Look, my child," and she held up a flask of coffee in one hand and a tin of condensed milk in the other.

Ilse savoured France. When the cheese was gone, she lingered over the crumbling pastry, licking the apricot jam from her fingers.

"Have another one?"

"Yes, please."

The more Ilse ate, the more Frau Ginsberg beamed. She herself nibbled daintily but continually at the sweet things, while her sister hardly ate at all.

"So, my child, you are going to meet somebody?"

Ilse smiled and nodded.

"What's a little girl like you doing all on your own?"

Good as the pastries were, she did not have to swallow the questions too. There was a time to speak and a time to be silent. Old Shatterhand, who had the strength of a bear and the cunning of a fox, understood this well. Not everyone could fathom his wisdom. He had made his plan, looking at the river, had thought through his dilemma and predicted the outcome. "Didn't I tell you that when I drown, then we are safe?"

"Won't you at least tell me your first name?"

"Ilse," said Ilse severely. "I think you must think I am younger than I am. You know, Frau Ginsberg, I am quite old already. Nearly fourteen." She was used to being taken for a ten-year-old.

"Ilse. What a pretty name." She was not offended, not at all. "It's good to be with somebody who speaks our language. And a young lady, too. We are lucky. We're two old women sick of each other's company, aren't we? We've been in France for six months. Before that Holland. And now we are going to South America. Who would have thought that I would travel so at my age? When I was a girl I wanted to. But now, I just think of Dahlem and the lovely house—all gone now."

She ignored the way her sister frowned and plucked at her sleeve. Ilse was tired suddenly and her head kept dropping forward, though she knew that it was rude. The fat lady talked on, while Ilse tried to keep awake. Snatches of her words reached her. ". . . the most beautiful coats," she heard. "What stitching, mink, beaver, anything. Such workmanship," and later she burst out indignantly, "He was a hero—in the Great War!" Ilse's head drooped. Frau Ginsberg should not talk so much. Telling people things did nobody any good. If you spoke, people pushed things out of you, but if you were quiet they would give up eventually.

"Ilse? Where are you headed for? Because you may be going the same way as us."

"Look how tired she is, poor darling," said the thin sister in a whisper. "Let her be." And she was the one who helped her to her feet and then up into the bunk.

The boat, which was supposed to sail at six, left much later. In the night, the weather became stormy. Ilse woke to see Fräulein Tischler kneeling between the bunks on the little strip of floor and supporting the big head with its coiled plaits while Frau Ginsberg was sick again and again until all the pastries had returned to the surface and there was nothing left to come up. Fräulein Tischler stroked her sister's head in the kindest way. She draped a small towel over the nasty basin. Then she sat on the edge of the bottom bunk and held it for a long time, not so much from solicitude as from the impossibility of putting it anywhere. No stewards would come, of course, even though there was a button to press to call for them. There was no help to be had from anyone.

Ilse lay very still and held herself in readiness, and thought through the many different things that might happen, until her imagination was tired from the effort and gave up. Each time the ship rolled one way the widow moaned, then gave a horrible groan as the vessel sank upon itself. Eventually she fell quiet. Ilse peeped down. Perhaps it was the dim bulb over the door, which could not be turned off, that had turned her puffy face such a peculiar sallow colour. Dark circles lay under her eyes.

Abandoning the basin, Fräulein Tischler climbed carefully up into her berth and looked across at Ilse, who pretended she was asleep. Ilse would have liked to read her book, sleep being out of the question with all the noise and motion, not to mention the smell, but she dared not put her reading light on. On the bunk opposite, the thin sister cried continuously and, it seemed, inconsolably. She did it silently, as though by practising the art she had grown expert. The little French nun, who had not spoken to any of them, was silent. Perhaps she slept, though it hardly seemed possible with so much suffering just a metre away.

Waking to the sound of the trolley bus creaking up the Wuppertal hill, to the faint singing of Tante Röschen in the bathroom and the drumming feet of cousins Max and David fighting on the stairs, Ilse lay with her eyes closed, exulting at her success. It was her most cherished ambition to stay overnight with her big cousins, no longer to be the baby who never could be left. Her mother put her to bed at her aunt's house, just the way she did at home in the Landsweg. The breakfast table had been set with an extra place, between the boys. A tiny spoon carved of horn lay ready for her speckled morning egg. Ilse would lie upstairs, listening to the soft farewell on the doorstep, the assurances that Tante Röschen would telephone at once if anything were amiss. Always before, the sounds of her mother leaving had made her lose her nerve and run down in her nightgown, desperate for the familiar, clamouring unreasonably to go home. Why then, as the noises of the house increased around her, was her anxiety growing? As she abruptly opened her eyes to wake for the second time, the deception was revealed. The world was a blur of unhappiness. Ilse scrubbed hard at her face with a grubby handkerchief. She scolded herself for her stupidity, for the feet belonged to passengers going on deck and the boys were long gone. Max and David must be young men by now. They had said goodbye in 1934, sold up and left for Palestine. The English let people in if they had enough money. Even then, it had cost 15,000 marks, the price of a house. After that there was no family left in Germany, since Grandfather Salomon did not count. Nor did her mother's only relative, Tante Käthe in Krefeld, so old that she had always to be reminded who Ilse was. She was the one who said that "that child is not one of us." In spite of this they visited her twice yearly, taking flowers and sugared almonds. Though she was the only relative they ever saw and Ilse wanted to love her, she was not able to bear the way the old lady ate the nuts, crunching them all up greedily and then picking little pieces out of her teeth with a sweeping and poking finger.

Ilse scrambled down and tried to spruce herself up. Frau Ginsberg lay with her eyes closed, seemingly asleep. Her sister was nowhere to be seen. The boat was no longer rocking. The nun, who had apparently not taken off her clothes at all and did not seem to have any luggage, folded up her bunk and clipped it to the wall. She went away. Ilse hurried up on deck. The sea was perfectly flat. The day grew hot and clear as she watched the glitter on the waves. It was March 26th, Ilse's thirteenth birthday. She thought of the present in the case, which her mother had packed in a brown box right at the bottom, so no temptation would come her way. She would open it in Meknès. Fräulein Tischler came wandering along the deck looking for her, offering something to eat. Ilse shook her head. She felt a constriction in her chest, a tightness which prevented even the thought of food.

By the afternoon, a dark smudged line could be seen, the North African coast. The guidebook had insisted that the first glimpse of the coastline was something no traveller to the Dark Continent should miss. Now that she had seen it, Ilse went down to fetch her case. She should be ready. Her uncle might be in a hurry to get away. Frau Ginsberg, restored and with her hair once more tightly braided, took a lace blouse out of the suitcase, one with a lilac trim, and put it on. She rummaged, found matching lilac leather gloves. She was smartly turned out in a suit of navy blue with silk stockings. Savagely, her sister attacked her jacket with a brush that removed lint. Back on deck, Ilse braced her suitcase between her legs for safety. The port of Oran was called Mers el-Kébir and for centuries had been a den of pirates. She looked for black sails but saw only a tugboat ahead and two small fishing boats.

Passengers were jammed up against the railings long before they steamed slowly into the quay past a long row of rusty boats, unloading not people, but huge crates. Ilse leant against the saloon walls and waited. When people got off she would have a better view. She wore the winter coat, which would not fit in the case, fearing that if she were to try and carry that too she would lose it. It was very hot inside the coat. Those at the railings were pointing and laughing, chattering loudly to one another.

People were starting to disembark. Spotting a gap a few metres away, she wriggled as near as she could to the railing and peered down, shading her eyes. Hundreds of people were standing below, some holding signs on pieces of paper or card. The writing was too small to read, too far away and the light too bright. She looked at men in headdresses and long robes, women in light clothes and high heels. Baggage was being unloaded in a hubbub of people shouting and pushing. Two women fell with screams into each other's arms. A customs officer with a blue uniform leant against the whitewashed building of the Douane and puffed a cheroot. Somebody pushed their way up against the flow and shouted up, "Hast du meine Blutwurst?"*

A hand touched her sleeve. Frau Ginsberg, reaching past a big bearded man, said that she should go with them. The sun showed up funny indentations in her thickly powdered face and released a wave of eau de cologne. Her sister looked apologetic. "Here is the plan, my child. We will all wait a little while until things ease and keep an eye on the luggage. I need a porter, and what about you—what if you got lost in the crowd?"

"I won't get lost," said Ilse.

"You're small, stand next to me. Who is coming for you?"

She was a kind woman; she meant well.

"Is somebody coming?"

Ilse did not speak. The two women gave each other meaningful glances. Ilse was not a baby but thirteen and capable of travelling on her own, and she wanted them to go. Her money was in a purse in the deepest pocket of the coat. She kept her hand round it. She had been very careful and it would be enough. It would get her to her uncle's house if necessary.

"Surely you're going to be collected, my dear?"

"Don't worry." Fräulein Tischler was hovering. "People never know what time these boats are arriving."

She thought that she was being helpful. Ilse did not look at them. She stared down at the quay.

Willy was awfully handsome, her mother had said. He would be easy to recognise, for he had hair her mother said was "just like yours." On the piano in their old home, their proper house, among the silver frames stood a photograph of a very tall young man, with his arm round a pretty girl. This doomed, romantic couple had only had a few years together. Her mother, generally so precise, would not say what had happened to the wife, though she evidently had had something to do with her only brother leaving Germany forever. Willy and his broken heart were part of general conversation. But her parents had said other things too, lowering their voices so she had to strain to hear. Willy, her mother had said once, could never say no. "Good thing he wasn't a girl."

*"Have you got my black pudding?"

She scanned from right to left and back again. In the crowd below she could not see a single redheaded person. Ilse touched each button on her coat from bottom to top and then each of the mother-of-pearl buttons on her cardigan, from top to bottom and never the other way round. Mother-of-pearl was precious and special. They were all there, as was the button on the back of the waistband of her skirt. Finally, bending quickly, she touched the laces on her shoes. They were done up tight in double bows. The arrangements for the long and difficult journey had actually been perfect. It was very natural that things could not be as she and her mother had imagined in the long evenings spent sitting together, sewing and practising French. She realised that they had been wonderful evenings. They had found plenty of things to laugh about in the guide. Lore had been so amused by the idea that the people of Marseilles, with the whole sea at their disposal, chose to eat bouillabaisse, a soup concocted out of odd bits of fish. Her mother had knitted the cardigan and had sewed each tiny button on with a double thread, stitching the ends in neatly to the back of the ribbon binding, making each safe. There was something about the tightness of the stitching and the care of it that was unbearable.

Ilse gulped, but the air did not go where it should. Her head ached. She was dissolving. Fräulein Tischler kept trying to give her a piece of paper, an address in Casablanca, the hotel where Ilse could stay with them. She whispered that Ilse was not to mind, her sister's interference was well meant. She was sad because of her little girl, who had died years ago. Ilse put the paper in the pocket of the coat that she hated, that was much too hot. There was no reason for her to care about a little girl she did not know, who had happened to have a look of her. If only she had not mentioned it. Why was it, then, that it was Fräulein Tischler, not her sister, who seemed the sad one? Ilse might have said this, had she been able to speak. There was sadness everywhere. It rose from the sea, a mist that slipped through the small gap between the ship and the land where all the strangers stood. Ilse was drowning, with no hope of ever coming up.

Something very big, something white was weaving through the crowd, catching the light as it edged to the very front. The letters shone and danced. They re-formed as she blinked, then blurred again unstoppably. The European in a cream suit and hat was taller than anyone else and the sign itself was simply enormous. He took off the hat and waved it in huge sweeps, from side to side. The brilliance was the sun irradiating thick reddish-blond hair. The scarlet letters, professionally executed, were huge: WILLKOMMEN IN ORAN, LIEBE ILSE!*

"You see," Ilse said. "You see!"

She waved with all her strength. He waved back. She explained to Fräulein Tischler that the sun here was very strong and it affected a person's eyes. Then everything speeded up and she was hurrying down to the docks, she was on the land, spirited through the crowd and he took hold of her and swung her up and round. He was laughing. He did look like Lore. She stared at his skin, which was tanned dark, his dazzling, very pale blue eyes. His laughter at her looking at him was delightful. His hair, thick and glossy, grew back in a wave just like a film star's, just the way her mother had always wanted hers to.

"Your friends want to say goodbye."

The sisters, looking incongruous, one tall and one fat, stood a little way off like an island lapped by a sea of cases and bags. Willy gave them his card, thanked them for keeping an eye on his niece. Ilse, who was not in the habit of embracing people she hardly knew, found herself giving Frau Ginsberg a kiss, at which the big face crumpled alarmingly. At that moment a porter picked up their leather bag, which was much too heavy for one man to lift, and its handle came off. Frau Ginsberg's lilac gloves twisted in lamentation and then Ilse saw no more, for Willy was off, swinging her case, and she was running to keep up with his long legs. They dashed through customs—nobody stopped Willy Lindemann. People knew him. They greeted him and smiled.

They drove all the way to Meknès in his big American car. It was a long way but Willy said he loved to drive, said he loved his car, which was so big that a person could comfortably lie full length in the back seat. When her uncle smiled, his mouth curled up and pleasure crinkled his face. He had long elegant hands, which smoked and gesticulated and loosely held the wheel. The car purred on. The day was bright and the sun laid down a blanket of comfort. Meknès was a royal city, a beautiful city. She would speak French. He and his wife, Toni, had a simple place but she would like it. The pleasures came in snatches as the nodding of her head woke her up. They would go to the cinema. Swimming. On picnics. He presented these marvels to her as though she was a normal child with the right to such things. Weariness and relief overwhelmed

*Welcome to Oran, dear Ilse!

her. He stopped the car, insisted that she stretch herself out on the back seat and put her coat over her; he gave her his jacket as a pillow. He did not care if it creased, what did that matter? They could stay the night somewhere if he felt tired or perhaps not. They would see. It would be good to get back to Toni. The motor hummed and the road curved in her head, and Toni was like Tante Röschen only younger, with a kind face and soft, warm body.

Willy was whistling. It took a moment for her to realise where she was and that this noise was intended to wake her, this gentle touch his hand on her shoulder.

"Wake, little one. You must see this."

Yawning, Ilse tried to get up. It was cold. Her legs were stiff. She rose from the darkness behind to the rim of light coming over the world. Meknès climbed out of the plain, minarets sharp-cut like a child's picture book of the *Arabian Nights*, ochre walls flushed pink by the dawn sky. They leant on the hot bonnet and marvelled. He had driven all night and he wasn't tired; he put his arm round her and Ilse laid her head upon his shoulder, and they sat quietly until the sun edged up above the towers.

They drove through the medina, which Willy explained was the name given to the old part around the great mosque, and skirted the hammam. Everything started early, stopped, went on until late. Some of the passers-by waved and saluted them. Ilse, sitting proudly beside him, saw how the cafés were already busy with groups of men drinking glasses of tea. Others wearing long dresses, which Willy said were called djellabas, led little donkeys to the souk, their panniers charged with merchandise. Young men in Western clothes wove in and out of the narrow streets on bicycles; one woman was modern in a short skirt and heels and stockings, though others wore long robes in bright colours. The big car nosed its way along the Rue de la Route, stopped beside an old stone wall with a tiny opening protected by an ancient metal grille. Below was a sign etched in brass: M. & MME LINDEMANN.

Willy opened a wooden door, which led into a long shady corridor and from there through to a big room. Beyond this was a courtyard lined with colonnades in dusty pink and a garden of an astonishing green. All the houses were like this, he said: plain outside, their treasures hidden away. The courtyard was flanked by two buildings: one had a kitchen and dining and living room, the other bedrooms and bathrooms. The third side was a big shed with ladders and painting gear and room enough to nose the car inside, to keep it cool.

"Quietly, now," he said. "We don't want to disturb Toni."

They crept in.

He balanced the case on his head, carried it Moroccan style into a room with a little white bed, a wardrobe and a chest of drawers on which stood a cut-glass vase full of white flowers. She washed in the beautiful white-tiled bathroom, took out a clean dress and put it on. Outside, the grass was dew-dropped, iridescent. The sun streamed through the window and slanted across the floor, warming her feet and bare legs.

In the kitchen Marie, a smiling woman with a singsong voice, introduced herself and, clucking that the little one was too thin, made her scrambled eggs with herbs. Famished, Ilse ate the whole panful with piece after piece of bread. At home they had white rolls in the morning and at night Vollkornbrot, or dark rye. This bread was flat and you pulled it apart with your fingers. When Willy came in, Marie made more eggs. She came every day, Willy said, for Toni did not care to have a woman living in. At her name, Marie smiled and nodded, though she did not understand any German. There was real coffee and fresh milk, and a big basket of croissants. Like a Frenchman, Willy dipped his in a big bowl of coffee and ate the soft, crumbling mass with a good appetite.

She was not to be any trouble; her mother had impressed this upon her. Ilse unpacked her case, laying all the things carefully in the chest of drawers, hanging up both dresses and arranging her slippers. There was her present at the bottom. She took out the shoebox, carefully wrapped with brown paper and string, and put it on the chest of drawers. She sat on the bed, thinking that she would open it—but she would just put her head on the pillow for a moment. But when the gentle beat of her heart turned into the sound of somebody knocking on the door, the room was the colour of amber in the setting sun. Though it scarcely seemed possible, she had slept the whole day away. "Come in!" called Ilse.

A head appeared: a child with blond hair hanging down to her shoulders. It wasn't a child, but a doll. Toni wore a dressing gown, a filmy pretty one in pale blue with a pattern of roses on it that, falling open, revealed golden-coloured legs and throat.

"How are you feeling?" She had a strong foreign accent.

"Fine."

"Come on, then. We need to talk."

Ilse rose and followed. Willy had gone to work and come back again, and now he sat on a big wicker chair facing out onto the garden, which was slanted grey and gold, winking at her.

"Can I come?"

"No."

"If you need me, little mouse, scream. I'll come and save you," he said, lighting a cigarette, inhaling deep and smiling through the smoke rings.

The bedroom was Toni's domain. Her dressing table, a beautiful sleek thing with a mirror on top, held a dozen elegant cut-glass bottles of scent. It was somehow just like Toni herself. A wall of cupboards filled one side of the long room and everything was very modern. In one corner stood a little trolley with glasses on it and ice. Toni picked up a cocktail shaker, shook it vigorously and poured the contents over ice.

"Want one?"

"No, thank you."

Nobody had ever offered her a drink before.

Sipping at hers, Toni looked at Ilse very carefully. "You're small for thirteen," she said. "Like me."

Ilse smiled. "Thank you for the flowers. You're very kind."

"Flowers? Oh, Willy must have bought them." Toni slipped off the dressing gown and looked at herself in the long mirrors. Ilse admired her wonderful figure. Tiny as she was, her bosoms and hips were womanly, her waist small. Her girdle and brassiere were very modern. "From America," she said, noticing the look. Her large eyes were a curious hazel colour with golden flecks, like those of a cat.

"So, what's going on in Germany?"

Ilse shrugged.

"How's your father's business doing now?"

Ilse hesitated.

"The import company. The new shop in Krefeld."

"It's not his anymore. You know. 'Wer vom Juden kauft ist ein Verräter.' "*

"Who says that?"

"The signs. In the street."

*"Whoever buys from a Jew is a traitor."

"They took it over?"

Ilse nodded and looked away. A distant memory surfaced, one she did not care to share with Toni, of her mother bent over papers, cross, her father's upraised voice: "Do you expect Otto Blumenthal to buy and sell dishes while the world starves?"

"My father's not a capitalist," she said.

Toni burst out laughing. "He spent enough time on the shop design. And money. All that glass and concrete. The very latest merchandise, Swedish glass. Italian ceramics. That expensive silverware. I suppose he got bored when it was finished."

With practised movements, her fingertips finding the hairpins without looking, Toni did up her bright hair in a sleek roll. "I saw the pictures. There was an article, in the Düsseldorf paper. Your mother sent it to Willy. The grand opening party?" She glanced over at Ilse. "I expect you were too young to go."

Ilse nodded.

"It was a very handsome shop. He should have put the business in your mother's name."

"It was Grandfather's business."

"So? Your mother isn't Jewish. She could have run it."

Ilse hung her head.

"Why not, then?"

"He's not like that. My grandfather."

"What is he like?"

"I don't know," said Ilse, shrugging helplessly.

"Don't you know him?"

Another truth to be kept from Toni was that Lore had never met Grandfather Salomon. He had refused to meet the divorced woman his son was marrying, a woman not of the Jewish faith.

"He had to retire," she said evasively. "He was too old."

Ilse watched as Toni wiggled herself into a tight dress, which clung alluringly across her hips and thighs. She had seen her grandfather twice. She had a clear memory of a vigorous man in his sixties who was small and stout where her father was skinny. He smoked a big cigar and he smelt very nice, of the smoke and perfume. She had liked him for his clever eyes, eyes that smiled even though the mouth seldom did. She could see that he liked her. He would have liked her mother too, had he not been so stubborn.

"Your parents were coming here," said Toni. "Willy fixed it. Anyone with any sense got out when the Nuremberg laws came in. They should have sold the business right away."

"My father fought in the war. He has a medal," she said.

Toni raised a quizzical eyebrow. "So?"

"Besides, people can't all run away, can they?"

But they could. Ilse saw it. They could all have been here in clean white beds, going to the cinema, speaking French, eating ice cream. She thought again. "Germany needs people to stay and fight against the fascists," she said.

Both Toni's eyebrows shot up. "The fascists? I see. So your father's still involved in politics."

"No!" She shook her head violently, her face burning. "Of course he isn't!"

Toni studied her. "A stateless bankrupt Jew, who could have got out. Still running around making crazy speeches?"

Ilse smiled a smile of sheer embarrassment.

"Well," said Toni, stubbing out her cigarette, "it's all too late now. Is your mother as pretty as Willy says she is?" She smoked cigarettes with long filters and every gesture was deliberate.

"Very pretty." Ilse thought of her mother's kind face and smile.

"To think, she married him for the money and then this happened. What bad luck."

"She didn't," said Ilse faintly.

"My dear, it certainly wasn't for his looks."

"How do you know? You haven't met them."

"Don't get on your high horse."

Carefully, she put bright red lipstick on her half-open mouth.

Though she might entertain dark thoughts about her father, Ilse could not bear for Toni to voice them. The truth was something even worse. Her father had been in and out of prison for years. He was what he called a "submarine," living underground and holding secret political meetings, always travelling from place to place. If the police picked him up, they would send him to prison or worse. Communists were banned. He was a Bolshevik and a Jew, doubly an enemy of the Reich.

The state had confiscated everything he owned. When the Gestapo took their house, Ilse and her mother had moved to a room in the Jews' House. They were lucky to get even that: they did not fit in anywhere.

Not being Jewish, her mother still had her German nationality and because of this, Ilse was still permitted to go to school when Jewish children were not. A slate hung beside her classroom door. It read: BOYS 19, GIRLS 18, JEWS 1. She was (yet was not) that Jew. In the Jews' House she trod softly, fearing to offend these people of whose customs she knew nothing. Trailing home with her satchel one day, she had heard her father's voice inside. "Lore, please, don't leave me."

She had frozen, her hand still on the doorknob.

"That's rich, coming from you," said her mother. "Keep your voice down, Otto. The child will be back any moment."

She had counted to ten. Shyly, then, she had opened the door, clearing her throat and making as much noise as she could. Her father was standing in the corner, smoking, still wearing his dark coat and hat. She reached up to kiss his stubbly cheek. She had not seen him for nearly a year and hardly knew what to say. His nose and chin were sharper, even his eyes more defined, as though he was turning into a cartoon version of himself. Before he even spoke, her mother asked her to fetch cake. Ilse had run all the way up the hill to the shops and breathlessly back, worrying that he would be gone before she returned. She shot up the two flights of stairs, the slice of cake sliding on its cardboard tray, the double fold of wrapping paper starting to gape. Then, more slowly, up the third flight, because she could hear them arguing still. The room was tiny, the house crammed; everyone heard everything.

Ilse had retreated down to the very bottom and waited, sitting on the last step balancing the little parcel on her knees, all the time smelling the rich dark poppy seeds, the black eye of the cake looking at her. She jumped up when anybody entered, stood aside politely to let each tenant pass. It was the usual quarrel. Her mother wanted the three of them to leave Germany and her father would not go. He had no money. Jews' bank accounts had been frozen long ago and he could neither work nor borrow anything. Her mother had a job as a waitress, enough to feed them and a little surplus. She saved every pfennig. Ilse remained on her stair. When she judged enough time had passed, she went up, pretending she only had just got back. Her father said that she had grown, though she had not. She looked at their faces, marked with all the feelings they tried to conceal in her presence, the way they avoided looking at each other. They drank the coffee, which was cold, and he crumbled the cake but ate none, though it was his favourite. Later it occurred to her that perhaps this was because his throat hurt, as hers did when she was upset. He had left almost immediately.

After this visit, her mother said that they would wait no longer. Ilse had to be sent out of Germany as soon as possible. That was why she went alone: because they could only afford one ticket to Oran. They had agonised over this decision. For the same money they could buy two tickets to France. In France, they would be together but penniless and her mother did not know how she could earn money. Willy had connections. He had achieved the near impossible, a visa for her to enter Morocco and stay six months. Once she was there, her mother had said, it could be extended indefinitely. With Willy, Ilse would be safe.

Toni slipped into black high-heeled shoes, paraded before the mirror, then kicked them off. From the cupboard she got out different shoes, tried them on. Finally she settled on a pair just as high but the red of her lipstick and made of the softest calf. With those shoes on, she was perfect. Ilse stared at her fine features, her skin which was a golden olive colour, her tiny feet and hands. She was the sort of person you could not ignore. You could not stop looking at her, once you had started.

"Why didn't she divorce him?"

It was the first time Ilse had heard a grown-up express this idea out loud, though it had crept into her own mind on numerous occasions. "I don't know," she said.

"Be honest. Weren't they as good as divorced?"

When they narrowed, Toni's eyes were just like a cat's. Ilse studied the carpet. The Gestapo had told her Lutheran Protestant mother to divorce the Jew. Her mother had refused. They had never discussed why. Soon, when she was back in her room, all the things that her mother must have said about her father would come back to her, remarks about his looks and his talents.

"My mother loves my father. She would never leave him."

Perhaps this was the truth. Behind her back, Ilse crossed all her fingers into four crosses. That undid the fib and also meant that no bad thing could happen.

"Then Lore is even more of a fool than I thought. Willy thought you were all coming years ago. He sent the money, after all. It was bad luck that it was confiscated. Fancy choosing to stay in Germany instead of getting out while she still could."

Toni picked up her bag, admired her rear view, twirled back round. "Ready?"

Ilse stood up. "She wants to come, she's working as hard as she can waitressing," she said. She rushed on, wanting Toni to stop doing that thing she did with her eyebrows. "Once Mutti's saved up enough for her ticket, she can apply for the exit visa. You have to have the ticket first, that's what takes so long."

Toni opened the bag, checked the contents and then snapped it shut.

"Look, when we're out, don't talk about these things. You don't look Jewish. It won't help with her visa, either, if people sniff it. And don't look so worried."

They walked to a nearby café, its elegant chrome tables full of men and women, all French-speaking and laughing and drinking. More than half of them were Europeans and she noticed quite a few Germans. They seemed to know everybody there and she strained to remember the names as she was introduced to this one and that. A very broad man with a kind, clever face took pity on her, told Willy in German to sit the poor girl down and let her absorb it slowly. This man was called Heinz Steinberg and reminded her of Grandfather Salomon. Ilse was grateful. He smelt of a lemony cologne, what she thought was a good, German sort of a smell. He spent a long time filling a pipe, first teasing out the tobacco then tamping it down while telling a joke about Hitler going fishing with Mussolini and Chamberlain.

"The British premier lights a pipe and waits and waits. After two hours he lands a big trout. Furious, il Duce throws himself into the water, catches a monster fish with his bare hands." Somebody called to Heinz. He laid his pipe carefully in an ashtray, got up and went to another table, looked at a chessboard and moved a piece, then moved to yet another table. He was playing three games of chess simultaneously. In a moment, he returned, recovering the pipe. "Now it's Hitler's turn. He orders the pond to be drained. The fish are all thrashing about. Chamberlain says, 'Why don't you scoop them up?' 'No,' says Hitler. 'They have to beg me first.'"

The grown-ups around all laughed. Ilse did too, not because it was funny exactly but because it was wonderful that here Hitler was just a joke. She had a citron pressé with spoon after spoon of sugar. She was hungry, but did not want to ask for something, when they were going to a special restaurant for dinner, later, in the old town. Willy bought her an ice cream with whipped cream and a cherry. In the end there was no dinner, for the cream—much too rich and gobbled up too fast—made her sick. They took her back to the house in a taxi.

"Poor little mouse, you'll be better tomorrow," said Willy. It was he who stroked her hair, who put her to bed. He tucked her in and pulled up the blanket so nicely. As sleep overtook her, she felt her very bones relaxing from the intense relief of being a child again.

TWO

~

Hamburg, March 1939

Glittering on the handlebars of his bicycle, the sun made even the grey Elbe sparkle as Nicolai freewheeled home along the Elbchaussee. The big house, freshly whitewashed, was so bright it almost hurt to look at. Dismounting, he pushed open the front gate, wheeled his bike round the side. The sun rolled softly blurring wheels along the white wall, turned a boy with a satchel into a hunchback. He blinked the shadows of the stucco scrolls around the drawing-room windows into faces with puffed-out cherub cheeks. He bumped the bike down the steps, parked it inside the cellar door and squeezed past. The food cellar was crammed. Last year they had just the one cupboard with baking tins and sugar for jam-making and preserves; now a row of them had eaten up the space. His mother, remembering the starvation of the Great War, said that they had to be provisioned. Her first husband had been a career officer and she was understood to have superior knowledge of military matters. He dawdled past her weapons of war, brushing against sacks of flour, trailing a finger along the stack of jars waiting to be filled, their rubber-seal mouths open in surprise. The usual prickle of irritation at her excess was suppressed with the usual effort.

"Be generous, Nico, be kind," his father often said, being himself both of those without any effort. Nicolai tried to comply. His mother held the monopoly of a certain kind of knowledge, sensible seeming and reasonable, that was never to be argued with. Always right, she completely missed the essence of things.

As he came up the stone steps into the back hallway, the aroma of veal sausage blended with the house smell of furniture polish and flowers. Winter and summer a huge bowl of flowers stood on the highly polished French table in the middle of the hall; the fire in the big marble hearth brought out their scent. ("In life," his mother said, "it's the little luxuries that make all the difference.") He slung his satchel onto the ornate coat stand, carried on into the long white kitchen.

"Good day at school?"

"Fine, thank you, Magda."

His pleasure dimmed at the sight, under the apron, of the telltale blue blouse that went with their cook's best suit of navy serge. An afternoon with his mother yawned ahead.

Careful of her going-out finery, Magda held the mashed potatoes comically, at arm's length. "Don't wriggle, Sabine, it's coming," she said.

Enthroned in her high chair, his baby sister was beaming at him under her crown of golden curls. "Ni-co! Ni-co!" She drummed her feet in anticipation, stretched out dimpled hands.

Magda slid the dishes on the table in the bustling way of a person with no time to waste. She had made white cabbage salad with caraway seeds: it was what he thought of as a white food day. The metal tips of her town shoes rang out in a businesslike way on the tiled floor; her thin face, cheeks flushed from the oven, wore its usual slightly anxious expression. She had grilled the Weißwurst, had gravy keeping warm. He spread mustard lavishly, relished the first succulent bite as he cracked the sausage skin. "Magda, it's heavenly," he said. "Actually, you're an angel."

Her rare smile made her almost pretty. Sabine suddenly stuck her finger into a mound of potatoes in which butter melted, then cried, because it was hot. Magda kissed the finger and shushed her. The trick was to stop the baby from eating so fast that she would be sick. Magda loaded her little spoon, blew on it while trying to stop fat little fingers from snatching and spilling.

Nicolai made fortifications with his potatoes, forked waves into a gravy moat. Caraway seed men attacked and defended; the sausage battering ram won through. Magda had saved a portion of fruit compote for him. She ladled on cream. He plunged a spoon through the white lake to the red currant depths, then swirled the two into a Catherine wheel. Magda was already washing the dishes; she would have no time to chat today. The three of them usually ate together in the kitchen; there had been a suggestion that when Sabine outgrew the high chair they would join their mother, who, when at home, lunched in dining-room splendour. Nicolai hoped not.

From his room on the fourth floor, he watched Magda hurrying off to catch the trolley bus into town. The curled feather on her best hat went bobbing along the other side of the hedge like a tall passing bird. He stepped over the track to the station house and picked up the young lady with a red dress and a little Scottie dog attached to her base. He placed her on platform 1 next to the sign for the express train to Munich, which never came. She would just have to wait. His father had laid out the roads and bridge, extended the track, which so completely colonised his room that he had to clamber over it to go to bed. They had spent hours on it. Often Nicolai, hovering on the brink of tedium and hating his own ingratitude, redoubled his efforts to be pleased. Trains were the dream of his loving father, who had been poor, whose boyhood had never known the comforts that time and money bought. He could never quite live up to the expectations of joy.

His father must have realised. For his thirteenth birthday the previous month, he had given him the new Leica IIIa, which lay distractingly on his desk. "You need something to engage heart and mind," he had said. "This will show you the world."

Nicolai undid the two studs and opened the tan leather case to admire its magnificence. He looked at himself in the lens. There seemed to be a faint fingerprint on the glass. He breathed on it, took a soft cloth, polished it away. He was waiting as patiently as he could. As soon as his university work eased, his father, whose own patience was endless, was going to demonstrate the camera's refinements. They were going to set up a darkroom in his bathroom. He felt a kind of advance nostalgia for the age of trains, for the simple time which was already passing.

Replacing the camera, Nicolai got down to inspect the station. He could lay a camouflage net over the roof to guard it from enemy attack. He needed new paint colours, a drab green and more brown. Flat on the floor, one ear pressed against the track, he stared across the platform and through the ticket office window. The ticket inspector's tiny black eyes and lacquered head looked back. His giant eye filling the whole window must terrify the little man. He winked. Then he opened his eyes as wide as he could. The little metal face remained impassive. Nicolai wondered whether, if he laid the young lady on the line and ran a train over her, her head might come off. In which case he might get out his old paints and dab some blood around her severed neck. He had derailed the train several times without denting her when a high thin wailing arose farther along the corridor. Sabine generally woke up miserable after her nap. Any minute now his mother would be along to get her up, intruding into his glorious free afternoon.

He opened the windows as wide as they would go. Using the chair, he stepped up onto the windowsill, climbed over the single safety bar and, still clutching it, lowered himself backwards so he was kneeling on the chilly ledge outside, head still in the room, legs and feet protruding precariously into space. He glanced out. There was nobody coming. He looked along the Elbchaussee. A trolley bus passed without stopping. It looked no bigger than the model one under his bridge. Thirty metres below, the front garden was an improbably neat green rug, the evergreen bushes sprouting heads of broccoli. The long black line on the Elbe beyond was a tugboat, probably pulling barges full of coal.

He forced himself to stand up on the sill, felt the old pull of the ground calling him, telling him to lean farther and farther out, to let go. He wouldn't do that. He let his weight sag experimentally against the window. The hinges of the shutters, on which fresh paint was already cracking, might be rusty underneath, might not take his weight. He might fall, screaming, onto the gravel far below. A vision came of his half-brother, Wolfgang, wearing a black leather coat over his brown shirt, leading a funeral procession full of Jungvolk.* The Jungvolk all sobbed. Wolfgang, come specially from Lübeck, opened his mouth wide for the oration. It remained open, stuck. Nicolai screwed up his eyes and stared up into the sun until black spots floated across his pupils. Still he could not imagine praise coming from Wolfgang's mouth.

He pulled himself farther forward, so his chest was resting more securely on the double ridges of the window and shutter, held together by their two interlocking handles. He got a purchase with his feet. A tiny spider, dislodged from its web, ran along the green-painted ridge with

*"Young folk," the branch of the Hitler Youth for ten- to fourteen-year-olds.

its band of dirt. He watched it scurry down the dark space between the wood and the glass. The sun warmed his back. His stomach fluttered with anticipation. One, two, go! Nicolai shoved his boots hard against the sill. The conjoined window and shutter swung open. His breathing constricted with an intensity between excitement and fear as he hung in space, cantilevered from the window, then his feet were scrabbling for the branch beyond. He scissored his legs round it. He edged backwards, holding on to the metal handles. Bark scraped his bare knees. This was the difficult part, letting go and falling, flailing through twigs for a handhold. Bang. He was safe on the branch. He got his breath back. The path below was still empty. His open window was innocent. He shuffled his bottom along the branch as fast as he could to the point where, from the house, a boy on the tree was invisible.

He was a squirrel, leaping from branch to branch, except anybody who leapt would crash down and smash his bones. Getting back in that way was impossible. He always shinnied down the tree, went in at the side door past the larder. Magda would not let anyone near her larder, not even him. But Magda was out.

"Nicolai!"

His mother's voice, quite near, was coming from the nursery.

"Nicolai, where are you?"

Now she was in his room, but even if she looked out of the window, she could not see him. He kept quiet.

"What's become of your brother? Say Ma-ma, my Süßelein, say Ma-ma."

"Da-da-da!"

He lay on the branch and waited. Soon, she and the baby would go off to the park where Sabine would inspect every ant and fallen leaf, and his mother would have nobody to quiz with her dull questions about school. He wondered what was taking them so long. A little figure turned off the Elbchaussee and shimmered around the corner. The woman came closer and closer to their house, turned in at the gate and came up the path. It was much too early for coffee and cake visitors. She made a funny figure, foreshortened and looking down at a piece of paper in her hand. She looked up and saw him. She stood there gazing at him with her blank face. Damn and hell. That was why his mother had not gone out. Now he remembered. Some woman was coming to be interviewed for the nursemaid's job. As the doorbell rang, she took off her hat, smoothed down her hair, repinned it.

Nicolai shinned down the tree, successfully conducted a raid on the larder, acquiring a piece of Magda's excellent cheesecake. Heading across the big hallway towards the stairs, sniffing the damp, lemony richness, he paused. The women were in his father's study. The door was closed. He sidled up to it; the keyhole was big and he could hear their voices quite clearly. It was important to obtain intelligence about the enemy. There had been three nursemaids in the past year and a half. He had disliked them all. They always had the room off the stairs that led to the cellar, for which he envied them. The small window onto the garden was overgrown with ivy, which gave it a magical green glimmer.

"You've come a long way, Fräulein Lindemann."

"The Ruhrgebiet."

"You worked in a shop and a restaurant. I see here that you took a degree in law. My goodness. That's quite unusual, isn't it?" His mother sounded puzzled. Balancing the cake on one outstretched hand, he grazed at it, soft-lipped like a horse, so as not to make a mess.

"Well, Frau Bucherer, I always loved to work. When I gave up the law I decided to work with children."

"You're sure this is the kind of work you want?"

Sabine was chuckling. Sliding on her bottom across the polished floor, she tended to work backwards around his father's vast mahogany desk.

"Very much so, Frau Bucherer. I love children."

"Inge Riemke spoke very highly of you," his mother said. "What is the connection?"

"How kind. My brother, Willy, was at art school with Frau Doktor Riemke."

"How interesting."

Nicolai wondered that the conversation could proceed with such dry inevitability, every question a stone falling into a hollow place as his mother, eliciting the usual answers, learnt nothing. Sabine began wailing. She often pulled herself up under the desk and banged the top of her head.

"Have you hurt yourself, Sabine?" His mother's voice changed. Nicolai wandered away upstairs. He did not succeed in decapitating the girl in the red dress.

In a while he heard his mother calling him down. Sabine was sitting on the woman's knee. He put out his hand. The woman's hand was cool. Smiling, his mother put her arm round him. This rare gesture told him that she had decided to take the woman on.

"This is Fräulein Lindemann, our new nursemaid. From Wuppertal."

"Very pleased to meet you, Nicolai," she said. She had quite a nice voice. He heard no trace of the Rheinland twang of their last chauffeur, who came from Mülheim an der Ruhr and made the same stupid joke every day about the way Hamburgers spoke, endlessly going on about how they walked on the spitzen stein.* He studied her. Her dress looked home-made. She had thin arms and legs; near her ankle one stocking had been darned with thread that almost matched. She was on the pale side with reddish hair, eyelids heavy over light greeny-blue eyes. Because her eyebrows were almost invisible, she seemed to have an endless forehead. She did not seem the hysterical type. It was quite hard to see what type she was. This one seemed calmer than Fräulein Schwartz, their previous nursemaid, who would certainly have thrown a fit if she had seen him up the tree. Because she had not ratted on him, he came to a decision. He would give her a chance.

Voices shrilled, the classroom roar went on and on. His classmates were baiting Jochen Dressler, calling him "Jew lover," though there were no Jews in their boys' Gymnasium, which was one of the finest in Hamburg. Langenscheidt, voice booming above all others, led them all on. Nicolai cast a sidelong glance at poor Jochen, whose parents were devout Catholics. Conspicuous in blue shirt and pullover, he stared stoically into space. Nicolai could not have borne persecution with such noble silence. His own father was also not a Party member; he had prevented Magda from hanging out her National Socialist flag. On festive days theirs was the only house along the street that did not display one. But it went no further. Nicolai opened his mouth; catching Langenscheidt's rolling eye, he shut it again. If he said anything, they would round on him too. Elbows on the desk, he propped his head in his hands, stuck a middle finger hard into each ear, crushed thumbs and

*"Sharp stone," i.e., "sch"-sounding words characteristically pronounced by Hamburgers with an "s."

knuckles tight up against his skull. The jeers and racketings flattened into underwater silence. The blood pumping in his head was deep diver breathing. He relaxed his fingers slightly, bringing a rushing sound. It was a waterfall cascading a thousand metres into a rock pool far below. From an immense height he contemplated the black meniscus of the tiny pool in its white ceramic rim. Then he dived. His shrunken body arced. The dark circle opened. He vanished into the inkwell. School drowned. Nicolai stretched out spectral fingertips, the porcelain walls receded and he swam free in a liquid the lustrous green of a Heineken bottle.

He found himself on his feet, having presumably risen with the class as a body.

"Good morning, boys!"

"Good morning, Herr Schacht." Papers were being handed out for the maths test.

"Half an hour. All those who do not finish the paper will get a zero," said Herr Schacht, without raising his voice. With exaggerated groans, the boys settled to their task. Beside Nicolai, Heini chewed a pencil, legs twisted in mute anxiety, though the sums were easy: *How many houses at 15,000 Reichsmarks could be built for the 6 million RM cost of constructing a lunatic asylum?*

Nicolai wrote large, angling his work so his friend could see. The bell pealed, the others stampeded; Herr Schacht held up a broad hand. "Bucherer—I hoped for more from you, my boy."

"What is it, sir?"

The master had seen him helping Heini. He watched the sun light up the tiny hairs growing from Herr Schacht's ears and glow through his lobes while he talked at length about how contrary any form of cheating was to the true sense of National Socialism. Nicolai, unable to disagree, could not find any way to wriggle out of blame since the obvious explanation—that Heini's father went mad when he got below a 3—would not do. A tumult of gibberish was rising from the yard below, where Langenscheidt and his pals capered feigned lunacy.

In the changing room, pulling on gym socks, thrusting long feet into plimsolls, Heini took the bad news in silence. He was to stay behind, do another paper. Nicolai studied the parting in his fair hair, the way he looped the lace over a finger. The white showing above his pupils gave him a startled air; maybe that was how his friend acquired his old childhood nickname, "Little Hare." Maybe there was another, hidden reason. There was no softening the blow. Already, his friend was up and darting away. Nicolai trailed behind. Friendship was a precarious, precious thing, liable to break at any time.

As energetically as he could, Nicolai jumped on the spot, arms swinging, already slightly out of breath though they had only just begun. They drilled with the medicine ball for half an hour, then it was sprinting or the long jump into wet sand. He jumped, fell awkwardly short of the mark, getting a mouthful of sand. He shot up, spat it out and looked round. Herr Blank, the sports master, had not noticed. Hours of drill in shorts and singlet in the cold had taught him never to answer back, never to do anything but try his utmost. They ran laps and relays. He ran, throat aching with the effort. To soothe himself, in his head he repeated an old marching song: one, two, twenty-two, that's how the farmer walks through the mud, three, four and thirty-four. Singing away to himself, he did not have to see Heini turning effortless cartwheels, talking to others and laughing. How did those dull boys find so much to say?

"Where's your uniform, Dressler?"

Herr Blank's face had gone dark red. In silence, the boys buttoned up brown shirts, pulled on shorts. Jochen, alone in their whole Gymnasium, did not wear the uniform of the Hitlerjugend or Jungvolk.

"You read the newspapers, boy? The Second Decree for Implementing the Youth Law came into effect on March twenty-fifth. Duty service is obligatory now." He was so near that their noses were almost touching. "Obligatory, Dressler. Do you imagine that you alone will not serve your country?"

Various boys were now sniggering. By contrast with the angry flush of the master, Jochen was very pale.

"No, sir."

"Understand, Dressler? I expect you in uniform by the end of the week. This school will have one hundred per cent membership. One hundred per cent. The years of struggle are over. We are all part of the German community now. Tell your father he will be prosecuted if he does not comply."

"Yes, sir."

Going home, as he drew level with Jochen, Nicolai backpedalled. The very shape of his body was defensive. Nicolai felt a painful empathy for him, yet knew that such feelings were negligible in comparison to the huge wound he bore daily.

"Jochen." He sought words to throw at the averted head. What could he possibly say? "Jochen, do you want a go on my bike?" But Jochen never looked up.

When his father was away or working late, Magda laid out supper in the dining room so his parents could eat whenever they chose. Foraging, Nicolai lifted the lid of the pot, sniffed the soup keeping hot over the little tea candles. Everything else was cold. He inspected the veal cutlets in aspic with a parsley sauce; noted the reappearance of the cabbage salad. There was a fruit tart and cream as well as the cheesecake. He dipped a finger in the cream, licked it. Then he took a lemon bonbon from the big crystal bowl and, on reflection, a couple more for later. His mother's high heels clicked across the parquet of the hall. She generally wore full-skirted evening clothes, in pale blue to match her eyes or in a grey-beige colour she called oyster that suited her golden hair. He was often called upon to admire her but that would not happen tonight; he was supposed to be reading in bed but had not even got his pyjamas on. He slid behind the door as she continued into the study. His parents always had a whisky and a chat before dinner. He could gather some intelligence on how his father's job was going and when he would have time off for important camera work.

"New shoes? Very fetching," his father said.

Ice clinked on the drinks tray.

"The others are so shabby. A person can't manage forever."

"It's not a reproach. I like them. Well, what's the week brought?"

"I've engaged a new nursemaid at last, seems quite decent. We can't afford her on your salary, she's asking a lot. I'll pay her out of my income. I hope she's worth it."

Why did she sound so angry? His father mumbled something. The heels clicked about some more. He wanted to go nearer. Nicolai took a pace; a floorboard groaned. Bending down, he stealthily undid his laces, wiggled out of his shoes.

"Darling. Did you think any more about what I said?"

"I'll go to the army when they make me. Not before."

He splayed dampish feet, was a spider, creeping along unseen and unheard.

"I can't understand you, Benno. You complain about the mediocrity of the work, yet you want to stay there. And you hardly earn anything."

"I'm on the top grade."

"If you'd joined the Party you'd be a professor by now. It's holding you back."

"I can't do it. Must we go over it again?"

There was a long silence. Nicolai waited.

"I only want the best for you," she said in a small voice.

"They took the best minds away, Hilde, that's how I got my promotion. How do you think I like that? I'm passing myself off as something I'm not."

"Darling—don't." A chair scraped.

"Just look at this. Just this. A paper at the conference. Go on. Read it."

" 'Heine's decadent poetry reflects the structure of the Jewish palate.' Well—it's absurd."

"But not impossible. That's the tragedy. It's something worse than absurd."

There came the clink of another drink being poured.

"But if you hate it so much, why do you stay?"

"The university needs a few decent people."

There was a long silence.

"Hilde, what is it that you want to change? Are you really unhappy?"

His mother made no reply.

"It's not money. You have plenty, you know you do, your parents' firm has seldom been busier. Do you still miss the old military glamour, my sweet?"

"Don't be silly."

"Are you unhappy with me, is that it?" His voice had dropped. Nicolai strained to hear. "Hilde. Don't let's quarrel."

"We're not quarrelling, darling. It's just a discussion. Let's eat. The soup will be quite cold and the cutlets warm."

The heels clicked across the floor towards the dining room and the spider, scuttling as fast as he could, got away safely, up the stairs, two at a time.

In bed he pondered the best minds, which had been taken away. Where to? That his even-tempered father should pass himself off as something he wasn't seemed impossible. That sort of thing happened at school, where bullies and cheats got the best reports because they were Herr Blank's favourites. And why did his father not go to the army? Perhaps he was the sort the boys at school pilloried as turncoats and traitors. This worried Nicolai. He brought to mind Heini's face, his big cheerful father, then Langenscheidt, whose broad smile showed more teeth than any person could reasonably need, whose father was high up in the Party. These fathers were all going to the armed forces, all except his father, who was a better man than any of them. He pressed his hands to his eyes hard until there was nothing but a dark red world with sparkly scratches. It was hot under the feather bed, he was stifling; he threw it onto the floor.

He crept out of bed, groped across the desk until he felt the Faber-Castell pencil, the unsharpened one, then the torch. Its blunt edge inched the grey metal base of the stationmaster in his smart cap and uniform through the door and right up to the ticket inspector. He turned him, so the two little men faced each other, unblinking in the harsh beam. The ticket money did not add up. The cheat was going to get a real wigging.

"Don't you have a true sense of National Socialism?" he admonished him.

The little face looked sad. "Are you unhappy with me, sir?"

"I certainly am. You're passing yourself off as something you're not."

He closed the ticket office, trapping both men inside, and set the local train to the fastest speed. While they neglected their duties, it would rocket through, perhaps jump the points, smashing into the buffers, or come right off the bridge and topple onto the autobahn. Innocent passengers would die. He sat on the edge of the rumpled bed, unmoving, waiting for the crash, but the train just whirred on and on and round and round in the dark.

THREE

Morocco, March 1939

Ilse felt down with one foot, then the other, extending the warm part where she lay into the cool part at the end of the bed where the sheet tucked in. As a foolish little child she had been scared of the cold places, never budging from the position she lay in when her mother kissed her good night. These sheets were soft and smelt of sunshine. One pillow was a bolster, the other square. She got up, pulled the blankets straight, folded the sheet carefully back over them, tucked the bedclothes in. A long cord swung from the blinds. She pulled the wooden acorn and light slanted in from a sky the colour of forget-me-nots. The cream bowl on the windowsill, crackle glazed, had a tiny grey mark near the bottom. Dressing, she put all these things into her head. Then she brushed her hair fifty times.

She tiptoed into the kitchen, found a sharp knife and sawed at the knots securing the box. The object inside, wrapped in layers of tissue, was her mother's leather jewellery roll. It contained her mother's pearl necklace, her flower brooch in platinum, her diamond ring and three heavy gold chains. She had not seen them for a long time. Ilse had assumed that they had all been sold long ago. There was a heavy object underneath, carefully wrapped in layers of newspaper, which she started to lift out, recognised and returned to its place. The photograph of her parents smiling on their wedding day, elaborately framed in silver, had stood in the drawing room on the piano. She could not bring herself to look at it. They never should have given it away. She rolled up and fastened the leather roll and put it back in the box and hid the box at the very back of the wardrobe.

She sat on the bed and waited. There was a noise, which might be Marie doing something in the kitchen. Just after seven o'clock there came a tap on the door.

"Come, little mouse," said Willy. She was to start school that day. He had prepared a little school case for her; a wooden pencil box with her name carved in it held a dozen sharp pencils and a beautiful new fountain pen. He was in charge of her, both father and mother to her now. Straight after breakfast, she took the new pen and wrote to her mother in Wuppertal on Toni's writing paper, which Willy fetched from the broad cedarwood desk in the sitting room. The cream-coloured paper was very thick and expensive, the envelopes lined with dark blue tissue. The ink was the exact same colour as the lining paper; the slant of the nib stretched out her hasty words into italic elegance. Marie promised to stamp and post the letter on her way home at noon. As soon as she had finished, they tiptoed out, so as not to disturb Toni; glancing through, Ilse saw her sitting at the desk surrounded by papers.

"She starts work early so she can have the afternoons off," Willy said.

"What is her work?"

"Bookkeeping. She pays the bills, keeps everything straight for my firm. I've always been hopeless with figures. I've never seen such beautiful accounts. Wonderful writing, too."

Being poor at maths suddenly became less shameful, because it was a link to Willy.

The school was in the Rue d'Agadir, in the new town, beyond the big shops and banks. It was not far but she could not walk there. Willy would drive her every day. Because the journey might be short and she could not pass the whole day without asking, she blurted the question out right away. "How do I know my parents aren't dead?"

"Of course they're not."

She looked at him very carefully. It did not seem possible that he would lie to her.

"Will they get out?"

Willy let the car float to the side of the road, lit a cigarette. He glanced at her face.

"Your father's an enterprising man. He'll find a way, if anyone can. What's all this about?"

"I found Mutti's jewellery in my case. Why did she put it there?"

"Ah," he said. "That's not sinister. That's clever. That's because if they found it in her case, they'd keep it. But she will have reckoned that they might not search you. Did they?"

She shook her head.

"There you are then. She didn't tell you so you wouldn't worry."

It was one of his gifts, knowing how to say the one thing that made everything all right. As they drove on, she remembered how her mother had failed to sell her silver. Though her collection was exceptional, handmade by Danish craftsmen, no German would give a fair price for Jewish property. Glutted with silverware, Herr Mönckeberg am Alten Markt had offered a small percentage of each sale. But nobody bought. When the Gestapo demanded a list of her possessions, her mother decided that the authorities would not get her collection. She polished each bowl and platter, laid them in their blue leather boxes lined with white silk and carried them to the next-door neighbours. Back and forth she went, until Gerhard and Paula had them all.

From their first chance encounter in the Landsweg, these neighbours had been close friends. One spring evening, her parents had taken three-year-old Ilse to jump over the cat's cradle of strings on sticks that laid out the cellars and stairs of their new house. They had seen a nice-looking couple walking over the adjoining plot with a little girl, just the same age, doing exactly the same thing. Ilse loved that story of how she and Lottchen first met. They moved in on the same day, ran in and out of each other's houses. When school began, they walked there together every day, hand in hand. Yet when Paula accepted the gift of silver, Lottchen started avoiding Ilse. It was as if Ilse's mother had done something bad, for which they were both to be shunned. Going home, Ilse pretended not to see her walking ahead, talking loudly with girls who lived much farther away, but whose family trees demonstrated that they were of the pure race. She had spoken to her just the once. That last bitter winter in Wuppertal, she had noticed Lottchen in her Bund deutscher Mädel* uniform as she passed the gate of the Schloßpark. Her former friend stood under the bare trees asking late afternoon strollers to donate to the Winter Relief collection for the poor and needy. Two beautiful dogs sat sedately beside her. Ilse, who generally tried to avoid seeing her, had paused just for a second. They were such good, patient dogs, each with a collecting tin for coins round his neck.

In that second Lottchen had seen her and beckoned, drawing her past the sign that excluded Jews. In the most natural way, as if nothing had ever come between them, Lottchen introduced her to Max, the chocolate Labrador, and Moritz, the Alsatian. They were police dogs, so well trained that if you dropped a coin in his box, Max would lift his deep eyes to you soulfully and half raise a paw, as if in thanks. Short as she was of pfennigs, Ilse had to try this and the two girls smiled at each other. Then, stamping icy feet, Lottchen went off to the kiosk where the policemen who had trained the dogs had gone, saying that she was desperate for hot chocolate too. So Ilse was permitted to take her place just for a moment, to stroke the silky ears and back of the gentle creature. Max had eyes that smiled, that were the exact same colour as his coat and he thumped his tail on the ground when he was caressed. From far away she watched them returning across the park, a girl skipping between two policemen and then slowing down, hanging back while they came forward. Something must have been said. Who was she? Why was she not in uniform? Something must have been said about Jews, for the taller policeman drawing near called out sharply that she should not be in the park and the other one gave a loud bark of a laugh and said to watch out, or he might set the dogs on her. Moritz, taking his cue from them, began to growl. His fangs were very sharp. Ilse, fleeing, saw that even gentle Max stood. A dumb animal could not know better; he had to do as he was told.

Willy stopped the car outside a long white building with a neat yard; nuns in long robes went in and out. A group of girls walked by, chattering, one of them swinging books in a strap. They seemed so absorbed in

---

*League of German Girls—the female equivalent of the Hitler Youth, known as BdM.

one another. She could not seem to make herself move. Uncertainties weighed so heavily, they glued her to the seat.

"Willy, please tell me. Mutti is coming, isn't she?"

"Of course she is," said Willy. He came round and opened the door for her.

"Tell them I'm a Lindemann," she whispered as they went in. She had always wanted that name. If she had been a Lindemann, the bad things would not have happened.

"Nobody here cares what you're called."

"Please."

"Don't worry. You can use any name you like. But you are still you," said Willy.

It was not for her father but because of Willy that she wrote Blumenthal and not Lindemann on the exercise books.

The school had a shady central courtyard where girls played hop-scotch at break. There were no boy pupils. Ilse looked at them nervously. She did not make friends easily and never had, so her expectations were not very high. Here, where everybody spoke French, it was bound to be yet more difficult. All the other girls were Catholics. They wore neat cotton dresses and had little crosses round their necks. Of course they all had their friends already.

At break time everybody went out into the big space in groups of three and four. A group started a skipping game, and Ilse stood at a little distance and watched. A girl from her class with long, smooth brown hair came by and smiled at her. Her name was Anne. She asked where Ilse lived. She gathered her courage to reply. Another girl drifted near and listened to her halting French, not in an unfriendly way. Ilse explained that she was the niece of Willy Lindemann.

"Ah," said Anne, "Lindemann. But I know your uncle." Her voice was soft and went up and down, as though everything was a lovely surprise. She explained that her father was an engineer who had worked with Monsieur Lindemann's building firm and that her uncle was très gentil. Together, easily, they watched the skipping. In a little while, when the next person was out and Anne was beckoned in, she pulled Ilse with her. Skipping was something Ilse was very good at.

Every second morning there was mass, an impressive service in a cool chapel adjoining the school. She watched as the others went forward and took communion and had wafers put on their tongues while

she remained at the rear. Her class had done their première communion only the term before and on the wall of the classroom there was a
big photograph of them all in beautiful white dresses and veils. After
the mass, though nobody had asked her what her religion was, she
announced that she was a Lutheran Protestant. This caused a lot of
interest and she then had to explain it, which she did badly. They seemed
to know only about their own religion and Islam and it seemed to her
that these girls had probably never heard of a Jew, let alone seen one.
She liked being a Lutheran Protestant, felt quietly superior.

The school was strictly run; there was a discipline and order in every
detail, which pleased Ilse. Good pupils were rewarded and everybody
knew their place. She saw that if she tried hard, she could learn to speak
French really well. She listened carefully and spoke when she was spoken to. Her mother had been insistent that she should learn as much as
she could. But without real mastery of the language, maths was impossible, history new and quite different, even geography hard because the
whole continent of Africa was unknown to her. She knew Europe. A
dozen times, Ilse had been made to trace the Elbe, the Rhine or the
Donau from their sources to the sea, never managing to get the shapes
into her head. Here the places had new names, which flowed from the
tongue. Cologne, Bâle, Genève and Milan were much softer than Köln,
Basel, Genf and Mailand. Paris was the centre of the universe and next
came the départements of France, divided into mellifluous and romantic
places all the way from Pas-de-Calais to Tarn et Garonne. She loved the
idea of France. Anne knew all these names and when Ilse was called
upon to recite them, her new friend watched her, nodding encouragement. She was not irritated when a person did not know things.

When Ilse told Toni how much she loved her new school, Toni was
amused and said that she was very unnatural. Tentatively—for fear of
imposing—she asked if she could please have a cotton dress and a smock
like the ones the others wore. Toni cast her eyes to heaven, but she took
out a tape measure and measured her carefully across her nonexistent
bosom and skinny hips. Ilse did not have the courage to ask for a cross,
for fear of Toni's mockery.

Toni took her to the souk to buy fabric. Water-sellers were ringing
their bells in the dusty square and a tooth-puller sat on a little stool with
his implements glittering on a soft cloth. Black-eyed children clustered
round Toni, chattering and offering to be her guide, each elbowing the

next. Toni, who had brought a big basket, distributed the treasures inside—pencils and sharpeners—but the children did not cease importuning until one of them had been chosen to accompany them into the shady interior.

"You see they want to lead the foreigners through the dangerous labyrinth and then back out to safety. Because without them, we would get completely lost and never come back."

Ilse had supposed, wrongly, that Toni did not care much for children. With these children Toni was at her ease, teasing one, then another, heaping her gifts into the outstretched hands of a single lucky boy, only to turn away and then back again, suddenly finding pencils for all of them. And they seemed to know her, for they ignored other Europeans and vied for position, stretching out their chests and knocking one another out of line. They were so intensely alive, jittering on thin legs, chattering like starlings. The first boy seized the empty basket and drew himself up with the air of a man of considerable responsibilities. Importantly, he led them on. Crisscrossed with thin laths, which gave a striped shade, the souk was cool after the heat of the square. Ilse breathed in the dizzying smells of spices, which each different corner overlaid with its specific stronger odour, whether of mint tea or leather or cedarwood. Toni did not need a guide. She showed Ilse where the potters plied their trade and that the hammering sound came from the beaters of copper bowls. She pointed out which meandering way would lead to the embroiderers, who made beautiful blouses, and where—should she chance to need them—Ilse might find the weavers and woodworkers.

The little boy Toni had selected fell back, trotting respectfully a step behind. From time to time, conscious of his duties when somebody came the other way, he would let out a cry of "Balek—balek!" This meant to take care. Ilse was drawn by each fresh vision. She longed to watch the leatherworker cross-legged on his sheepskin in his Aladdin's cave of soft, pointed slippers, but she dared not stop. The golden figure of Toni, so precise in her heels and brilliantly coloured dress, moved ahead, blurring and twisting in the dappled light like the skeins of wool and cloth dyed in rainbow colours. If she looked away for too long, Toni might vanish into the pattern of a carpet or be absorbed into a red-threaded jar of saffron. She, whose moods were so various, might filter through the heaped baskets of ginger and chick peas, fava beans and split peas into some other realm. And so Ilse kept up until, suddenly slackening her pace to a crawl, Toni neared a particular trader's stall and dawdled before it and the one next to it, touching muslins and velvets and then asking the price of a heavily gold-embroidered cloth, then moving on, a person with all the time in the world and no particular interest in anything. When at last she flicked a finger at the cotton fabrics the girls wore, it was a random and disinterested selection. The stall-keeper was a broad middle-aged man who, bringing forth glasses of tea almost too hot to hold, tirelessly unrolled bales of magnificent silks and velvets from every corner, pressing their virtues on Toni, who saw everything, liked nothing, and finally, in a leisurely way, got up to go. They eyed each other. Perhaps she would have some of the cotton. Now the bargaining began in French too rapid for her to understand. Ilse, who would never have disputed the price anyone asked and would have been ashamed to ask for a reduction, watched Toni's animated face. Her pouts and sighs and exclamations of dismay were well matched by the hand-wringing of the seller until—agreeing to a price that would ruin a poor man like him—he was suddenly transformed into smiles. He wrapped up the cotton and then cut a long length of silk in a deep amber colour and reached down an apple green velvet, smiling at Ilse. He bowed extravagantly. "All for Mademoiselle, says Madame."

Ilse, open-mouthed at the magnificence, turned to Toni, who was not to be thanked, ever.

"These are your colours," she said. "Always remember that."

Ilse had been at school for two weeks when the nun from the boat reappeared. The small woman came to the door of the classroom and stood just inside it until the chatterbox girls noticed her presence and, falling silent, slipped back to their desks. The very outline of her head indicated authority. Ilse knew how recognisable she herself was. Although the nun said nothing, her eyes signalled that she remembered. Ilse felt sick. The maths lesson began. In the bustle of handing out exercise books, Anne whispered that Soeur Marie-Joseph was the principal of the school, had just visited France and then been on her annual retreat.

Ilse waited for her to denounce the Jew. She felt an acute consciousness imprinting itself on her brain. The words of the others floated by her, she was inside a bubble and set aside. She was aware of where Soeur Marie-Joseph was, of the precise angle of her slight figure at the blackboard, of the slanting light on the chalk and the raising and falling of her hand against the darkness. She could not take in anything the quiet voice said. Though the nun did not address her, it was only a matter of time.

At mid-morning there was a quiet moment when everyone rested. Ilse, itchy with misery, could not stand it one minute longer. She walked through the courtyard, pushed open the gates and picked her way down the long dusty road. She knew that she was not supposed to go anywhere on her own. She wandered around, looking at the streets and the houses. Some had courtyards with palm trees and green gardens glimpsed through half-open doors. Her head was milling with confused thoughts. Her skin was too white and she could feel it burning. She did not know where she was going or what she would do when she got there. A woman in a veil smiled at her and gave her dates to eat. After a while, because her legs had started to feel wobbly, she sat on a wall. A big dog barked. She got up and walked away. Men driving a lorry called something to her. She trudged on and on. She was hopelessly lost.

Around the next corner, low brick walls rose above a concrete slab. The bold red letters of Willy's company sign shone out. With sandals dusted white and feet aching from tiredness, she ventured onto the building site; a dozen men were working. He might be angry, but she could not go on. One of the men pointed. Another joined him. They were talking about her.

"Do you know where to find Monsieur Lindemann?" she said.

The first man ran over to a little wooden hut in the corner. She knelt in the dust. The man came back with a bottle of lemonade, offered it to her. She refused; her mother would not have liked her to drink from it. Her head felt buzzy and light. She stared up at the sky and a black bird far away. The two men were joined by others, who stood around and looked at her as the first one fanned her hot face. They said things. Time passed. The men started shouting.

Willy's car came round the corner. "You must get out of the sun," he said. The hut with its corrugated tin roof was very stuffy inside. He did not scold her, but knelt and told her that she had to drink something and now, obediently, she did. He gave her a handkerchief and she wiped her hands and face. It came away grimed with sweat and dust. When she was feeling better, he introduced her to all the workers, one by one. My only niece, he said, my precious girl. The men nodded and smiled. When they finished their day's work and left the site, Willy drove her slowly back to school. All the other girls had gone home. They sat for a time in silence outside the gates.

"This is the best school for girls in Meknès," he said. "Of course I'm no expert, but everyone says it."

She could not get out of the car. She felt weak.

"The nuns have a fine reputation for good works."

Ilse could not meet his eye.

"It's not a Gymnasium. I realise that it must seem very different from Germany."

When he started to open the car door, Ilse pulled him back. She begged him not to go in, said that they did not like her. His face was grave. She said that they had mocked her red hair, that the girls had been unkind, that the nuns were very cruel. He sat for a long time looking at the steering wheel without saying a word.

"Are you sure, Ilse?"

Tears sprang from her. She cried, with great sobs, both for the wickedness of the lies that she had told and for all the lies that there were in the world. She had wept like this when her teacher in Wuppertal had snapped at her that she was an idiot, that a half Jew was not permitted to join the Bund deutscher Mädel. Then she had realised that, though she knew nothing about Jews and their beliefs, she would never wear the uniform the others proudly displayed. Jews could not attend a Gymnasium; she was tolerated only because her mother was not Jewish. She was extremely lucky that they had not expelled her when they got rid of "the other dirty yids." She could never manage breakfast because her stomach churned with fear of what her teacher might say and do, and of the little rod he used so freely. She never spoke to anyone in her class and learnt to avoid meeting anybody's eyes. They said hateful things, and there were boys who enjoyed twisting her arm and yanking at her hair. But after that first shock, she had schooled herself never to react. She would not let them see that she suffered.

"Ilse?" He was looking at her still. "What is it?"

"I don't know," she said, trying to control her voice. Then, because the lie made her uncomfortable, she added to it. "It's my parents. It's not knowing about them."

"You mustn't worry about them. They'll be all right." He lit a cigarette, waited.

"Not Vati. Nobody would give him a visa. Nobody would have

him." She blew her nose. True words had come out of her mouth before she knew what she was going to say.

"Your father is a fine man. He's a good German. There aren't many of them left."

"I know all about that," she said. "For years, I've heard about fighting the fascists. But what if you can't fight them?"

He smoked and thought for a moment.

"Nobody can promise that it will all be all right. But your father will look after your mother."

"You don't know how it is," she said, not wanting to say straight out that it was the other way round. Mutti was the one who worked and earned money. "He's always away or in prison. So he can't look after her, can he?"

Willy's eyes were kind. "They'll find a way. I haven't seen him for years. But I know what he's like. You know, when Lore said she was marrying again, I interviewed him." Willy laughed. "I said I wanted to look him over, meet for a meal. He told me to get lost. Said he was going to marry her no matter what."

"Really?"

"He didn't care what anybody said or felt. We had a meal anyway. I liked him. Is he still like that?" She nodded.

"He gets his own way. Doesn't he? You see, it's the defining thing about him." Ilse saw. "You have to have confidence in that."

"I'm all right now," she said. Willy turned everything round in her head. She had been wrong to imagine that her parents would separate as soon as she was gone, if they had not done so already.

"All right enough to go in?"

She nodded. When the puffiness round the eyes had gone down, they went in. Soeur Marie-Joseph greeted them in her quiet voice, said she had been worried. What had happened? Ilse opened her mouth to speak.

"It is all my fault," said Willy rapidly. He had made a mistake, had offered to take Ilse swimming—she had thought it was a half day and gone to meet him. He blamed himself entirely. The nun, who held her head to one side, looked from one to the other and must have seen her red eyes, but did not mention it. Ilse stared at her knees, which still had streaks of dust upon them. There was a long pause when he finished.

Soeur Marie-Joseph leant back in her chair. She looked at Willy and gave her head a little shake, then stood. Willy stood and so did Ilse.

"Fräulein Blumenthal," said the nun in careful German, "I speak to you in your language because I want you to understand exactly what I say. I am responsible for every girl. I must know that every girl is safe. You must not go away in the middle of the day. Will you give me your word that it will not happen again?"

"Never. I promise." They shook hands on it.

Ilse floated to the car, she felt so light.

"I can't tell a nun a lie," said Willy, shaking his head. "I'm going to have to buy you a bathing suit right this minute."

Because in the afternoons Toni had her siesta, Willy collected Ilse after school and took her to the club, which was shady with long beautiful lawns sprinkled each morning to keep them velvety green. Girls she knew from school swam and drank Coca-Cola and ate baguettes, the fresh soft bread split in two and stuffed with squares of chocolate which melted deliciously as you bit in. People dived in and called to one another across the water, and Ilse swam with Anne, who was like a fish. She had long been afraid of the water, but would jump in if Willy was watching. He, who was so tanned, said her white skin was beautiful and that she need not mind being skinny. Toni had been skinny as a girl. She might grow, later, and if she didn't, she must not mind being small. Toni was petite and look at her. As for him, it was breaking stones in the desert that had turned him that colour and that was not to be recommended. He stretched out on a towel luxuriantly. "My friend Heinz developed shoulders like an ox."

"Why were you breaking stones?"

He laughed at her big eyes, staring at him. "Breaking up big stones into little ones to make roads. In the French Foreign Legion."

"Why?"

"For hundreds of years, generations of Legionnaires have sweated in the desert, handling these stones. Discipline. They like to keep you busy."

"It's terrible."

"It's a hard life. But Heinz was clever. He got us moved into the kitchen, said we were cooks. He learnt fast. He can make salami out of a donkey."

"But why did you join up?"

"I looked so good in the kepi." He was laughing again.

"Really?"

"I had to get out of Germany. But I loved the Legion."

"Why did you have to get out?"

"A woman. With me it's always cherchez la femme."

"Please, tell me about her."

"When you're older."

"I'll understand, I'm old enough."

He groaned and bent his back and hobbled, pretending he had a stick and was a very old man. "This old?" She had felt that she was old, very old. Here, she was just a girl of thirteen, the same as other girls.

Willy never talked about the past if Toni was there. She always said that they had to live for each day. Toni could not stand anything sentimental and especially not what she called Willy's soft butter side. Germans were all like that, she said, civilised and soppy until you gave them a knock and then they turned as hard as flint. When she shouted at him (the two of them always spoke German though her occasional endearments came out in French), Willy held his tongue. That annoyed her the most.

"He is perfect," Toni said sarcastically. "The perfect German knight." Ilse did not understand.

"Ask him about the Ritterpflicht,"* she said. "He knows all about that."

When she wagged her finger, Willy shrank back, pretending to be scared. He loved doing that.

"She thinks I'm some kind of medieval knight errant. That it's my quest to protect a lady with my life. I'll have to be a cat with nine lives, now that I have two ladies."

"You see? He doesn't have a single bit of common sense," said Toni. "It's deep in the psyche of the nation. Germans can't help themselves. Like the holy fool, Parsifal, swearing fine oaths and sent out to fight for a noble cause without even knowing what it is."

Ilse, puzzled, cast a look of appeal at Willy.

"Don't worry. She's crazy," he whispered, loud enough for Toni to hear. He waited for her to respond, but she would not. Ilse watched the

*The duties of the courtly knight.

stubborn, beautiful little face and was struck by an obvious thing she had nearly overlooked: how very seriously Toni took things.

Every night, they went out to dinner. Toni never cooked; she said it was no fun eating in your own house. Ilse was expected to dress up. She now owned three cotton dresses as well as the silk and velvet. Willy had insisted that she must have decent clothes. Since putting a clean dress on and brushing her hair only took five minutes, she would be ready, skipping up and down while they waited. Toni always took her time. While they were on their own, Willy could be persuaded to tell her secrets her parents had never disclosed.

"Tell me about Mutti's first husband."

"Rainer? A big fellow, very nice looking but also very weak. Very good old legal family, a long line of judges. He was the precious only son, but they all disowned him in the end. Lore married him for all the wrong reasons. Remember, Ilse, always beware of your first great love."

"But Jewish?"

"No. Why should he be?"

He puffed a beautiful smoke ring.

"Oh."

Ilse had always assumed that the first husband, a wraithlike figure compared to her substantial father, must have been Jewish too. This was a great surprise. She might have been the wholly Aryan child of that first husband, who had gone to the bad and after the divorce had vanished from all their lives. She could not stop turning this over in her head, wondering how bad he really was and whether, if he had been her father, she would still have been herself.

If Toni decided to have another martini, Willy would use the time to tend his garden. The planting was all his work. When he left the Legion and bought the house, he had planted the three cedar trees along the path, which now shaded the bedrooms. These were flanked with junipers and thuyas. The great mass of vivid pink flowers were bougainvilleas. Willy said that Meknès, like Fez, was watered by wet westerly winds; still, there was never enough rain for a really beautiful lawn. He loved to make the spray of the hose arc high into the air and threaten her with it.

"Dare me. Go on."

Hopping and squeaking "I dare you! I dare you!" she would dart about the courtyard in and out of the columns and behind the cedars, and he would aim and fire and turn the marble a slippery pink until in the end he would get her and soak her, helpless from laughing too much, from head to foot. Then, so Toni would not be annoyed, she would have to scramble into another dress in half a minute. Rubbing at her hair, she would stare through half-closed eyes at the photograph of her parents which she had rescued from obscurity and which now stood on the chest of drawers. She was trying to put her mother into the arms of a big man, quite nice looking, with a weak chin. Always, though, Otto came back in full strength.

A letter in her mother's writing addressed to Willy lay on the breakfast table. Ilse shot past Toni at her desk, ran shouting to the big bathroom and dragged Willy into the kitchen with shaving foam still on his face. He opened it, scanned the first line. "For you," he said, smiling and handing it over. "Am I allowed to shave now?"

She devoured it instantly, then read it again. Her mother wrote that she was overjoyed that Ilse was safe and happy. She could not wait to see her and be with her. She said that she had sent a previous letter, which had been returned to her stamped *Opened by the Reichs Post Office in order to ascertain sender* because she had foolishly forgotten to put her address on the envelope. So this time she would remember to give it. Ilse turned over the back of the envelope, where she read Tante Käthe's name and address in Krefeld. Of course she had to put an Absender.* Anything from a Jews' House would always be opened by the authorities. Did that mean she was now living with Tante Käthe? Ilse frowned. She could not imagine that. The letter was rather shorter than she had hoped. Her mother sent much love, thanked Willy for the introduction and said the job possibility he had mentioned was looking very hopeful.

"Why is it so short? Why doesn't it sound like her?"

Ilse watched his face as Willy scanned it.

"It's fine. I think she's saying to be very careful because she's scared of the censor. We have to write to Krefeld now and old Käthe will send the letters on. I hope my aunt doesn't throw your letters away. She's not quite there. You know, not all the cups are in the cupboard," said Willy, winking. This expression amused Ilse.

"What did she mean about the job?"

"I got in touch with a family I know in Hamburg, the Riemkes, old friends of mine. They know everyone, and I thought they might find her

*Return addressee.

something. She needs to earn decent money, fast. In a city it's much easier."

"It's so far," she said. It was odd to imagine her mother undertaking such a thing without her.

"Wuppertal is so small. In Hamburg she can make a fresh start."

"How clever you are," said Ilse, rejoicing in the thought of her mother freed from the claustrophobia of that crowded house, earning plenty of money. "I wonder how Mutti got permission to travel to Hamburg?"

"Permission?"

"Only Aryans travel," she said.

"She is an Aryan. If she doesn't use your father's name, that is."

She thought about this. It had never occurred to her before that her mother could behave like an Aryan. But she was one and perhaps now she could. Of course things went on and were different, without her. Ilse wrote back at once, telling her mother about school and the smooth way the nuns walked, as though they ran on little castors under their skirts. How incoherent her last letter must have been, all pleasures and sensations jumbled up. Sucking the end of the pen, Ilse waited for the right words to come. They seemed to lie elsewhere, in the pauses between the careful strokes of the pen. "Please come soon," she wrote, "it is so lovely here," when she wanted to write that her mother should get out as fast as she could. Willy had warned her not to say anything contentious. She knew that she certainly should not mention a ticket, or the hope of an exit visa. So she wished her mother good luck with the job and that she hoped it would pay very well and underlined that twice. She would understand. Then she sucked some more on the pen. It gave Ilse a pang to think of Mutti alone in Hamburg when she had so many people now. Meknès was full of Willy's and Toni's friends.

After dinner, if they were not going to the cinema, Willy and Toni would drop Ilse back and go out to a nightclub with Heinz and one of his girls. Heinz's love life enjoyed continual shifts and turns. Toni explained that he generally had three women in his life. There was the current favourite, the last one—who was being eased out very gently—and the next, who was being brought on. Ilse had got used to Toni's breathtaking frankness. This being a school night, she was supposed to sleep, but could not. Ilse lay with her mother's letter under her pillow, looking at the stripes the moonlight made coming through the blinds and imagining her getting the good job. She wondered what it would be. She had tried so many things to earn money. It should be better than being a waitress, though not as good as being a lawyer. Three years earlier Hitler had stopped all women from being lawyers; how upset her mother had been.

She was still awake when they returned. The house was so quiet, she could hear the faint sound of Willy and Toni talking. Sometimes she could not sleep because of the way they argued, her voice high against his low occasional rumble. Toni was like a storm which raged but then blew over quickly, bringing clear skies.

"A hundred reasons for being an atheist," announced Willy in the car.

"We've done them all," she said.

"We can't have—"

"You told me the one about the priest and the housekeeper. And the one about the bleeding statue made of red clay. You told me last week." She was glad that he did not know about her wanting the cross.

"Those are Catholic ones. This is a Mohammedan one, about the great prophet Sidi Aïssa, who performed so many miracles that it was not possible to count them. His admirers were legion, too many to count. Too many to handle. That's his house over there."

It was an ordinary-looking white building with a green roof.

"Go on."

"So he summoned them to the square in front of his house and said, The prophet demands the sacrifice of the most faithful. Who of you are that? What do you think happened?"

"They ran away?"

"No. One man stepped forward. The crowd waited, and from the house there came a terrible scream. Blood ran over the doorstep. What do you think the believers did then?"

"They all ran away."

"They had faith, Ilse. A second went in and a third—and more blood flowed, but the square began to empty."

"See? They weren't stupid after all."

"They withdrew. Then Sidi Aïssa came out of his house leading the forty sacrifices. Allah had given them the power to let their blood flow without dying. But it was the blood of forty sheep."

"Poor sheep."

"They had a feast. Ate them. Did I tell you about the time I was offered the sheep's eyeballs, as a special delicacy at the wedding of my friends?"

"Yes! Yes! Don't!" Ilse was squeamish.

"Don't worry. Nobody really eats them," but he mimed putting them into his mouth and making the imaginary balls pop from one cheek to the next until she begged him to stop.

"Where there's religion, something has to be sacrificed. Always."

"All right." She thought for a moment. "Are you saying religion is always a bad thing?"

"I'm saying it shouldn't count. That it doesn't matter. It's the great tragedy of the twentieth century that it does. Ask Toni."

Of course she didn't. Ilse knew not to ask Toni anything unless she was perfectly sure that she wanted to know the answer. At night, snug in the neat little white bed in the room she loved so much, she would go over in her head the things Toni had been right about. There was the business, which her mother could and should have taken charge of. Now the shop belonged to the Aryan manager. There was politics and also religion. Her father said that religion was irrelevant in the twentieth century. That was why she had never been inside a synagogue, nor eaten kosher food, except at Tante Röschen's. Otto had been wrong about that, too. Sleepily her thoughts drifted away from that unreal Germany where everything was so difficult. She was never going to go back there. Nobody could force her. She thought instead about the food Marie was making for the picnic on Sunday, spicy lamb with mint and rice and a huge tagine with couscous. She was growing, putting on weight. She wrote to tell her mother that, carefully licking the envelope shut and writing Tante Käthe's address in her best writing. The old lady would not forget, she would send the letters on. Mutti would be so pleased. She thought dreamily about how, when she arrived, her mother would love the couscous and the silk. Their colours would be exactly the same. They would forget all about Germany and never talk about it ever again.

In Ifran, the air was so clear that the mountains looked like picture post-cards. The pretty villas with their lush green gardens in the European style made the people who had not been home for a long time feel very nostalgic. Heinz had brought his new girlfriend and there was another German couple and a French one and a Moroccan lawyer from Fez and his wife and their baby. As they lay eating a lazy lunch, it seemed impossible that their nations could fight each other. Ahmed, their Moroccan friend, asked the men whether they supported France or Germany.

"France," said Toni right away. "We're French by naturalisation and champagne."

Toni had not spoken much French before she came to Morocco but now she was as quick as anybody, rattling it off and making the men laugh.

"Neither," said Heinz. "We belong to the Legion. The treizième demi-brigade owns our souls."

"Our friends are the kinds of Germans Hitler doesn't like, and we're the kind of French nobody likes," said Willy and then the men got into a discussion about independence and what would happen to Morocco if war came.

Ilse cuddled the baby and watched Willy, languidly laid out on a rug enjoying a smoke but always turning his face and screwing up his eyes against the sun to see where his wife had got to. If she talked too long to some other man then Willy would fidget, losing the thread of his own conversation. When Toni wandered down to the pine trees at the water's edge, scuffing her high-heeled sandals through the soft ridges of pine needles, Willy and Ilse went too. Monkeys were running wild. Willy said there was always snow here in the winter, that she would love it at Christmas. They would go dancing at one of the smarter hotels, see "les palmiers en fête."

"Will Mutti be with us by then?"

"She'll dance us all off our feet," he said and winked.

Heinz and Ahmed wanted to go fishing. Ilse went with them to rent a boat at the Châlet du Lac. She was allowed to row it, proud of her prowess though it raised little blisters on her palms and thumbs. From her position on the still waters she could see, but not hear, Willy and Toni walking and talking, back and forth at the edge of the water. They looked serious. But when she got back from the rowing, Willy lay at his ease under the pine trees at the water's edge and smiled his usual smile.

Her French was improving rapidly. She and her friend did homework together. With Anne as her dictionary, she looked up fewer words and wrote more fluently. She made up a story about a little monkey separated from its tribe. The monkey, which had wanted to be free, found itself threatened by wild animals. By swinging through the trees, always letting the sun flash a certain way through the palm fronds, it managed to find its way back to its people and safety. Soeur Mathilde congratulated her on her story, said it was an allegory, one of the few words that was exactly the same in French, German and English. She was learning English now.

At the end of term, Ilse was awarded the prize for the best story and was called up to receive a silver cup, which was hers until the next term began. Lots of girls applauded. Proudly she placed it on her chest of drawers alongside the photograph of her parents. She polished them both with a special liquid Marie had. Ilse would have been completely happy, were it not for the news. The Europeans in the cafés were disagreeing noisily, pointing to the newspapers and speculating. The talk was all about the coming war, about Hitler's aggression and whether the Munich agreement would hold. When war came, German citizens would be interned. No, they would all be repatriated. Not to worry, Willy said. They should all take French citizenship, as he had. The French had a huge army, they would defeat the Germans, providing, of course, that the Legion was in on the fight. Then they heard that there would be peace. The British minister had fixed it.

Toni scoffed at that. She was the first to join in the endless speculation, driven to know the latest rumour and then to analyse it. Willy asked her to stop, saying that he was sick of listening to stories of German aggression, but Toni would or could not.

Ilse tugged at his arm. She whispered, "We should be frightened of the Germans."

"I was born German, wasn't I? Are you frightened of me?" His eyes were sad.

"Never."

She felt free with these adults, with their complicated but carefree lives. She knew that Willy loved her and she loved him without reservation.

At night Willy and Toni took to arguing with a different tone. These were long discussions. It was about where they would go when war came and what to do with her. Her visa would soon expire, so a decision had to be made, to apply for residence or not. If Willy chose to fight, Toni said that they had to send her back. She mentioned Belgium or France. Willy said they could not do that. They had a promise to keep. Toni said a good deal about the duties of parents. She kept saying that they had to be practical. Ilse, who knew that Toni was very practical indeed, could not bear to hear any more and put her pillow over her head. She thought that if she kept quiet on the subject, she might be able to conceal her stubbornness—a fault so great that her mother had once said it extended to the point of wilfulness. She passionately wanted not to be sent back, for clearly her mother had made the right decision in sending her here. Yet she could not oppose whatever Toni chose to do. Ilse understood and admired Toni's terrible straightforwardness, which made her unlike any other woman.

For Toni's birthday they went away for a week, driving first to Rabat, then purring along the good tarmacadamed coastal highway to Casablanca, which, as its name suggested, was a city of white buildings with the most elegant shops. They spent one night in a hotel looking onto the grey rolling sea and early the next morning they took the road up to the broad plain of Blad el Hamra. Marrakech was two hundred and fifty kilometres away, said Willy. Ilse watched the mountains coming ever nearer, until they were passing through hundreds of palm trees with the red ramparts of the city ahead. It was, as Willy had promised, a broad city of gardens and very green. Their hotel lay on the edge of the city walls, surrounded by palms and fruit trees, and looking towards the high Atlas Mountains. Willy went right away to look at plots of land while Ilse and Toni wandered in the sun-striped alleyways of the souk. Toni was even younger than she had imagined, confiding in Ilse that it was her thirtieth birthday, a great event. She bargained for carpets and bought herself jangling gold bracelets for her birthday present and threw in another one, finely hammered with an elaborate curling pattern, for Ilse. She would not be thanked, skipping ahead and shaking off any hint of gratitude.

They sipped mint tea and ate cakes on the terrace of a café overlooking Place Djemaa El Fna and watched the dancing monkeys, the snake charmers and fire-eaters. From the little height where they sat, Ilse could see a very old snake charmer, almost bent double, with a very dark face and a very white turban. He sat cross-legged and with his face twisted up, shaking a tambourine and playing his wooden flute. In front of him, a blue wooden box sat in the centre of a piece of dingy carpet. It was from this that the head of a cobra rose. The old man never looked right or left, never took his eyes off the snake and did not seem to care or notice what went on around him. They had the same eyes, man and snake, which they kept fixed upon each other. Ilse sat for a long time paralysed by them, quite unable to move her feet, though she badly wanted to rise and get away from the place. It was the snake which hypnotised the man.

Toni's birthday dinner was chicken under egg pancake and Ilse's favourite, lamb with peas and aubergines roasted in an earthenware pot with couscous. Full as they were, Willy ordered pastilla au lait, which you ate with your hands, layers of crunchy mille-feuille pastry with sesame seeds on top and milk poured over. Ilse loved this best.

A large lady came on swathed in veils with heavy makeup and a gold brassiere with dangling beads, the sleeves separate and attached with strings. Even the French couples who talked all the time fell silent to watch her strike a pose. The musicians struck up a high note and she started to shake and turn, and the beads glittered and turned with her. One by one the veils came off, pink, blue, black, green, red and then cream, leaving only the orange one under which could be seen a big wobbling belly. The men applauded as the big woman gyrated her hips more and more rapidly, shaking out the beads. As she began to pull the orange one off, Ilse noticed the French proprietor, a small man in a dinner jacket. He was going from table to table, his palms facing outwards in supplication, talking intently. Behind him, the orange veil came off and the big woman shook and shimmied more violently than ever.

"Messieurs, dames, forgive me for disturbing you," said the little man. The German army had invaded Poland.

Toni got up and went straight out of the room. Willy followed her. They were gone for a long time, and Ilse, licking a finger to catch the last crumbs of the pastry, waited anxiously for their return. When they came back, Willy said that they had to leave the restaurant straight away.

In the car, Toni hissed at Willy, "Don't tell me you're going to go and fight, because you're not."

"Do we stand aside while they overrun Poland?"

"You know what I feel about Poland."

"If the Legion fights, my darling, the treizième DBLE will need every man."

"Not you."

"Toni. Please, look at me."

But she looked away and would not talk to either of them.

At the hotel, as Toni clicked angrily away across the marble lobby in her high heels for a last drink at the bar, Willy took Ilse's arm and saw her to her door. All the way up in the lift, she kept thinking the same silly thought about how she might persuade Willy to be her blood brother. The way to do it was to make a little cut and collect a few drops of blood in a basin. They could mingle them and drink the liquid, dissolved in water. That meant that they were one soul with two bodies. But there was not time to suggest this, for Willy was hurrying back to his wife.

Willy took her for a drive very early in the morning. The weather was beautiful, the air so clear, the mountain peaks tinged with pink. As soon as they got out of town and onto the open road, he stopped the car and told Ilse to drive. She, still small for her age, sat on his lap while he worked the pedals, peering over the steering wheel on which he rested one negligent arm. Willy, looking over the top of her head at her reflection in the mirror, kept laughing at her serious face. She was concentrating. The air smelt fresh and good. Driving the car was her favourite thing in the world. But even through the intense happiness of smelling his shaving lotion and being in his arms, Ilse felt, louder and louder, the knocking of her anxious heart.

"Life goes on," he said. "It's important to enjoy each day. Things change. That is what life is."

Mutely, Ilse shook her head.

"When my first wife died, I thought I could never smile again. But look at me. Look at me and Toni. How happy we are."

Ilse thought of Toni's beautiful little face, set in an angry pout.

"What happened to your first wife?" She tried to control her wobbly voice. But the secret was a sad one, even worse than she had imagined, for young Liesel had died tragically in childbirth. Then she did not want to drive anymore.

Willy turned the car round in a cloud of pale dust. "I must get back—I'm concerned about Toni," he said. "She's worried about her people."

"What people?"

"Her family. In Warsaw."

"But what are they doing in Poland?"

"They are all Poles, my darling. Like her. Her family couldn't get out, you see. Same problem as you. And now, who knows?"

Ilse was very stupid. She had not realised that Toni was Polish, let alone Jewish.

FOUR

Hamburg, October 1939

Nicolai chewed at his pen, watched water running down his tree, slicking it black against a grey world. Rain drummed on the roof of his dormer window. His exercise book lay open. He had enjoyed Bible study, which was interestingly full of miracles and disasters, floods and plagues. Now the headmaster taught Lebenskunde* instead, stories about the leader's youth and the history of the Party. It was very dull. The essays he set for homework all had the same titles: *"We want to work and we shall work."* Or: *"We were a broken people but now we are one."*

He flicked ink on the blotter, doodled the blots into giant Zeppelins. His father might have mocked the titles, but he would have helped him with the work. Now that he had gone to officer training school the house was too quiet. Nicolai had taken one particularly good photograph of him laughing, head thrown back, elegant in the field-grey uniform. He reached for the camera. Smoothly, he removed the 35mm lens, screwed on the 50mm, pulled it out and twisted it. There was a faint

---

*Life studies / philosophy of life.

chance that his father might buy him the Elmar telephoto, if he came on leave, if one could be found. He slotted the viewfinder onto the bayonet shoe, adjusted the knurled ring. The optics were the finest available; the very smallness of the camera was astonishing. He relished the weight and solid feel of it in his hand for a moment, then lifted it to his eye, framed a couple of shots, carefully focused: the window, sheeting with rain, the room. No point wasting film.

His mother was out. Roaming through the house, a dog sniffing his usual places, he tiptoed into his father's study, swooshed the whisky round the decanter, poured himself a tot and drank it down. It caught in his throat, its fiery progress down his chest made him shudder. The old faint cigar smell lingered. He played with the lighter. His father would have pulled out a book from the back of the shelves, one of the banned ones behind the innocent front ones; he would have found something to make him laugh. The house was so dull, Nicolai would even have welcomed Wolfgang. But his half-brother had written to tell their mother that he would be visiting less often; Hitler Youth and sports rallies took up all his weekends. At breakfast she had read the letter twice in her proud Wolfgang voice, unbearable now that his father was not there to deflate it with his twinkling eyebrows or sidelong wink.

If only Sabine had not caught those stupid measles. Fräulein Lindemann would have given him ideas for his essay. She was very clever at history and at turning a phrase, but she had been busy with his little sister all week. Sabine, though sweet, was not company. She greeted Nicolai with yelps of delight, she laughed because he did, but she was not a person one could talk to. He had clicked at the big silver lighter too often; it was out of fuel and would not light. He banged it down.

"War is using us all up," he declaimed dramatically.

The empty room mocked him. Everything was annoying. He trailed past the forbidden territory of the kitchen; Magda had banished Nicolai until suppertime. Hot-faced, she slaved in clouds of steam, scalding rubber seals and glass jars, stirring the vat of slowly bubbling sugary fruit. Purple damsons, split and stoned to show their yellow hearts, massed along the wooden board. He descended the cellar staircase, dragging his feet. The supplies multiplied; gleaming jars of peas and red cabbage lined the cellar wall. Shelves filled the space where he used to park his bicycle, which now had to live in the garden shed. Passing Fräulein Lindemann's room, Nicolai spotted a suitcase open on her bed. What was that for? She wasn't going anywhere. He paused. He was not supposed to enter her room, nor Magda's. Dubbed "the sentimental shrine" by his father, Magda's room was crammed. Little china animals and flowers hid every surface, hand-hooked rugs covered the floor. Next to the Führer portrait hung a large, wobbly watercolour of her home, a farm on the Eifel, and beside that a photo of her brother, who looked exactly like her. His father called them the holy triptych, because she worshipped all three.

He put his head round the door. Fräulein Lindemann's room was so bare. There was nothing on the walls at all. Perhaps she was going to leave them. Perhaps she had packed her things already. An anticipatory dread tugged at him. He stepped over the threshold. Her spare navy uniform hung on the wardrobe door, cuffs and collar starched vivid in the dim greenish light from the high window. On the bedside table a clock emitted four chimes. Though late for the Jungvolk, he took a further tentative step on the spotless linoleum floor. The room smelt faintly of talcum powder. A pile of household linen lay stacked on the desk alongside cotton reels, a wooden mushroom for darning and a fat pincushion. She mended and embroidered. Everyone agreed that she was the best nursemaid they had ever had (certainly the best paid, his mother said tartly). His mother, who enjoyed finding fault with her staff, complained that the Fräulein kept running into town upon any whim. This seemed unfair. Even he had noticed that in the six months she had been with them she had scarcely taken a day off, always offering to look after Sabine on Sundays. Occasionally, driving to church they passed her, walking fast, head down, hands deep in the pockets of the grey coat she always wore. She never looked up. He wondered where she went. She was the first nursemaid he liked, because she didn't fuss him.

The suitcase lay open, expectantly. It was a cheap cardboard one with frail metal clasps, lined with tartan paper, part of which was peeling away. Inside was a brown crocodile handbag. With a quick glance at the door, he opened it. There was an identity document, a fat envelope. The young face of Fräulein Lindemann of Seiterstraße 11, Wuppertal, looked just about to smile. A mass of hair fell to her shoulders. The woman he knew wore a faintly pained expression, as if the hair had been strained back too tight, the hairpins holding up the thick twist of hair on the back of her head pushed in too hard. The envelope contained a lot of money, hundreds of Reichsmarks. He riffled along it with an envious finger. It reminded him that he needed money for the Winter Relief collection. Upon an impulse he took a ten-Reichsmark note. She would never miss it. Quickly, he pushed the envelope back into the bag. He really had to hurry.

"The Führer has made Germany live again," a solemn voice intoned. "Nothing will divide us from our leader."

The troop sat cross-legged round the shiny brown Volksempfänger.*

"Nothing will divide us," breathed Peter on his left, a boy about whom a sour smell hung, acute even over the general damp doggy one. He had the irritating habit of repeating every word he heard and a big, slack mouth that tended to hang open.

The Führer was speaking next. They scrambled to their feet. "My only desire is peace with France and Great Britain. Peace with honour," he said.

"With honour," whispered Peter wetly.

Peace was supposedly the objective, though it was obvious to Nicolai that everyone there was mad for war. When the broadcast was over, their leader drew back the curtain and lit the candles, which, nearly spent, guttered dramatically in the draught under the cellar door. One wall was draped in black cloth, emphasising the white of the Siegrune† on the bloodred flag. A steel helmet with real combat dents sat in front of the big poster with the text of the "Horst Wessel Lied."‡ Friedrich announced that every boy had to donate thirty pfennigs for new candles, and distributed the text for the week. The theme was "Martyrs of Germany." Peter opened the pamphlet and his mouth; he mumbled along, even when others were doing the reading.

Nicolai, gazing at dead heroes with chiselled features, could not stand the accompanying monotone. "Peter. My brother Wolfgang's a Stammführer§ over in Lübeck," he whispered.

Peter swivelled his pale eyes round. "A Stammführer? So what. My father's in the army," he said. "And my brother."

Nicolai saw that he had done scant justice to Wolf's glory. "He's in

*People's radio receiver.
†White lightning flash emblem (literally, "victory rune").
‡The most important Nazi song.
§Cadre leader in the Hitler Youth.

charge of six hundred boys. Before that he was a Fahnleinführer* train-ing forty boys his own age, and that's a fact." He was babbling. "Of course he's my half-brother, not a full brother really—"

"Shut up, Bucherer!" called out Friedrich.

"Shut up!" repeated Peter, smirking and looked down at his text. The boy on the other side was sniggering. Eyes fixed on the coarse paper, in dull concentration on the exact spot where the grainy half-tones of the unknown hero's dead cheeks gave way to the darker dots of his mouth, blood beat through Nicolai's head in slow waves of shame. Boasting was futile. Every attempt to connect went wrong. The readings went on and on. Floating up to the smoke marks on the ceiling, looking down at the circle of cross-legged Jungvolk, heads bowed, partings neat, fingers on text, he observed with distant interest his own long legs, his distinctive dark head, shaped, he saw, just like his father's.

The group divided into pairs. One group was learning how to repair a bicycle, the remainder laying telephone wires. He would have far pre-ferred the bicycle, but nobody chose him. Perhaps he gave off the wrong smell to these boys. Over half were the children of workers; he got on equally badly with the boys who went to Gymnasien like his. Paying out the heavy cable on his own, he felt its weight like an affront, while they flicked at chains and pumped air. They loved the work and belonging and the whole idea of Gleichschaltung.† There was always talk about the workers knowing best, about youth being one heart, one soul, one body for the cause. Only one thing was worse than being in the troop and that was being excluded. Weeks earlier, Jochen had disappeared from their Gymnasium. His fortitude, amplified by absence, grew more heroic. From this safe distance, Nicolai could imagine himself sharing it. One true word from Jochen, always so quiet in the babble of idiocies at school, would have been worth having. But he had not dared try for a real friendship. He could never have borne humiliation as Jochen had. He had no expectation of finding a friend in the Hitler Youth proper; big boys would be worse. They would all be like Wolfgang.

"Have you brought your donation for the Winter Relief Fund, Bucherer?"

"Yes sir."

*Standard-bearer.
†Conformity; making all equal, especially through the wearing of uniforms.

He delved in his pocket. Their eternal struggle was to beat the Blankenese troop, the one Heini belonged to—Häschen, who no longer wanted to be his friend and who said cruel things behind his back. Not that he cared. He had ten Reichsmarks, much more than anyone else. Friedrich, pocketing the cash, did not even smile at him.

Released from the smoky basement into the clean air, Nicolai saw that it was still light. The rain had stopped. He did not have to go home. He could close his eyes, cross his arms, let the bike go where it would, let the air carry him. With the petrol shortages there were few cars to worry about. He let the bicycle run free, enjoying the swish of rubber on the wet road. He calculated the exhilarating seconds before he opened one eye a crack in time to catch the handlebars, to swerve away from the kerb where a bicycle might tip, where a boy's skull might crack open like a nut, spilling his brains onto the pavement. He kept going all the way to Blankenese, head down for the uphill struggle, then along Ferdinands Höh, peeling away in the direction of the Sülldorfer Kirchenweg. He wheeled into the graceful curve of the Bismarckstein. It was a green and private place, the road winding round a thickly wooded hill, the few houses half hidden under the overhang and nestling into the slope. Nicolai got off the bicycle, crept up to the hedge and peered through it. A table was set for dinner, a big man sat with his hands clasped, head low. With so many children, their house was always full. Slowly, the maid carried in a brimming tureen. There sat his friend, his long, paler face distinctive among the ruddy ones. He framed the shot with his hands. Häschen could not be praying, for his eyes were open, he was laughing at one of his brothers who was making a face behind their father's back. No, it was that idiot, Langenscheidt, his teeth, his fat smile. How could he choose to befriend such a fool? Somebody came forward and pulled the blackout down, closed the shutters. Turning, returning, the light was gone. Luckily there was a moon. All along the gleaming river under the malevolent blind stare of blacked-out houses, he sang the sad song of the Lorelei: I don't know, what can it mean, that I should feel so sad? But he did know.

He went in at the cellar entrance; blundering past the cupboards because there was not enough light, his jacket caught on something. He tugged. The crash of the jar breaking on the hard floor was shockingly loud. He crouched down, feeling for the shards with both hands and hearing glass crunch under his boots, hardly caring if he cut himself or not. A triangle of light fanned out of the doorway and spilled down the stairs. As she stepped forward, the loose tendrils of hair caught the light in a brilliant fuzzy halo. Fräulein Lindemann wore something white, a nightgown; her figure was distinctly outlined. He could not help staring.

"Can I help?"

She was always calm. He liked that.

"It's only me. I broke some glass."

"Stay where you are."

He waited. Wearing slippers and a dressing gown, she came past him with the brush pan and swept the pieces up. He did not move. She smelt, very faintly, of vanilla.

"Is anything the matter?"

Then he followed her to her room, wanting something, hardly knowing what. He needed to be with her, just for a moment. "Fräulein Lindemann, I wondered—"

"Yes?"

He hoped for some word of reassurance. But because she had her back to the light, he could not read her expression.

"Will you want to stay? You're not like the others."

"That depends, I suppose."

He could hardly bear his own awkwardness, could not look or think straight.

"We're not so bad, are we?"

"No. Not so very bad."

"Well," he said with thundering clumsiness, "that's good then."

"It's simple enough, Nicolai. I work for money."

"You have so much—" He shut up, dumbstruck at his own idiocy. A brilliant red stain shot up her throat and spread, mottling her face. She knew. Nicolai fled, feeling on each alternate step the ugly scratching of broken glass embedded in the leather of one sole.

Sunday morning, usually so precious, dawned bleak. He waited on the top landing until the weary hour had ticked away. Stealing down through the silent house, he rapped on the door; she opened it at once. She looked drawn and tired. She must have stayed up late with Sabine.

"What is it, Nicolai?"

He hung his head. "I couldn't sleep. I'm sorry. I took your money."

He held out a ten-Reichsmark note which he had wiggled out of his savings box the night before. She showed no surprise. He was a thief and she knew it.

"I would rather, Nicolai, that you didn't go through my things." She made to close the door.

"You think I stole it," he said, despairing.

Those large, pale eyes saw right through him. "I expect you were just borrowing it," she said.

Now his cheeks burnt at the kind lie. "I did steal it. I'm so sorry. I won't ever come in your room again. I swear it on my life."

"Thank you, Nicolai."

The door closed quietly and for a long moment he stood there, hands balled in frustration and self-hatred.

FIVE

Paris, October 1939

From time to time, Ilse left the Red Cross post to walk around the Gare d'Austerlitz. She paced slowly past the people waiting in the queue for tickets and those embracing near the platforms. Each middle-aged couple standing with suitcases gave her a tremor of hope and then disappointment. It was better not to look at all, but she could not stop herself. She had thought that she might go to the zoo or just walk along the river, but as the grey day drew on she knew that these were dreams. Her suitcase was in the Consigne, *Winnetou* locked safe inside it. German was the language of the enemy. She passed the long hours studying the railway map of France on the wall, reacquainting and then testing herself on the départements of France. She listened to the conversations around her, understanding just about everything. It might be a long wait. No definite arrangement could be made with people trapped in the strange world of Germany. Her thoughts ceaselessly bumped up against the worst eventuality, only to veer away again.

Around seven o'clock, as people drifted over to the station buffet, the room cleared completely. Stretching out on the bench, Ilse was irritated that the door opened, obliging her to sit up properly, to wriggle back into her shoes.

The slight man in a raincoat came straight up to her and touched her arm. "Ilse," he said. "Ilse."

Ilse jumped up and put her arms round her father. He smelt of staleness and tobacco, his cheek was rough with stubble. Surely he used to be taller and better-looking? His hair, which she remembered as dark and abundant, was stippled white.

"I'm late, I'm sorry," he said, "I overslept."

But it was already the evening.

"Where's Mutti?"

He gripped her arm briefly, then let go.

"Come on," he said. They collected her suitcase and she remembered, as he stood silent beside her, that he spoke no French. They left the station and walked along a wide road beside the Seine with Ilse carrying her small case. Otto walked ahead and went fast. Paris was not so very cold, but her father, shivering in his raincoat and thin shoes, his hands dug deep into his pockets, brought winter with him.

She had to hurry, throwing her question into the gap between them. "Is she at the hotel?"

"Shh," he said, putting his finger to his lips. "Not in the street."

Her mother must have gone ahead with the luggage. Ilse planned how to greet her in French, considered the words she would say. How pleased her mother would be that she had learnt so much and that she had grown. They walked for ten minutes, then turned into another wide boulevard, the Saint-Germain, and from there plunged into a maze of side streets. The buildings were old and had a shabby charm. Paris was beautiful. Together, she and her mother would visit every sight. Ilse smiled at the thought.

They turned into a side street and then another. Her father stopped at a set of old wooden doors, pushed one open. Behind was a courtyard and to one side a glass-sided room where a concierge sat, a man who nodded; Vati nodded back. They climbed the stairs and went on and on.

She whispered, "Which floor?"

"The fifth," he said.

Impatient, Ilse ran ahead. There were two doors. She danced from one foot to the other. She could hear her father's footsteps as he came up behind. He was wheezing. He fumbled for a key and unlocked the first door, which was on the courtyard side. They went in. There was nobody there. The room was small, its two little beds covered with grey bed-spreads.

She spun round, looked, did not understand. "Where is she?"

"She's coming as soon as she can. When she's got her visa. You'd bet-ter unpack."

Apart from a toothbrush in a glass on the washbasin, the room looked as if nobody lived there at all.

"How long have you been here?"

"Ten days."

"But there's nothing here."

"I came with nothing. Over the border to Belgium on foot. Then on and off goods trains."

"Why didn't she come with you?"

"Too risky. I came through the underground. She needs a proper visa. Without papers she'll be sent straight back if she's picked up— we're at war. The enemy. It's different for me. I have no papers anyway. I lost the last lot to a nosy official. An idiot who thought I'd wait while he checked."

Her father laughed abruptly, took off his raincoat, flung it on the bed, paced back and forth. She saw the familiar truncated middle finger of his right hand, where a piece had been shot off in the Great War.

"Unpack," he said. "Make yourself at home. How was the journey?"

It had been a bad crossing in stormy weather and nervous excite-ment had made her so light-headed that she had thought she might faint. She had had to go up on deck for fresh air. Then there had been a very long wait for the train north. But she could not say these things while her father kept moving about.

"Fine," she said.

The wardrobe was crooked with a door that hung forward and creaked when she opened it. The dark space had a musty smell. In slow-motion disbelief, Ilse hung up her new warm winter coat and the tam-o'-shanter and matching scarf. The coat, chosen by Willy, smelt of happiness and was dimmed by going into this place. She opened her case, took out her dresses and shook them out, found hangers for them all and hung them up. She turned. He was watching her.

"How could that woman send you back, just like that? What if I'd not been able to meet you?"

"In times of war, children need to be with their parents," said Ilse. These words, which Toni had uttered with such weight, made her father snort. "Willy didn't want me to come. He's going to fight against Hitler. He's a good German, like you, Vati."

"Willy's a complete fool. Any pretty girl could wind him round her little finger. Toni must be a beauty. I've got you a sandwich. Are you hungry?"

Her face was burning. She could not bear it, that he criticised them. She was wearing Toni's bracelet, carefully tucked under the sleeve of her knitted cardigan for fear of thieves. When she came to the brown box she hesitated, then left it. There was also a bottle of perfume in the case, another present from Toni. She snapped it shut and slid the case under the bed. She would not show him these treasures. She did not know how to behave with him. To be alone with her father was so unusual, she could not remember it ever happening before.

She looked at him, pacing and turning. Ilse was shivering. She undressed and got into bed as quietly as she could. It was warmer under the grey blanket and she pulled it over her head and closed her eyes. Nothing like this had ever been imagined in discussions with her mother, nor in her goodbye talks with Willy. His footsteps stopped and she heard the rustling of paper. He was eating something. Then the feet started up again and went on and on.

"Ilse?"

"I'm very tired," she said.

"Of course you are. Go to sleep."

But he kept walking and the noise of his feet on the bare floor reverberated through her head. The disappointment was overwhelming. Her mother had always been the important one, overshadowing her father, who was so often away. As though to teach him how to behave, she lay completely still and, sliding into darkness, breathed as quietly as she could.

In the morning, her father did not stir when she dressed. Ilse had French money Willy had given her. She took her purse and found her way back to the wide boulevard, glad to be out of the stale smell of the room and in the crisp autumnal air. A woman just behind was talking German. Ilse whipped round, anxiety mingled with hope. It was not Mutti, of course not: it was two middle-aged women, arm in arm, who at once fell silent.

She studied the shops. There was a boulangerie and a charcuterie, a quincaillerie full of pots and pans, a horsemeat butcher with a horse's head projecting over the sign, a couple of restaurants. No placard announced Judenrein.* She could not think what the French equivalent would be. Perhaps Juifs interdits or Juifs non admis. Seven weeks ago war had been declared, but she saw no sign of it. Shops were full of people with normal lives doing their daily tasks. The leaves of the plane trees lining the boulevard were turning gold. The sun slanting onto them lit the whole street with colour; in Meknès, it still gave real heat.

In a tobacco kiosk she chose two postcards of Paris, asked for stamps for Germany and Morocco. The bread in the boulangerie was cheap and smelt delicious. How hungry she was. French people actually ate in the street. Boldly, Ilse broke off a piece of crust and nibbled at it. She bought coffee next, and milk. Climbing the stairs, she suddenly thought of all the other things they needed and went back down the boulevard to the hardware place she had spotted. There she bought a coffeepot and a saucepan, the right size for the little gas ring in the corner, three plates and cups, a knife, fork and spoon each. She carried the heavy parcel back, lugged it up the stairs. Her father's eyes opened as the water boiled. Measuring out the coffee, her spirits lifted at the rich smell filling the room. In the Jews' House, she had prewarmed the coffeepot, waiting for her mother's weary tread on the stairs before she poured the milk to heat. The restaurant often kept her late; Mutti used to say that it was the thought of Ilse's good coffee that sustained her through the dark journey back.

Ilse had milk with a splash of coffee; her father the reverse. The coffee gave his face some colour.

"What a good housekeeper you are," he said.

"Thank you."

Ilse poured out more.

"How long until Mutti comes?"

He shrugged. "However long it takes. We just have to wait."

"Do they have a school with nuns here?"

"Why nuns?" He smiled. "You are a funny girl."

"It's the system," she said in an offhand way. He knew nothing about the system.

*Cleansed of Jews.

"You can't go to school, Ilse. We have to be invisible," he said. "The French have interned a lot of German men. Very few have got out again."

"But you're not a Nazi. You're on their side."

"The French don't know that. And if they know, they don't care. France and Germany are at war. The French don't make any distinction between ordinary Germans and Jews or others exiled for political reasons." This smile he made was an ironical one; she remembered that this was his way of underlining his point. She noticed with a little stab of anguish that one front tooth was badly cracked that had not been before. "I'm not German, as it happens. I'm stateless. But that makes no difference either."

"And me?"

"Children under seventeen are exempt. Don't worry. You'll be fine." Adults seemed to imagine that she would believe such talk.

"Then what are we going to do?"

He shrugged his shoulders. "Wait for your mother."

"Mutti must be missing us," she said. She knew how her mother felt from the heaviness of her own heart. There was a kind of gravity shift in her. Sorrow lay like a sick child, to be tiptoed around.

While her father went to wash, Ilse found her wooden box and carefully filled her beautiful pen with ink. "Chère Maman," she wrote, "Paris est tellement belle! On se sent si libre. Nous pensons à toi."* She had copied their address from the street sign onto a scrap of paper and now printed it in the top corner in block letters. She wrote the second postcard to Willy and Toni, saying that she had arrived safely and had been met by her father. They had found a room for the two of them. She did not mention her mother. Toni would just have to think whatever she thought. She wondered what address she should use for her mother.

Returning, her father picked it up and shook his head. "You can't write to Germany."

"Then how will Mutti know where to find us?"

"We have ways of communicating, but never openly. That would be insane."

"I can't write once?"

"Not unless you want the Gestapo to know she's communicating

*"Dear Mummy, how lovely Paris is! One feels so free. We are thinking of you."

illegally with an enemy of the Reich. And where to find her. And where to pick us up, naturally."

He dressed with his back to her. She watched his thin shoulders shrugging on the shirt with a feeling of complete helplessness.

"This communicating you do. Will you be able to send my love, properly, to Mutti when you do it? Promise?"

When he turned, he smiled. "Come on. Let's go for a walk," he said.

"Can we go to the zoo?" A thought struck her. "Or the palace of Versailles?" The guide emphasised that this, of all the great sights in Paris, was not to be missed.

"Something better. I'll show you a little piece of home."

They walked together to the Boulevard Saint-Michel and through the Jardin du Luxembourg. Much of the open area was not green at all, but wide paths of flat-packed earth with a little scattered gravel. It did not seem much of a garden. They came out to a narrow street called the Rue de Tournon. There was a small café a few metres along. Her father pushed in through the double doors in the centre to a wave of heat, of smoke and babbling noise. People leant against the bar which, made of shiny copper, took up half the room to the right; they were rapping on it with coins to attract the attention of a scowling waiter.

"Otto! Du hast uns gefehlt!"* a man shouted out. A middle-aged woman got up and kissed him; her father said vaguely that she was a friend, from the old days. The noise was Russian and German and Czech. He pushed his way through to a big table in the corner. The woman followed. Ilse sat beside him and looked around. This warm, busy place where exiles and Jews congregated, this was what he thought of as home.

"So you're the daughter," said the woman, shaking her hand. "He said you were coming. What would we do without your father? Now, Otto, what's the latest news from Germany?" She drew up a chair. Her father lowered his voice, turned away.

Ilse sat warming her fingers on a cup of hot chocolate. They all spoke in their own languages and if the Germans were supposed to be hiding, they gave no sign of it. They were discussing where to live and where they should go next, how to get the permits and pieces of paper they needed to be en règle.† The rules apparently changed all the time.

---

*"Otto, we missed you!"
†Police permission to remain in France.

Her father told a little woman with frizzy hair tied up in a knot about dollar bank accounts. Someone else asked about visas to Ecuador. Ilse watched his hands swooping as he explained the intricate details of medical certificates and exemptions and where, if you had the money, a Czech or German national passport could be obtained, one without the "J" for Jude stamp, a good fake but not—of course—as good as the ones the German underground made.

She tugged cautiously at his sleeve and whispered, "Vati, why didn't you buy one of those very good fakes for Mutti and you?"

"No time," he said shortly.

Ilse remembered the long year of his absence during which she and her mother had prepared the journey, had waited for the visa, which had been so hard to obtain, being—of course—in her real name.

At noon he stood up. Lunchtime. On the way back they did the shopping. Ilse's French did not have the giveaway German accent that others had, which made some French people turn away and shopkeepers act as though they were invisible. It seemed to Ilse a strange reversal. Before, they had been hated for being Jewish and not German; now they were hated because they were Germans and the enemy. Her father stayed outside the shops while Ilse did the talking, then helped carry the food. It helped that she looked so young. She looked Aryan, he said, with her white, intense face and flaming red hair, whereas he looked "like a thousand Jews." She was not sure that he was right, but it did not matter. In France, luckily, they did not hate Jews.

They carried the potatoes and cabbage up the long flights of stairs.

"Let me," he said, scraping at the potatoes while Ilse attacked the vegetables. Neither of them was good at cooking and they found worms and black parts in the potatoes.

"What if Mutti can't get out of Germany?"

"Of course she can. The Gestapo are delighted to assist with the emigration of Jews and their associates, at a price, naturally," he said. Again, he gave the ironic smile.

"But she doesn't have a lot of money."

"Ilse, we discussed it. It was urgent for me to leave—not so for her."

Ilse shivered. "You're upsetting me," she said.

"She needs real papers, properly stamped, that's all. It's nothing to be upset about. It's less dangerous that way. It's her choice to do it all properly and then nobody can touch her. She'll come."

This was more reassuring.

"When she comes—where shall we go?"

"She'll decide. Italy, maybe. You know your mother."

She did know her mother, but she could not think why he mentioned Italy, when the obvious choice was Morocco. She decided not to ask. She did not like his explanations, which did not make sense of things—in fact, rather made them worse.

Ilse turned up the gas and boiled potatoes and cabbage in the saucepan with violence. That was their lunch. A system developed. She learnt to put the potatoes in first, then the cabbage. Otherwise everything disintegrated into a wet mess. Occasionally, she cracked an egg over the results while hot or threw in a cooked slice of meat from the charcuterie. Sometimes the combination was horrible, but he never complained. She bought lamb, but it was thick and fatty, and boiling it turned out to be a mistake. She could not bring herself to eat the grey blubbery mass, though her father did not mind. The room smelt awful for days. She found couscous in the shops, but when she cooked it, it stayed hard and then suddenly turned to mush. She had found dried apricots and added these to the soggy mixture, hoping for a taste of Morocco, but the effect was peculiar and they were far too expensive to try a second time.

After lunch, she washed socks and underwear or Vati's second shirt and tidied the room while he smoked two cigarettes, never more. Often he slept in the afternoons. He was alert or asleep, never anything in-between. Ilse lay on her bed and studied the *Paris-Soir*, which she bought every couple of days, underlining the words she did not know and looking them up in the dictionary Willy had bought for her. In her head she attempted increasingly ambitious conversations with Anne, imagining her nodding encouragement. Anne was at school learning useful things while she was trapped in a room which stank of cabbage. Sometimes, on a boulevard, the smell of an American cigarette like Willy's or a sudden burst of laughter carried her to Meknès, piercing her with longing.

She began to worry about money. Her father had hardly any. Her precious stock of francs dwindled; she eked it out. She haunted stalls that sold fruit and vegetables looking for curly kale, which was very cheap, or for purple turnips, which she hated but which cost next to nothing and filled a person up. Sometimes a stall-keeper would throw in a couple of onions or a bundle of cress for nothing; once even a bag of potatoes.

Toni's beautiful bracelet turned out to be very pure twenty-two-carat gold. It fed them for a month. When Ilse went out with her little string bag to buy food, she always felt the same thump of anticipation when she passed the concierge. She was certain that her mother would write and explain why it was taking so long. But weeks passed and no letter came.

As they pushed through the double doors of the café one morning, a very tall thin man jumped up and came over and embraced her father, who stared at him in shock.

"Kennst du mich nicht?"*

"Albert, what have they done to you?"

The thin man gestured at his loose clothes. "Three months in concentration camp." He was terribly ugly, with a squint.

"You're so skinny. I wouldn't have known you."

"I was fat under the Nazis. The French have done wonders for my waistline."

"Where were you?"

"I've been at 'Hotel La Falaise'† peeling potatoes in the mud. Got picked up in the first roundup of foreigners. If I hadn't been a writer with a few friends, they'd have left me there to rot with the others. Who's this?" He was staring.

"My daughter, Ilse. Albert Rothberg, the writer and poet—an old friend of mine from Hamburg." They shook hands. "We used to see a lot of each other in my travelling days," said Otto. "Ilse, find the waiter and order us coffee and one petit marc, and you can have a hot chocolate. We have to celebrate."

"Two petits marcs," called out the stranger. "One for your girl. She is very pretty, isn't she! A beauty."

Nobody had ever said such a thing about her. Before Ilse, blushing, had taken more than two steps towards the copper counter, the waiter was ready to take the order. She turned to get another peep at the man who could command such attention and saw that he was still staring at her. His jet-black hair was too long. His sallow skin hung down around his long jaw and even his strange eyes sagged—he really was an exceptionally ugly man, with big hands. His face in repose was positively

*"Don't you know me?"
†La Falaise concentration camp.

sinister. But when he winked at her, as now, his eyebrows shot up and down energetically and he radiated amusement.

"Albert, what are you going to do? Will you stay in Paris?"

He shrugged. "If they leave me alone, I will. Write, if I can. I have my foreign royalties. A few articles. There's the possibility of a play. Do you know a good translator?"

"Three dozen. I wish I did it myself. But I never had any gift for languages. I've written a few articles nobody wants. Where are you living?"

That her father was writing something was news to Ilse.

"Hotel l'Univers—while the dollar royalties still come through. It's a dump but it's all right. You can visit me there. Ilse can read to me. I need a good reader."

"Read what?"

"Plays. Poems, prose, anything." Albert was looking at her again. "I think you'd be wonderful."

"Me?" said Ilse.

"You. How far away are you?"

"We're in a little pension a few streets away." Her father reached out and squeezed Ilse's hand. "My little girl looks after me very well. Where'd I be without her?" When her father smiled at her or was kind, as he was now, his expression was very sweet and his whole face was different. At moments like these, she felt that they were perhaps only one step away from really understanding each other.

"Albert Rothberg! Wonderful!" A woman was bearing down on them, followed by a tight-faced man in a very smart suit.

"Excuse me?"

The woman, who wore a lot of makeup, was very pretty, her blond hair expertly waved. She leaned over to embrace Albert. Her scent was very strong. "Don't tell me you've forgotten poor old Tilly. Tilly and Franz Wolff—you know, we met years ago. With Franzi Heiden—don't ask about him. I suppose we're all shadows of ourselves."

Albert's good eye looked at her bosom and then her lips. "Not you," he said gallantly. "You're more beautiful than ever. You must sit with us."

Chairs were found, drinks arrived. Albert pushed one across to Ilse and ordered two more, looking at the blonde. Ilse's faint chagrin surprised her. She dipped her tongue into the drink, feeling grown-up. The marc was extremely strong; she knew she wouldn't finish half of it.

"We don't know where to go. Paris is so crowded. Where are you staying?" The pretty woman smiled and pulled her chair closer to Albert.

"Here's a good one!" Vati suddenly stood up, swaying a little, as though he was the one who had drunk the marc. "Hitler's in heaven—where else? And he says to Moses, You can tell me this in confidence, Herr Moses. Wasn't it you yourself who set the bush on fire?"

Everyone burst out laughing, and her father, leaning over Albert, said something to him. Looking around at their amused faces, Ilse noticed that the man in the smart suit barely smiled. Albert stood up and started shrugging on his coat.

"Come on, or we'll be late for our outing," said Vati, smiling round at them all broadly and drawing his arm through that of Albert. He gestured to Ilse to hurry up.

Outside, as they moved away down the Rue de Tournon in the opposite direction to home, Ilse plucked at Albert's arm. He was still chuckling.

"What was so funny?" She had never heard her father joke like that before.

"The Reichstag fire."

She had no idea what he meant.

"The joke is based on the Nazi claim that the Jews destroy their own synagogues—"

"Just tell me, do you actually know them? Her?" Her father, interrupting, wasn't drunk after all, though his cheeks had a fiery red tinge. Albert shook his head. "Albert, you're a bloody fool to even talk to her."

"Why, Vati?"

"Can't you see she's poison? Celebrated people like Albert, who are wanted in Germany—they're on a list. They're trophies to be bagged."

"Some trophy. He thinks I'm a lion, but I'm not. I'm a donkey."

Donkeys were gentle beasts. She liked the idea of being a donkey.

"What happens if you're on a list?" she asked.

"If the Gestapo catch up with you, you're finished. You disappear. That's what happens." Her father was curt.

"The Gestapo are not operating in France, my dear Otto."

"If you believe that, then you're a complete fool."

Her father strode ahead. His angry haste brought home the deep truth of why she could not write openly to her mother. Her father had to be on a list. B for Blumenthal. His was probably the very first name on it.

All the way back to their pension, Albert kept disappearing into shops, so she had to catch up with Vati each time and tell him to wait. He folded his great height into their one chair and, with the two of them sitting on her narrow bed opposite, laid out a roast chicken, which he took apart neatly with a pearl-handled penknife, peering at it shortsightedly. It smelt wonderful. There was cheese and a slab of goose liver pâté, which he said he was addicted to. They relished the rich food. The men drank a bottle of wine between them and then Albert produced a small bottle of brandy from his briefcase. They drank from the big cups, Albert becoming the first to use her mother's cup, fork and plate. Her father fell asleep and they put a pillow under his head. Ilse felt very happy to see him sleeping peacefully, his thin chest rising and falling gently.

Ilse made "muckefuck" coffee out of ground-up barley, real coffee now being beyond their means, and Albert accepted it gracefully though he clearly was not used to it. Afterwards, he persuaded her to read to him. His eyes really were very bad and she saw that he could not puzzle out the small print. She read a poem by Heine and another by Rilke.

"Good," he said. "Really. Try these."

He delved once more into his red leather briefcase, fanned out a sheaf of papers. After a while she realised that these had to be his poems. She read, hesitantly. It was odd what he wrote, very sharp and savage, and completely unlike the person he appeared to be. But it had rhythm and a kind of clever roughness. She stopped at the bad words, but he laughed at her and made her say them. Next he produced a manuscript written in the tiniest writing. After an hour, putting down the papers to get her breath back, she felt that she had known him all her life.

"Faster, go on. Giddy up."

"I'm not a horse. Or a donkey, like you." That made him laugh.

"You'd make a lovely donkey. Well, Ilse, you're bursting. What do you want to ask?"

"Why do you write about death and sadness and people killing each other? Why can't you be amusing in your stories? In real life you're funny."

"Somebody has to do the dirty work."

"I mean it."

"I only have a certain amount of funniness in me. I have to eke it out. I might live a long time."

She did not know what to say to that.

"Anyway," he said, "I'm saving myself for you, when you grow up."

"I'm thirteen. It's too long. You'll be all used up by the time I'm twenty-one."

"That's why I eat. To keep up. Look," he said, showing her as he moved the notches on his belt. "It is my duty as a good German to fatten myself for the kill. Of course, in Paris they don't have geese like the Hamburg geese."

"Albert, how did you meet Vati?"

"The great and noble cause." He saw that she didn't understand. "The fight against fascism. He came to Hamburg to speak to a group of writers. He was full of mad ideals. How the comrades would overthrow Hitler and bring about a social revolution with our pens. But the other side had guns. Rather more effective, you see."

"Vati has lots of ideals."

"Your father's a great hero. His ideals are the only thing that spoil him."

Ilse laughed out loud. Albert was very different, of course, especially in looks, but somehow he reminded her of Willy.

Albert had proper papers and permission to be in France. He was en règle, wholly official with special status as a celebrated writer, even though he was a Jew on the list of those proscribed and sought by the Nazis. Prominent writers had petitioned for him to be given French citizenship—which, ironically, he said he had no desire to take.

"Don't you want to be French?" she asked.

"In the years I've lived away from Germany I've come to live more inside my head, more inside the language. German is my fatherland. I've not become French in any sense."

How odd that was, when she so yearned to be French herself.

"It's always best to keep all your options open. If I'm to change nationality, I'll decide when I must."

For years, Albert's royalties had come through twice annually from the United States and Canada in handsome sums held on deposit in a dollar account. He could even take his money in dollars, which more than doubled its value. In the Café Tournon, he held court at his "own" table and grandly played the part of the poet. He talked of literature and art, proclaimed himself uninterested in the politics that preoccupied the others, bored by the trivia that swept through the place in waves of gossip and rumour. Others discussed who was in Paris and where, how much a bribe to this or that official cost. Albert told her about the politics of Heinrich Heine, exiled in Paris a century ago, just as he was now. He flirted all the time; it took a while for her to understand that that was what he was doing.

"Do you want to know a secret?"

He leant across the table confidingly.

"Go on."

"About women. The uglier they are, the more fascinating and beddable. Much more so than the pretty ones."

"Why?"

"Because they try harder. Pretty women can be so dull."

Ilse did not think that any woman would say no to him, once she knew him. When she saw him with a new beauty, Ilse would wink to remind him of his principles on ugliness and he would catch her eye and signal back with his one good bulldog's droopy eye, the other one always staring across his nose at some other place.

Waiting for her mother made them both restless. It drove her father to the café whereas Ilse, loving calm, preferred churches. Something about the three great archways at the Cathédrale de Notre-Dame de Paris repelled her; the building did not have a human aspect. She liked Saint-Michel better. There, kneeling, she made sure that all her coat buttons were in order, each one from bottom to top, touching each lightly and saying her mother's name.

"Dear Lord," she said, "keep Lore Blumenthal alive and well and I will always honour you. Do not let them find us and take us back, Lord."

Saint-Sulpice, being closest to the café, became her favourite. She attended mass or slipped in behind wedding parties. So many took place in these strange weeks; it seemed a curious way to prepare for war. Rituals and holy smells soothed her, as did the Latin, unfamiliar and rich sounding. On clear, sunny days she checked the progress of the sun calendar. Two centuries earlier, the curé of the church had commissioned a gnomon, a device to measure the passage of the sun through the sky. He had wanted to know when the glory of the resurrection would come: Easter Sunday was always the first full moon after the equinox. Sitting in the quiet of the north transept, she observed how the low winter light shafted across above her head. By the summer solstice, when the sun was at its highest point, the beam would have retrenched to the southern side of the church, falling directly upon the floor plaque the good man had inscribed in 1745. She would not see this. Her mother would come long before then and they would all be in Africa. But Ilse could sit in her chilly corner and warm herself imagining how a priest, standing on the oval brass plaque before the altar on a sunny Easter Sunday, might delight in feeling God's light directly on his face.

The winter was extreme, with twenty degrees of frost. Paris rooms had either no heating at all or elderly radiators, which on their top floor barely worked. A man came to turn them on. For days afterwards they made hammering and gurgling noises. Still no heat came out. They had very little money left; she was scared that she would have to sell her mother's things. She had not yet revealed to her father that she had these treasures. Each time she felt that the moment might have come to sell them, Albert offered them money. Her father took it, always with reluctance, though all three of them knew that they were dependent upon it and him.

"Not to worry," Albert said. "The year's-end American royalties are looking good." He said that she was worth it and more, for the excellence of her reading aloud. He was, as she told him, a terrible flatterer.

"Make the most of Paris," said her father abruptly in the third week of December, as though they might be leaving soon. Perhaps he had divined her thoughts, her conviction that surely, surely, her mother would be there for the holy solemnity of Heiligabend.* She wondered what she and Mutti would fabricate by way of a tree. She tried and failed to imagine the three of them celebrating Christmas together, something they had not done for years. In their old house, in the Landsweg, she and Mutti had always carried up the big wooden box from the cellar between them. Together they unwrapped the beautiful glass baubles that were special, because they had belonged to her mother's mother, who died before Ilse was born. Ilse might decorate the tree, which other less careful children were not permitted to do. Even in the Jews' House, Sankt Nicholas had found them.

In her case she had a photograph of Willy, in the uniform of the French Foreign Legion and wearing his kepi, bearing a great resemblance to his sister. She had begged it from Toni. When her father was

*Christmas Eve.

out she studied it, his eyes deep-shadowed by the hot sun but always smiling at her. She also had a snapshot of the three of them larking around. She was in the middle, laughing, wearing a pretty dress and with her arm slung through both theirs. Ilse could almost feel the heat, if she concentrated hard. When she closed her eyes she saw the early light slanting through the blinds of her room and the flowers on the chest of drawers, and the grey spot on the crackle glaze. Willy's dares: Could she hop and skip without stopping all the way from where the car was parked to the café? Dared she ring all the doorbells in their street and run away? She did. With him she had been as free as a monkey swinging through the palm trees, finding its way into the light. These places and people still existed; they were all safe.

Her father, coming in unexpectedly early, caught her with this photograph. He looked at it for a long time, his expression strange. "It's so long since we all lived together properly," he said. "How long is it?"

"Five years?"

"And you're much older, not a little girl anymore. I don't know what people your age want." In the three months they had been living together his eyes, so dark that they were nearly black, had never looked at her so intently. It made her feel almost breathless.

"I don't want anything," she said.

"Do you remember us all living together? We were happy, weren't we?"

"Yes," she said. How sharply her parents had quarrelled, each time they met.

"When your mother comes it'll be a new start for all of us. Real family life, Ilse. I didn't understand how much I needed it, you see, until it was too late. Then, because of you, this happened. I'm a very lucky man."

Their real life together was so far in the past that she had forgotten it. She remembered the very first time her father had been arrested. The police said they were looking for illegal weapons. They found the pistol her father had kept as a souvenir from the Great War lying in a drawer with the Iron Cross, which he had been awarded for valour. For some reason this made them very angry. For four months he was interned in a camp. When they brought him back, he had two black eyes and a bad look on his face. He had something of the same look now. He gazed around at the cramped room which she had done her best to tidy. " 'Ein Volk ohne Raum.'* That's us."

Ilse tried to smile.

"You're such a good girl. Almost too good. Do you want anything? A present?"

"I'm fine," she said.

It gave her a pang, that she had not thought to get him anything.

Very early the next morning, Ilse stole out to buy a Christmas present for her father. She ran past the concierge, who waved something white. The letter was addressed to her in her mother's writing. A sudden rush of blood to her head made her giddy; she steadied herself against the wall, ripped it open.

Darling Ilse,

I am enjoying the new job in Hamburg and the house is lovely, in a magnificent avenue lined with old trees and a view of the river. You will love it. Well, darling girl, it is nearly time to come home. What a pity you lost your papers, but don't worry, the certified copies will be with you soon. Meanwhile enjoy Paris and be a good girl and give a big kiss to your uncle, who is so kind. All my love, darling,

Mutti

As Absender she had written her maiden name: Lore Lindemann, but no address.

Ilse, folding the letter doubly safe inside her pocket, went to buy the warm scarf for Vati as planned. She returned home in an exalted mood, hid the present in the wardrobe and took the letter out. Her father slept on. Mutti had got the job, was earning money, there was a plan; that was the thing, even if the details were mystifying. Her mother's plans were always excellent. Why did she say her papers were lost? The wonderful thing was the way she and Mutti had both had the same idea, about reverting to her maiden name, Willy's name. Struck by the physical exis-

---

*"A people with no space" (title of Hans Grimm's 1926 epic novel; its message was that the decent, industrious white German nation needed more space and lived within too narrow frontiers).

tence of the piece of paper that her mother had held, by the continuing reality of her mother, the dam of misery inside broke and she found herself sobbing, making a hard barking noise she could not subdue that shocked her father awake.

"What's happened?"

She handed him the letter.

"She's not coming," he said in a flat voice, almost immediately dropping the letter onto the bed.

"But she must—"

Ilse's throat was so dry it came out a croak.

"She's betrayed me. She's abandoned us."

"How could she? What do you mean?"

"She's played a double game. Making false excuses, delaying, needing more money—all along I suspected something."

He rose, with frenetic haste threw his clothes on.

"What excuses?"

Then she understood that things had been said in their communications, things he had kept from her.

"Vati, tell me what she said. What excuses?"

The door slammed. In an agony of anticipation she waited. After an hour he returned, still livid.

"I've sent a message."

"Vati, what's happened? Where have you been?"

"We'll soon find out. Your mother has evidently decided to stay in Germany."

He was stubbly and unshaven, with a wild look, his hands shaking with emotion as he lit a cigarette from the stub of its predecessor. His breath smelt bad.

"Why would she want to?"

"I don't know why. I assume she doesn't want to be a refugee. I assume she wants to celebrate the thousand-year Reich. She is enjoying Hamburg," he said. "The opera house, the theatre, the gardens—"

"Please, Vati, please, don't—what does she mean about the copies and Willy, me coming home? What has she said? Are we going back to our proper house?"

"Is that what you want?" he said savagely.

Ilse said she did not know. Or rather, she knew that that was an impossible dream.

It seemed that Ilse did not know any number of things.

"Take your Toni. You think she's wonderful, don't you? Clever Toni, a woman who sold herself to the highest bidder." Toni, he said, was a lecturer in psychology and not thirty but nearly forty. She had sent a photograph of herself to the Legionnaires' Club requesting sponsorship ("all dolled up like a tart") and Willy ("a hopeless romantic, what a fool") had been an idiot to reply, gallantly offering his hand in marriage. He had thought it romantic to save her. "Willy's a soft touch, like his sister. He fell in love with a pretty face."

Ilse hung her head, willing him to stop. But he would not.

"Do you know why you had to come back on your own? Because the Red Cross wanted to charge too much. Toni got the bill. She wouldn't let Willy waste the money a second time."

"It's not true. The Red Cross is free."

"Rubbish. She wrote to your mother that you were very capable, more than most. You'd look after yourself all right. Anyway, you didn't look Jewish. Nobody would think you were."

Ilse waited for him to finish. It wasn't true. Even if it was, that was just the way Toni spoke, her manner. This had nothing to do with Toni, nor with her. This was just a new form of the eternal quarrel between her parents, which went on even here, in Paris.

"Your mother was outraged. Couldn't believe her precious Willy had let her down. So she summoned me. Told me it was time I got out of Germany. Sent me to meet you. With her false promises." He was shouting now. "How we'd be together. A family, the three of us. I should have known. How she used to go on and on about getting out of Germany. All lies."

"It wasn't lies."

"She made me go, knowing I didn't want to, knowing my work, knowing it was more important than any individual. I'd sworn never to abandon the struggle and my comrades. She knew that."

"Why did you leave, then?"

"She forced my hand. I told you. Claimed she was saving me. Saving you."

"She did save you. And me."

"She used me. Because of you. She doesn't want me, or she'd be here, with us. But she wants you all right. My God. She actually thinks I'll send you back. I can't go back, she knows that. Madness. Madness—"

"Why not?"

"And abandon you?"

"But it was Mutti I wanted—"

The words burst out of her, the "not you" remaining unspoken. For a long time neither of them spoke. The words had been said and there was no taking them back. He lay on the bed with his face to the wall. In a while, there came a muffled noise, a dry kind of hoarse breathing. Ilse listened to the anguished sound of his sadness. She pretended not to hear. It was strange that her father should discover that he loved her mother so much. He had never shown signs of it when they were together.

Late in the afternoon, he got up. She was reading her book. In the long silence, he started looking at her things lined up on the little bed-side table, picking up and discarding them with jerky movements.

"Haven't you got something more intelligent to read?"

"I like *Winnetou*."

They could not afford books. He knew that. Not being French, she couldn't join a library.

"Karl May never once went to America. All that sentimental stuff about Apaches and the Wild West. He made it all up."

"He can't have done that."

"He never left Europe. And he was blind."

"Blind?" She was shocked.

"So he couldn't ride a horse, could he?"

"That doesn't matter." She was getting angry.

"Think of it. Trapped in a room all his life. Making things up, all pretence."

He took the book from her, flicked through it, then tossed it onto the bed.

Ilse picked up her mending and stitched on. It was an art, to make the tiniest of stitches, so minute they were almost invisible. A person could not possibly look up while doing such fine work. She waited for him to go out, which he did soon enough, slamming the door. When very unhappy, he needed more space to pace. She had made him unhappy and he her. She put down the cloth and closed her eyes. Out of his darkness, she conjured forth the brilliant heat and light of the Moroccan sun. Her Indians, with their fierce, keen eyes and their noble spirits, could still ride there. Old Shatterhand, with his code of honour and all his thorough German skills, got on his horse and smiled at her.

He was waving goodbye. He was gone. She opened her eyes. The sky outside was a leaden grey.

On Christmas Eve Ilse put on her green velvet dress. When at midnight she gave him the scarf, he wept. She had assumed that he would have forgotten about Christmas, but he drew something out from under his bed. It was a complete edition of Albert's works, signed and dedicated to her. When her father embraced her, she felt how thin he had become, each jutting bone clearly delineated. The next day Albert took them both to a private room in a fancy restaurant. His present to them was a radio. Her father drank fine wines instead of eating. He threw back glass after glass, with elaborate and ironic toasts. His unhappiness was almost palpable. When he was out of the room, she asked Albert what she should do about him.

"It will pass. It's not your fault he's unhappy."

"He's waiting to hear more from Mutti. He thinks she won't come. She will, I know she will. She made another plan, but we can't understand it. You see, she can't write proper letters, because of the censor. I don't know what she told him. They always quarrel. But it's not just her. He's unhappy because he left Germany and he can never go back. The awful thing is he did it for me," she said. It struck her hard; this statement was actually true.

Albert sighed. "No, my dear little donkey. It's that he's thought too much about ideas. In emotions, he's just a baby. Don't worry about him. It's a father's duty to be with his daughter. A father's pleasure." He sighed again. "I wish I was your father." Part of her wished it too.

Ilse thought about her mother all the time. The letter was code, it meant something which neither of them could fathom. Otto's love for his wife, remaining locked up within him, seemed to Ilse to grow. From time to time an outburst of rage confirmed it. It was much better to be the product of this enduring passion than of no love at all. It seemed to her that just one level under the darkness that shrouded him there had to be a huge golden space, full of light. This space, which could not be seen from the outside, contained all the love he had for both of them but in these circumstances could not be expressed. When Mutti's answering message came, these things would become clear.

Her father lay in bed, eating when she forced him to. She played a game in her head that this was not her father who might be expected to look after her, but Otto, a good old man who for some reason could not speak. Sometimes she pretended to be a nurse, who would take his temperature and make him well, though he was not ill. With the volume turned low, Ilse listened to news of the Russian invasion of Finland on the radio, always choosing the French channel, which he could not understand, as news from Germany upset him. War would not come to France, the radio said, because their troops were so strong. Food rationing was introduced, but without proper papers they could not claim ration books. Without Albert, they might have starved; certainly, she would have gone crazy. Luckily, when Albert was not there she still possessed him. She read each volume twice, for they were all so different, sitting very quietly, turning the pages softly so as not to disturb her father, who just stared at the ceiling. She feared that her father was jealous of her. Perhaps that explained his silence. She could understand that. Had her mother not loved her she would have been heartbroken. She dared from time to time to ask Otto whether there was a message from Hamburg and would he please check. Always, he shook his head.

On an icy February morning a stranger walked up the stairs, knocking on all the doors and asking for Lindemann. Ilse, chopping vegetables, heard the sounds ascending, the strong voice with its German accent getting louder. The concierge had sent him on up, without telling him which floor they were on. She went to the door and stood rigidly at attention in front of it, hearing the footfalls coming nearer and nearer. The young German clicked his heels when he saw her.

"Guten Morgen," she said.

"Fräulein Lindemann?"

Automatically, Ilse did a little girl's bob and curtsy.

He held out a little card. "This is something sent for you. From Germany."

The card had his name on it. Then he showed her a bigger envelope. There was a form she had to sign, with a big official crest on it from the embassy.

"Now you have your papers, you have to get back home as quickly as you can, Fräulein. All German nationals must leave France. Especially a young lady all on her own. You must travel right away."

"I will," she said. "Thank you very much."

She willed him to go before her father, asleep inside, made some noise. From the landing she watched the wide shoulders and the blond head disappear down the stairs, then exhaled her relief. The hair was exactly the same colour as Toni's; she thought of how civilised and soppy Germans were until, of course, you gave them a knock.

Back in the room she sat on the bed. Carefully Ilse opened the envelope. She looked at the official stamp, the double-headed eagle, that black bird, which Heine had hated so much. She admired the name Ilse Lindemann, which she thought well suited the girl in the picture with the long plaits who was just like somebody she had been once. There was no "J" for Jude stamp on this passport. She was an Aryan. She was en règle. Her father's eyes were open.

"Show me what she's sent you. Well. First quality," he said, tossing the documents onto the floor. Quickly she retrieved them.

"There's your message. Your mother wants you back in Germany."

"But why has she changed her mind about coming?"

Abruptly Otto laughed, and went on laughing until the laugh turned into a cough and she had to get him water, then hold it for him because it slopped over. When he lay back, his face had a glassy look.

"I wouldn't have thought she had such cunning. Such subterfuges, such complexities, just to get rid of one poor old Jew."

Ilse shook her head, knowing this was not possible. "Vati, you know that's not true. She wanted to save you."

"Are you going to tell me next that she loves me?"

She could not meet his eye. It was a long while before she dared to speak again. "Vati? Should I go back?"

"No. No Jew is safe in Germany. No half Jew. It's madness."

Sick at heart, she knelt beside the bed, tentatively stroked his hand. "Are you so sure she's not coming?"

His look was full of pain.

"Can you still believe it?" She could, but dared not say so.

"Of course, if you want, I can take you back to Germany myself. My fatherland. I never wanted to leave it."

She knew what would happen to him in Germany.

"Vati, can't we go to Morocco?"

He smiled a very twisted smile.

"I can't go anywhere by boat. No papers and no visa. I can only creep across borders by night. It's France or Germany, nothing else. You can try to get a visa for Morocco, with these fine new papers. Who will look after you there? Toni won't. Willy's off to fight."

His eyes closed; he had such a defeated look.

Ilse felt defeated too. "You'll look after me, Vati. I've got good papers now. You can buy new papers. Mutti can join us there."

"I'm finished with false papers. Every set I've had, something went wrong. My face shouts Jew, a blind man could see it. Besides, we don't have the money."

Ilse tiptoed away, knelt beside her bed, pulled out her suitcase, opened the brown box and unwrapped the jewellery roll. Piece by piece, she laid out the jewellery her father had bought for her mother so long ago on the edge of the coarse blanket.

"Vati, we have these. Please look. We can sell them."

He turned over. Then he covered his face with one hand. For a long time he held the precious objects in his hand, turning and turning them over. There were tears in his eyes, which he wiped away.

"Vati," she whispered. "Shall I sell them?"

"She'll leave Germany for you. She saved these for you, when she had nothing. Ilse, you must write. You tell her to come. Tell her properly." He stood up, started to pace, his bare feet slapping the cold floor. "That's the answer. Quick, do it now."

Ilse scribbled on a piece of paper. *Dearest Mutti.* How often she had wanted to write and not been permitted to. Now she could not think what to say.

"Go on. She'll listen to you."

"What about the censor?"

"It'll go through the underground."

Deep anger filled her that he had not permitted her to write before. While Otto paced and fidgeted, she scrawled a note, explaining that she could not return, that Vati said it was a bad idea, that they both so much wanted her to come to Paris and that she should please, please come as soon as she could. Otto snatched the paper up, read it before the ink was even dry. It was all much too fast. Pulling on trousers over his pyjama bottoms, thrusting bare feet into shoes, he was gone. She sat at the little table feeling sick and empty. Somehow, though she did not know how it had come about, or even how it was wrong, he had persuaded her into an act of betrayal. Somehow, she had taken his side.

Surely, though, this was the right thing to do. Mutti had to come.

She longed for her. They would buy papers for Vati, the three of them would go on together. She did not want to go back on her own. She could not, not when there was no guidebook in her head for this journey and no directions to be had from anyone. Mutti would read her letter and then she would come. In a moment Ilse got up, took the big envelope and slid it into her suitcase. Carefully, she put the jewellery away, sat staring at her hands, the wall, the cupboard, the scuffed toes of her brown shoes.

Her father returned within an hour. When she said she did not want either of them to go back to Germany, he smiled. It was a victory for fear.

The next day Otto rose and resumed his café visits, as though something had been settled, as though the way they spent their days was real life. The spring brought more and more air-raid alerts: in the shelter they dared not speak. On the street they had to be silent. Even in the room, silence spilled out over them. Every day the news on Albert's radio worsened. The Germans pushed into Denmark and Norway. On Easter Sunday, a day of dull cloud and drizzle, God did not shine on Saint-Sulpice. Ilse stared through the gloom at the failure of her hopes. She prayed intensely for her mother to come very soon. The battles for Narvik were intensive; the German air force was strong. British cruisers were being destroyed. Hitler attacked at a speed of forty miles an hour. His planes all but destroyed the Allied forces on the ground.

Café talk concentrated on the terrifying speed of the German advance. No army in history had moved so fast. Belgium would be next and then France. At the corner table in the Rue de Tournon, Albert ignored it all and held court.

"Mein Kopf ist ein zwitscherndes Vogelnest von konfiszierlichen Büchern,"* he said sonorously. Sitting here, he liked to work on his satirical poem of exile, which he said echoed Heine's account of his German journey. The poem was a useful distraction from his main work, the book he had been writing for so many years. Albert had got Ilse to read the poem out loud to him several times, especially the Hamburg section, which he said made him feel so homesick.

"You see, Ilse, Heine was a rapier, but I'm just a scattergun aiming at all my enemies.

*"My head is a chirruping bird's nest of confiscatable books," from *Deutschland ein Wintermärchen* by Heinrich Heine.

"Ihr Toren, die im Café Tournon sucht!
Hier werdet ihr nichts entdecken!
Die Konterbande, die mit mir reist,
Die hab ich im Kopfe stecken . . ." *

Albert declaimed.

Denmark fell in four hours and people started making plans to flee. There was talk about sharing cars, pooling petrol, train tickets and where to go. Some carried suitcases with them all the time, even to the café. Wild rumours ran around the room, claims that the German supermen raped all the women and cut off the hands of children so they would not grow up to fight. She heard a bearded man holding forth at the next table about how the Grande Armée was invincible. They would easily defeat the Germans. They would defend Paris to the last citizen fighting on the last barricade. Ilse remembered Willy saying that the Maginot Line was impregnable. He had explained that it was a kind of extended fortress that protected France from Germany. She had asked, half jokingly, what would happen if the Germans invaded France anyway? "Then I will come to France with the Legion and save you," he had replied. They had laughed about it. Another voice rose, claiming good authority. Hitler had a timetable and by August 1st German troops would be in London. Jews were already fleeing England. A woman called out with a note of real despair, "Then nowhere is safe!"

Ilse went over to where her father sat; he, like Albert, had his regular spot. "Vati, we must leave Paris," she said. "When are we going to buy your papers?"

"When your mother comes."

"But we can't stay here," she said despairingly. "Nobody is staying here. Can't we go to America?" Everyone was on some list for America, the promised land, though hardly anyone ever got in.

"Do you expect me to live in a nation of outright capitalists?"

Ilse looked at her father, whose cheeks had grown very red.

"What do you take me for?"

"How should I know what to take you for?" she cried out.

He calmed down at once. "Forgive me. You're right, Ilse, you're right."

"Where are we going to go, Vati?"

*"You idiots, looking for my contraband in the Café Tournon—you won't find anything. It is hidden in my head."

"Where does a Jew go?" He said it with a kind of cunning, as if he was trying to catch her out.

"Palestine?" That was where Tante Röschen was and the boys, all safe now.

"Ah, Palestine. We could have done it. We had the money once. But I was against it, and you know why? It was wrong. Because the Jews want to exploit the Arabs and take their lands. Like Winnetou. Like the native Red Indians. Exploited by the white man. They stole away their souls."

It hurt her, that he said this when his sister was such a kind and good woman. Ilse knew that after Kristallnacht Tante Röschen had tried to help them, sending a large sum of money, which had been confiscated along with the other assets. Vati's hands, marked with nicotine, were trembling. Ilse could not stop looking at them and then at the faces of the people at the tables beyond, in the real world of today, who were all leaving as fast as they possibly could. Perhaps he had forgotten about their shop, and Grandfather's business and that lost capitalist life they had led which had seemed so normal and, to her at least, enjoyable.

People at the next table were saying their farewells; they rose to embrace one another. A woman was crying. The café was emptying.

"Vati. Shall we go south?"

"What? It doesn't matter where we are. There is no escape. Nobody wants me. Not even my wife. An enemy, a German who isn't a German and a Jew who isn't a Jew. A null, that's me. A blank," and he leant back in his chair, threw back his arms and laughed.

There was, at this moment, a lull in the hubbub. Behind her, Ilse heard somebody call out, "Good old Otto. Nothing gets him down."

She gazed at her father, seeing how bright his eyes were. Perhaps the truth was something as simple as this. Sitting here, at this moment, he truly was happy. Surely, he had not simply given up?

The weather was remarkable; day after day the sun shone out of cloudless skies. The shops were open and a few elegant women in bright summer dresses and high heels still tip-tapped along the boulevards with their packages, but the streets were empty of traffic. All the rich people in their smart cars were gone. On the 13th of May, German panzers rolled over the border into France. Refugees not already interned had joined the exodus. When Ilse, head down, walked past the Café Tournon, the waiter leant on a broom or swept round empty tables. It was too dangerous to go there now. The French police arrested anyone heard speaking German. Crossing the Boulevard Saint-Germain on her way to Saint-Sulpice, Ilse noticed a huge placard lettered in red: the word "allemand" leapt out. There was another one, down towards the Luxembourg gardens. She went to read it. All "ressortissants allemands"* were to be interned in "camps de concentration." Perhaps they were the only three left, still free. All German women, Frau Wolff included, had had to report to the Vélodrome d'Hiver, the ice-skating rink, where they apparently remained still, herded like cattle under the great glass roof. Anxiously Ilse wondered if she should just destroy the precious Aryan documents. She could not bring herself to do it, when her mother must have spent a fortune obtaining them. She dared not ask her father, in case he destroyed them himself. She told herself to keep her options open.

She walked for hours on the dusty boulevards, stopping when parched at some little café to buy lemonade, always sitting outside to sip it. They heard that the whole French government had gone to the Cathédrale de Notre-Dame to pray for a miracle. Otto laughed long and helplessly at this, as she had not heard him laugh for weeks. "Sheer animal superstition," he said.

"These bastards can pray all they like," said Albert, "but it won't help. What's wrong with these people, that they won't fight?"

"Europe bows to the inevitable," said Otto. "The French have always been magnificent realists."

"Can't we be realists, Vati?"

"Our reality is different."

"Otto, you are not going to just sit here and wait for the tanks to roll in?"

"I am waiting for my wife," he said. "Or are you suggesting I should abandon her?"

Ilse winced. When Albert shook his head, his long jowls shook too and he looked more like a bloodhound than ever.

"Otto, are you listening to me?"

"I'm hardly allowed to do anything else these days. I note that you're still here, my friend."

Albert had all his visas; yet he, too, lingered. Grateful as she was for his presence, she feared it was on their account.

"Albert, please say," whispered Ilse, "where are you going?"

*German nationals.

"Brittany. I want to get evacuated to England when the British get kicked out. English women are fascinating. Beautiful skin, rotten teeth. I'm looking forward to it."

"Don't joke. When are you leaving, really?"

"Very soon." His face grew serious. "Will you come with me?"

She shook her head, smiled, shrugged. "Just as soon as Vati's ready," she said, and moved away to sit with him, because otherwise Albert would press her and she could not bear to discuss it again. Vati insisted that the message had got through. But what if it hadn't? What if her mother in Hamburg was expecting her, was waiting, just as they were, hoping for some sign?

Ilse sat beside the radio waiting for the French and British to unite and stop the Germans. But the German army swept across the north of France, heading for Boulogne and Calais, and by May 22nd they were at the English Channel. The British resistance at Arras was overcome. Boulogne came under fire. When King Leopold of Belgium surrendered, the newscaster expressed outrage and said the French would never surrender. Otto smiled his smile. News came that the British were withdrawing, evacuating their troops from Dunkirk. On May 29th, Ilse heard that some French troops were joining in the exodus.

The sun inched across the sky towards the summer solstice. On the first of June, Albert came to the pension and dragged Ilse out onto the stairwell. "The government's getting out. You're coming with me. Pack your things, I'll be back in two hours."

"What about Vati?"

"I'm sick of telling him. He knows. I'm not going to waste more breath arguing with Otto. Or you. You have to save yourself."

She looked at him in despair, shook her head.

"Darling little donkey, can't you see he is glorying in being rejected? Just wallowing in it? He's lost the will to do anything."

She did see it. Ilse got out her case. As in a dream, she put on one of her treasured school dresses, smoothing down the creased cotton. She had got over her dislike of dressing and undressing in front of her father, merely turning her back, as he did. She packed the brown cardboard box of treasures under her clothes, then got it out again and looked at the tarnished silver photograph frame with its image of two young people smiling at the photographer. Two little silver clasps on the back twisted round against the soft blue leather at the back of the frame, so the photograph could be replaced. The back came off easily. Inside, concealed behind the photograph, was a green paper, which she took out and opened and stared at for a moment before she understood that it was an American fifty-dollar note. Something small and dry fell onto her lap. It was the little blue flower, Vergißmeinnicht,* which her mother loved so much. Carefully, she folded the flower back into the centre of the note, replaced it and the frame. She touched her mother's face. Albert's books made the case very heavy; then she thought that she would not need them, if they were travelling together. It was a happy thought.

"Shall I pack for you, Vati?"

She had long since bought a small case for her father. Now she took it out and opened it, ready, but did not dare touch her father's few possessions. Otto shook his head. She placed her suitcase at the door alongside the sack of potatoes and the cooking pots and the few dishes they had. Too nervous to remain in the room, she went out into the baking heat. At the Comédie Française they were showing *Cyrano de Bergerac*. A poster said that that night's performance was sold out. Though Jews were not excluded, she and her father had not been to the theatre once in her months in France and now she regretted it. Albert would have given her money for a ticket.

All the cars Ilse saw were going in the same direction, heading south and heavily laden, often with mattresses strapped to their roofs, to protect against machine guns. Along the Boulevard des Italiens there was a street vendor selling porcelain figures laid out on a long bench. A middle-aged man crossed the road to look and then bought one. Going closer, Ilse saw that they were dogs. Each little figure had a leg cocked over an opened copy of *Mein Kampf*. She walked back and, turning into their building, saw a taxi waiting in the courtyard.

Her father did not move. His face was the colour of his grey hair. He sat, a small pale man with outspread hands, touching and retouching his truncated finger.

Albert shook his head. "It's over, Otto. There are clerks running around filling up cars and vans with their papers. Pushing typewriters onto rubbish trucks. They're all getting out. We can still get to England. Come on, Ilse." He put a hand on her shoulder. Then he started shouting. "Now! Get your things!"

*Forget-me-not.

Her father shook his head. "I can't," he said. "I have no documents, no visa. I'll never get out of France."

"Up and on, comrade, remember? I'll help you," said Albert. "You're not alone."

"You have papers. You're a writer. The Allies will take you. They'll turn us back. They don't want a Jewish troublemaker. I'm not going like a lamb to the slaughter for the Nazis to finish me off. We're safer in the city. The people of Paris will fight. I'd rather die on the barricades." His tone was indescribably bitter.

"Ilse has papers," said Albert. "She's below the age of internment. She could get out."

"The outcome of the war is inevitable, it makes no difference where we are."

"Otto," said Albert in a sharp tone. "Let the child go. She at least should be saved."

"Vati, please! Can't we all go, the three of us?"

When her father took hold of one hand, squeezing it in his cold one, Ilse realised how moist hers was. Her back was dripping with sweat.

"My old comrade is right. You're just a child, they can't intern you. Go with Albert."

Ilse looked from one man to the other. It had come down to this moment, the shabby room with the dusty potatoes at the door and the dry light falling on her father's grey skin, this view of Albert turning and turning the signet ring with its blue crest on the little finger of his left hand, something he only did when distressed.

"Vati, please, what shall I do?"

"Go with Albert," he repeated.

Ilse stayed with her father at the window until Albert's distinctive lanky figure emerged in the courtyard below. People were trying to commandeer his taxi and Albert was holding them off. "I am going, Vati," she said. Her voice did not sound real.

"Good luck, my darling girl." He spoke so tenderly, why did he do that? He squeezed her arm. He embraced Ilse, a dry kiss. His stubble rasped her cheek.

Ilse took her case and went slowly down the five flights of stairs. At each turn there was a window through which she saw brilliant sunshine. At the courtyard she stopped, turned her face up into the light, squinting into the sun. Her father was at the window upstairs, looking down. He waved and smiled, and made motions that she should go. Albert sat in the back of the taxi. His good eye watched her. She looked back up at her father. He was very small. In a moment, when the taxi drove off, he would turn and lie down on the bed. He would never move if she were not there to make him. She could see exactly how he would lie and how he would turn his face to the wall. He would starve to death within a week. Albert, sitting in the taxi between two piles of suitcases, saw. He slumped.

Ilse put her case down on the pavement and embraced her friend. "Break a leg! Good luck!" she said.

"Take this." He reached into his trouser pocket, shoved a roll of francs into her hand. She saw that he had tears in his eyes. Then she could not prevent tears springing to hers, but she held them back as best she could, unable to utter a word and, waving, watched the taxi go.

Retreating to the shade of the concierge's little room, she wiped her face. Slowly, she climbed the stairs. Her heart had ceased its racket and was now at peace. She went into their room. Otto was lying on the bed. He gave a sort of convulsive jerk as the door opened and turned his head away. Ilse went and sat next to him, feeling him turn as his slight body sagged towards her on the mattress, breathing in the familiar faint smells of tobacco and the sourness of clothes that needed washing and something that was decaying, deep inside. She reached for his hand.

He squeezed hers back. "Such a good girl," he said.

SIX

~

Hamburg, April 1940

Nicolai threaded the black scarf under the collar of the brown shirt, adjusted the leather fastener, put the end of it in his top pocket and buttoned the pocket shut. He pulled the shirt straight, checked in the mirror. He had thrown up from nerves the night before. The Staatstheater was packed, the street outside thick with people, inside would be even hotter. Hundreds lined the stairs where he stood; more waited in anterooms. There must have been a thousand in all. Girls with braided hair and pink cheeks stood beside boys with hair neatly combed, smelling of carbolic soap and starch and sweat. Two girls lugged around a big tin bucket with a mug hooked over the side, giving people drinks. The prettier of the two made sheep's eyes at him; he noticed that her lips and cheeks were rouged. He would have liked some for his parched throat, but the water looked cloudy.

"Nothing else you want from me, then?"

"No."

Laughing, the girls went on. He reminded himself that his grandmother was taking him for lunch at the yacht club; the day could only improve.

The boy at the top, who was leading them in, stood in a kind of trance with his head unnaturally high. The signal was given; Nicolai lifted his standard. By the time he had got up the second flight of stairs, his arms shook from the effort. They were on. To a continuous drum roll, his section marched into the hall from the back, a line three deep going straight into the blinding lights and up the shallow stairs to the platform, tramp-tramp-tramp, the thunder of feet, girls on one side and boys to the other. They lined up, filling the stage from the back, row upon row, to either side of the Hitler portrait. An awed silence fell. He became aware of the huge audience beyond the lights.

"Youth, forward!"

In through the lights came a stream of boys and girls in perfect marching formation: first the thump-thump-thump, then outlines appearing though a haze of brilliance, up past the trembling leaves decorating the platform to become flesh and blood until the entire stage was packed. The leader raised his baton. Nicolai, already feeling slightly faint, rehearsed his line; upon the signal, their voices rose in unison:

"Joyfully we enter through this door,
With courage we face our fate
For fate defeats the coward, but God will help the brave!"

An SS officer stepped to the microphone.

"Our Führer has said: 'Let the young generation be hard and strong. We want our youth to be reliable, loyal, to obey orders and behave decently.' "

The band started up. They sang "We carry in our beating hearts faith in Germany." The SS man stepped forward again.

"German youth! German parents! This ceremony marks the moment at which the young person between fourteen and fifteen enters a new stage of life. Before, your parents spoke for you; now you speak for yourselves. A nation fights for its future, so its youth must support the battle and fight with all its energy."

The words flowed. His arms hurt. His head buzzed. He wondered if he was going to keel over. To keep a fixed point, he stared at the dark scorch mark on the back of the shirt of the boy in front of him where an overeager mother had applied an unnecessary finishing touch. The triangular shape came and went until he felt dizzy. A girl opposite was blinking back tears; he too felt his throat constricting with emotion, he hardly knew what.

"Let us together affirm the German oath."

They intoned: "We affirm that the German people has been created by the will of God. It is our wish to fight for this German Reich, for our home. We will never forget that we are German. This is our will."

But what if a person did not want to fight? He didn't.

The SS man shouted, "Let the flags fly!"

With straining arms, Nicolai lifted his standard as high as it would go. Above his head the sea of red flags hung. The usual chords were struck; thousands of voices thunderously sang the "Horst Wessel Lied." The roar invaded him. His arms ached; he mimed the song while uncontrollable shivers ran up and down his spine and a cold trickle of sweat started in the middle of his back and ran down.

> *"Die Straße frei den braunen Bataillonen,*
> *Die Straße frei dem Sturmabteilungsmann!*
> *Es schau'n aufs Hakenkreuz voll Hoffnung schon Millionen*
> *Der Tag für Freiheit und für Brot bricht an."**

As the row in front turned to march out, and with relief he lowered his standard to rest it on the floor, he saw the officer was giving each one a book. Smooth-skinned and unsmiling, he offered it with his gloved hand, for a second his sharp eye rested on Nicolai. Then it was over. Outside, gulping in the fresh air, waiting for his mother and grandmother to find him in the milling, babbling throng, Nicolai steadied himself. The book was called *Remember That You Are a German*. A paper label was pasted inside with the insignia of the HJ in red, with a signature scrawled across it. It read: *Presented on the day when you took on obligations for the life of your people*. Nicolai snapped it shut. It was just words. He had not signed anything. They could not own him, body and soul, because of those words.

The house was very still. Sabine slept upstairs. The sun slanted through the gaps in the ivy leaves and, reflected on their shiny surfaces, made shifting double patterns on the linoleum, on his bare outstretched legs.

---

*"Clear the street for the brown battalions, / Make way for the SA man; / Millions full of hope gaze at the swastika, / For the day of bread and freedom has come."

Sitting on the floor of Fräulein Lore's room, for every other surface was covered with fabric, he played with her pin box, inserting half a dozen pins the tiniest bit into his fingertips, waving steel-tipped fingers.

"Ouch," she said.

"It doesn't hurt. Fräulein Lore, what does Ilse look like?"

He was very curious about this child who was going to live in his house and be his friend. Putting down her sewing, she opened the drawer beside her bed and drew out a framed studio portrait of a sweet-faced child about eight years old, with hair in two thick plaits and big questioning eyes. The hair was hand-coloured a vivid auburn, eyes painted a startling unnatural turquoise.

"And this is the passport photograph. She was twelve. She'll have grown, of course, in a year. It's over a year."

Her lips curved into a faint smile when she looked at her daughter. The older girl in this tiny second picture stared at him directly with a serious look, her hair drawn tightly back. He was fascinated by this other secret life that had been hidden inside the woman he knew. She was like the Russian dolls Sabine was so fond of, with their round red cheeks and bright headscarves, their invisible join where a smaller, nearly identical person was hidden inside. The little doll Ilse was the image of her mother. A month younger than he was, Ilse would not be a silly flirt like some girls. She would be clever like her mother; they would ride on bicycles, go on picnics. They would walk and talk with Sabine between them, laughing as they swung the little one off her feet. She would speak French fluently, naturally, and perhaps she would teach him. Then they would share a secret language. Ilse's life seemed very romantic; the great good fortune of being sent away to Paris to stay with her uncle and learn French balanced by the misfortune of being stranded there when war broke out, the further bad luck of having lost her papers. It had taken a long time and a fight with officialdom to obtain another set. (It had been expensive, too; he blushed at the memory of his theft, forgiven and forgotten, now that they were friends.) Who could have anticipated that the army would invade France as fast as it had, causing further confusion? All this time, Fräulein Lore had kept her secret well; she had not wanted to tell her employer about this loved, absent child until she knew that she would be coming home. She was a woman of mysteries and secrets. It would take time and all his patience, but he would unravel them all.

The little green room was crammed with acquisitions for Ilse. First she had obtained the bedstead, which stood against the far wall. A pile of blankets and pillows sat on it. A new feather-and-down bed was rolled up, its cover white striped with a tiny pink and green sprig design, quite unlike anything else in the house. It was frivolous; he liked it. New celluloid hairbrushes were laid out in a row. She noticed him looking.

"Such hair she has," Fräulein Lore said, sighing and mock grumbling. "Such long curly hair, it needs a lot of brushing." How proud she was of those curls. She picked up another two of the pieces of grey flannel fabric laid out in an elaborate jigsaw covering the bed, laid them together and tacked neatly along one side. It was a dress for her daughter.

"How long now?"

"Soon, any day." Neatly, she snipped the thread with tiny scissors. He watched the little thimble flash as she sewed. She stitched all the time, never sat still.

"You're doing it again."

"Am I?"

She smiled, pressed a hand to her forehead and rubbed it. When she frowned, she deepened the two little creases of perpetual worry in the middle of her forehead that never quite went away. He wanted to put his hands on her forehead and smooth them out; he imagined how soft the skin would be. He wanted to touch the delicate skin at her temples where the faint blue vein throbbed.

Tight-lipped at the revelation that the nursemaid was a divorcée with a child of her own, his mother had said that there could be no question of taking in another mouth to feed. Magda could not be expected to work harder. When she understood that the alternative was losing the Fräulein to a more generous-minded household, she had relented.

"You see, darling, it's so hard to find good domestics these days," she told Nicolai. "And we must think of the poor child." As the idea grew in her mind, she became almost enthusiastic: the little girl would be a helpmeet, a big sister to Sabine and a friend to him. Nicolai knew how essential Fräulein Lore was. Every day his mother was busy. She went lunching, dancing and dining with her friends in the Vier Jahreszeiten or the Hotel Atlantik. Hamburg was full of officers and there was a succession of tea dances and war drives; war, or the absence of their men, had released some frivolous part of them. Colonised by his mother's friends, without his father to provide the balance with his good sense and reasonableness, the house had become enemy territory.

Nicolai's world shrank to his room and this one. He felt at peace here, knowing that Ilse had received her papers and was coming home to safety. Any day the call would come and she would be there, at the station.

"I can't wait to meet her."

"I can't wait either. Toi, toi, toi,"* she said, rapping the wooden mushroom. She tacked the seam, was threading the needle again, then reaching for pins. Leaning forward to pass the box, he took in the very faint vanilla smell of her skin.

"Fräulein Lore! Please come upstairs!" Magda was calling down the stairs with a note of urgency. "Fräulein Lore, please! The Luftschutzverein† are here."

She had given a painful start, then sunk back; he felt for her. How swiftly hope rose again, only to be suppressed.

"I'll go, you're busy." He ran up to the hall.

"They were at the Reemtsma house last week," hissed Magda. "Poking around. Inspecting everyone's air-raid defences, noses in every cupboard. Their maid told me."

He peeped out of the window. A dozen fierce-looking ladies with steel helmets and grey mackintoshes over their arms stood at the front door.

"We can't let these busybodies in the cellar to see our supplies. Frau Bucherer is lunching at the Vier Jahreszeiten. What do I do?"

"Fräulein Lore will know," he said.

She came up to the front door and let them in. The ladies crowded into the hallway, saying things all at once. There was a new decree. All cellars had to be reinforced, new emergency exits provided. Everything had to be inspected. They were looking around at the paintings and furniture and flowers.

"I'm so sorry," Fräulein Lore said. "The cellars are locked."

"Where is the key?"

There was a pause. Nicolai hung over the banisters and watched her face.

*Touch wood.
†Air Defence League.

"It is in the offices of Colonel Oster."

"Colonel Oster?"

"Of the SS. Currently based in Lübeck. A family friend who has been helping Frau Bucherer with the necessary building works. Of course, with young children in the house, one doesn't want to risk any accidents. The Colonel is very precise about these matters."

The ladies whispered together for a moment.

"The Colonel is a busy man. But if you insist, I will inform him."

Suddenly, all smiles, they withdrew. Nicolai admired her quick thinking. He knew perfectly well where his mother kept the cellar key; they all did, for air raids. The RAF had bombed Hamburg, and though they had rushed to shelter in their deeper cellar, there had been no need. The British hadn't hit a single target, had killed women and children. "Germany will exact a terrible revenge for these crimes," his father's newspaper said. He had formed the habit of reading it in his father's study. Nobody else went there and the room still smelt faintly of him. Unlike Magda, who listened avidly to every radio announcement, Fräulein Lore hated war news. She was like his father, wanting peace, praying for it to be over soon.

She stitched pleats together, folding and measuring the fabric so they were all the same width. Nicolai dreamt on, lost somewhere in the folds. He could not imagine why Colonel Oster should be invoked. Wolfgang's godfather and guardian was so awe-inspiring that Nicolai had never dared address him. Nicolai's own godfather was a wishy-washy second cousin who lived in Elmsbüttel but only turned up once a year, if that. Before Wolfgang turned twelve and went away to live with him and be trained up for the military academy, the Colonel had visited regularly, bringing wonderful presents: binoculars, quarter-size model engines that really worked, even a rifle with real bullets. He had taught Wolfgang to shoot, he treated him like his own son. Their mother's first husband had been the Colonel's dearest friend in the army. Nicolai still remembered Wolfgang bragging about the car and how he had been driven away to his new life, puffed up with pride because the chauffeur had saluted him.

"Does Colonel Oster really have a key?"

She shrugged, nodded.

"I suppose the Colonel's only supervising the cellar work because Father's so far away."

"I suppose," she said.

Nicolai could not utter the word "father" without a twinge of sorrow and, alongside that, a sharper pang that his mother did not seem to miss him as he did, as she should have. Pushing the thought away, he studied the way Fräulein Lore's lashes swept up and then down. She scrutinised her work. He had managed to take one good picture of her, in profile, minimising that little frown of hers, which even now remained.

"We don't need officers here. I can look after my womenfolk," he said. The glance she sent him was very sweet. It was a little victory, to make her smile.

Uniformed boys flocked around the station buffet; the train seethed brown. The annual summer camp took not just his whole school year, but fourteen-year-olds from two other schools. They blurred together, the shorts above bony knees the same, even the backs of their necks and haircuts seemingly identical, so that he no longer knew which his troop was or barely who he himself might be. In younger, sadder years, camp week had passed in terror at this uniformity. He had been on constant alert, fearful that if he once ducked into the wrong tent, he might find himself forever trapped in somebody else's life.

Pushing his kitbag onto the train, Nicolai felt deep relief that he was not going to be with this gang the whole time. His family would be at the other end. Though for many months she had been busy with other things, his mother had really bucked up at the reminder of his obligatory week of camp, had insisted, wonderfully, that this must be a family affair. She and Sabine and Fräulein Lore had already driven up to Timmendorfer Strand; even Wolfgang would be coming. All this was for his benefit. The only ones left out were his father, of course, and his grandmother. Though she usually came away with them, she had decided this time to stay in Hamburg. All the way in the noisy compartment with boys flicking things and squabbling, boys eating salami and Leberwurst sandwiches out of greasy paper and belching, like idiots, straight in one another's faces, he felt grateful to his mother for such generosity of spirit. In a week, all these boys would go home and a new set would arrive. But he would stay on and spend an additional week at the hotel. That would be a real holiday.

Rows of tents stretched across the sand dunes. They were put to work, sweeping them out and gathering driftwood for the fires, then assembling in long rows.

"We owe to our leader, Adolf Hitler, the fact that we can open our camp today," said the camp leader, Herr Francke, then they all sang "Onward, Onward." "Tonight, boys, community hour is omitted as the group is still very tired."

Nicolai would not have to sleep in a tent on the hard ground, nor drink his breakfast milk from a tin mug. He stood to one side longing to go, not quite daring to leave.

"Where's our official photographer? Ah, Bucherer. There you are. Good. I must come over to the hotel with you and greet your delightful mother."

They walked in a group; Herr Francke and two other boys, who soon peeled off. They too had obtained permission to stay with their families in hotels, though none was as grand as the Strandhotel, which gave right onto the beach, the crisp white building now visible, its blue shutters flung open in welcome.

Clicking his heels, Herr Francke kissed his mother's hand. Dressed in silk, she had makeup on and her shining blond hair was swept up in a different style. She looked very pretty. Lugging over his kitbag, Nicolai felt a wave of pride.

"Frau Bucherer, what a pleasure. I am honoured to meet the famous daughter of the equally famous shipbuilding firm."

"Goodness, I don't have anything to do with the business," she said. "We have managers for that. One day this young man will take it over, I hope," and she leant over and ruffled his hair. Nicolai squirmed between pleasure and embarrassment. She usually said that about Wolfgang, not him. Everybody knew who her favourites were. "Herr Francke—my husband is away in the army of course—an intelligence officer. We miss him so. Now, it will be lovely to have some clever conversation for a change. I am hoping you are going to tell me about the war and what's happening."

"At your command." Overcome, the camp leader clicked once more.

Dimpling, his mother beckoned a waiter, who came over with a bottle of Sekt and glasses on a tray. She looked at him. "Your kit, darling—run along and find Fräulein Lore and put it in your room."

From his high attic room he watched the attendant down on the beach in front of the hotel rolling up the bright striped awnings of the little beach baskets and closing up their doors for the night. In the adjoining room Fräulein Lore slept peacefully; Sabine lay, arms flung wide, in her cot. Herr Francke and his mother were on the terrace with other people she knew, having drinks and laughing. He had had crayfish for dinner and potato salad, then cake and cream. Over at the camp, they had had to cook pea soup, which always formed a disgusting frothy scum. In pyjamas, he stood at the high window and sniffed the salt wind coming from the grey sea beyond.

Fräulein Lore had brought his camera and equipment safely; he needed to prepare some film. He got out the lightproof cassette, took his scissors and neatly slit open a fresh packet. Sitting on his bed, holding the loading cassette under the blanket, he carefully placed the film inside and snapped the lid to in the dark. By moonlight, he dropped the bobbin into the narrow end, attached the end of the film, closed the lid and turned the handle to wind it on, not needing the counter to tell him when he had reached thirty-six. His hands knew. Reaching under the blanket, he slotted the two halves of the cassette together. In the morning he would trim the tongue of film so it was ready for loading. He was going to take dozens of excellent photographs and make his father proud. When three films had been prepared, he tiptoed over the scrubbed pine floorboards to the partly opened door, crept over to the bed. Just for an instant he lowered his head beside hers, intoxicated by the clean, lovely smell of her skin and her warm breath on his cheek.

The sound of seagulls came on the breeze. The hot June sun shone. Midges seemed to love him, and the black shorts, new and still stiff with starch, chafed badly.

"Password?"

They roared it out: "Blood!"

"Motto for the day?"

"To remain pure and become mature."

It was only ten o'clock but Nicolai was sweating. He had emptied his water bottle and thought with longing of the cool water in pitchers with ice, back at the hotel. It was too hot to bother to get out the exposure metre. He set the camera to a 250th of a second at F8 and pointed it. It was best to pick one figure from the many. He chose one boy, very athletic and concentrated. The Leica was perfect for action shots. The sun burnt the back of his neck: he was Robert Capa on a hill in Spain, with the smell of death in the air, aiming as troops were dodging bullets. His father had shown him photographs of the Spanish Civil War in an American magazine. His hero used a Leica too. Together, they had marvelled at them.

"Down!"

The boys sprang forward, noses in the sand. They did twenty push-ups.

"Twenty more!" He clicked, wound on, clicked. The sound the Leica made, that silky soft zipping noise as the focal-plane shutter moved across, was intensely satisfying.

"Up! Forward march! Run!"

To the rear of the disappearing column, a boy was making faces at him, a small lad with big protruding ears and a cheeky face; he was waggling his hands and sticking his tongue out.

"Jammy bugger. I know you. You're the one staying in the fancy hotel." The funny-faced boy sauntered forward. He had lagged so far behind that the troop had run off without him. "Bloated member of the bourgeoisie, that's what you are."

Nicolai put the camera in the bag, did it up and put it on the ground a little way away where it would be safe, then turned and squared up to him. His heart had already set up a steady thump of alarm.

"You and the other softies missed a right treat last night. Our Herbert got us up in the middle of the night, down on the beach, marching for hours. You should have heard him. *'Mummy's boys can lie on soft pillows. Our country needs strong fellows, not cowards. We will be hard, hard with ourselves.'* We stumbled back into camp, half dead. Where are our leaders in the morning? Down at the hotel having breakfast with you lot while we're still trying to light the bloody fire and shit in a bucket."

The tone of outrage rose high; Nicolai could not help smiling. The boy smiled back. It wasn't going to be a fight after all.

"Nicolai Bucherer," he said.

The other held out his hand. "Klaus Losch. They haven't noticed I've gone. They don't do roll call till the evening. Let's bunk off. We can swim and then go back to your hotel. You can buy me an ice cream."

Nicolai had never bunked off anything.

"Well? Got any better ideas?"

He shook his head.

They tore out sharp blades of seagrass, whistled through them, then rolled down the dunes until they grew bored of shaking sand from their hair. Klaus knew the routine, it was his third year at this camp. Though much smaller than Nicolai he was nearly two years older, almost sixteen. All along the beach he tried in vain to get Nicolai to hand over his camera, claiming he could persuade girls to do handstands and lasciviously miming how he would take pictures of them.

"That one." Klaus pointed. "The redhead. What a figure." He wolf whistled, then blew out his scrawny chest and beat on it. "Me Johnny Weissmuller—she Jane."

He meant Fräulein Lore. Wearing her bathing suit, she sat in the shade of a rented basket helping Sabine build sand castles. Each time the little girl in her huge floppy sunhat marched purposefully down the beach to fill another bucket with water, Fräulein Lore raised her head and stared out to sea. They made a pretty sight.

"Let's go and talk to her."

"No. We'll swim," he said.

He could not have borne it if Klaus had tried to make her do a handstand. Though opinionated, his new friend was easily persuaded and they headed towards the water. Fräulein Lore did have a figure like a young girl's. His mother had remarked upon it, said something about eating less herself. Nicolai lingered. This was the picture he wanted; the woman in the dappled shade, the light falling obliquely across her, the lovely curve of slender legs against the weave of the basket, the hair falling down her back, loosely tied. Quietly, he took the camera from his bag, felt for the 90mm lens. As he turned the knurled wheel, the black frame closed on a tiny, perfect image. In a moment she looked up. She waved. He waved back. Happiness pierced him.

They swam, ducking each other, lay in secret dips in the sand dunes staring at the sky. Trips like this to the mountains or seaside were the only holiday Klaus ever got. He liked the swimming and the football, hated the drill and so got out of it.

"You waste your energy complaining. You can pick and choose, idiot. Francke fancies your mother. So you can do what you like, see?" said Klaus. Nicolai digested this.

"How do you know he fancies her?"

"Pretty obvious. You can see it. She's a real sexpot."

"You're mad."

Batting away Nicolai's incredulity with both hands, Klaus claimed expertise. "It's the way they walk, obviously. The ones who want it walk differently from the ones who don't."

One foot placed directly in front of the other, he minced along the sand dunes, thin hips sticking out, swaying from side to side, one red-knuckled fist poised delicately above the brown leather belt. "See? When they do that it's because they're mad for it. Some of the really desperate ones lick their lips when they look at you."

Nicolai burst out laughing; but Klaus, frowning at his disbelief, skidded back down the dune, showering him with sand.

"If they look at you straight, without blinking, they really like you. God's truth. Like this."

They practised their blank stares, the winner being the one who made the other blink first. Klaus won every time. Then they ran through their BdM jokes.

"A class is set the essay: Would young Werther have committed suicide if he'd been in the Hitler Youth? The top boy writes an excellent piece and he gets to choose the next topic. He thinks for a long time—then inspiration strikes. Would the Maid of Orleans have remained a virgin if she'd joined the BdM?"

"Do you ever think of anything else?"

"What else is there?"

"You should be a writer, Klaus."

"Fat chance. I'll probably end up on the railways, like my dad. We bloody workers never get a look in at any decent kind of a job. My dad doesn't hold with any of this 'born to die for Germany' nonsense. He says we're born to live. I know what I'll do when I get in the army."

"What?"

"Sabotage. Sugar in the petrol tanks."

"What does that do?"

"Stops them dead in their tracks. But it doesn't do it straight away, see, so you don't get caught. The engine snarls up a kilometre or two away. You have to be clever about it. I'll defuse the bombs. Or even better, prime them so they blow up the generals. Finish them all off."

"You are insane."

"Just wait."

"Why go to the army, if you're so against it?"

"What choice have I got? That's what happens to the proletariat. When they talk about shedding German blood, it's the workers they've got in mind. We're cannon fodder. We're innocent. So we have to defend ourselves."

His defence of the innocent was so bloodthirsty, it made Nicolai laugh.

"My half-brother believes in all that German blood and honour stuff," he said. "He's really dedicated, he's an officer cadet, wants to join the Schutzstaffel as soon as he can." This was the wrong thing to say.

For a long time, Klaus remained silent, chewing at bits of the wiry grass. Eventually, he spat out an indigestible matted mess. "People like your brother. That's the heart of the problem," he said. "If educated people believe in the Party, then there's no hope. The masses just want jobs. And beer."

His new friend, always begging for ice creams and sandwiches, was not so much greedy as hungry. Klaus had never gone home from school to the certainty of a hot lunch. His mother was dead; he and his father lived in St. Pauli "in a stinking tenement. Cockroach hotel, I call it." When pushed, he described the filth and decay, not with shame but with hot anger.

On the last day of camp, wandering around the hotel, they ran into his mother. When Klaus was introduced to her, he bowed. "Delighted to meet you, dear lady." He clicked his heels and bent over her hand and almost kissed it in a way Nicolai found very ironic, though she did not seem to notice, or mind.

"But aren't you boys supposed to be up at the camp?"

"We got lost in the forest," said Klaus, urging her to write a note to excuse them, which she did. Waiting for her to finish it, they exchanged addresses on the grand hotel paper. He wrote an immaculate copperplate hand, with all sorts of curlicues and flourishes. Nicolai marvelled at the beauty of it. They said goodbye out on the sands: camp was breaking up and already parents were turning up to collect their boys. Delighted to be free, Nicolai turned the first cartwheel of his life. Klaus was his witness. He watched him out of sight, running down the beach backwards and waving the note like a trophy.

"Who was that peculiar boy?" his mother asked, on her way up to change.

"A leading member of the Hitler Youth," he said. "About to graduate with honour. It really is true that the workers show us the way, isn't it?"

His mother carried on up the stairs. She had probably never met a real worker.

Everybody gathered in the salon to hear radio news of the war in France before the early dinner sitting, the one the children went to. His mother dined in solitary state. Sitting in the comfort of their cosy evening together, of Sabine safe asleep upstairs, he noticed how thin Fräulein Lore was becoming. She was leaning slightly forward, listening intently, and the summer dress she wore each evening gaped at the back. At supper, she had one spoonful of soup, crumbled a roll. He looked at her very directly, trying to make her look back at him properly, as a woman might look at a man. Though she smiled at him very nicely, she always blinked. At night, she fell asleep at once, as if exhausted. He tiptoed into her room and studied her by moonlight, examining the freckles, darker spots on her clear skin, trembling to touch her long pale lashes, worrying that his breath might wake her.

The sun woke him early. He had a week of real holiday and wanted to relish every minute. The maids had laid the tables for breakfast but nobody was there except for him. He poured a glass of milk, took one of the delicious morning rolls. Breaking the crisp crust, he dug a finger into the soft white bread. With the knife, he raised a thick curl of white butter and plopped a spoonful of bilberry jam on top. He bit hard, squeaking through the butter, leaving teeth marks. A church bell nearby started ringing; it went on and on. He turned on the radio. Von Kluge's Fourth Army had entered Dunkirk, capturing thousands of French troops, the announcer said. Hitler had ordered all church bells in Germany to be rung to announce the end of the greatest battle in world history. Like the wind, he ran upstairs. The bells ringing meant the end of the war. His father would come home; perhaps he would even join them here. Determined to be the first to tell his mother the great news, he threw open the door to his mother's dressing room, which gave onto her bedroom.

Colonel Oster's jacket lay on the sofa. Two highly polished black shoes stood neatly, side by side. A pair of black trousers hung over the chair beside the dressing table. The door to the bedroom was closed. Nicolai went back downstairs. He went out to the porch and sat for a long time and thought about it. What a fool he had been not to realise that the Colonel came here. That was why his mother dined late every night and not with them. That was why she had been so keen to come to camp. And he had imagined that it was for his benefit.

In the afternoon, Wolfgang arrived. From his attic window Nicolai watched the chauffeur open the passenger door of the long black car, its high polish flashing white against the haze of sand and sky. The sheen and curve of the bonnet had the iridescence of a tenement cockroach. The white-blond head got out; the door clicked shut, the chauffeur carried a case in, came out again and the insect scuttled down the ramp and away, underground. Wolfgang had a room to himself. It would be easy to avoid him: his half-brother never wasted his valuable time with inferiors. Perhaps he knew about the affair. Perhaps everyone knew except for him. Nicolai stood for a long time, watching the day fall away. Slowly, the red ball of the sun dropped from the sky into the water, and the sea, instead of boiling, swallowed it.

"What's the matter, Nicolai?" asked Fräulein Lore.

"Nothing," he said. "Time to dress for dinner."

He was dining with the adults. From outside the glass door, striving for the right expression, Nicolai saw Colonel Oster standing in the middle of the dining room as waiters scurried round him. His mother reached up to embrace Wolfgang, now as tall as the Colonel, elegant in his cadet's uniform. As she kissed her firstborn, he saw how exactly alike they were in colouring, their neat oval faces the same. The three of them could have been a family; the Colonel clean-shaven, still handsome with his grey-blond hair and pale glinting eyes. He was probably in his early forties, just a few years older than his mother, but the long cruel furrows from nose to chin aged him. Nicolai, with his dark hair and his father's long face, belonged to a different race.

Wolf stood with his mother's arm loosely round his waist, very erect, smiling with that utter confidence he always had which actually stole something away from every person. Nicolai wished his father was there to wink, to make a Wolfgang joke, to make the world safe again. The bitter jolt of knowledge shuddered down, that he could never tell his father what he knew. He felt them all receding, continuing their lives from a great distance. Then he put a face on and pushed through the doors, into a clamour of voices and glasses. Champagne had been ordered and Nicolai was given a glass.

"Aren't we lucky," his mother said. "Some good things aren't rationed." She dimpled and smiled with the tiny black balls of caviar caught between her teeth. If he waited all his life, she would not say one original thing.

Colonel Oster proffered a hand. It was frightening when those hard pebble eyes remained fixed on him. "Where's your uniform, my boy?"

He had been so happy to take it off, had chucked it into the corner of the room.

"I didn't like to wear a dirty one, sir. The other's in the wash."

"Remind me to give you a very fine pair of binoculars from the Oster factory. We make the best ones, you know."

"Thank you, Herr Oberst."

After that he ignored Nicolai, who picked at his fish while they talked military talk about reparations and how they would make the French pay. History, the Colonel said, was written by the winners. He explained the success of their strategy; said everything was legitimate, if you won. Everybody laughed. Wolfgang talked loudly of blood and honour, pushing back the fine hair, which kept flopping over his forehead. His mother hung on his words and patted his hand and adored her big boy. Nicolai drank his wine down in two long fizzy draughts. Wolfgang had very neat features, cut out of a paper pattern and tacked invisibly together by an expert hand so the seams did not show. Other people were not so precisely assembled; he was himself jagged. Nicolai observed that, for the others, he was barely there. He was a shadow of Wolf, a lesser version. The waiter refilled the glasses. He drank.

A boy got his strength from his father. Wolfgang's father, hero of the Great War, had been carried off in the influenza epidemic of 1923, when Wolfgang was a baby. So he couldn't have been that strong, could he? His mother went on smiling and nodding and agreeing with everything the pair of them said, and laughing at the Colonel's jokes. She behaved as though nobody would notice her extreme good humour.

"My father will be a colonel," said Nicolai unexpectedly. They looked at him. He felt his face flushing and, emboldened, he seized his moment. "He's brave. He'll be a great war hero. Better than Wolfgang's father. Much better."

His voice had come out too loud; the adjoining table hushed. The Colonel opened his mouth. Laughter burst out of him. Wolfgang, aping him, started laughing his false ha-ha-ha. The Colonel's eyes shut, shoulders shaking with mirth; his mother's mouth was open, showing her white teeth, pink tongue, the smear of lipstick at the corners of her mouth. He was drawn out of himself, sucked into their hot stream of noise. Before he could disappear down their open red gullets, Nicolai shrank back into his body. He let himself concentrate on the man's black shoulder and fell, dizzyingly, into its depths, pulled down and down. Somebody had a hand on his shoulder. In a little moment his mother swam back into focus.

"You'd better go to bed, Nicolai," she said, smiling brilliantly. "I think you got a little too much sun today, darling."

He got up, bowed, said good night. He hated his mother. He marched down the corridor that led to the salon. The waiters were busy serving dinner. He hated them all. He turned towards the kitchen and went past the rooms where the maids clattered and chattered. Two of them were piling up dirty glasses. The second room was empty. All the clean things were here, the morning salt and pepper pots, the coffee cups and eggcups and saucers lined up and waiting to go back on the breakfast tables. The sugar sifters were in his hands before he knew why he wanted them.

It was very quiet in the underground garage. The Colonel's car was at the far side. Nicolai unscrewed the top of the sugar sifter, cupped his hand and carefully directed the white sugar into the petrol tank. Wars were about winning. He emptied the second sifter in. Then he licked a finger and wiped away the little white granules around the rim. He screwed the cap back on, feeling the sugar crackle as he turned it as tight as it would go. He crept back upstairs, returned the sifters to their place. He wondered how far the car would travel before the sugar got into the engine. He hoped that it would break down irretrievably.

Because, afterwards, he could not sleep he stood for a long time at his window feeling strange, feeling the breeze on his hair, staring at the full moon, which lit everything up. He might turn into a werewolf. He unbuttoned his pyjama top, let the moonlight cover him. Hair would grow all over his body and claws erupt. His skin was already crawling. The beach was so white that he was not sure at first if the figure at the water's edge staring out to sea was real or not. It was a ghostly apparition that shimmered in and out of the silvery water, going forward and back, ever farther and deeper. Was it going to swim away or drown itself? Then he recognised her. Fräulein Lore was the werewolf.

SEVEN

Paris, June 1940

Anti-aircraft batteries rattled all the time; the distant boom was the Germans bombing factories and airports outside Paris. No bombs had hit the centre, the announcer said. One ear pressed to the radio to blank out the whine of aircraft, Ilse listened to announcements of great French successes. The Germans had been decimated in battles to the north, the "glorieuse Armée" had triumphed. The evacuation of the British from Dunkirk had been achieved "successfully" using an armada of British boats; French forces were "successfully" holding the enemy in check. The RAF was conducting numerous "successful" sorties against the enemy. Albert, surely, was safe in London now. She switched the radio off.

Bathed in a beautiful June light, Paris was deserted. The concierge had left. The landlady disappeared and nobody came to collect the rent. Most shops had put their shutters up. Luckily Albert's money had bought tins of meat and fruit and dry goods and rusks, butter and oil. The boulangerie was still open. Returning home with two warm baguettes, Ilse passed a queue of women standing in the street, each holding a dog or a cat. The long row stretched round their corner and to the doors of the veterinary surgeon. In the room, she sliced the bread, spread it recklessly with butter.

"What were they doing?"

"Putting the animals down."

"Poor animals."

"They've grown soft. The last time the Parisians defended their city, it was a siege," Otto said. "They ate them all, to the last cat and rat."

Lunch was a tin of ham with potatoes and haricots verts. Otto drank his glass of wine and then permitted himself a second. Because there was nowhere to buy wine and only a few bottles left, he had been rationing himself for a week. They even shared a chocolate bar.

"What are we celebrating?" she asked.

"That it's not rat."

Signs like mushrooms sprang up everywhere: CITOYENS! AUX ARMES! The radio announced that Mussolini had declared war on Great Britain and France. "The people of Paris are ready to defend their city to every last stone and lamp-post," the announcer said. They should prepare for street fighting. Her father spoke of manning the barricades, said that she would hide while he fought. She looked at him, incredulous. There were no soldiers anywhere. All they saw from the window was one old lady carrying a shopping bag. Otto had another swig of his wine, pointed to her and laughed.

"What's funny?"

"The troops are out in force. Nothing's funny. I need a gun."

She thought of the pistol he had kept locked in the drawer of his beautiful modern desk in the Landsweg until the Gestapo took it away; she remembered the cherry-wood panelling and the glass-fronted cabinet. He went out, saying that Ilse had to stay behind and keep the door locked. She sat at the window and looked out for two hours, thinking in a kind of dull stupor that he would be arrested and taken away, and that she would never see him again. Otto returned. He said that he had spotted half a dozen stray Tommies drinking tea out of big tin mugs and looking cheerful. "The French forces must be here. They are lying low," he said.

The next morning, even the boulangerie had closed and no trams or buses ran. The only sound was the barking of stray dogs. The electric light flickered and when, in the evening, she wanted to cook potatoes, there was no gas. In the night they smelt a sharp smell and woke on Wednesday to find a thick pall of smoke filling the sky.

"They might have set the city on fire—to defend it," he said. "Why no alarms? Why didn't they warn us?"

By the middle of the morning the smoke had gone; the sun shone once more. Everything seemed very unreal. The radio announced that the government had left Paris and that it had been declared an open city. As she translated, Otto flew into a fury, kicking over the saucepan of water for the potatoes.

"What's an open city?"

"The bastards are handing it over. There'll be no defence, they're abandoning Paris to the Germans. Abandoning their capital without firing one shot. It's impossible."

"What are we going to do?"

"We're going now," he said. "Immediately."

A hot jet of bile rose in her gorge. "Now?"

"I would have fought for Paris," he said. "Cowards. All cowards."

Mechanically, she picked up the potatoes, some of which had rolled under the bed, looked at his feet tracking water across dry floorboards. With angry haste, her father started putting his few things into the small case and filling it up with tins of food. He kicked the wardrobe door shut. The automaton Ilse collected the rest of the food together and said nothing. He went out first. She picked up her case; once more she carried it down the five floors to the street door. Her father carried the bag and the cooking gear plus the potatoes, staggering under the load. They waited for a long time near the bridge, but there was no hope of a taxi. They would have to walk to the station. They set off, carrying the sack of potatoes between them. Ilse wore her coat, which was so hot that she began to feel giddy and sick. She took it off and her father carried it for her. For a while, neither of them spoke.

"Where are we going?" She would not look at him as she asked. "Dunkirk, I suppose?" She spat the words out with fury. It was far too late, didn't he realise anything?

"They're coming from the north," Otto said. "We'll head south. What's the nearest station?"

"Montparnasse."

From several streets away it was obvious that others had had the same idea. Along the approach roads to the Gare Montparnasse, the crowd became so thick that they could not get anywhere near. Men and women stood shoulder to shoulder, the ground jammed with their suitcases; weeping or listless children clung to their parents. Ilse and Otto eased their way into the line, still carrying the sack of potatoes. When they stopped they rested it, now against her legs, now against Otto's. Her arms ached and so did her feet; she longed to sit down but did not dare. Grimly, the crowd pressed forward up the gentle incline. The people seemed sullen, hostile even. Something hard in her father's raincoat pocket kept pressing against her hip. After some time it occurred to her that he must have found himself a gun. This scared her. She worked her way round him, so it was on the other side. The blank hopelessness of it kept coming over her in waves, alongside incredulity that her father had actually remained in Paris in order to fight.

Rumours went back and forth: there would be trains in the evening, somebody said. The trains were running but they were not long distance, said another. They were just shunting people out to the suburbs, shuttling back and forth to clear the station. No, they were going south, right to Marseilles, not stopping anywhere. An old man kept repeating that they would all have to spend the night there, in the open, where the Germans could bomb them. A woman with bleached blond hair and a shrill voice said that she knew it on good authority from her cousin who lived there that the Germans had set the northern suburbs on fire. The Germans were going to torch Paris, section by section, until they surrendered. By the late afternoon, when they had hardly moved more than a couple of dozen metres, more and more people began to sit down until most were sitting on the pavement and in the road, leaning on their bundles and suitcases. A sudden screaming sound came from up ahead. They craned to see. Another scream came, the extreme noise of great pain. Two women stood holding up a blanket and a coat. Some poor woman was giving birth, right there on the pavement. Up ahead, an old grandmother held in her arms a baby that was clearly dead; flies kept settling on it and from time to time the old woman, who mostly just stared ahead, came alive and swatted at them, kissing the little face with passion. A thick-set man in a railway porter's uniform came stepping through. People accosted him, cajoling or shouting, demanding to know what was going on. He said he had no information.

"Go away! Go away all of you! They've blown up the railway lines! No trains can get out!"

Nobody believed him.

By ten o'clock in the evening, pressing on inch by inch with the mass, they had got inside the station but no closer to the trains. It was impossible to get anywhere near the guichets where tickets were sold. A woman beside them told another that no ticket was given without a French identity card. But without a ticket there was no chance of a train. Only one train had apparently left that afternoon, jammed solid with people, and another, equally jammed, was standing in a siding, but there was no chance of getting on it, nor of finding out where it might be going. A new rumour swept the crowd: that the Germans were already in Paris and had begun to massacre the population. There was an enormous surge forward, women started screaming and fainting. Ilse saw a child pushed to his knees, crushed, his face disappearing. Then she saw a baby being passed over the heads of the people, shifted from hand to hand, then another, bigger child. The gendarmes were ordering that all children were to be passed forward over the heads of the crowd to a place of greater safety. Everyone started shouting and calling out names. She looked up at the huge vault of ceiling, where there was all the space anyone could need.

Ilse was hungry and her throat was desperately dry. She looked at her father, crushed against her side. She did not dare address him, even in whispers. A vein was throbbing above his left eye like a blue worm under the skin. She started to shove and squeeze through the crowd to fetch water. It took over an hour of pushing to get to the Red Cross post thirty metres away. There was a nurse there, giving a drink to children, dozens of them on their own collected together. She saw that the small ones were howling, some seeming ill.

"Please," Ilse said, "can I have water?"

Wordlessly, the woman held out a mug. Ilse took it and turned to go.

"Oh no," she said, "I need that."

Ilse drank. She could smell soup, her mouth watered, but she had to get back to her father. Outside, she thought, behind the shuttered shops, Paris was full of food. It took so long to get back; people were lying down now and she felt a kind of panic that she might not recognise him among the bundles of clothes. Then she spotted the suitcase, the one she had bought him. Between the heat of bodies and the cool night air, the cold concrete floor, which made her spine ache, and the smell of unwashed people, the night was got through somehow. There was the occasional flash as gunfire, far away, lit the dark sky. She even slept, waking around three o'clock. She listened to the conversations around them. The train they had hoped for had left. No other train had come in.

Otto kept squeezing her elbow, then struggled to his feet, indicating that she should stand. He began to climb over the sleepers. Silently, unable to remonstrate, she was forced to follow suit. She thought of Willy, standing tall and shouldering his way through a crowd with her suitcase on his head, then looked at the stooped figure of her father. It took a long time and her feet were burning, her mouth was like dust, her head thudding. Bit by bit, the crowd parted and let them out. As soon as they got to a place with slightly fewer people she pulled at him, put her mouth close to his ear.

"You don't want to try?"

"No. It's impossible. The Germans will be here before a train leaves."

"Then what do we do?"

"Go back."

"Where? The pension? The south? Germany?"

He tugged her on. Outside, a car started hooting at the mêlée around the station; they moved out of the road to let it pass. A bunch of men ran after it and then surrounded it, shouting "Salauds." There was a middle-aged couple inside, looking terrified. The mob pulled them out and started beating and kicking them. Ilse looked away from the flailing fists, the boots, the thud of flesh being damaged, the woman's face puffing up, the pretty blue dress ripping as she fell.

"What did they do?"

"Belgians," said her father. She remembered that a few weeks back, when Belgium surrendered, the radio had said they were all traitors. They walked on, the crowd thinning. A few minutes later the car passed, accelerating away, now full of men. Away from the station, the city was deserted.

It was broad daylight when they arrived back at the room. Too tired to unpack, Ilse lay down fully dressed on the bed. Her whole body ached. She fell asleep immediately. Otto tried to persuade her to get up but she could not and when he saw how worn out she was he desisted. She rose each time from the darkest and blackest sleep to the same nightmare. She was on a cliff and terrified, but unable to move, knowing that one step would dash her to the rocks below. With all her strength she tried to turn, but could not. She could not even make a single sound. At last, the dream receded and she fell asleep once more. She did not get up until the evening and even then, washing in cold water, she only had the energy to swallow a few mouthfuls of fruit from a tin before going back to bed. Even this luxury could not revive her. She listened. Paris was as still as death; all the dogs must have died.

"Are you ill?"

"No."

She fell back into the blackness.

The sudden roar of a motorbike racing by somewhere near woke Ilse. A heavy, rusty, scraping sound arose to a thunderous squealing that went on and on and on. After the long silence it was shocking.

"What is it?"

"Tanks."

The Germans had arrived. There was no gas to light the ring so they drank a little cold water, filled water bottles and prepared to go. He picked up her case and frowned.

"Why so heavy?" Ilse said nothing. He saw that she had put in three of Albert's books. She so wanted to take him with her.

"These will finish us, if the Wehrmacht* stop us."

She nodded. She arranged them with his others in a neat line on the table.

"Come on."

Once more, Ilse plodded down the stairs. Crossing the Boulevard Saint-Germain, the noise of the trucks and tanks was tremendous. With the bag of potatoes once more slung between them they crossed the Rue St. Dominique in the direction of Montparnasse, skirting the crowded area near the station. Ilse nudged her father in the correct direction. Looking left as they passed Les Invalides, Ilse saw the glint of shiny metal. A long column of German troops was drawn up along the huge square in a formal line. They were presenting arms, bayonets glittering in the sun. They could not have fought a battle: their boots shone and they were immaculate. Then, yet more incongruous, she saw that opposite them there was a whole line of policemen drawn up, French policemen looking correct in their proper uniforms with their white batons, as though they were all part of a military display, their faces as rigid as waxworks.

"What is it?"

*German army.

"A formal surrender. Cowards. Come on."

German soldiers were everywhere, truck after truck of young men each holding a rifle between his knees. They looked young and tired. Some were fast asleep and only woke as the truck jerked to a halt. Behind each convoy of trucks roared motorcycles with sidecars. Other people had come out onto the streets: French men and women stood like statues. As they trudged by, Ilse noticed that most of the women were weeping. The men stared at the invading army with dazed expressions. All the time the tremendous noise continued. She understood it now. It was the scrape of tanks bumping over cobblestones.

A huge black Mercedes limousine passed. They carried on, always choosing the side streets just behind the main boulevards. Ilse guided them using her mental map of the city's landmarks, turning not towards the Luxembourg Gardens but away, following the signs for Montparnasse. When they were past the cemetery, they would head south towards Châtillon. Her feet hurt. Her hand sprouted blisters. She said nothing.

In every avenue, men were setting up machine guns.

A small car drove past with a loudspeaker blaring out a wireless announcement in such good French, she could not believe it was a German talking. "No demonstration is permitted while our troops march in. The Paris police will function normally. Any hostile act will be punishable by death." Troops in another car going very slowly were giving out leaflets to people. They took them awkwardly; nobody read them, but they dared not crumple them either. A passing truck suddenly braked and came to an abrupt halt just in front of them. Half a dozen soldiers jumped out, one carrying a ladder. Beckoning frantically, Otto disappeared into the next courtyard. Ilse was frozen to the spot. One young man went up to a poster and tore it down. It was one of the French war-bond posters, with the slogan "We shall win because we are the stronger." Another man followed with a big roll of paper under his arm and a pot of paste. Expertly, he unfurled the roll, stepping up onto the ladder. Dipping in a long brush, he pasted up a brightly coloured image of a smiling German soldier holding a scruffy urchin in his arms while others clustered round. He had evidently just given the little girl a tartine and she was biting into it and smiling. "Populations abandonées," the poster read, "faites confiance au soldat allemand!"* With another dip of the brush, he slicked over it and admired his handiwork.

---

*"Abandoned populations: have confidence in the German soldier!"

Noticing Ilse, the first young soldier waved. "You're free, Mademoiselle, to go wherever you like," he said in excellent French. Then he reached into his pocket and smiled. "Would you like some chocolate?"

She nodded. He came nearer and gave it to her: a handsome young man with bright blue eyes and a strong chin, the sort of face she had seen a thousand times before, the face of her schoolmates in Wuppertal. The truck took off again with a roar. Waking from her paralysis, Ilse looked down and saw the German chocolate in her hand. She put it in the pocket of her coat.

In the suburbs, the empty streets betrayed signs of panic: cars abandoned, suitcases dropped, doors gaping open. A mattress lay in the middle of one road with a pillow and folded blanket resting neatly on one end as if waiting for its occupant. Passing a bar, Ilse heard a snatch of German: "Paris is calm," a familiar voice said. It was the rich, reasonable sound of the Voice of Germany. As they walked on, she heard music swell up.

"Wagner," said Otto with his most ironic smile.

She was desperately thirsty again and hot. Among many resentments Ilse numbered the fact that, with her father there, she could not go into a church. They passed several. Tired as she was, she had a yearning to sit where it was cool and pray and go through her little routine. The sun beat on her head, which ached all the time. Eventually she stopped to rest. Her father looked at her with the look she could never fathom. Perhaps he was annoyed with her. Was she the burden he almost, but never quite, had the nerve to shake off? She shook with a rage so deep that for a time she could not speak.

"What is it? What's the matter?" He said it in a kindly way. "You're tired. Shall we rest a little longer?"

She shook her head. They went on. Very few people were on the streets here. Once a German motorbike went thundering past and they jumped to get out of the way, then a truck passed, then four more bikes. When the sound of their engines died away abruptly just up ahead, Otto held up a hand, told her to wait with the suitcases in the garden of a villa. He would go and see what was going on.

Her feet hurt; they had been walking for four or five hours. Ilse stumbled through the ornate gate. The house was quite large, painted blue with green shutters. She went round the side and lay down on the grass in the shade to rest and looked at the flowers that belonged to another, happier world. Albert was sitting in an English garden, with a pale-skinned beauty who, when she smiled, revealed her bad teeth. He was flirting with her. She turned to the sky and let it scorch her.

Otto returned. "It's a roadblock," he said. "They are stopping everyone. Nobody is being let through."

"What do we do?"

"There'll always be another way."

She followed him round to the back of the house. The villa seemed to be abandoned; Otto kicked the door open. They went in and drank and drank the water until they were satisfied. Then they sat at the kitchen table and ate, helping themselves to preserves from the larder and butter, and a couple of pieces of the German chocolate. With the taste of her childhood dissolving in her mouth, she watched her father. A dog whined at the door; when Ilse told it to come in, it ran away.

"What happened to the people who live here?"

"Panicked, probably, when they saw all the Parisians coming through."

He went out to scout the area.

In the big upper bedroom with a mahogany bed, Ilse knelt in front of the little plaster saints on the shelf sheltering in their red and blue cloaks and wished she knew their names.

"Dear Lord," she prayed, "keep Lore Blumenthal safe and I will always honour you. And Otto Blumenthal." God could not know who all these little people were, so she used their proper names. It struck her that this was the first time she had included her father in her prayers. She lay on the bed, then got up to keep watch from the window. After quite a long time a German soldier passed with a rifle. She saw the dog she had invited in before, the last dog in Paris. It started to bark. The German took aim. Ilse jumped to her feet, screamed, "Nein!" Did he hear? He turned and looked at the house. Then he walked on. Five minutes later she heard the sound of a shot. She was rigid.

A moment afterwards, her father returned. "I can see a way," he said.

She did not dare ask him about the shot. They went downstairs. He led her through the garden of a white villa, piling the suitcases up to help her climb the fence, then pushing them over, letting them fall to the other side and scrambling over himself as best he could. She heard the clunk of the gun in his pocket against the wooden fence, worried that it might go off and wound him. They went through half a dozen gardens and alleyways, once through the back door of a house to come out on the other side. It was nearly dark. After a while, he said they had passed the roadblock. Now they needed to go as fast as they could. They heard the occasional roar of a military motorbike. They walked on, disappearing into doorways at any traffic noise.

Around midnight, a lorry rumbled up behind. Otto went into the middle of the road, stretched out his arms wide. The headlamps lit up his face, his scalp shone under the fuzz of his hair. At the last moment it stopped. Ilse spoke to the man driving, a deserter, for he wore half uniform and half normal clothes. She asked where he had come from, wanting to know where the fighting was. But he misunderstood, said that he came from the Dordogne and wanted to get home fast. He was quite young, short and stocky, and spoke with a thick accent Ilse could just about puzzle out. He said he would give them a ride for five hundred francs. She conferred in whispers with Otto, who said that they had no choice. He got Albert's money out, then took it back and tore the notes in half. Ilse held one half out to the soldier, who pocketed it. "At the other end," she said. He understood.

They climbed up into the back, where a woman lay and a very old man sat bent almost double. The driver had chalked a message on the back of the lorry, a military one that he had presumably appropriated: VENDU PAS VAINCU. Later, Ilse thought, she would explain to Otto that this meant "betrayed not beaten." She wondered who the betrayer had been. The woman lay very still holding a little bundle of blanket that probably had a baby in it, though Ilse did not care to look for it never moved or cried. It was a bad night to be born; all over France babies were dying. Perhaps some were refusing to be born. She herself with deliberation looked outwards, all the time.

They were jerked about, the lorry went so fast and swerved so much. Often, though, the driver spotted something in the road and braked suddenly, jumping down and looking for useful items, heaving the odd suitcase into the back, discarding shirt and then trousers for a better pair. He took his time about it, sifting through all kinds of objects. Each time, he would throw off a remark, saying words she could not understand. Perhaps he was explaining himself to himself. He picked up a pram and a bicycle, half a dozen mattresses and many suitcases. Ilse and Otto dragged the mattresses flat, so they could lie on them, trying to make the woman comfortable. They had been hot all day. Now it was cool. One time he stopped and filled his cap with apricots from somebody's trees and as they drove he ate them, grimacing and spitting out the ones that were not good. Ilse watched through the glass panel as he put them in his mouth and then spat fruit or stone through the open window. He stopped at a café, smashed the window in and came back with a whole case of wine. Nobody seemed to care about anything anymore. Otto went in after him and came back with bottles of lemonade, which he handed round. Ilse and the old man drank eagerly. Another "fuyard"* in uniform charged at them out of a side street and climbed into the cab, wrestling at the wheel and thinking to take the lorry away from the driver. With sidelong worried glances at one another, the passengers watched the two men scuffle and swear, the usurper desisting only when threatened with a gun. They drove off. The driver was drinking wine now.

Desperate men and women tried to flag them down, begging for a lift. Their driver honked and kept going, swerving wildly so anyone trying to jump up on the back was forced to leap out of the way. The road was an obstacle course. Cars stood with their doors open and carts stacked with things lay at crazy angles. Some people were mad and screaming, and some quiet and some, it seemed, dead. Ilse stared at the mattresses abandoned on the road and carts attached to dead horses and people lying down, little children who had not run fast enough. They passed many scores of men and women who were sitting down and looking as if they could not go any farther. Most just kept on going, pushing prams or carts laden high. One family rode in a hearse.

It grew much quieter as dusk fell. Once, though it happened with such slowness that it felt as though it was not happening to her, a Stuka flew low over the slow column, the heavy drone retreating only to return with bursts of fire that did not seem to hit anyone before it flew, dreamily, away. Night came. She saw that her father—fitfully visible in the flare of a match—did not sleep, but sat hunched to one side and separate from the others. Through her slits of eyes, she was aware that his gaze rested upon her more and more frequently. It took a long time to place the emotion, but eventually Ilse understood it. He was worried about her. He did know that she was a child, his child; he did know that she was scared. It was just that he had no idea of what he himself felt about her.

The lorry had come to a stop. The driver stood beside it, talking

*"Fugitive," i.e., deserter.

quietly at her in his difficult French. He sounded annoyed, but he also smiled at her. She struggled to make out what he was saying. They had run out of petrol. She had to get out, to come down to where he was. He was swaying from side to side. It was hard, very hard, even to open her eyes. Stiffly, Ilse climbed down. She stood in the road, yawning, cold. The sky was very clear; the faintest rim of light lit the horizon. Among dozens of stars there was one bright one. She pulled at and got out her little case and put it under her arm. She was waking up. The woman with the baby bundle had gone. She waited for her father to get out. When he didn't, she climbed back up and looked around. There was nobody left on the lorry.

Sliding back down, she fell into the arms of the driver who pinned her against the tailgate and jammed his mouth against hers. Ilse could smell the wine on his breath. She shoved him away as hard as she could. He tottered. She pushed again. He lost his footing and tilted, looking at her with an air of surprise, toppling slowly into the ditch at the side of the road.

"Oh, la pute,"* he said. She watched. In a moment, he stirred and then he was on his knees, flailing and crashing around. She turned and ran at full pelt down the country road. The air rushed against her face. She felt the thud of her feet, the hard plane of the suitcase against her chest and her whole body reacting still to his hand wrenching her shoulder, to his thrusting knee, to the bad taste of his mouth. Her feet, already sore, hurt at every step. She made them keep moving. Somewhere nearby a voice was calling out. It sounded weird, inhuman.

She stumbled across the ruts, recovered, stumbled. Her legs were not working properly. Getting down to pick up the case, she fell forward and scraped her knee on something unseen, something sharp. She shot up, then bent again for the case and felt the warmth which flowed down her leg, comfortingly, her own blood. Beyond the line of trees lay the darkness and the smell of the countryside. The ditch separated her from the welcome dark. It looked deep. With an effort, she made herself jump. A scramble; the good knee hitting uneven ground, her hand reaching to steady herself grasped something with thorns on it. Snatching her hand back, she got up the slope and ran, dodging around trees, going well, getting away. Her breath rasped in her throat. Here it was

*"You slut."

much darker, the branches hid the moonlight. Her awkward flapping feet tripped and then got caught in a root. Wrenching her foot she fell hard, banging her shoulder. She lay, winded. The blood, thundering through her head, gradually slowed. She sat up. Her hand was throbbing. In a while, she got herself to a crouch. She walked, limping now, deeper into the trees. It was too dark to see much. Her shoes kicked through dry leaves. Resting her back against a tree, Ilse slid down, clutching the case to her chest. There was no pursuit. Her feet hurt, her head, her leg, her hand.

She shuddered herself awake perhaps an hour later. The faint smear of light had brightened to day. The forest stung her nose, a sweet, rotting smell like an overripe melon. It was good that she had the warm coat. She touched her head, winced at the bruise. Turning her head the other way, she saw a blue boot. Beyond was a greeny-white leg. She sat up. It was the body of a child, head turned up. A dead fly-festering eye was looking at her. That was the smell. Hand over her mouth, forcing back the sour flux that kept rising, she got to her feet and backed away. She ran, feeling the thorns in her hands, angry red bumps. Her legs carrying her away were stranger's legs, one brown with blood, the knee forming a large scab that was already splitting and oozing. Her socks were saturated, the knitted welt crisped with dried blood. She reached out a hand, pushed back her hair. Her hand touched burrs. A leaf floated down.

Approaching the road she crouched, opened the case; there might be something to drink or some food. Thirst was parching her throat. There was nothing. She remembered. The food was in her father's case. Walking in the safety of the field beyond the ditch and hidden from the road by the trees, she started back in the direction of the lorry. A cart track ran parallel with the road. She could stay on this side and look through, keeping a safe distance, toiling across the ruts. The sun was starting to burn. She took off her coat. There was no shade on this side of the ditch. After another ten minutes or so, she stopped. Her eyes hurt too much. Wearily, she slid back down into the ditch, her leg burning when she bent it, then scrambled past the nettles and up on the other side. Limping, she started back down the road, heading north, the way she had come. It was easier walking in the shade of the trees. They were a long grey band, a stripe of light first white, then dark, that blurred together and pulled her on.

Daylight had brought people back onto the road, picking their way past the occasional car or cart. Those on foot were the tail end of the exodus, those who could still walk. In some of the cars people were sleeping or dead, their heads tipped back. Calmly, she let her face slide over them. They were not real. An old man approached pushing a cart with pots and pans and a brass bed on it. A goat was tethered to the handles. His wife plodded along behind him, staring down at her feet. They passed without looking at her. It did not matter. It was just a kind of game they were all playing.

From a long way down the straight road, shifting from one foot to the other, she made the sun wink at her, dazzling on the windscreen. The lorry itself was a dark patch against the shimmering road. The driver's door stood open. She stayed near the ditch, ready to run or hide, just looking. There was no sign of the driver. From time to time, someone in the oncoming trickle of people—always a man—would stop and climb up into the cab, as if it might miraculously be full of fuel and ready to go. She knew more than they did. She went closer and closer. The mattresses had been pulled off and lay on the road nearby. There was something white in the road that drew her. A little scrap of paper, on which she recognised her mother's writing.

A tremor went through her as she bent—to snatch up another, and another—and she turned and swivelled and looked right and left and then straight up to the sky. These were messages from heaven. Like Dr. Faustus, her father had vanished into the dry cracks of the earth. Her mother had come to save her. Where was she hiding? She was up behind the sun. She was too bright to be seen.

"Kannst jetzt rauskommen, Mutti,"* she sang out. It was time to end the game. But her mother didn't come out. Ilse turned and turned again. She was a spinning top, too fast to be seen. She would see everything in the world if she went fast enough. But the motion made her so dizzy that she had to stop. Nobody noticed. Among the confusion of adults, a child was invisible. Some people talked to themselves, others cried. Three children, one quite small and wearing a school smock, plodded by. The big girl tugged the little one on. Where were their parents? The small one started to cry and the big girl picked her little sister up. They did not look at her. Perhaps she was not there. A woman came behind them

*"You can come out now, Mummy."

walking in bare feet, carrying a pair of high heels. She did not look at Ilse either.

"I don't like any of you," she said. She, facing against the flow, was different from all of them. She was either invisible or dead. This explained everything. She climbed onto the lorry and looked. There was one mattress left. She lay down. She would wait here for her mother to come.

Her head was resting on something hard, but she could not move it. After a while she realised that it had to be Pumpf. Pumpf always slept in her bed though he never appeared to be asleep at all. This was because he stood very upright and his legs were stiff, so he could not be made to lie down. The nicest thing about him was his ears, which stuck up straight and made him look very alert and interested in everything, which he was. His hard sawdust head often became wedged between the sides of her wooden bed and her pillow, not that he minded. He liked it. She was at home, in her wooden bed in the Landsweg. If she reached forward she would feel the loose knot in the wood that could be jiggled from side to side and nearly but never quite pushed through. She often fiddled with it, pushing it from side to side until she fell asleep. The reddish glow through her eyelids was her night lamp. It had a crescent moon on the sides and on the top there were little cut-out stars. If she were to open her eyes now—not that she would—she would see little white stars on her ceiling. She heard the distant rattle of the last tram. Then the sounds all died away. Now that the tram had gone by, she had to keep her promise to sleep and not wake up till the morning.

"I miss you, my darling girl."

"Me too," she said. "I miss you so much."

"We shall be together soon. Listen to me. Please give all my love, all my love, Ilse." Her mother's voice grew more insistent. "You must learn to go into a café. They won't bite your head off."

She was so tired, she just wanted to stay where she was. Ilse thought about it. It was true that she was hungry and also very thirsty. Reaching out for Pumpf, she opened her eyes. Her face was burning. Her arm scrabbled around, hit something hard. There was no little grey dog anywhere.

The flies, buzzing, were terrible. She opened her hand, looked at the scraps of paper. She clambered down, stiffly, picked up all the pieces that she could find in the weeds at the roadside. They were letters that had been ripped up. Most must have blown away. She found an envelope Toni had posted in Casablanca addressed to Mademoiselle Blumenthal in beautiful calligraphy. Of the letter itself there was no sign. She put the little pieces into the envelope. Her head was banging. Though it was very hot, she was shivering with cold. Her eyes could not focus properly. She climbed into the front of the cab, which gave a little shade, and concentrated on her mother's special messages, taking out and smoothing each crumpled piece. They were so small, as if somebody had torn and torn again. *"Paris was not,"* her mother had written, and *"wicked."* There were other words: *"Ilse," "you," "we never," "found together," "Because," "a line," "very hard," "not," "visa."* There were bits of words that might have been anything.

Carefully Ilse shook all the little white squares back into the envelope. Her hands were very dirty and smeary, she noticed, the nails black with dirt. The place where the thorn was embedded still throbbed, but it no longer concerned her. Climbing down once more, she went down into the ditch like a crab, sideways, so she could keep the leg with the scab straight, and looked for more paper. She went along the ditch for a long way in each direction without finding any. In the nettles there was something blue: Otto's pyjamas. She picked them up. They smelt strong and unmistakably of him; there was his suitcase, open and upended. She rolled up the pyjamas and put them in the case. Ilse zigzagged back and forth across the road. She found her father's shaving brush. She put this in the case. Of the tins of food there was no sign. There was a man coming. She stood behind the lorry until he was gone, slipping round the side as he approached. He did not see her. He was a crazy laughing man, walking down the middle of the road talking to himself. Back on the lorry, she stared at the empty road.

A small figure moving in the wrong direction, blurry against the heat coming off the road, gradually solidified into Otto. He must have been certain of her long before she was sure that it was him. She could tell from the way he lifted up his hands and signalled. He started to run towards her. As he approached the lorry, they were still held up in the ancient gesture of distress, of lost and found.

"I went to find shelter for us," he said. "I lost my way. I signed to the driver to look after you."

She said nothing. He leant against the truck, panting a little. Ilse stared past him.

"I couldn't work out which way to go. I asked—of course, nobody understood what I wanted. Some fool thought I was a German spy. Thank God I found you. The best part of the day lost. I thought I would never see you again," he said. "Can you get up?"

"I don't know."

He climbed up onto the back of the truck.

"Your leg," he said.

"I fell. Did you shoot the spy?"

"No. Show me your hands."

She held them out. He tried to pick out the thorns but they were in too deep, in any case his cracked yellow nails were too brittle to get a grip. The thorns were much worse than the knee.

He stroked her cheek. "I couldn't wake you," he said. "I thought, better let you sleep. Can you try to get up?"

"They took the food."

He dug in his pockets: there was a piece of bread and an apple, a wizened thing. Out fell the other halves of the hundred-franc notes torn in two: the bribe to the driver, to take them. He folded the money, put it back in the pocket. She ate.

"Look at me," he said, "managing to find something to eat. And I never was a practical man. Can you get up? We're going to have to walk." He climbed down, stretched out a hand. She could see that he was trying to be nice.

"Mutti wrote," she said. "Somebody tore her letters up." Her hand shook, holding out the scraps; it no longer looked like a part of her. "I'm not going anywhere if you don't tell me what she said."

"Let me jump you down."

"No. I mean it," she said. "I'll stay here."

Weary though he was, Otto started pacing in the road.

"Vati, please. Her exact words."

"That I should send you back to her. That in Germany you would be safe."

"The exact words. Please, please, tell me."

"Your mother decided that in Germany you would be safe with her. Because she's Aryan. She imagines she can conceal you. Remake you. With that new passport. It's insane. I told her that. I see this, Ilse, as a gigantic conspiracy that she wanted a child, you, but not a man. Not me. Hitler made that possible."

"I'm possible because of Hitler?"

"I mean she saw her chance. She thought she would get away with it."

"Get away with what?"

He sat down with his back against the lorry. She leant forward, shadowing him. When she bent her knee, the blood started running again, so she straightened up. His hair was covered with dust and his face was very dirty. She probably looked the same.

"Vati. Get away with what?"

"Your mother wouldn't divorce me. I don't know why not. It was the most practical solution. For years she said we should all go abroad. She urged me to leave, to save myself. Of course, she knew that I had to stay in Germany, that I could not abandon the fight against fascism, I had sworn it on my life to my comrades. I told her that when I went underground. Then she sent for me. The last time I saw her she said I had to meet you in Paris. It was a last chance to redeem myself. We would be together, she said. We would be a family. Then, when she had persuaded me out of my country, she wrote to say she had changed her mind, that it would be better if we were apart. What a fool I've been. Duped on a false promise. I should have remembered that she hates me."

Listening to his flat voice, Ilse was much too tired to argue. She made an effort, kept her voice steady. "I think that you hate her. I think you're mad."

Perhaps he was actually mad. Abruptly, she understood.

"Vati. How could you tear up her letters?" Then, when he did not reply, "She wrote to *me*, didn't she?" She heard the outrage in her voice. "I'll never forgive you. Never."

"Ilse. That's enough. Get down at once." He spoke sharply. She pushed herself along to the edge of the lorry, struggled down. They started to walk. Ilse stumped along stiffly, determined not to speak. Otto remarked that a number of cars had been abandoned near a turnoff to a village. Perhaps there would be food there, or shelter. Walking was slow, for Ilse was having trouble keeping going. Rounding the last bend, she saw three old men sitting on upright wooden chairs, which they had brought out from their houses. All the other houses were shuttered and the shops closed, but these three sat in a row, to see the spectacle. The old men watched them plod slowly past.

At the end of the village a low wooden platform had been put up in a little square. A middle-aged man was overseeing the distribution of food. He wore a black suit in spite of the heat, around it a tricolor sash. People were queuing; they moved quietly to join them. Each was being given a metal dish, turnips, bread and salt. There was a mug to fill with water. On the other side of the square half a dozen soldiers with tattered uniforms sat in front of a little café, smoking and drinking. Little white cards were tacked up against the wooden posts of the platform, overlapping, from top to bottom, dozens of them. She read them.

Lost on the road near here on June 9th my son aged five Jacques Lemorel dark hair blue eyes: write to Madame Lemorel poste restante Chartres.

Madame Bois requests information about her daughters Marie-Hélène and Monique, eight and six, lost ten kilometres from Chartres. Response please to Chartres town hall.

The queue inched forward. Towards the front, a young man in a soldier's trousers and jacket drew the eye. He was exceptionally tall, with blond hair so light that it was almost white. Something about him pulled at her. A moment later he turned and glanced directly at Ilse and then at Otto, then back at her. His eyes were very blue; he looked like the young man in the poster, the pinup for the Hitlerjugend. She watched him. The soldier balanced his piece of bread, his salt and his vegetables in the dish, then sauntered across to the café. He sat, lit a cigarette, flicked the match into the air. He actually smoked before eating: such lack of urgency seemed remarkable. The queue shuffled slowly forward. Ilse took her ration. "Your billeting slip," the official said, handing her father a chit of paper. She took it from him. It was an address: Rue du Marché. She asked the official where they were: he said eleven kilometres from Chartres. They went to the far side of the square, away from everyone else, and sat on a low wall. Ilse forced herself to eat the bread slowly. It was dry country bread and very coarse. Eating made her feel so tired. She looked at the turnip. Who could eat a turnip raw? She closed her eyes. When she opened them again, the blond soldier was squatting close beside Otto. He was saying something very quietly which she could not hear, but it had to be in German, for Otto nodded. How could he be French and German too? It was very interesting, but even so, her eyes could not stay open.

Otto was pulling at her arm, getting her to her feet. "We have to get to Marseilles. It's the only overseas port still open," he said. "We'll head for Chartres. If we can get to the next village down the road we should be able to get transport."

The young soldier who knew so much about where to go had not left. He was still in the square. He came out of the café with a glass of beer, sat down and started joking and talking to the other soldiers.

"I want to stay. I want to go to the Rue du Marché," she said. "You go."

"No. You're coming," he said.

They laboured along the stretch of road, following the sign for Chartres. In a while they heard the low rumbling of a motor. It passed them, going very fast—a shining black official car. With a squealing of brakes, it stopped fifty metres on. An arm beckoned, the white-blond head stuck out of the passenger-side window to smile at them. They hurried up to the car, her father wheezing with the strain, got in and propped their cases up on their knees. Of course, she thought, a gendarme would still have petrol.

"Il faut les aider, quand même, ces pauvres Flamands,"* said the blond soldier to the gendarme at the wheel. He winked at her, indicating that she should say nothing. She could not think what quality it was Flemish people had that made others help them, when the Belgians were hated. He sat at his ease in the front, smoking and laughing with the gendarme, his arm stretched along the seat, the arm of a man among friends. The driver was a local man, young and friendly and excited; he had a round, freckled face. He seemed almost pleased that war had come at last. He drove as fast as the road permitted and asked many questions, and the blond soldier talked about troop movements and panzers and les sales Boches.† Once the gendarme threw a remark over his shoulder at Otto. The blond soldier interjected, said something that made the other man laugh. He was called François. She stared at the way his hand with its faint dusting of pale hair lightly rode the seat and seemed to hold them too. She was supporting him, silently, by trying her hardest to appear normal.

"My God," the gendarme said, every time they passed another column of straggling people labouring along with their possessions. "What chaos." The local authorities had evacuated all the hospitals, the schools, everything. The lame and the sick were all on the road. Soon, he said, the Germans would overtake the whole lot of them. She rose from darkness as she felt the car slowing down. Her father slept, his head occa-

---

*"We've got to help these poor Flemish people all the same."
†Dirty Krauts.

sionally bobbing against hers. Another gendarme put his head in at the window; he and the driver knew each other.

"The panzers are twenty kilometres away at most." He nodded his head at the soldier and looked towards Ilse.

"Hitchhikers," said the driver, waving a cheery arm in their direction. The man grunted and waved them on.

The gendarme dropped the three of them somewhere on the outskirts of Chartres and pointed out the direction in which they were to walk. There was a great deal of traffic; cars passed going slowly, full of baggage and people.

"Rich Parisians," said François. When, footsore, they reached the huge main square below the great cathedral Ilse saw that it was jammed with cars parked edge to edge. They stopped at a café, but could not find a single seat. It was the same at the next and the next, with bad-tempered people who were hungry like them standing outside. In front of every hotel was a big hand-lettered sign, saying that every room was taken. "The bourgeoisie got here first."

François extracted a cigarette and took his time smoking it, looking around the Place des Epars. Ilse and Otto stood a little distance away. There was not even space on a park bench for them to sit. François ground out the cigarette. He came over, touched her shoulder. "Wait here, siostrzyszka,"* he said. She watched as he headed into the biggest restaurant on the square, threading his way through the tables.

Otto and Ilse stood under the lime trees. A woman in high heels carrying a fur coat, incongruous in the heat, was making some kind of scene on the pavement. Her companion, a man in a suit sweating and dabbing at his bald head, stood ineffectually beside her, patting her arm. She stopped shouting. He put his arm round her and she started to cry. Eventually they walked on. Ilse watched, as if through a pane of glass. The dappled light made patterns on the dry ground, the trees were the fresh green of her beautiful best dress. If she half closed her eyes, she could see the bolt of velvet unrolling and being cut.

François touched her arm. He was laughing, balancing three deep soup plates of meat stew with a baguette under his arm. She saw three spoons tucked into his belt. "For our heroic boys. Come on."

He led them over to the fountain. They sat on the rim. A small boy

*Little sister.

came up to her and looked at her plate. His mother called him away. The meat was savoury. Ilse gulped the first mouthful down. She saw a tiny bone. She pushed at it with her spoon. Otto was cramming the food into his mouth.

"What is it?" asked Ilse. "It's not rabbit, is it?" Her voice sounded very small. She was so hungry. It looked wonderful but it had a telltale aroma. She would eat anything but she could not bear rabbit. If it was rabbit, she would throw up immediately.

"Eat," said Otto. She put her spoon back onto the plate.

"Monkey," said François. "In the glorious French army—currently existing in its individual scattered molecules and not as an entity—we live on it. We call all meat monkey. Monkey with potatoes, monkey with noodles." She liked his voice, wanted it to go on.

"People don't eat monkey," she said. "Where are you from?"

"And you? What beautiful French," he said. "If you eat, I'll tell you. Can you guess?"

She picked up the spoon once more, took a spoonful, swallowed. She thought of all the mellifluous and romantic places.

"Pas-de-Calais to Tarn et Garonne," she said.

"You funny girl. Paris, for my first ten years," he said. "But really I am from Warsaw. My real name is Franciszek." His smile transformed his beautiful but very serious face, lighting up his eyes. Perhaps he knew Toni; she wished that she had been told her maiden name. He was twenty-three, a student. He had got on a train to Paris to go and fight Hitler when the Germans invaded, had joined the Polish Legion. He broke off pieces of the bread, passed them to her. She used them to mop up the gravy. After the food, she felt so much better. All the time, he looked at everything all around them with his bright eyes that understood everything. With a stick, he drew pictures of birds and spiders in the dust. He used his spoon to feather the bodies of ostriches with silly necks and big eyes. He used her empty plate to carry water from the fountain, made a splash on the dusty ground and then turned it into a giant ladybird.

Her father was silent. He sat hunched forward and very still, warming himself in the sun. François traced a long squiggly line that could have turned into anything but chose to become the outline of Otto, his despairing arms gripped between his knees, somebody who could not be anything but Jewish. He saw her recognising it, started to erase it. She kicked at the dirt until the figure was gone. He seemed to know exactly what she was thinking. She felt embarrassed.

"In the fighting, did you kill lots of Germans?" she asked.

"No." François got up and stretched his legs. "Let's go."

She had said a stupid thing. He was impatient now, probably eager to be rid of them. He walked on ahead into the back streets. Ilse, hurrying behind, found no moment to say how very sorry she was. A food shop was open. On the shelves were bags of flour and rice and tins; they bought sardines, as many as they could carry; François said they were rich in vitamins. They put them in their cases. He led them to a little park near the bus station. Otto sat down; his eyes closed and his chest rose and fell in a deep sleep. Ilse sat beside him. François went away into the bus station. With her arms round the case, Ilse also permitted her eyes to close. She awoke abruptly, feeling a warm breath in her ear. The shadows were lengthening, the day cooler.

François spoke quietly. "There's nowhere in Chartres for you to sleep. Stay here until the bus station opens at six. Then get on the bus, the first one that runs, and get out."

"How do you know there'll be a bus?"

"I asked."

"Can't we get a billeting paper? In the village, they gave the people those." She shook Otto's arm, but he did not wake.

"Do you have papers, proper papers?"

"No."

"I wouldn't risk anything, if I were you."

"Not even for one night?"

He looked at her for a long moment. "Do you want to live?"

She nodded.

"Then ask yourself not what are the others doing, but what am I going to do? How do I get out? What's the safest way? Do you understand?"

"I understand."

"One in ten thousand really understands. With no papers, you have to be invisible. Another thing. When you get to Marseilles, don't go to the centre d'acceuil.* They're locking up all Germans. Find an out-of-the-way hotel. Get out of France as soon as you can. Do you understand?"

She nodded.

"Good luck."

*Municipal welcome centre.

He took her hand to shake it. She winced and when he saw the swelling he kept hold of her wrist and lifted her hand up and examined it. "What's this?"

"Thorns."

He took the other hand, compared them. One hand, she now saw, was much bigger than the other.

"This needs water. You soak it for a long time, till it's very soft. Then if the thorn doesn't come out, you cut it out. Just a neat cut over the swelling. With a razor blade. Remember, only use a clean blade."

She nodded. He still held her hands, turning them over and inspecting them. They were calloused and grubby with broken nails, belonging to someone else.

"You have a long life line. You'll be 'old monkey.' What a strong heart line. See where it splits here? At least two husbands. Well, two great loves. Two children."

His hand, tracing the line, left its own invisible mark. He was smiling.

"But I don't want to have children."

"That's because you're a child yourself. Later you will."

"Boy or girl children?"

"If I knew, I wouldn't say. The future must always hold a bit of a surprise. Au revoir, Mademoiselle."

"Aren't you coming to Marseilles?"

"No, siostrzyszka, I'm going to go back and kill lots of Germans."

"Oh!" She looked. He was still smiling. She liked the funny name. She wanted to know what the word meant; she wanted to ask how he knew so many things, but could not. She only had the wrong questions. And in that pause, he waved and melted into the dusk. As the pale flame of his head disappeared it became obvious that he was not a man at all but an angel. For a long time, Ilse could feel the line on her hand that he had traced. She sat in that awareness looking at the trees which had taken François until it was too dark to see.

At six in the morning a man unlocked the gates to the bus station and went into the little kiosk there, turning on the light. She woke Otto. The man inside the kiosk sneezed several times.

"We'll get on the bus now," she said. Stiff and shivering, they stood. Very carefully, watching the door of the kiosk all the time, they crept onto the bus that stood there. Otto lay down on the back seats. At the very back there was a small curtain that could be drawn. From the outside, or to anyone looking in from the front, they were invisible. At seven o'clock a policeman appeared beside the bus and started checking the papers of everyone who got on. But because he did not look inside, nobody asked for theirs, nor did they check that they had a valid ticket for the journey.

In Poitiers, using Albert's money, Ilse bought two tickets to Marseilles. There would be a train to Limoges. From Limoges there would be a train to Toulouse, one that stopped at numerous stations. Then it was a question of getting across to Montpellier. They got on trains, got off, waited on platforms in places with no names, watched the yawning clerk chalk up the delay on a board and waited some more. Eventually, there was always another train. They were getting nearer to the south. The sardines, so oily, were somehow also dry and unpleasant. They ate them all the same. Otto was more and more tired and kept falling asleep. In a station waiting room she saw her face in the mirror, her hair. She looked like a scarecrow. She tried to comb her hair with her fingers. People avoided them, which was good.

At Montpellier the train stood so long at the platform in the heat that Ilse's head began to throb. Nobody knew when it would leave. Otto slept. Her father's lips were cracked, he looked grey. She opened her case, found the tin mug. There had to be water somewhere. The guard pointed her to the waiting room, where there was a drinking fountain. She drank, filled her mug and, turning, saw the train with her father on it jerk, gather itself, slowly move away. She saw the dust eddying up from the dry stones as the train began to gather speed, saw faces looking out, slow-motion faces that swivelled to see her—she was screaming as the carriage passed with him in it, eyes closed. She turned, began to run with the train, not able to grasp the doors that were passing as she thudded alongside. It was the end. The guard moved to block her and she evaded him, her chest constricting with the effort as the train speeded up and then a door opened, a man in shirtsleeves was beckoning, steadying himself on a handle and stretching out the other hand towards her. He leant out. She sped on, frenzied, seeing the end of the platform approach, seeing how she would fall, how the end of the train would pass—she jumped. One foot on the step, the door banging against her side, his hands sliding away then seizing and pulling, the anguish of his grasp on her wounded hand such that she screamed again. She hung in the air. She was inside, falling forward. The door slammed shut. Ilse collapsed onto the floor of the corridor. She lay on the dirty floor, unable to move or speak.

"Are you all right?"

She nodded. Finally, she got up, tried to smooth herself down, thanked him. With quivering legs she made her way back to the carriage where Otto, unwitting, slept on. She looked at him. He sat with his mouth half open, his breath rattling in his throat. A very bad smell was coming from him, sardines mixed with the putrid stench of rotting vegetables. He had turned into the old man she had imagined him being six months ago. She sat beside him, closed her eyes and waited.

They rattled into the Gare St. Charles at midday. It was almost impossible to wake Otto. She held on to her father as they came across the broad concourse of the station, propping him up as they went through the crowd, fearful that they would be stopped. Her hand was red and shiny, and very swollen. Its pulse went right through her. Otto was ashen. His skin was sagging and his face stubbly. His eyes, which were half closed, shut tight against the overwhelming light as they came out. A radiant map of wrinkles spread out from his eyes and over his forehead, a grid that went on and intersected with itself like the roads of the big city spread out below.

The wind was strong. Marseilles smelt just as it had the previous year. Down there, she thought, was the sea. Her father was making a kind of moaning noise.

"What is it? Is it your head that hurts?"

"Only strangers help," said Otto. His eyes had opened and he was staring at her. "What was his other name? You know, François?" His eyes were flickering all the time. They could not focus properly.

"I don't know," said Ilse.

"François," said Otto. "You know."

"He didn't tell us his real name."

"Yes," said her father. "It's Franke. Famke. Frante."

"Franciszek," she said. "Vati, why did he help us?"

"He's one of ours."

"One of ours?"

Ilse did not understand. His eyes started darting from left to right, looking for someone or something. He made her feel very nervous.

"What is it?"

"I'm looking for strangers. People have helped us. We have to keep in touch."

"What people, Vati? François helped us."

"Who?"

"Franciszek. The soldier who helped us. You know."

"He's dead," he said with great firmness. "You will never see him again."

All at once tears started from his eyes. He ducked his head.

"Come on, we're nearly there."

The steps down were very difficult. She was holding him up; he was not heavy but because he was leaning so desperately against her, she nearly fell. Luckily he kept hold of his case. He wept silently. The boulevard below was very crowded. They were on the Boulevard d'Athènes, the big main road dropping from the station's steps down to the centre of town below. They steered an unsteady course, bumping up against people.

"This way," she said, "not far." She had no idea where to go. The first big building on the right was a hotel called the Splendide. She left her father leaning against the imposing façade, walked up to the desk and asked for a double room. Just for one night, she thought.

The concierge laughed. "There is no room here, Mademoiselle," he said. "Every hotel is full. There are thousands of people looking for a room."

"Thank you."

She kept her head high.

As she walked away he called after her, "Do you have your billeting slip?"

"Of course. I'll be back."

In her coat pocket she found a handkerchief to dry Otto's face. She saw a taxi turning in towards the station and prayed. She did not think that she could drag him back up the steps to the taxi rank, not with the cases, not now. The taxi saw her and turned.

"Thank you," she said, "thank you." She pushed her father in.

"Where to?"

She looked at the man blankly.

"Well?"

"Notre-Dame-de-la-Garde."

Otto kept his eyes closed; the sound of his breathing was shallow, difficult, with an unpleasant thick rattling noise deep in his chest. She looked out. The taxi went down a broad main road with shops and cinemas and restaurants, down to the port and along past the boats, then it took a very steep winding road up the hill and stopped. There were a dozen steps beyond up to the church. High above, the Holy Virgin glittered. Otto was asleep. He would never manage the steps. In any case, she did not need him with her in the church.

"Please," she said, "would you kindly wait for a minute?" The taxi driver turned the engine off and lit a cigarette.

Halfway up the steep path to the church she remembered and went back for her coat. She pushed open the wooden door and tiptoed inside, putting it on as she went. The church was huge and cool. There was nobody there. She chose a side chapel that looked popular for it had the most candles burning, took a candle and lit it and found a small coin to drop into the box. The marble martyred body of a saint occupied one wall, his pale face turned enquiringly up towards the stained glass at the rear. Kneeling, she buttoned the coat. When all were in order, buttoned up tight from bottom to top, she touched each lightly and said her prayer.

"Dear Lord, help us today, we so need help. We need to become invisible. Look after us and I will always honour you, Lord." She ran down the buttons and said the prayer twice, changing the words a little, giving them a different emphasis. Kneeling was very painful, the scab cracked and was oozing pus, but she had to do it or God would not hear. The ritual soothed her, as did the holy smell. She bent to touch the laces on her shoes. They were filthy but the laces were tied tight and secured with a double bow.

Outside, the sea stretched out its glittering lines as far as she could see. The harbour, guarded by its two forts, was full of boats. She frowned. Nothing was as she remembered it. The driver was looking at her.

"To the quay, please," she said. Otto's head slipped down onto her shoulder. She put her arm round him.

"We'll get a boat," she whispered. "To Oran."

As the taxi turned to go back the way it had come, she realised with a pang that she had not mentioned her mother. She had not protected her. Now it was too late. The taxi went down the hill, turned onto the quay and stopped. Carefully, Ilse counted the coins into the driver's hand, thanked him. He drove off. She sat her father down on a fat metal post.

The quay, piled with barrels and coils of ropes, was not as she remembered it. A sign said QUAI DE RIVE NEUVE. Fishing boats jostled for space; the whole harbour was alive with them, but they were too small to take passengers. She asked an old woman scurrying by where La Joliette was. She pointed. Marseilles had two ports. The other one was far away, on the opposite side of the harbour. Her instructions had failed, as she had failed her mother. Otto's eyes had a blank look and he could barely stand. There was no question of him walking so far. The old woman stretched her mouth into a gappy smile. A gold tooth winked at the back. She pointed up. Two huge pylons carried a slender bridge suspended high in the air. It was a giant toy, a beautiful Meccano set which straddled the port like a colossus. Tiny figures moved across at the top. The old woman smiled and pointed, indicating that they could cross this way.

"Come on, get up." Ilse pulled and pushed Otto onto the jetty. They stood at the base of the huge pylon, anchored on two enormous disks of concrete. She pointed to the lift. "You must," she whispered. Otto, giddy at the prospect, shook his head. Even if she got him up to the top, he might not be able to walk across. Looking up into the sun, she had a blurred vision of him tumbling down and into the water. The old woman had caught up, was just behind them, pointing again.

"Mademoiselle. The transporter bridge," she said.

An extraordinary vision was moving across the water towards them. God had heard her prayer. He had sent her a magic carpet to ride across the water, with a delicate pagoda perched on top. She blinked, looked again. Strung below the bridge on cables was a broad platform ten metres wide gliding at great speed, floating above the water nearly at their level. It eased to a halt. The pagoda held an operator, who let down a low metal ramp. The old woman opened her hand, showed Ilse a fifty-centimes coin in her palm. A car drove off and a dozen passengers stepped on. Ilse paid a franc, urged Otto on. He clung to the railing. Looking up, she watched the shimmering cables that drew it across. After a minute or two they were halfway across the water. Looking back at the city, she could see how the wide main street, stretching away from the deep recession of this smaller port, seemed to split the city neatly in half. Perhaps there was a good side and a bad side, as there was with people. Out on the water a chill wind blew. Ahead the city rose steeply from the waterfront in a semicircle of façades, shuttered against the day, with alleys behind them as steep and black as knife cuts.

"Le vieux quartier," said the old woman. The port was on the further side of this final hill.

Alighting, they crossed the old stone flags of the road, Ilse supporting Otto, who was slipping on the smooth tram tracks. At once the light was gone, the streets rising too close together for any sun to penetrate, so steep that steps were needed, too narrow for any car. Washing lines stretched from one side to the other. A gutter right down the middle had dirty water running in it, which stank; it was not water but sewage. Head lowered, Ilse clutched the case with one arm. With the other she pushed Otto. From the top, they would see where to go. A girl with long black hair leaned out of one of the windows above them. She said something that Ilse did not quite understand, something about red hair. At the window opposite sat a fat bleached blonde with a strong Roman nose. They were laughing at each other. They were laughing at her with their horrible eyes. Another girl stuck her head out of a window farther up the hill and blew a kiss. A man in a vest appeared and leant out beside her. Someone shouted.

Otto sagged into her arms. She tried to hold him up. She could not manage it. He sank down onto the dirty street. His case tumbled down and toppled over. Ilse bent over to look at him. He lay on his side on the cobblestones.

"Please," she said, "please get up." She pulled at his arm. She did not have the strength to pick him up. Kneeling on the road, she tried to put her arms round him and lift him. She could not do it. He was a dead weight. The fat woman emerged from a doorway and came up the street towards them. She walked very delicately and carefully in high heels, setting her feet down like an acrobat. She squatted down and felt Otto's pulse with one white hand, then pulled down his eyelids and looked at his eyes, which were rolling up. She had bright red fingernails. She pursed her lips and sighed. Her eyes, two dark currants lost in puffy cheeks, were very sharp. Her eyelids were a brilliant artificial blue.

She bent forward and pulled him up into a sitting position.

"Leave him alone," said Ilse.

Otto stirred and moaned. The woman put her arm round him and, raising him up, half carried him back down towards her door.

"What are you waiting for! Come on!"

Scrambling for the cases, she followed. The woman pushed at the door with her dainty shoe; it opened into complete darkness. Ilse hesitated. There was a click and a light came on, a dim bulb draped with a scarf at the far end of a long corridor. She made out that the corridor was papered with huge blue roses. The woman pulled back a very dark, thick curtain half revealing a door. While Ilse supported her father, the woman unlocked it.

The room had an enormous bed. The woman laid Otto onto it and looked at him, opening his eyes and again feeling his pulse. Very adroitly, she began to take his clothes off, peeling them away, then pulling up the sheet to cover his nakedness. Ilse was shocked. He was very dirty. He stank. The woman went away. She stood in the middle of the room, listening to the rasping sound that her father made. Perhaps he was going to die. The woman came back carrying a bowl of water and soap, a sponge and a towel. She began to wash him, starting with his feet, uncovering each limb carefully and then scrubbing with both hands and kneading his skin before drying him with a towel. It was done with delicacy but so firmly. Perhaps she was some sort of nurse. Ilse had never seen a naked man before and looked away from his private parts, which, worryingly, seemed to be a dark reddish colour as though there was something wrong with them. The water running from the sponge was grey.

The woman went away, returned with fresh water, carried on. It was vigorous work and a light film of perspiration covered her face. Close up, she had very beautiful skin, pink and rosy like that of a child, and she smelt of perfume. Her yellow hair was black at the roots. Ilse helped as best she could. Together, they could turn him over. He was so thin that his hip bones stuck out and his ribs could be counted. When he was clean, Ilse went to the case and fetched the pyjamas. The woman shook her head, wrinkled up her nose. They smelt. She used a corner of the towel to wash his face and then patted eau de cologne around his temples. She looked at Ilse.

"You need a bath too," she said. "At the end of the corridor."

"Thank you, Madame."

"I'm called Renée," she said. "And you?"

"Ilse."

"And him?"

"Otto. Madame Renée, does he need a doctor?"

Madame Renée wagged her finger negatively, making a clucking noise. She took Otto's pyjamas, then stooped with the same graceful sway to pick up his other clothes, holding them at arm's length. She took all the clothes with her, leaving clean towels on the table.

"We can pay," Ilse called as she retreated. Madame Renée, already at the far end of the corridor, shrugged massive shoulders without looking round. Ilse tiptoed around the room. There was the bed and a chair and a table, a rug on the oil-waxed floor; a wardrobe, a cupboard. She opened a door. From top to bottom the entire depth was layered with fine linen: tablecloths and antimacassars and sheets, all very stiff as though still brand-new. She pulled one piece a few centimetres forward in the tightly configured pile. It was a perfectly folded linen sheet with an embroidered border. The room was extremely clean and smelt of polish. She sat for a moment on the chair. She must have nodded off. There was a scratching noise. She went to the door, opened it: a tray stood there with a big bowl of hot broth. She brought it in to her father, but could not get him to open his eyes. He was making a heavy, honking sound. The soup smelt wonderful. Water rushed to her mouth and, unable to make herself stop, she drank down every drop herself.

Otto slept on and on. Ilse went and looked in the bathroom. There was a packet of razor blades on a little shelf with a shaving brush and cake of soap. When she got back, Otto was still sleeping but restless and muttering and very hot. She took the little towel, wrung it in cold water and placed it on his head. Then she took the bigger towel and went to the bathroom. There was a big, deep bath. When she turned the tap on, hot water spurted out. She lay in the bath for a long time. The dirt did not come off at once. Her body was skinny, weightless, smeared, her belly distended from the soup. She was never going to grow breasts. She was never going to grow up. When the water was cold, she got out of the bath, let all the water out and ran another one. This time she scrubbed harder. It was impossible to get the tangles out of her hair. Clean, she let the bad hand lie submerged, adding hot water. When her skin was very soft and wrinkled she set to work. It was very awkward, because it was the right hand and she was right-handed. She held the injured hand carefully against the metal side of the bath so it would not move and, holding the razor blade tight, cut the red flesh into strips, then held the hand under water, squeezing hard. The long clean cuts pleased her. So much blood came out; she was surprised. It stained the whole bath but hardly hurt at all. The thorn came out, long and curved, and she placed it on the rim of the bath and looked at it for a time. She got out of the bath. The walls ducked and swirled. Giddily, she held on to the rim and watched the red water gurgle round until it was all gone. A stream of blood flowed down and down the side of the bath. Then she wrapped the hand in her dirty dress and with the other hand tried to clean the bath. Holding the towel round her, she went back along the corridor to the room, bumping the soft hand against the wall, feeling her way to the curtains. She found the door. She turned the knob and lay down beside her father.

EIGHT

Hamburg, June 1940

Weaving adroitly to one side each time an army truck tore out of the barracks and thundered by, churning up a cloud of dust, Nicolai coasted along the Alster, in and out of sun, shade, the dappled freshness of the limes. He kept well behind the pale blue dress, the pram, the child in red starting to wail. Sabine did not care to be pushed in a pram; that was beneath the dignity of her three years. But his sister soon tired of walking and held up her arms and fussed. Fräulein Lore stopped, lifted her up. Sabine was too heavy to be carried so far; it was much too hot. The little couple vanished into the portico of a white stone building. Long red flags hung limp in the heat.

He waited, leaning on his bicycle. That Tuesday, she had visited the French embassy, had stood a long time at the gate in a crowd of people without gaining entrance. The next day she had spent over an hour and a half in the town hall. She was worried sick about her daughter, still in France, of whom there was no news. He longed to help, if only she would let him. He got the camera out of the saddlebag, slipped off the lens cap, focused on the dazzling brass nameplate. The sun was directly on it. Nicolai moved to one side, looked again: Central Institute, Hamburg branch. He had no idea what that might signify. He moved closer. They had arranged to meet in front of the Alsterhaus: Fräulein Lore had said that she was doing some shopping for his mother. Why did she not trust him?

"Ni-co! Ni-co!"

He swung the baby up into his arms. Looking very white, the Fräulein leant back against the plate-glass window full of women's straw hats, with some kind of tape stuck over to protect it.

"Are you all right?"

"It's just that we didn't find what we were looking for," she said, unable to smile.

Worry made Nicolai grow breezy. "Shopping is tiring, isn't it? Großmama won't mind if we're late. What if I buy you coffee and cake here, on the Alster, now? Sabine, you'd like ice cream, wouldn't you?" Holding his jubilant sister on the seat of the bicycle, he steered them across the Lombardsbrücke towards the Hotel Atlantik, the nearest place for tea. All along the bridge, victory flags were strung out. As they walked into the lobby, the smell of perfume was overpowering. Trays of cakes and drinks were being carried across, and the big hall and salon beyond were full of men in uniform with Iron Crosses prominent, women in silk dresses and high heels. Draped casually over the backs of their chairs were furs from Norway, despite the heat. The band struck up the current favourite: "Denn wir fahren, denn wir fahren gegen Engelland."* Fräulein Lore shrank back; he too felt a kind of revulsion. He remembered that this was one of his mother's favourite places.

"Are you all right to go a bit farther?" She nodded. He hoped she would manage the extra distance, reassured himself that his grandmother would know what to do.

The flat in the Rothenbaumchaussee was delightfully cool. Großmama was overjoyed to see them. Clucking and tutting that they had walked so far on such a warm day, she fetched a glass of water for Fräulein Lore. They sat in the vast drawing room full of heavy Biedermeier furniture. Käthchen, her elderly maid, slowly spread an undercloth on the polished dining-room table and then unfolded a heavy damask cloth, its hundred shades of white smoothing into one.

*"We're going, we're going against England."

She shuffled back and forth with the best Meissen china cups and saucers. The rattle was her extracting silver cake forks from drawers lined with green baize. Watercolours of the shipyard hung in the corridor leading to the kitchen, photographs of Großpapa and various dignitaries launching ships stood on the piano. Above the drawing-room fireplace was a full-length portrait of Großpapa when he was president of the Hamburg Yacht Club, wearing his badge of office. He wandered around, waiting for his grandmother to make tea in her special silver samovar, looking at the oil portraits of his mother as a young woman. To make her eyes sparkle, the painter had put a white dot on each eye. They hung alongside the delicate charcoal sketches his father had drawn of his children. He remembered how Sabine, still tiny, had wriggled and squirmed, and his father, giving up, had taken the charcoal twigs and laid them on the rejected sketch, had brushed on blobs of Coccoina glue to hold them fast, snipping at the thick, creamy paper. He had magicked a beautiful little paper cottage into existence, cutting windows and a door that opened and drawing on shutters, the art paper held up by its twig structure. Remembering the delicious almond smell the glue paste gave off, Nicolai suddenly understood that it was because of this that he loved marzipan so. The paper had long since curled up at the corners to reveal its delicate undertracery, but the little house existed. He would find it, would give it a position of honour on his desk.

"Tea is ready, my darlings."

Käthchen brought the cake platter, served them and withdrew. Großmama kissed and tickled Sabine and chattered on. Her hair, which must have been blond once, like his mother's, was pure white now, but her eyes were very sharp and did not miss a thing. Sabine, on her knee, devoured forkfuls of strawberry tart, leaning forward, mouth open in perpetual readiness.

"I was cross today," Großmama said, and she nodded at Nicolai. "One of your 'little Hitlers' stopped me from going into Finkelstein's department store."

"They're not mine," he said.

"You wear the uniform every day, my boy. You're wearing it now."

"But they force you to," he said. However, his grandmother, embarking on a story, was not to be deflected.

" 'Must you buy from a Jew?' he asked me. A boy, perhaps fifteen. I shook my stick at him. 'Young man,' I said, 'you get out of my way. I will buy where I always do.' We've always had English tea, pure Assam. From Fortnum and Mason's, imported by Finkelstein's and it's the finest, war or no war. But my dear, there was not a soul apart from me in the store. I fear they will go out of business, or worse." She lowered her voice. "Our good Jewish doctor in the clinic here, who was ordered not to lay a hand on an Aryan child—can you imagine? He emigrated two years ago to Holland. His wife wrote to tell me that he committed suicide when the invasion came. I remember when he came and told me he was leaving. Twenty years I was his patient. And there is nothing one can do. Nothing at all."

Fräulein Lore leant forward and for a moment her hand hovered above that of his grandmother. "May I ask for your advice on a serious matter?"

"What is it? What has happened?"

"About my daughter."

"Who lost her papers? Hilde has told me all about the poor dear child."

Nicolai blinked, thinking how annoyed his mother had been.

Fräulein Lore edged her chair a little closer; her voice sank lower. "I don't know where she is."

Großmama looked startled and glanced at Nicolai, who made big eyes and shrugged at the strangeness of the disclosure, though the story was now so familiar to him.

"The invasion—she was in Paris. She was leaving to travel to me. Then she sent word that I must go to her—and now she's lost."

Großmama put down her cup and deliberated. "Do not be alarmed, Fräulein. Who will harm a little girl? Civilians will not be touched. When everything settles down a little, her uncle will return her."

Sabine had had enough cake. She wriggled down, ran off down the corridor.

"Nico my love, will you keep an eye on the baby?"

"Of course." He stood and followed Sabine out. Käthchen was amusing her in the kitchen. He moved soundlessly through into the drawing room; from here, he could hear the two women talking quietly in the dining room.

"The population of Paris fled. She's not with her uncle. She could be anywhere—" She drew breath, made an effort to be calm. "Today I spoke to a senior officer in Maschinelles Berichtwesen.* It's a new office, part of the Statistical Institute, which registers the entire population in each country. They have a special system of cards, they can find people. They require the birth certificate and travel document. If she is registered anywhere in France, they say they will find her."

"Why do you think she will not return to Paris, when people do? My dear, forgive me, but perhaps you are being overdramatic."

"Circumstances change," Fräulein Lore said. "Sometimes people don't do what they have promised to do. I have come to believe that she will not be returned to me."

"Why ever not? I don't understand you."

"Forgive me—it's complicated—for all these reasons I see that I must go to France myself. I have enquired. To travel to France requires a special reason, a further permit beyond the usual ones, then one needs the same set of papers twice over. Without them, I'll be sent back. I don't have the connections." Fräulein Lore's voice started shaking. "My reason is apparently not good enough. It is hopeless. Perhaps—I wondered—you are so kind, perhaps you might know someone? At the visa office."

"In the Gestapo, to issue a visa?" His grandmother made this sound very unlikely.

"Sometimes rules can be bent, even in a war."

"But all this makes no sense. You must wait, Fräulein, first of all. What if she came and you were gone? If no news comes then you can go back to this office you went to, this Berichtwesen, with her papers."

"I have no papers. Her travel documents were sent to Paris."

"But the state and local archives keep everything. Give them your birth certificate, pay the fee, then they can find your marriage records and divorce papers and all the other records for the child and issue certified copies."

"I can't. Please advise me—you spoke so sympathetically just now."

"My dear, I simply don't understand you."

In the long silence, Nicolai inched closer, determined not to miss a word.

"My birth certificate is no good," she said wearily. "It leads to the wedding certificate, the grandparents, the family tree. There is a requirement for a certificate of Aryan purity. She doesn't have it. I need

*Office of Automated Reporting.

to find someone prepared to waive all those requirements. Or someone who will give me a permit to leave and won't ask questions."

"I see."

This silence seemed to go on and on. Nicolai waited in acute anxiety.

"On the father's side I assume?" Großmama sounded very stiff.

"Yes. What do I do?"

He strained to hear.

"I think that it might be better to leave the child where she is. You must hope for the best, Fräulein. You were very wise to send her away."

Then neither of them said anything.

At ten o'clock Nicolai crept down through the silent house. His bicycle stood ready near the garden gate. He carried the thick black cloth from his darkroom rolled up neatly under his arm; with that over his head as a hood, he would be able to train his torch on the map and find out where he was without violating the blackout. The Elbchaussee was quiet; when traffic came along, he ducked under the trees. It took three separate attempts before he found the narrow alleyway winding through St. Pauli, not far from the docks. The building, six storeys high, was dirty and rough-looking. Strange people hung around, girls who might be prostitutes. Not liking to leave his bicycle in that dark hallway where anyone might take it, he struggled with it, sweating profusely, up five flights of stairs.

He half fell against the door of 55G; Klaus opened it almost immediately. They stared at each other, both surprised. Klaus wore trousers so wide they nearly concealed his shoes, a navy-blue tailored jacket, starched collar, a homburg, a white silk scarf.

"Look who it is." He hauled Nicolai through the door. "What do you think? All black market stuff," and, revolving in a slow circle, he waited to be admired. He looked a real spiv, but a classy one.

"Where are you going?"

"Jazz club. Funny time to visit. What're you doing out, slumming?"

"I wondered how you were," he said lamely.

"I'm working. Finished with school."

"What's your job?" Nicolai thought of his beautiful writing, then of the ignoramuses at school, stupid boys who could box or run fast and so came top of the year.

"I'd hoped for a top shipyard. Blohm & Voß or Deutsche Werft—no chance. Not enough influence, see. But I've landed an apprenticeship all right. As a fitter at a boiler works. It's not bad. Dirty place, but not bad. I like welding. I'm going to be good at it. There's a lot of my sort there, you know. People with the right ideas. It's only my first week but I reckon I've landed on my feet."

Nicolai was uneasily aware that he had never told Klaus that his mother's family owned a substantial shipyard. Perhaps he could have obtained an apprenticeship for him. A real friend would have done that. He opened his mouth; closed it again.

Klaus looked quizzical. "Well? And you?"

He did not know how to edge up to the numerous reasons for his visit. "Nothing much. You know, school, the usual."

"Sit down."

Nicolai looked: there was a stool, one rickety-looking wooden chair, a table covered with newspaper, a bed in the corner. They had so little, not even a kitchen. He was not sure where to put himself. Klaus, looking at him steadily, seemed to read his thoughts.

Reddening a little, he stood his ground. "I came because I need something," he said. "Papers. Documents for a woman who wants to leave Germany and can't do it legally. I thought you might know how to get them."

Klaus whistled softly, sucked his teeth. "So you thought of me."

"Thought you must be good for something." Klaus smiled ironically. "I'd not have come without this. That's the truth of it."

"It's all right. I'd not have come your way either, would I?"

He laughed; everything eased.

"Nice bike. And it even climbs stairs."

They shared a beer, kept on the windowsill because his father said it cooled better, at night. Klaus did not know how to help him, had no contacts for a venture so dangerous and ill-advised.

"She'll have to sleep with somebody important in the Gestapo," he said.

"Typical suggestion from you. Very practical."

They both laughed.

"Look, I'm going, or I'll miss the first set."

"Can I come with you?" Nicolai asked.

"You might get yourself into trouble," said Klaus.

"I'm not scared."

Klaus punched his arm in a friendly way; they clattered down the stairs mock-fighting, carrying the bike between them. He could feel something shifting, as though his future could take a different shape. He had spent too long in a world of women, he wanted something hard and male, something real.

"You can't wear that stupid getup." Klaus gestured at his uniform. "Come back in civvies and I'll get you in."

"All right."

Nicolai watched from the corner of the street as people trickled into the Café König. The man at the door belonged to the Party, he wore his badge prominently displayed on his collar, not pinned underneath it the way most members did. That was intimidating. He was scrutinising identity cards; he refused entry to quite a lot of people. Nobody under eighteen was allowed in a nightclub; but then jazz was banned altogether and a good Party member would know that. Nicolai could not work it out at all. Klaus claimed that he was always let in; he was a shrimp, mind, and Nicolai was a good head taller. He turned up the collar of his father's raincoat. That wouldn't hide his face. He turned it down again. He probably looked a fool as it was.

"Second thoughts?" said the voice in his ear.

"What's in it for him, the doorman?"

"Dunno. Must like jazz. He could be arrested. That's what makes it exciting. Come on."

Shouldering his bag, he followed Klaus.

"Official photographer," said his friend.

The hand on his shoulder swung him round. The doorman looked at him. "Got your ID, son?"

Nicolai held up the Leica and, folded small, a twenty-Reichsmark note. It disappeared. They were inside.

Klaus winked. "If you're lucky, he'll let you have a print at cost," he called back cheekily.

The room was hot, smoky, dark. The phonograph was on. A trumpet played. He had never heard music like this. On the phonograph at home they played classical music or his mother's favourite dance tunes. Couples were dancing in a way he had not seen before, swaying from side to side and rolling up and down on the balls of their feet. Perhaps this was the notorious jitterbug.

"Louis Armstrong," said Klaus knowledgeably. "Negro music is the best."

As his eyes became accustomed to the gloom, he began to spot the Swing Boys. They had long hair, long sideburns; all except one, dressed exactly like Klaus, who had been razored nearly bald. Long, angry-looking scratches furrowed one side of his head.

"The Hitler Youth got him last week," said Klaus. "They shove in here and God help you if they catch you. We're the opposite, see?"

He saw. A pair of girls, not much older than himself, sat to one side. Both were smoking; one, with her hair hanging loose down her back and lipstick that turned her full mouth almost black, crossed her legs ostentatiously when she saw him looking; there was a flash of petticoat over tanned legs. Her sweater was tight over high breasts. Some act was announced; he didn't catch the name. The whole place rose, applauding as the members of the group started to come out.

"Tenor sax—drums, and he's the bass," murmured Klaus. Nicolai stared from one face to the next in disbelief. The room fell entirely silent; they started to play. The drumbeat thrilled up his spine. Then the sax soared out the melody, sweet, breathy and sure. Like a human voice, it penetrated right through to the roots of his hair. The girl with the tight sweater started dancing on her own, hips gyrating, eyes closed. Klaus was grinning like a maniac. In a moment, his friend got up and pushed his way through until he was dancing as close to the girl as he could reasonably get. Feeling down in the dark, Nicolai found the camera. He reached down to the flashgun in his bag. He fanned out the reflector, splayed delicate fingertips and felt very carefully for a bulb. His index finger touched one, then retreated. Just getting out the apparatus was disruptive. Instead, he set the shutter to a quarter of a second, the slowest possible speed, at F2. Holding the camera in his lap, he waited for the musician to move closer to the light.

Nicolai moved the strip of film in the enlarger on to the final frame, edged another sheet of photographic paper into place. He had four blurred discards already; he had had to push the film to get any kind of image. He had been up half the night, waiting for the film to dry; he could not give up now. This was the last one. He had studied all five negatives with a magnifying glass. They might all be blurred; there was no telling until he saw the detail. He moved the head up and down, adjusted, focused, turned the enlarger on for a few seconds, waited for the image to develop. Then, still by the dim red light, he lifted the print into the tray of acetic acid and, counting to sixty, swooshed the print back and forward in the fixing tray. Then, fingers crossed, he pulled the cord of the bathroom light and held the dripping print up.

Sweat gleamed on the profile of the tenor sax player, a coal-black man in a dark suit, head thrown back, the white shirt in crisp contrast. His head and throat were huge, magnificent. His exhalation of breath was a fuzzy glinting cloud; smoke from the cigarette he had just delicately placed on the edge of the table curled up around the back of his head. There had been just enough light to lift the image from a grainy blur to this perfection. A prickling course of pleasure ran through Nicolai. He could still smell that smoke in his hair; he could still hear the jazz beat pulsating, the sax soaring and curving new shapes inside his head.

NINE

Marseilles, July 1940

"Wo sind die Nutten?"* Voices in the corridor shouted and laughed. Heavy footsteps came right up to their door, the curtain rattled and the knob was turned several times. The door shuddered under a barrage of kicks. Ilse gestured to her father, awake and white-faced, that he must do and say nothing. The door, always bolted from the inside, strained under the onslaught.

"Shit," the German voice said. The deep voice of Paul, the barman, called down from above: the gentlemen should come upstairs. Soldiers' boots hammered up the stairs, they heard the distant laughter of women. Her father's face had the rigidity of fear and was hazed with sweat. She took his hand to reassure him. Relaxing, he turned over. Soon he would sleep. Ilse, who could not get used to the clamour, who could not help imagining all that went on up above, lay awake.

Rising at seven to the silence of the house, she crept about in the shuttered gloom and felt for her clothes. The wardrobe let out a

*"Where are the whores?"

depressing odour of mothballs. Renée's elderly mother had died two months earlier. The linen in the cupboard was new and the finest quality, destined for a country house that had not been bought and now never would be. Upstairs, the house stank of cigarettes and wine, rank smells of sex and excitement. She went out, pulling the curtain to behind her, and tiptoed along the corridor past Renée's rooms. She made her way along the alleyway that ran past the Clocher des Accoules. Jumping down the stairs along the handsome old façade of the Maison Diamantée, she trailed a hand, for luck, across the faceted stones which gave it its name. She hurried towards the light, the sun. The fishermen were stringing out their nets to dry. In the port a person could breathe.

On the quay, she headed straight for the Hôtel de Ville. The city, with its generally shabby but always knowing air, was growing familiar. She admired the purposeful way the Marseilles housewives trotted about with their baguettes and their little string shopping bags, their demeanour suggesting that they were real working women, not dawdlers. Crowds were forever coming down from the station or going to it, there was a crush up and down the Boulevard Dugommier and along the Canebière, and trickling into the Vieux Port. By mid-morning, the hot, dusty streets were packed. It was easy to pick out the refugees with their heavy coats and hangdog expressions. Whenever she heard a snatch of German she walked a step or two behind her compatriots, hoping for a hint as to what they were planning. Most wandered about as she did, aimlessly going from place to place. It was still possible that her mother would come to find them in France. Then she would surely turn up here. Everyone had to pass through Marseilles, the only port the Germans did not control directly. The Kriegsmarine was in charge of all the Atlantic ports.

Every day, trainloads of French soldiers arrived, waiting to be let out of the army and sent home. The process seemed to go at a snail's pace. They packed out the front and rear platforms of the trams, an endless flow of dirty-looking infantrymen or colonials with bright red fezes or chechias.* She noticed a group of Senegalese, proud, elegant men, their turbaned heads held high and pinned with a great gilt star. She looked hard at the Foreign Legion volunteers who carried their kepis in dust covers. One day the treizième DBLE would arrive in Marseilles, ready

*Tarbooshes.

to embark for home. One fine morning, surely, Willy would be among them. She walked and looked and hoped a little longer. At the corner, she would stop to buy the *Petit Marseillais:* "Donnez-moi le menteur,"* the Marseillais said. The radio told lies, just like the newspapers. Everybody knew it.

The people who had laughed at the Führer and made jokes had all been wrong. France had surrendered unconditionally. They signed the document in the very same wagon-lit and in the very piece of forest where the Germans had surrendered to Maréchal Foch in November 1918. Army engineers had towed the carriage from the museum built to hold it all the way to the siding; Hitler had insisted on it. Every newspaper had carried the picture. The Germans occupied Paris and the north, along a line north and west of Geneva going nearly up to Tours and skirting Poitiers, then going down the Atlantic coast and right to the Spanish border. The new French government under Maréchal Pétain and his cabinet, subservient to the rights of the occupying power, had gone to a little town called Vichy, not far from Lyons.

At the corner by La Sainte Trinité, an old woman swept the pavement vigorously. Ilse paused. She looked too frail for this good work.

"Let me help, Madame," she said, reaching for the broom. While Ilse swept up cigarette butts in little eddies of dirt, the old lady watched critically, pointing out places she had missed.

"Would you like a lemonade?"

She was not from the church at all, but the owner of the tiny café-bar on the adjoining corner. Amused, Ilse went in. In the semi-gloom a labourer nursed a marc with his morning coffee. Otherwise the bar was empty. The old lady reached down a bottle of lemonade and unstoppered it, pouring the liquid slowly into a tall glass. Ilse liked the darkness of this place, the old rich smells. She had no idea what a bar in Wuppertal smelt like, or Krefeld. She had never been in one. The lemonade was very good. Ilse savoured the treat.

"You're a good girl. Look at the time. You'd better be off to school," she said.

"Thank you, Madame."

"Come back tomorrow!" the bar owner called.

She had gone into a bar and nothing bad had happened. She hurried

*"Give me the liar."

away, pretending she had a school to go to, then doubled back to the church. Inside, she knelt, concentrated.

"Dear God," she prayed, "please make my father be all right. Bring him to life, please. And help us to get to safety."

She did not mention her mother because of a new fear she had. Like a snatch of song she could not get out of her head, like a bad dream, the idea of her mother being wrong kept recurring. Why had she not come? Ilse had been forced to choose and she had chosen her father. As a result, everything had gone wrong. God was punishing her.

The short figure of La Tatie was stumping up ahead, wheezing and coughing. Ilse caught up with her just before she reached the house. Together, they cleared up the bottles and glasses, emptied brimming ashtrays and swept the two main rooms. In her kitchen along the corridor, Renée's voice rose just before noon, the rich, soaring contralto singing one popular song after another. Through all this, her father slept. Day after day, he either slept or lay silent. Ilse went to wake him, tapping his hand or cheek. His skin had become pink and healthy-looking.

"Wake up. Renée will come soon," she said.

She and her father had lived in solitude for ten months. But it was here, over these last four weeks surrounded by people and noise, that Ilse had come to understand what real loneliness was. It was the absence of hope.

"She's cooking now. Very good food. You should wake up now." He opened his eyes.

"Vati, talk to me. Please."

He sat up. He seemed properly awake. "Good food," he said. "Yes. We've fallen on our feet."

"Yes, you're right." She tried an even brighter tone. "On your feet, Vati. If you were, Renée wouldn't have to wash you, would she?" She knelt at the side of the bed. It was not much of a joke, but he could have tried to smile. He was looking at the door, waiting.

"Won't you try and get up, Vati?"

She wanted to shake him really hard, until his bones rattled.

Renée sat on the bed, tipping Otto a little to one side. Though big, she was muscle rather than fat, with exquisite hands and feet. She unfolded a fresh white linen napkin, placed it round him and creased it, with care, under his chin. He opened his mouth and drank his soup obediently. She dabbed a dribble of soup from his chin and fed him another spoonful, her mouth curving down in concentration. In profile, as now, with her solid jowls and dramatic nose, she looked like a smooth-faced Roman emperor of great cruelty and strength. Ilse shuddered. Her father opened his mouth and closed it again, like a baby. He smiled at Renée. They both liked it, the baby-feeding, just as they liked her washing him.

Renée, an excellent cook, used ingredients that did not exist in the markets, where meat was scarce and butter nonexistent. In the black market, where she bought her wine and spirits, she could get her hands on butter and chickens and real coffee. She had boiled beef just as Otto liked it, thick sliced with boiled potatoes and horseradish sauce. She cut the meat up, held the fork out. Otto chewed, smiling his appreciation. He had gained three kilos in as many weeks.

"German soldiers nearly broke in here last night," Ilse said abruptly, her voice shaking a little.

"Not soldiers," said Renée calmly. "Officials, bureaucrats; they belong to the Armistice Commission stationed in Marseilles. It's good that they come here. Then my girls can find out what those bastards are up to. Don't worry. They'll soon learn where to go."

Her father tugged at her arm: that meant that she should translate what Renée said. Ilse ignored him.

"What's the Commission?"

"Officials sent from Germany. Why should the Germans bother to occupy the south, when our diligent French do all their work for them?" She did not call it work, she called it "conneries," a bad word which Ilse would have been hard put to translate, had she wished to try. But she did not wish to. She picked up the little bag she had prepared and went out. Going along the corridor with the blue roses, she heard the bolt shoot to behind her. The roses on the next floor were pink and those on the floor above yellow. She knew many untranslatable things that she was not supposed to know at all.

The best jewellers were on the Canebière. She chose one that, being neither too luxurious nor too mean, seemed to represent the right milieu. The doorbell jangled as she went in. An old man came out of a back room and squinted at the pieces in her mother's jewellery roll with his loupe. Everybody was selling things; he had too much already. Ilse turned to go.

"Mademoiselle," he said casually, "I'll take the brooch. The chains are ordinary, but perhaps I will put them in the window of the shop for a couple of weeks. If they sell you can have a third of the money."

Suppressing her anger, she said that she would think about it. Without cash, they would never get out of France.

"Madame Renée, may I ask you something?"

"Of course." She was sitting at the little bureau, doing some sort of paperwork.

"Madame, where's a good place to sell jewellery?"

"What've you got?"

With reluctance, she held out her jewellery. Turning on a reading light, Renée unrolled the leather case. Her sitting room gave onto a tiny and very dark courtyard full of plants shedding a greeny pallor. A huge, elaborate armoire with glass fronts was crammed with china, another contained crystal glasses; even the chandelier was cut glass. The diamond ring was far too small for Renée's fingers, which were very smooth and dimpled. But the pearl necklace with its lovely lustre sat well on her fine skin. She stood and went to the glass to admire it. Then, sitting down once more, she ran the gold chains through her fingers, weighed them mentally. She touched the platinum brooch with her long fingernail; it was a caress.

"I'll take the pearls."

It could not be helped; Ilse tried to disguise the blow.

Renée took a roll of money from the drawer of her cupboard and peeled off half a dozen big notes. She saw Ilse's surprise. "For the time being business is good," she said. "I have always helped my friends. That is my luxury."

She smiled and Ilse tried to smile back, though she could not put much life into it. The pearls her mother had only ever worn on special occasions, the ones she wore in her wedding photograph, now lay around Renée's throat.

"I want to buy visas and tickets to get out of France."

"Tickets? That's only for the high-ups. Our police check everybody. The Germans have given them nice long lists of who to catch." "Salauds" was the word she used for the police. "Unofficially, when your father is better, we will find a way. But first he must get stronger."

"He is stronger."

She shook her head.

"Surely, Madame, surely you want to get rid of us," Ilse said, choosing her words carefully.

"Ilse. A man like your father must be very careful."

Ilse frowned. She wondered how this woman knew all that she did. With one long finger, Renée tapped the side of her nose. She could not begin to imagine what her father had managed to communicate when they did not share a language and he hardly spoke, even to his own daughter.

Renée's mother kept two books beside her Bible: a life of the saints with much emphasis on the martyrdom of the blessed Sainte Cathérine, and *L'Abbé Tigrane* by Ferdinand Fabre, tales of provincial life. The old lady must have been very religious. Each time she read them, Ilse knew more words and skipped fewer. When her eyes were too tired to carry on, she would sit staring into the near darkness listening to her father's breathing and to the noises of the house. The way the linens lay folded in perfect alignment seemed to Ilse to be just like the parallel scars on her hand, which were healing nicely, little train tracks which she ran her thumb across. She wondered if she had changed her destiny by making those marks. She thought about her guardian angel when, with drooping eyes, she finally lay down in the big bed next to a clean-shaven Otto smelling of eau de cologne. Once he had suggested that she might prefer to sleep alone. Wordlessly, she shook her head. She could not bear to be alone, listening to the noises of the night, wondering what bed he had gone to, in a house which had so many.

"Komm herein, mein Schatz,"* said La Petite Louise. She said this to everyone, even the English soldiers who came in drunk from the bars on the quai. Prisoners of war were locked up in Fort Saint-Jean, but the French guards let them out on day passes.

"Herein!"

She had sharp little yellow teeth like a rat and a boy's figure. Though she scared Ilse, she was always friendly, always seeking company. She was not unlike a Toni, or rather a Toni that might have been. There was another Louise, known for obvious reasons as La Grande, a country girl who hardly ever opened her mouth. On the few occasions when she did, she had a strong accent of the Midi. La Petite's door was always half

*"Come in, my treasure."

open, to hook in passers-by for a chat. Some of the girls appeared simpleminded or just strange. Ilse worried that one of them might one day reveal to a German client that she and Otto were there.

"We won't tell. Anyway, I'm the darling of the German Commission. We're more afraid of Renée." She laughed. La Petite looked so much better when she did not smile, though Ilse could hardly tell her so.

"Why?"

"Don't cross her and you'll never find out. She has a finger in every pie in Marseilles. Knows all the big shots. Gangsters and so on. She trades her information, does her deals. Of course, she loves money. Don't we all," and she lit a cigarette and mimed flicking through a thick wad of it. La Petite was brewing coffee on a little gas ring in the corner. It smelt very good. She always had real coffee, never ersatz.

"Want some?"

It was dark and delicious. Gratefully, Ilse sipped it.

There was a sharp knock at the door.

"I can smell contraband. Come out at once. Customs!"

"Raymond!"

A small man, laughing, ducked his head and pretended to charge like a bull, pointing fingers for horns. La Petite embraced him. He was a real Marseillais, stocky and short and full of cockiness. Thick black hair grew on his arms and chest, springing forth with vigour.

"Ilse, you know Raymond? The brother of Paul. My friend Ilse—Raymond Leboeuf, look at him, a real bull."

"Paul is the ox. I am more of a calf. You're the girl from Germany. Paul told me about you."

She could see the family resemblance; the oversized barman must dwarf him.

"What have you got for me, mein Schatz?"

"Coffee, sugar, tobacco." Raymond winked. He drew a packet out from under his shirt. La Petite counted out notes, then poured him a cup. He lit up a cigarette. Ilse sniffed the strong smell of real Virginia tobacco.

"Raymond, Ilse and her father want to get out. Raymond works in the docks," said La Petite.

"Where do you want to go?"

Hope sprang up at once.

"To Morocco, to my uncle, to Oran," she said. "If we can get places on a boat."

"Raymond will smuggle you out, won't you, darling?" said La Petite.

But he was shaking his head. "They search every ship. The coast is patrolled by the Germans for illegal boats. They stop fishing vessels just beyond the port, they get a nice catch that way. But they don't search soldiers, nor troopships. They're the only ones."

"Oh."

"One thing, mind, I heard about Morocco. Some of the French soldiers being demobilised get free passage there, if that's where they come from. Don't look so sad. Something will come up."

He had kind eyes. Ilse stored the information away. Later, she asked Renée about it.

"You think Vati could pass as a French soldier?"

They both looked at him. Clearly not.

It was wicked to waste money on a book, but what could she do? She could not join a library and did not have the nerve to sit in one without a card. She went to the big bookshop near the station that was always full. Scanning the yellow softbacks for something cheap, she chose a book by François Mauriac. Returning with her prize, Ilse very quietly drew back the curtain. She was curious to know how they managed to talk, when she was not there. They had not locked the door from the inside. Opening it noiselessly, she peeped in. Renée was kneeling on the bed astride her stretched-out father, her black dress pulled up around her waist and her mound of flesh engulfing him, his face in a rictus, his arms gripping her white thighs, her pink heels turned up.

Ilse stepped back. She heard him crying out, a hoarse sound. She went straight out of the house, marching with stiff knees to the top of the hill. Without seeing it, she looked down at the harbour. She did not feel anything very clearly. She was not even surprised. Renée was simple, made no demands, she was action and reaction, she was flesh. She was a whore. That was what whores did. It came to her that she had no memory of her mother and father doing anything like that. She did not remember her mother ever touching her father. In a little while, leaning against the side of a house, she began to read, brutally ripping the pages where uncut. The book was about an old man full of rage. It used many words she did not know, important words that in a moment, when she returned, she would look up in the dictionary Willy had given her.

These angry words would be dwelt upon in silence; she would stretch them out and make them occupy the evening. The thunder of blood in her head was slowing. The stones were warm against her back. There was no hurry. Up here it stayed light until nine o'clock, when the alleyways below were dark. The door was open when she returned, but her father was not there. She sat listening to the noises of the house until, overcome by weariness, she lay down to sleep.

Otto had woken before her, was up and dressed.

"There's so much to do."

Ilse looked at him in blank amazement. Otto began to pace. He was going to start writing again: pamphlets which would be translated into French. The issue right now was the paper supply. A man Renée knew who came to the house could supply most things. Matters would be arranged. It had to be Raymond. Why did her father never tell her the important things? As usual, he treated her like a child.

"I need to learn French," he said.

"So you can talk to Renée?"

"So I can talk to everyone."

He seemed to be in an extraordinarily good mood. From his pocket he drew a pack of cards and started to shuffle them. Ilse recognised the Pierrot and Pierrette motif she had seen in Renée's kitchen. He laid out the cards. The king of clubs came out, went down in the vacant position. But the hand then replayed itself, on and on, with no new cards to put anywhere. Doggedly her father, who had no patience at all, ran through the pack several times to be quite sure. His hands never stopped moving.

"Vati, now you're feeling better, we have to get out of France," she said.

"I like France," he said.

"You like Renée."

"She's a fantastic woman. In another world, she'd have been an opera singer. She has the body for it."

"Instead of the madame d'un lupanar."*

"What's that?"

She translated.

"Perhaps both."

He was laughing. A red tide of rage swept up her face and she bit her

*A brothel.

cheek, so she would not say anything rash. She needed to be in his confidence, but the free way he spoke depressed her. She told herself to be clever, to be reasonable.

"We have to let Mutti know where we are. That's the first thing. I'm going to write to Willy and ask for the address of those friends of his in Hamburg."

"Willy enlisted. What a fool, at his age. You told me yourself. He's probably in Algeria somewhere. Who knows?"

"But Toni will know where he is, she might have the address."

"Ilse. Must we go through all this again?"

"But she needs to know about us." She steadied her voice. "She wrote to me, you know she did. You tore the letters up."

"All that's past. Your mother could not bring herself to leave Germany. It's a pitiful thing, but there it is."

"You didn't want to leave either."

"I wanted to fight them from the inside. Your mother's a different case. She's Aryan, she could not be one with the refugees and outcasts."

This shocked her. Ilse felt the truth of this, a stab in her own body. She did not want to be a refugee either. This was a hard lump, which she could not swallow, a fishbone sticking in her throat.

"But I want to write to her."

"No. In any case, we have no address. She never gave it to me. She has severed her connection with the underground. Even if I knew where she was, I would not permit it. It's not safe."

She did not believe him. He knew how to twist words to his advantage. The conversation, like so many with her father, was meant to go differently. The faint sound of the cards went on and on. She picked up the *Petit Marseillais*. The newspapers carried page after page of classified advertisements, families trying to find one another: lost brothers and sisters and fathers and mothers who might never see one another again. She looked at the small print with eyes that would not focus. She had chosen her father, though she did not much care to be with him and she could not trust him to save her.

She pressed her old school dress and cleaned her shoes, which were very tight. She was growing, even her feet were. She got out her set of fine Aryan papers. That was the first on her list when, desperate to fall asleep, she ran through her possessions in ascending order of importance. Last of all and most precious was the photograph of her mother, which she now kept safe in her suitcase inside the cupboard. The American embassy was at No. 6 Place St. Ferréol. It was not hard to find: an enormous queue of people stretched all down the street, and right round the corner and along the next street. Ilse attached herself to the back of it. After an hour, a man came down the queue telling people something. They began to melt away. Ilse was not near enough to understand him. When people stayed, he came over and explained it again: this was not the place for visas. This office was for Americans. They had to go to the visa office at Montrédon, in the outskirts of Marseilles.

Early the next morning she crept out while the whole house slept. Others had had the same idea for the tram was jammed with people. They rode out into the hills, standing much too close for comfort. Sweat trickled down the back of her dress, gathered damply in the belt. She felt very conspicuous, when other children were at school, but nobody seemed to notice her. All the people on the tram got off at the same place and headed along the hot, dry road towards a big brick villa. Many people were already standing outside. Large notices were wired to the railings: APPLICATIONS FROM CENTRAL EUROPE ARE NOW CLOSED. Another read: VISAS VIA SOUTH AMERICA CURRENTLY SUSPENDED. She joined the end of the queue. The next tram brought another sardineload of hopefuls. A lot of the women were dressed up, wearing high heels, which the dusty road covered with a fine powder.

Germans in the queue talked to each other. It was odd to hear her language spoken so freely. As they shuffled slowly forward, Ilse listened to them exchange information. To exit by sea seemed to be most people's hope but all passages from Lisbon or Marseilles to any place outside Europe were sold out for months in advance. They talked about the exchange rate and the impossibility of buying dollars even at the official rate. A woman, shrill and sharp-faced, who reminded Ilse a little of Frau Wolff, was standing just in front. They fell into conversation.

"Do you have your transit visa?"

Ilse shook her head.

"But you've got the American visa?"

Ilse looked at her feet. The woman looked at her pityingly as she explained the system. First she had to obtain the visa for America— generally considered impossible. Only with the American visa could she apply for Portuguese and Spanish transit visas. With a boat ticket from Marseilles, one did not need the transit visas, but the only ships leaving Marseilles were French ships for Oran and Algiers. Tickets on these could only be bought for dollars and special permission was needed, which foreigners were unlikely to get since only Vichy officials were permitted to go to Africa. Without exit visas, you couldn't put your name down for any ticket.

"I queued for three days just at the Spanish consulate," the woman said. The Portuguese visa was essential to get the French exit visa. That was given only by the Vichy government. "In other words," she whispered, "it's all controlled by the Gestapo."

Ilse smiled and nodded and said thank you and stood, dully, in the queue for another hour, for some stupid reason too proud to do the obvious thing, which was to walk away. Rattling back down into town, the tram was empty, and she took a seat and stared out. Walking disconsolately along the Canebière, her eye was caught by a woman rolling down the blinds of a patisserie. It was a café too, a big, pretty one with a yellow and blue striped canopy and little tables inside. She stood on the street outside and looked at it, feeling the sun on her shoulders. An image of the braided head of Frau Ginsberg and of her lilac gloves floated into her mind. Her mouth was suddenly watering. She could almost taste the apricot pastries. She could see the sisters waving, the handle of the leather bag and the clear light of Oran. Suddenly, she wanted Willy so badly.

Walking nearer, she saw the window was nearly empty. There could be no pastries when there was no butter and no eggs. On the glass shelves stood a dozen gaudy confections. These were cakes—if you could call something a cake that was made without eggs, butter, sugar or flour. They were a mass of solidified pink foam with a cherry on top. She was staring at them without really seeing them, rather seeing herself reflected there. It took much longer than it should have for her to discern, inside looking out, the tall ugly man whose mouth, like that of a fish, opened and closed, and who was waving like a madman. Albert came out into the street and put his arms round her. She saw tears in his eyes. He drew her back inside and they sat at a table near the door. He blew his nose loudly several times. He came here for breakfast each day, he said. But for the visit to the American embassy, she would never have seen him.

"You should be in England," she said. "Beautiful skin, rotten teeth." He patted her hand. "What are you doing here?"

"I was an idiot to think I could get out—the British left behind forty thousand French troops at Dunkirk, and some of their own. I'd left it too late. So I made my own way down here durch Nacht und Nebel,"* and he squeezed her hand. A curious little tingle went right through her. "And you, my darling girl?"

"We got out at the last minute," she said. "You know." The journey from Paris was something she wanted to suppress forever. "Albert, I don't suppose you could afford a cake?"

They had four of the cakes that tasted of froth and coffee made out of barley ground fine, sweetened with saccharine that left a sour aftertaste. She ate three cakes; he crumbled one, laughing that she had such an appetite.

"How old are you now?"

"Much older. Fourteen and a bit."

He was amused. "Oh, so much older." With one good eye, Albert seemed to look at her. The other was fixed on the door. "I'm nervous for you," he said. "Any foreigner without a sauf-conduit† is sent to a concentration camp immediately."

"Nobody sees me."

"I saw you. Don't you read the newspapers? The French are already cracking down on Jews. They have made themselves a nice Statut des Juifs, so they can round them up more easily."

"Don't worry," she said airily. "I'm en règle. Sort of. Anyway, I'm not Jewish."

"Indeed. And you'll be interested to hear that I'm now Czech," he said.

Albert really was en règle. He had a fine, expensive new passport from the Czech consul in Marseilles in an unpronounceable name; he took it out of his cream linen jacket and showed it to her as they walked down towards the port. She admired its pink cover and gold stamp, the visas for China and Siam and, most important, a sauf-conduit from the military authorities. Albert had been promised a visa for America. With his pass, he could leave France and wait for the visa anywhere: in neutral

*"Through night and fog": sinister German expression.
†Pass.

Lisbon perhaps, or somewhere safer along the Portuguese coast. From America, he could go anywhere in the world. But he had not gone. Only one in ten thousand really understands, she told herself.

"But why haven't you left?"

"I've been working. Ilse, something important has happened. The book—I'm going to finish it. I've started to write again." He had been working on "the" book for years, on and off. "Or rather, I could finish it, if I had someone. A special girl to read back to me what I've written."

Deep joy surged up. The sun shone and the boats with their gay pennants danced upon the water. He would not go to America; only the book mattered. For the book, for her, he would stay in Marseilles. She could have danced up the Montée des Accoules.

The door was locked from the inside.

"We can't go in just now," she said. "Vati and the madame. You know," she said, shrugging. Albert raised his eyebrows. In Renée's kitchen, she put water on to boil for tisane. A big piece of meat sat on a plate to one side in a pool of blood, covered with a net dome to keep off flies; alongside were a dozen eggs. When she turned, Albert's good eye swivelled from these luxuries back to her.

"My friend!"

Otto and Albert embraced. Renée was just behind. They shook hands and Albert looked from Otto to Renée and back again, and Ilse saw her father's face set. For a moment neither of them said anything. Then Renée went out and everyone spoke at once. Ilse explained how she had run into Albert and where he was staying.

"Albert's going to America. He's just waiting for his visa," she said.

"You'd better be careful. Vichy controls all the exits. Walk over the mountains into Spain and hope not to be caught—that's your way out, on foot through Lisbon. Forget the papers."

"It sounds much too energetic, my dear Otto."

"You'll catch the express, will you? From the Gare St. Charles, where the police have set up a permanent barrier?" Her father was laughing at Albert. "You and your papers. Clinging to a world that's gone. To a belief in order, it's incredible. What are these papers?"

"A Czech passport in a false name. A real one."

"I doubt it. The consul gives his anti-fascist friends a document with a pink cover, not the official green one. It'll do. Until the French authorities realise these are just interim documents. Your real problem is that you're so recognisable, Albert."

Ilse, making the tisane, was gripping the pan of boiling water much too tight. How was it that her father always knew everything and yet arranged nothing for himself? Distressed, she looked at Albert, who raised a hand, signalling to her to be calm. "All these crackpot schemes and permits and visas for Peru and Panama—it's all hopeless. We're shunned like the plague by every neutral country." Otto was warming to his theme. "Even with connections and money it's impossible to get a real visa for anywhere. Nobody wants refugees. Especially not German Jews. We have to accept that our destiny is to fight."

Albert set his cup down with a bang. "Too much red meat has heated your blood, Otto. And the child, what is her duty? Is she supposed to fight too? This is no place for Ilse."

"This house is safe. You're ten times more likely to be picked up in a hotel which the police visit every week than living as we are. Even with your fine new papers." Her father's voice was getting louder. Ilse stood with her back to the dresser and felt its knobs sticking into her. It was like sitting on the stairs while her parents fought over her. "The French are already locking up their Jews. Kicking them out of the professions. They've given themselves the right to arrest foreign Jews and put them into concentration camps or wherever they like. It's another Germany. Nobody's affected. Nobody protests. Then it's too late. But there has to be protest, Albert, there has to be a voice raised."

They bristled at each other.

"Forget it. The only thing to do is to get out. Don't be wilful, Otto. You know what I'm talking about. Ilse can't live here with prostitutes. My dear friend, think of Paris and learn—let's both try to grow wiser—"

"You are such a bourgeois, Albert," her father snapped. "I'd forgotten. You never cared about the proletariat. Only saving yourself. And your work."

Albert's good eye glared at him. "You're right. I have work to do." He picked up his hat.

Ilse looked from one to the other. "Please, Albert, don't go."

"Sit down, Ilse," her father said. "It's not safe for you to walk the streets. Or to be in this den of vice. Didn't you hear what Albert said?"

"Please, Vati, don't—" But already Albert was in the hallway. "I'll come to your hotel later," she whispered. Of course her father had spoken sarcastically.

But later he said it again: "I forbid you to go out." Head down, concentrating on her mending, Ilse nodded.

She waited a week. School started in September and Ilse reckoned that children, out with their satchels, would not be stopped. On the street, she wore her lucky school dresses and stayed on the outside of the pavement. That way she could get away if the police suddenly blocked the streets. People whispered about these roundups, called the police vans "paniers à salade"* because they took anyone and everyone. She had her safe way. She crossed the road at a certain corner, stepped off the same lucky sloping piece of kerb at the little patch of tired green where the blind man sat. It was lucky to say hello to Madame Dumont, to sweep in front of the church in case God was watching.

"Did you hear? They tried to invade England," the old woman whispered, pouring the lemonade. "The English are so clever. They poured oil onto La Manche† and lit it. They say all Paris is full of the burn cases. All the German military hospitals are full. So many men burnt, thousands of them. And of course plenty drowned, also. Go on, my girl, eat," said the old lady, seeing her looking at the bowl with the hard-boiled eggs on the counter. "Thank God, England's safe." Ilse thanked her and took one.

"Give it to me, my pet." Expertly, she cracked and peeled an egg, and cut it into neat quarters, shaking on salt and pepper, and arranging the pieces prettily on a plate with a gherkin. Now that she avoided eating with her father, Ilse was often hungry. She tried not to eat too fast. Smiling, Madame Dumont took another one, cracked it on the zinc counter. Ilse savoured the second egg.

"I must go. School," she said.

"Welcome!" Albert's room, tucked away in the attic, was very private. Ilse sat down. The pile of paper waited in the exact centre of the desk.

"How many pages did you do?"

"Seven," he said, beaming.

*Salad spinners.
†The English Channel.

"How many more will there be? Make it a long book, Albert."

"I wonder. You see, the war combined with the additional complexities of your helping me just makes it go faster."

"Explain. Or else this donkey won't walk another step," she said, happily reviving the nickname.

"It's a lovely donkey. Listen, this is Goethe's sonnet about a sonnet.

"This is the way with all kinds of creation
Useless for an unbridled spirit
To try to achieve the summit of perfection
Only self-discipline can lead to greatness.
Accepting limits will reveal the master,
And only the law can give us freedom."

He meant that the constraints were making the book better. That made sense. The difference was that he wanted the book to go fast while she was desperate for it to be as slow as possible. She had her stratagems. Sometimes she stalled by making barley coffee before they started work; sometimes it was tea.

She scanned the pages, then read out loud. Albert said that when she read, he heard the words flowing in a way he could not when, with his bad eyes, he had to puzzle them out for himself. Once she had put it back into his head, he could write. Nearly two hours went in this way, with her reading out loud and him telling her what to change and her writing corrections on yesterday's pieces of paper. Then Albert took a fresh sheet of paper and started to work, rewriting what they had done in his tiny neat hand while she read the corrected version out slowly. Only then could he continue and add words. This he did rapidly, head down, in an unstoppable flow. The well would run out in perhaps five or, on a very good day, ten pages, but in the morning it was always renewed. She had to keep an eye on the time, to remember to leave at lunchtime when the streets filled with children going home with their satchels. She was back when the house woke up. Sometimes her father was not in the room; sometimes he sat and wrote at Renée's table, scribbling away or reading proofs of his pamphlets and posters. He never asked where she had been; she did not enquire what he was doing. He seemed not to notice that she went out. Perhaps he was avoiding noticing. Perhaps it did not occur to Otto that she might simply disobey him.

Afternoons dragged until the six o'clock mass. Kneeling in the quiet pew, she would close her eyes and use the words, which she was getting to know by heart, as a kind of stepping stone to a calm place where things would be made right. She was no longer a child, to believe in buttons. This was the place for prayer, and if she sat very still and never scratched her nose, even if it itched, if she truly concentrated, then the God of the Catholics might help them. She worried about getting what she prayed for; perhaps God was laughing at her when he sent Renée. She had been wrong to try and cheat him, to ask him for things when she did not have the right. Only those who belonged had the right. The priest who seemed so kind had a mouth that turned down in a disapproving line when she started to explain that she had been brought up as a Lutheran Protestant and now she wanted to become a Catholic. The saints hid their faces behind their smooth blue cloaks.

"I want to be christened and then confirmed," she said in a small voice. "I have faith, Father."

The small man looked at his feet, then looked back at her. He knew. "It will take a little time," he said in a whisper. Jews probably asked him for this all the time.

"Of course, mon Père. Thank you very much."

Her father and Renée occupied the kitchen like a married couple.

"La soupe c'est bon," her father said laboriously. "Un peu de poivre, peut-être."*

"Bonne, it's feminine soup, of course." Renée mocked him for his mistakes and for liking spicy food; he seemed to enjoy her making fun of him. When, after supper, Renée went upstairs to look to her clients, Ilse had her chance.

"Vati," she said, "what does it mean to be a Jew? Will you explain it to me?"

"Nothing. It is the same as being a Christian, or a Muslim. Or a communist. Or a Buddhist. It's a name. A sect. In the modern world, nobody believes in these archaic things."

"Some people have faith."

"People who think—intelligent people—know it's all superstition."

She felt a surge of anger which she tried to suppress. "So all Germans are superstitious? They believe in Jews, don't they?"

*"Perhaps a little pepper."

He shrugged. "They need somebody to blame. Somebody to hate. They picked the Jews for economic reasons. Maybe they envied us our beautiful names. After all, they are called miller and tradesman and smith. But we are flower-filled valleys, fields of roses, golden stars, mountains of blooms."

She had never heard him say anything so fanciful.

The next morning, still puffed from climbing the attic stairs, it was the first thing she asked. "Albert, doesn't anybody believe in God anymore?"

"I believe in literature," he replied.

"But I'm serious."

"So am I."

"So, is there a God in heaven?"

"We will leave heaven for angels and sparrows,"* said Albert. "I wish I'd written that. It's Heine, of course."

"Of course. How would I know? I haven't read anything," she said mournfully.

"There'll be books in Lisbon. I'll buy you whatever you want."

Nothing he said was predictable. Ilse never knew what Otto would say either, but as the words came out, his face always made just the expression she expected. It was that she could not bear.

"Albert, when did you decide to leave Germany?"

"When I saw that books by Jews wouldn't be published. When non-Aryans could not study, just before the Nuremberg laws. A thousand conversations went on about when the regime would fall, but it became clear that people loved it. They were all happy," he said, shrugging his shoulders.

"When was that?"

"I suppose—1933."

"And it was easy to get out then?"

"Simple. People left in droves—off to London and New York and Stockholm or Constantinople. Canada, South Africa. You know, Ilse, I can give you a precise moment—in 1934, I went to see *Don Carlos*.† In Hamburg, in the Staatstheater—and when Posa said, 'Sire, allow freedom of thought!' people clapped for a long time, maybe five or ten min-

---

*"Den Himmel überlassen wir den Engeln und den Spatzen." Heinrich Heine, *Deutschland, ein Wintermärchen*.
†Schiller's tragedy of 1787 in blank verse.

utes. And straight afterwards *Don Carlos* was banned from every theatre. And then I knew that there would be no limit to how far it would go and no detail they would overlook."

"Why did it take you so long to go?"

"I think in German. My dreams are German."

"And why didn't you go straight to America, Albert?"

He looked at her with his good eye. "It's one thing to be in Europe and another to choose to go outside. I didn't want to go outside. I still don't."

"Not even to save your life?"

"You do anything to save your life, but actually the choices aren't like that. It's not if somebody says if you want to live, join this queue. That queue is for those who'll die. It's never that obvious."

"Then you're not going to America? Or Palestine?"

"An immigrant arrives in Tel Aviv," he said. "The immigration officer looks at him. First question: Tell me, are you coming from conviction or from Germany?"

Albert's face had a special way of crinkling up when making a joke, which she found delightful. His face was peculiar and yet so full of intelligence that she never tired of looking at it. He had been fat and now he was thin. The skin that hung down at his chin line and neck had a kind of special softness, which other flesh did not have, a buttery-toffee feeling to it. It made her think of the ruins of an ancient building, which could be reconstructed and imagined in any number of different ways. Though he twinkled at her now, Ilse could not laugh at such jokes.

"It's very expensive," she said. "My cousins took fifteen thousand marks with them. The English won't let anybody in with less. And America—it's just impossible."

Albert saw through her right away. "Your father would never contemplate it," he said. "The money is not even the problem."

"I won't be spending the rest of my life with my father," she said.

"No. You're coming with me."

She loved him for saying that.

"Albert, if we didn't know where we were—or how or where to meet—where would it be?"

"Paris. That's where I'll be, after the war. Café Tournon," he said at once.

"Three o'clock in the afternoon on Tuesday. Every Tuesday. I'll wait for you."

"Three o'clock on a Tuesday."

He took her hand in his big one; they shook on it.

"Come, let's work."

She picked up the paper, read aloud. "It was the land that the people needed, the land that drew them." She worried about these people. A tiny band moved across a desert landscape of rocks and sand, subsisting on very little and bickering eternally with one another about where they were going and why. Their shadows lay so heavily and so long across the landscape that they seemed to mark it. She had long since worked out that under this pitiless light, under the ironic scrutiny of their creator, their end could only be sad or bad. In these pages the language was extremely simple, in contrast to previous parts of the book, some of which were written in a kind of free verse that was complicated and full of allusions. His work was like a necklace with different beads, she thought, the effect of the conjunctions not becoming visible until the next bead had been added.

Head bowed, his good eye two centimetres from the pen as it scratched across the page, his nose nearly touching it and frowning with the strain, Albert wrote. The pen went fast. The book was nearly done; he spoke of going farther down the coast, to Cassis, where things were quieter. In Lisbon or wherever he was going, in a safe place where noise did not betray a person, he would engage a woman secretary. Somebody else would read all his new words. Then that lucky person would type them out. He would like the text much better when it was typed. Albert claimed that there was greater clarity, when the words themselves were exactly even. Ilse had nimble fingers. She found a piece of cardboard and drew the keys of a typewriter, copying the one she saw in the window of the Bon Marché. She put it on the table in the kitchen and closed her eyes to practise. Rumours persisted that the Germans would occupy the south. But perhaps they would not come. If Otto stayed with Renée, if it was safe, then she would be free to go with Albert. If she could type, she would be indispensable to him. Then she would be worth what-ever it cost to buy her freedom. Her fingers flew over the imaginary keyboard.

When Otto came for supper, washing ink-stained fingers at the kitchen sink, the words came out in a stupid rush. "Marseilles is very dangerous, but Cassis is safe. Albert is going to go there and we could stay with him. He'd like it. He's found a house."

"Three Jews in a French fishing village? Speaking German? How very inconspicuous," Otto said. "When did Albert call? Did I miss him?"

She would not answer that.

"We can't just sit here and wait to be picked up. Please, Vati." Her voice rose querulously, she could not help it.

"I'm not sitting, I have work to do. Albert can leave. For us, the safest thing is to lie low."

Ilse stood up. "The safest thing is to get out of France. If I only had a visa, I would go with him. I'd give anything to do that. To get away from you. Anything."

Before her father could say anything, she brushed past him and went out, slamming the door.

On the stairs leading to Albert's attic room the next day, she heard her father's voice booming out. Shocked, Ilse stopped dead.

"What insane fantasies are these? Visas and leaving—what right do you have to interfere with my child?"

"What right do you have to neglect her?" Albert shouted back.

She hurried up and into the room.

"Shh! The whole hotel can hear you!"

"I'm going to take her with me. Out of France."

"Vati—please—Albert!"

The two men were facing each other across the table. Hectic spots burned on Otto's cheeks.

"Why don't you have papers? Why haven't you even tried to organise some? Living in a brothel. You have a duty to get your child to safety. Trailing her about. What life is this for her? Who even knew in Hamburg that you had wife or child? You're completely irresponsible."

This was a painful revelation to Ilse.

Her father slammed his hand on the table. "Ilse, come with me. You are forbidden to come here."

"You don't behave like a father!" Albert started shouting. "You behave as if she doesn't exist!"

"*I'm* irresponsible. *I'm* insane. And you? Encouraging her to traipse all over Marseilles in broad daylight, risking her life so she can read to you? Duplicity and madness, selfish madness. But your book's worth the risk, isn't it, Albert? Come, Ilse."

Head down, she followed Otto. He paused in the door.

"Goodbye, Albert." Her father's mouth was working as he spoke. "I don't wish to see you again."

She did not, could not, say goodbye. With flaming face, impossibly conspicuous, she followed her father as he marched down the Canebière.

On a bright Sunday morning in October when the bells were calling the early worshippers, Albert sent word that he was moving to Cassis sur Mer. Ilse stole from the house, determined to see him one last time. He insisted on showing her the place he had chosen to settle in. She had the honour of carrying his manuscript in the little red leather briefcase. As the train chugged along the coast, he tried to amuse her, telling how he had obtained his permis de séjour* the previous week by giving somebody at the Hôtel de Ville a very hefty bribe. She could not smile. Cassis was over twenty kilometres away, much too far for her to dare to visit.

"Your passport is good, isn't it?"

"My darling girl, it should be at that price. Don't worry."

Cassis was a fishing village with two sandy beaches and one of shingle, with white limestone cliffs, a summer place. A cold wind was blowing. The season was shifting. The little house high on the rough cliffs was set apart from all the rest. It was bare but pleasant, with a wonderful view of the sea. She walked from room to room and looked at it all blankly.

"You'll stay in this room when you come on holiday. Or would you rather have the one at the side?" If not for Otto, she could have occupied that side room now. The kitchen also had a view of the sea. A dozen aluminium saucepans hung in a row, scoured bright. It had a big table that a person could sit and write at and where bowls of coffee would be drunk. The massive wooden dresser held dozens of elaborately scalloped green plates in every size, the cheap kind the markets sold, in colours that were almost iridescent. She would never eat from one of these.

"There'll be sea urchins and fresh sardines every day," said Albert. "I expect I shall get fat again."

"You don't even like fish."

*Residence permit.

"When you visit, I shall cook for you," he said—Albert, who could not boil an egg.

As a parting gift, he gave her the little red case, which she had often admired. They walked down the hill hand in hand with her holding the light case in her other hand and swinging it, high and low, just as though she did not care. When he kissed her, four times in the French way, she clung to him. Then she rushed away.

The train was busier going back and she stood, hugging the precious case in her arms. At the Gare St. Charles, without meeting anyone's eye, she walked from the station into the restaurant. It was now lunchtime and the place was full. She threaded her way through the tables. The kitchen connected by a short corridor to the Hôtel Terminus; that door opened directly onto the street. That was the safe way. Inside the station, the police were a permanent presence, holding inspections at the ticket barrier to see if papers were en règle. This was where most people were picked up, just when they thought they had made it. She had no sauf-conduit: she knew very well that even a child could be picked up and sent away. As it happened, she had not brought any papers with her. Only now did she wonder at her own naivety. Upon an impulse she paused, opened the case. When she saw the big roll of French francs, she slammed it shut. She understood that Albert did not expect to see her again.

Not knowing what to do with the empty hours ahead, she walked down to the harbour and right along to the other side of the transporter bridge, to prolong the moment of the return. The days were drawing in and she needed a new coat: the old one, much too small, seemed shrunken and the cardigan she wore underneath for warmth was stretched tight. She paid her fifty centimes and got onto the platform. As it drew rapidly away from the quay and floated across the water, she saw police vans roar in from both directions at once, blocking any escape route along the waterfront. A woman standing beside her crossed herself; Ilse did likewise. These events were dreamlike and strange, the sharp wind and the blurred city unreal, as were the little figures being herded together near the "salad spinners" and then separated out into smaller groups.

As the transporter slowed at the far end of its journey, she saw the gendarmes single out one figure and lead towards the van a man who might have been her father, were it not that her father never went out.

The raincoat was like his; there was something in the bowed angle of the head. Some twenty metres farther along, a woman who had a slight resemblance to Renée, but who of course could not possibly be her, pivoted on high heels and was engulfed by the dark porch of Saint-Ferréol.

He was not in the kitchen. Two packs of cards lay neatly on the table. The bed was made. For a long time Ilse sat in the silent room with the cupboard open checking every few minutes that his coat really was gone. The feeling grew that if she looked away for long enough then the coat might reappear and with it the sound of the cards snapping on the table. The piece of cardboard with the typewriter keys drawn on it mocked her. The emptiness of the room was that of a person holding their breath, a person who might asphyxiate from the waiting.

The noises of the house went on, the occasional shriek and laughter, the banging of new clients on the front door, the thudding of feet on the stairs. The world continued to turn as if nothing had happened. It was nearly midnight when Renée came through the curtain with a heavy tread. She locked the door behind her, shooting the bolt and clicking the small table lamp on. "He's been taken to Les Milles. It's a detention camp near Aix. I'll get him in the morning."

"I don't understand. What was he doing away from the house?"

"We went to the photographic studio, just across the road. He didn't have a decent photograph. We never got there. It was bad luck. Where were you?"

"I went to Cassis."

"I see." She had had her hair done and it glinted an unnatural gold. Her mouth turned down, the petulant folds etched deep into each corner. Ilse could not summon any emotion beyond disbelief.

"The photographic studio?"

"He needed a photograph. To make false papers. For an exit visa."

"An exit visa?" Ilse repeated stupidly.

"Yes. Wasn't that what you wanted?"

Ilse felt sick.

"You can spring anyone for cash. I've been to the Préfecture, I know people there. I'll go back in the morning."

The bed was big without him. The smell of eau de cologne brought a lump to her throat. Though she did not expect to sleep at all, Ilse at once fell into a complete darkness.

. . .

The next day, rising through varying levels of sound and greyness to a dull consciousness of everything being strange, she was astonished to see how late it was, nearly noon. Renée reported back that Otto had been transferred elsewhere, she did not know where. One source said that he might be in transit to Paris; another that he was in Gurs, one of the worst such places, in the Pyrenees. It cost money even for this inadequate information. Renée bribed a man of authority in the Commission de Criblage.* The going rate for releasing a refugee picked up in a rafle†️ was two or three thousand francs. A Jew cost more. She went out again in the afternoon to see Carbone, the man she called the emperor of Marseilles. Even he was not able to discover where Otto was.

"You could have bought the Pope himself for what I offered. No deal."

Sitting at the kitchen table, she lit a cigarette. Ilse had never seen her smoke before. It was Virginia tobacco, the kind Raymond brought. Her shoulders sagged.

"Unfortunately, I think he might have been carrying a gun."

There was no point going out and nowhere to go. A moment came in the dull afternoon, as the sky darkened into night, when Ilse began to play patience, shuffling the pack as her father had. The silence in the room had an entirely different quality from the silence she and her father had shared. She noticed the way her hands were made and the cuticles shaped; she noticed the grain of the wood of the table, which ran the opposite way to the grain of the floorboards. She heard the voices in the alleyways. Though the queens came out again and again, of the kings there was no sign.

*The Selection Committee.
†️Police roundup/raid.

TEN

Near Dortmund, January 1941

Even the inside of the carriage had iced up. Frost had eventually silenced the tongue of the heavy fellow who got in with them at Hanover. After Bielefeld, they and he were the last ones left in the compartment. The fat man wiggled a jar of goose fat from his coat pocket, smeared it thickly onto bread with a pocketknife and crammed great chunks into his mouth, rapidly chewing and gulping. The rich smell in the small space was a provocation. Nicolai and Lore exchanged a look. Poor hungry Sabine cried herself to sleep, her breath a cloudy mist. The train inched to a halt just outside Dortmund station. Stamping to warm his feet, the black marketeer heaved down his case from the rack with self-pitying exhalations; it was so heavy, it had to be full of similar jars. He dragged it along the corridor. Nicolai sprang up, pulled the blackout blind down over the compartment door, held tight to the chilly handle. The station came, doors slammed, the train moved on. Nobody tried to come in. He sat.

"My husband hates such men," said Lore. "They make him shake with anger, literally shake."

"He made me feel hungry."

She smiled wearily. "Rest, Nicolai. Try and sleep."

Sabine slept on, cheeks scarlet in the knitted bonnet. The train juddered, buffeted by one passing the other way. Easing up the blackout blind by the width of a curious finger, Nicolai peered out. A long black troop train slid by, an eel through dark waters.

Lore was drooping. He sat, conscious of her head on his shoulder, the weight of a woman's body, slight but definite, her warmth. He sat still and upright, so as not to disturb her. In February he would be fifteen. Already the height of a man, he towered over her. Everything about her touched him: the faint shine on her good stockings, that she had dressed up for the journey, the scuffed shoes, her hand, with a hard bump on the thumb from sewing. He looked at the way her hair fell from the parting, the hairpin, which was working its way out from under the little hat. One side of him was warm, where she lay against his heart.

All through that Christmas of victory celebrations, he had been conscious of her holding herself together, waiting. She was desperate to go to Wuppertal and seek news of her daughter, but had only the statutory day off. Magda was celebrating the coming of Christ with her brother at their farm in the Eifel. The temporary cook was not accomplished; tempers wore thin. Fräulein Lore held their household together. His mother said she could not go away now; she complained that the party season was the worst possible time, that her annual holiday was not yet due. It was true, but she was, as usual, missing the point. The alternative was to lose her altogether. Nicolai had chosen a morning when the house was quiet.

"I've had a wonderful idea, Mutti," he said, smiling broadly. Fräulein Lore had taken Sabine sledding, and his mother, paying bills, which she hated to do, was glad of a distraction. He and Sabine longed to go on a little trip with the Fräulein. It would do them good to visit the countryside; it would be a little holiday. While he fabricated, she played with the gold cigarette box the Colonel had given her, running a finger across its polished shagreen lid.

"Wouldn't you like a bit of time on your own? Away from your bothersome children?" Cunningly, he slipped the bait onto the hook. "You could visit Wolf in Lübeck. He'd love it. It can't be fair that we have you all the time."

"You're being very sweet, darling," and she flicked open the case.

The lighting of a cigarette, for her still a daring gesture, gave him his answer.

It was easy to manage someone when you had stopped caring what that person thought of you, and vice versa. His mother was not wicked; she was just lax. Without his father there, she had become a sloppy version of herself. Plenty of women of her class were loose; he had seen them out on the streets, gallivanting with officers. The war had shaken people up like a kaleidoscope, re-forming them into different colours and shapes. When another shake came, they would sort themselves anew. Her moments with Colonel Oster would submerge into a forgotten past. He would not let it affect him. What mattered was that his father should not find out. The anguish he felt on his father's behalf was so acute, that even now it made his chest ache.

He pushed the thoughts away, went back to studying Lore's face. Even in sleep the little frown remained. Inside her lay the lost child, his lost friend. As the compartment swayed, as his eyes flickered with tiredness, the Ilse of the passport photograph surfaced, the contour map of her features pushing up inside her mother's. The young face emerged sharp for an instant, only to sink down again inside the older one, submerging in a sea of sadness.

"Nicolai, wake up. We're in Wuppertal." Smiling, she touched his shoulder.

He picked up Sabine; her curls lay bright against the velvet collar of her coat. The train, going on to Köln, pulled out. They stood on the dark platform, shivering. There was a trolley bus, but the train had been delayed and they had missed it. She took the case, which was light. They walked from the station, slipping on icy cobblestones through blacked-out streets; Elberfeld announced itself "Jew-free" with a shiny enamelled sign.

"When I was a child it was two villages, this one and Barmen, joined by the railway. When they connected, they gave the valley a new name. Elberfeld was famous from the twelfth century."

"What for?"

"Weaving, beer. The water from the Wupper, you see. In the nineteenth century it was the first place in Germany to introduce legislation for the relief of the poor. I wrote a thesis about it." She gave an ironic smile. "There must have been plenty of poor. It's an industrial town."

"Making?"

"Textiles? I don't know anymore. Who knows what they make in a Jew-free town." She was still smiling.

They struggled up the stairs; he carried the suitcase and the still sleeping child.

"What beautiful children, what a good boy," said the innkeeper's wife, taking off Sabine's bonnet and stroking her cheek. "How old is this little sweetheart?"

Her eyes opened, she stared accusingly. "I'm not little! I'm big. I'm going to be four."

The kind woman came back twice, once with milk, once with a big plate of bread and butter, which the three of them devoured.

They breakfasted late in a wood-panelled dining room. The inn, newly constructed, was substantial. Coming in and out with breakfast, the woman confided that business was good, "bigwigs" stayed there. There was real coffee and rye bread and butter, the coffee boiled bitter but still good with hot milk. A speckled egg appeared, "for the baby," and no ration card was asked for. Sabine soon disappeared after her into the kitchen and did not return. Thick crocheted lace curtains hung at the windows. Heat radiated from the stove, covered with blue Delft pattern tiles. Two sets of windows, an inner pane and an outer, kept the warmth in. The deep sills were crammed with those spiteful green spikes known as mother-in-law's tongue; the scratchiness of them against the lace hurt his eyes.

"What should we do while you're gone?"

He knew that she wanted to go alone.

She shrugged. "There's always the Schwebebahn. It's a special train. The Kaiser rode in it. When I was a child we used to dress up one day a year and ride in the emperor's carriage. Best bonnets and bibs." She was being as cheerful as anyone could. Nicolai smiled back. A very, very long time ago he had been interested in trains.

By mid-morning he had finished the local newspaper and was bored. In the big kitchen a row of peg dollies with smiling faces pencilled on lay on the table. Small squares of check material were going to be their skirts.

"Sabine, we're going on a train. Look, here's your coat."

Standing on a stool, busy gluing fabric to her fingers, Sabine shook her head. In the yard behind the inn were chickens and she had helped feed them. She was going to tickle the pig's back with a stick. There were potato pancakes for lunch and afterwards an apple, specially baked for her in the oven with sugar. His sister did not look up from the dollies, she concentrated, sticking out her little tongue. Wiping wet hands on the apron, picking up a bucket of slops and potato peelings for the pig, the woman could not stop smiling at the child.

"One ticket, please, there and back."

Alter Markt was the nearest stop. Inside the first of the three double cars, a brass plaque explained that the Schwebebahn was the only monorail system in the world to be suspended from a steel rail. The cars rode on the rail, carried by thick metal arms extending down around the rail and mounted to the top of the car. Ten metres above the ground, he enjoyed the novelty, gliding by the black cobweb lace of the trees on the riverbank as the rail followed the curve of the frozen Wupper, the white ice gleaming below. Tilting and turning on the corners, the carriage cut close to the trees; below, thick mounds of virgin snow that had dropped from the branches showed where there had been a thaw, then another frost. A neat track, perhaps that of a fox, disappeared into the woods. Then there were rooftops. The rail hummed over streets for a brief moment, a kilometre or two, before making a neat U-turn within the station house and returning on its track.

On the return journey, obliquely through the trees, a woman who could have been Lore was walking alongside an old fellow leaning on a stick. Closer up, he recognised her grey coat and hat. The man was very shabby with a black coat. A Jew. He knew it at once. How did he know it? Was it the gestures, hands rising and falling? Or was it his anticipation, preknowledge about the Jewish husband? He would trust only the evidence of his eyes. Nicolai got off at the next stop and waited. When she did not come he regretted his impetuosity. Now he had to wait in the cold for the next train. A moment later the old man came round the corner alone, heading away from town.

He followed. When he slowed, so did Nicolai. Peering back over his shoulder, the old man walked faster. So did he, wishing he were not in uniform. Abruptly the fellow fled. Veering right off the icy road, pushing through the hedgerow and losing his stick in the process, he galloped away over the hard ruts of the ploughed field. Nicolai picked up the stick and sprinted along the road bordering the field; the steel tips of his toes and heels rang out on the frosty ground. Across the fields, the black diminishing figure was slipping and stumbling on the rough terrain, the soles of his shoes flapping. Could this tragic clown be her husband? Surely not. He was a rusty old thing, a raven, flapping arms to keep his balance, a black-on-white photographic negative for a comic print.

"Wait!"

He set off across the fields; with his excellent boots, he could easily catch up, leaping across the furrows. Through a long-distance lens, Nicolai saw himself, a brown spider chasing a black beetle along a length of striped mattress ticking.

"Hello! Stop! Your stick!"

He was nearly upon him when the old man bent double, stopped dead. Wheezing terribly, he fought to get his breath, nose dripping. Water swam in his eyes where the cold had hit him, drops which suddenly gathered in one pouchy eye and ran down his cheek. Nicolai saw himself blurring, re-forming, in that terrible stricken gaze.

"It's still the day," he got out at last.

"What?"

"The day."

Nicolai shook his head in puzzlement. There was a place where the plough had sheared the sod, forming a convenient blank ledge; carefully he placed the stick on it and backed off.

"Jews are permitted outside. In the day. Until eight in the evening."

"I mean you no harm. I'm sorry I frightened you. Please. Your stick."

Inching forward, he retrieved it, shaking in his hand.

"Who are you, please?"

"Who am I? Who am I?" The hands rose again. "Whoever you want me to be." He had a gentle, melodic voice. His was a clever face, but the eyes were tragic.

"Where do you live?"

"Nowhere." The old man took a step backwards. Of course, he could not possibly understand.

"I'm Nicolai Bucherer. Forgive me. I should have introduced myself—I'm with Lore."

Again he edged away.

"I mean, are you the husband of Lore Lindemann?"

He shook his head. Another step and another, furtively done, as though these were not his feet taking him away, but someone else's.

"I am a widower," he croaked. "I don't know anyone called Lore."

It was getting worse and worse. Nicolai wanted to say that he was a

Swing Boy, a secret enemy of the state, and not at all what he appeared to be. He wanted to say that he loved jazz and America, and that Jews were his friends. Instead, he felt in his pockets, took all the money he had and held it out. "Please, take it. Please."

The old man looked at the money with contempt. Holding the stick defensively against Nicolai—a dangerous dog to be kept at bay—he retreated.

They whispered in the room, though there was nobody there to hear. Salomon Blumenthal, the old raven, was her father-in-law; it was very strange that Lore had never met him before.

"I was scared of him once. Of the idea of him. But he's so small."

"Is he?"

He dared not say what he had done. In his head, a tiny figure ran in terror across the white fields, no bigger than the peg dollies twirling on a string across the cot in which Sabine slept. If he waited, she would tell him more. The closer they came to her birthplace, the more she had felt the need to confide in him. She had started by telling him that she and her husband had never divorced, had whispered of "Otto" in a station waiting room and the name "Blumenthal" in the quietest outbreath; she had murmured her secrets in quiet patches when a crowded train cleared. All the facts were very peculiar. He watched her frown deepen.

"Otto might have been in touch with his father. What kind of a son does not send a message? But Father Salomon doesn't trust me. Even if he knows, he won't say—not to me. He said his children have all left, only he remains. I don't know if I believe him."

"Why wouldn't he tell you what he knows?"

"Why? What manner of mother is not with her daughter?"

He looked not at Lore's face but at the floorboards painted chocolate brown. Every length bore its pale wounded circle where a boot had scraped paint from the raised knots. "Don't get upset," he said.

"Of course I'm upset."

"Your husband has her. It's not as if she was on her own."

In the long silence, looking at her bowed head, he tried to form a picture of this husband of hers who was wealthy but had lost all his money; a Jew with no religion, a talker who would have joined an army, if there had been one where people like him could fight. The husband was all contradictions.

"He'll look after her. You told me what an idealist he is, a fighter."

"Otto doesn't think like other people. He wouldn't leave Germany. I forced him to. I broke his heart."

Her voice held the deep note of real despair.

"But now he's there, he'll look after her."

She shook her head. "I counted on Willy to save her. And he sent her back. How then can I count on Otto?"

Willy was her brother in Morocco; his friend Ilse had already travelled so very far. "Who could know that France would fall? And so fast."

"Nobody could know," he said.

"I should have gone myself to Paris and fetched her. But I didn't have the money for the documents and the journey, both. I couldn't arrange it. I sent perfect documents, perfect."

Her voice went lower all the time.

"You don't know, Nicolai, how terrible it is to live an unsafe life. I was going to France, to follow him. We had agreed it. We would live in Paris, the three of us together. But I kept thinking, how would we manage? We had no money. What would life on the run be like with a man who can't even provide for himself? Every time I imagined being with him and Ilse, I just couldn't. He's so difficult. We'd never even travelled together." She drew a long, shuddering breath. "I changed my mind. I thought, Rely on yourself. Work hard. Make a home for her here. You can do better."

She dropped her head in her hands.

He waited.

"Otto never loved her, not like I did. She was just any little girl to him—perhaps with a boy, things would have been different. He didn't see how precious she was. When she was leaving forever, he didn't come to say goodbye. That's when I stopped loving him. He only thought of himself."

She wasn't really talking to him, but to herself. These were the thoughts that ran ceaselessly through her mind, causing that little muscle to tug its electrical impulse at the side of her mouth.

"How could I give her to him? I must have been mad. How could he not send her back to me?"

"I don't know."

"I couldn't just walk over the border. I couldn't. They'd have picked me up right away, I don't have the nerves for it. Then there would have been more problems, with papers, more troubles. I couldn't. I knew I'd be trapped, then, in his life. I can't stand his life." She sighed, deeply. "I wanted to make it all safe and right."

"You were right," he said.

"I have been terribly punished," she said. "Was it such a bad decision, to bring my child back into a safe world? Was that so wrong?"

He looked at her helplessly. What did he know? "It wasn't wrong," he said.

"If only Willy had kept her. In Morocco she was safe—I can't forgive him for sending her away. But I did the same thing myself. I sent her away on her own. He did what I did."

She went endlessly over the same thing like the Schwebebahn, which, reaching the end of its route, was forced to turn along the preordained track and retrace the whole circuit.

When he woke in the night, she was still sitting in the same chair. Her eyes were closed, face impassive, but he could almost hear the sharp thoughts running in their circles, blades etching their deep track.

"Please. You must sleep," he said.

"I know why Otto wouldn't return her. To punish me. It is like a bad dream where you run and run and stay in the same place. All the choices were right. I took everything into account. But not his peculiar sense of things, what's right and wrong. I never could think like him. You're right. I think that they are together. They are together in death."

In the morning when he woke she was pacing about, dressed in her coat and hat. "I'm going to my old house in the Landsweg to see the garden I planted. A big, beautiful house, we built it ourselves. Ilse was so happy there."

At the door she turned, smiling brilliantly. "I've been thinking— perhaps I will see her there. Perhaps, who knows? If I wait long enough, she might come to the window and wave."

It was quite hard getting Sabine out of the warm kitchen and away from the innkeeper's wife, who had no children of her own, but Nicolai did not care to be alone. Ilse's face recurred and recurred, locked into his mental album as if he had taken her photograph himself, pored over hundreds of negatives and finally passed just two through the enlarger: little girl, eight, happy; little girl, twelve, sad. Sabine enjoyed the train; he held her up to see the view and, as it tilted on the turns, she laughed. Late in the evening Lore crept in, shivering. She must have spent the whole day wandering the icy streets. The bedrooms at the inn were very warm because the windows had two panes of glass in them, but even beside the stove she could not bake away her chill.

The next day, Sabine refused to leave the kitchen. She stirred puddings, eating half the mixture, her stomach tight as a drum from being fed too much. She made endless paper chains of dollies, regularly decapitating them with scissors her hostess had blunted specially for her use. Lore, who in Hamburg was never still, sat motionless in the bedroom.

"Did Father Salomon say anything?"

"He knows nothing. I can tell that he believes the worst."

Then she did not speak at all. When she went away from him like this, Nicolai felt so lonely. He needed to do something; inactivity made him itch.

"It's stopped snowing. We could take a walk. I'll bring the camera and take some more pictures for you to keep."

She shook her head.

She was a double reflection in the glass and so was he. Everybody had an inner and an outer self. Everyone led a double life in the real world; as children grew, they built an outer shell for themselves. The inner person was tender and had to be protected. The trick to staying alive seemed to be to make the gap between the outside pane and the inner one as narrow as possible. He saw that if the gap was too big, as it was for Lore, a person might perish inside that void.

ELEVEN

Marseilles, January 1941

Ilse suffered with violent stomachache and cramps. She had never felt so ill. When the blood flowed, she understood. La Petite Louise showed her how to make up the pads of cloth and attach them to an elastic belt with safety pins; she told her to wash them out in cold water, never hot.

"How old are you, Schätzchen?"

"Fifteen in March."

"High time you became a woman."

In the night she felt feverish. Then Renée was there, pulling the tangled sheets straight. For a long time the big woman sat holding a damp cloth to her forehead. Ilse did not want to move. She could have lain in that position forever, held in place by Renée's firm hands.

"I'm sorry, so sorry," she said, "about the exit visa." The big hands pressed down. Since her father was taken, she had said this often. "No, child, it's nobody's fault. In war things happen. We'll find him and get him back."

Her father, moved from one place to another, was still in France.

They knew that because, though three months had passed, his name never appeared on the weekly list of deportees.

"But what if the authorities find out that he's the one who wrote the pamphlets?"

"Otto won't tell them. Your father's a veteran when it comes to prisons. He'll have kept his mouth shut. That's the first thing they teach them in the underground." Perhaps Renée was part of the underground too. In the dark her voice sounded different, dampened; they were both depressed. Ilse had known about the gun. She was to blame: she should have taken it and dropped it in the harbour.

She was not a woman. She was a child, alone, wanting Willy, wanting Albert, wanting her parents. In dreams, she climbed the hill in Cassis, knocked at the unyielding house until her hands turned into hammers. An evil old witch barred the door, but Ilse pushed her aside, insisting on going in. Laughter came from behind a door; Albert had only been hiding. He cooked fish, laid sardines in a perfect row alternating heads and tails on a green plate. She typed at the kitchen table. The words came out beautifully even but, like the fish, every other one was upside down. This made his text impossible to read. Albert grew angry and accusing. The book would never be finished because of her mistakes. She woke in a sweat of anxiety, lonelier than ever, and stared sightlessly at the blackout, waiting for the first faint shimmer of day, remembering.

It had been her first impulse to go to Cassis. Albert would know what to do. Faintly alarmed when the door was opened by an old woman, Ilse had stayed, irresolute, in the doorway, unable to believe that he was not there.

"Where did the monsieur go? When did he leave?"

"Last week."

"Are you sure?"

The old woman had shrugged, as if to say she could not understand it either.

"Come and see for yourself, Mademoiselle."

She walked from room to room. There was no trace of Albert. Fear clutched her that he, too, had been taken away.

"No police came, nobody from the military?" asked Ilse in a whisper.

"No, Mademoiselle."

Perhaps the old woman with her hooded eyes had known more than she had said. Perhaps Albert had received his visa for America: that was the only explanation that calmed her. It seemed incredible that he would have left France so abruptly without saying goodbye. Perhaps it was a decision he made because of his book, a good decision. Nothing lessened the feeling of desolation. Nightly, the bad dreams returned.

Renée continued to search for Otto, but Ilse knew not to have hope. She trailed most days to the poste restante, where nobody knew whether letters sent abroad were delivered or not. Everything went through the German authorities. All correspondence was in any case limited to preprinted postcards on which you crossed out words and filled in blanks: . . . *in good health . . . tired . . . slightly / seriously ill, wounded . . . killed . . . prisoner . . . died . . . without news of . . . in need of supplies / money / . . . is working in / is going to / is being put up at.* She sent three of these carefully worded, official postcards to Toni, saying that she was "in good health" but "my father" was a prisoner; she signed them "your friend." No answer came.

Her parents had disappeared out of the world; they existed only in dark places in her head. When her father tried to come into her dreams she woke at once, terrified of what he might accuse her of. In these slow hours her wickedness lay heavily in the corners of the room. She had disobeyed him and as a consequence had lost both him and Albert. She had challenged Otto to bring her to safety and here was the evil result. Often she had woken to his snores and, turning sharply, had pressed the pillow over her head to shut them out, longing for a bed of her own. His absence oppressed Ilse far more than his rasping breathing. She would not lie in the centre in sole occupancy, for that meant he would never come back. Again and again, she shifted over just a few millimetres. Because the mattress sagged in the centre, she had to be vigilant. The old bedstead creaked its protest. On these bitter winter mornings it would not grow light for hours.

Without Otto, she was losing her sense of her mother. Even when they did not speak of her, Mutti had continued to exist in her full strength between them. Her careful mother had made an irretrievable error in imagining that her father would send her back. If only she had joined them in Paris. If only she had realised how much Vati loved her. Love was a more powerful force than she had imagined. "Mutti," she whispered, "what do I do? How shall I ever find you now?" Dry-eyed, she stared at the ceiling, waiting for the drab day.

The girls felt sorry for her. They had a jacket made for her, a poor relation to the beautiful coat Willy had bought her, now outgrown, the nap worn bare. The wool substitute material they clubbed together to buy was thin and scratchy. It absorbed water when it rained and never recovered its shape.

"Look at your tits," said La Petite. "That miserable dress is so skimpy it's indecent."

"You should know," snapped Ilse, then bit her tongue. What was wrong, that she was so bad-tempered? They found her some underwear. The brassiere they offered was pink satin. Tart's underwear. She would have preferred something white, something simpler. Ilse knew that she should be grateful but it was too hard.

"Raymond has got us a man," said Renée. "Un drôle de mec" she called him. That meant an oddity. "A bit of a maniac," she said. "He knows his way round the camps." He would find Otto.

"How do you know he's to be trusted?"

"I've met him, he's not a stranger. He's been here a few times before. This one's not the usual type that'll do anything for money. He's more sophisticated. And he speaks German, so he'll be able to talk to Otto. His speciality is getting people out of France."

"Have you warned him about Vati? About his work?"

"Don't worry. That's a recommendation to this fellow. They're on the same side."

The knock at her door woke her.

"You've got a visitor." It was Raymond's voice. Scrambling into her clothes to unbolt the door, Ilse had an oblique view of a very tall young man with jet-black hair, his head bowed. The stranger smiled. His eyes were so incredibly blue. She stared at the drôle de mec who was going to find her father.

"I'll stay out here, keep an eye on things," said Raymond, shutting the door on them.

"Keep an eye on the girls, he means," said François. "What a bad memory you have, don't you know me?"

She nodded. He took her hand and kept it, turning it over to look at the long scars along the fleshy part of the thumb. Dismayed, Ilse found herself blushing a bright red.

"Did you do what I said?"

Still she could not speak.

"The wound has healed nicely."

"My father—" She was stammering.

"I know. Madame Renée has told me everything. I am going to try and help you."

"You know Madame Renée?"

"Everybody in Marseilles knows her. I've been to this house before. Often." He was smiling. "Some good friends of mine come here a lot."

"Oh," said Ilse. "And this is what you do?"

"I do lots of things."

He was looking around the room, thinking whatever he thought. Then he was once more looking at her.

"Do you have a photograph of him? Just as an aide-mémoire."

Ilse took out the silver frame, turned the little clasp at the back, carefully took out the glass and removed the photograph of the two young strangers. Who would recognise her father from this? She felt a strong urge to keep the little figure of her mother; because her parents stood with their arms entwined, there was no way of keeping one without losing a piece of the other.

"I'll return it, I promise," he said. He studied the photograph. Then she dared to dart glances at him, the beautiful skin, his eyelashes, which were naturally dark.

"What happened to your hair?"

He turned and pulled back the fringe. She saw that the rim of hair at his scalp was growing through, half a centimetre that was almost white. He laughed. "I shall ask the girls to help me dye it. I look just like a German otherwise. Much too obvious." He was already at the door, turning back. "It's curious, when she told me about a father and daughter, I thought it might be you. You see, Mademoiselle, it was obviously meant to be that we should meet again."

The blush returned and did not fade for a long time.

The commotion in the big room above hers started early. François lounged in the bar with his long legs propped up on a bar stool and flirted with the girls, who, fussing around him, were much nicer than their usual morning selves. There was something almost tender in the way the green eyes of La Petite rested on him. Sitting with a towel round his shoulders, waiting for the girl who knew hairdressing best, he read their fortunes.

"You have a long life line. You'll be 'vieux singe.'* But terrible trouble with the heart line. See where it splits here? And here? Three great loves or four. What a terrible flirt you are."

Ilse refused her hand. Evidently he did not remember. Evidently he said these special things to anyone.

"What about children?"

La Grande Louise was serious. For her he predicted six.

"Oh, la pute," said La Petite Louise.

But La Grande was pleased. When the big girl smiled—and it happened so seldom that it was a surprise—she revealed wonderful white teeth, strong and regular. A girl Ilse did not know well, one with round bosoms falling out of her clothes, came in and took charge of the dyeing process. Marielle kept running her hands through François's hair. She had been a hairdresser, but it did not pay so well. She said that they would use vinegar to set it. His problem was that the white halo encircling his head grew so fast. His skin, the pale colour of toffee, which Ilse could not stop staring at, was very smooth and clean-looking, especially when the dye the girl was putting on splashed and had to be rubbed off. When he talked to the girls and laughed with them, Ilse felt a strong burning sensation in her chest. She leant over and took a cigarette from La Petite, saying "I'm nearly fifteen" to deflect any looks, but then dared not light it for fear of coughing. While the dye took, he drew birds on a piece of paper.

"Not bad," said La Petite. The flock wheeled over the page as if at any moment it could leave the edge and fly away. The piece of paper passed from hand to hand. One of the girls dropped it as she grabbed a cigarette and it fluttered behind a sofa. Later Ilse crept back to retrieve it.

She got out her good dresses, too tiny for her to squeeze into, and took them up to Pauline, who worked for Renée part-time. She was a seamstress by trade with a sewing machine at home. She cut the apple-green velvet to pieces, made a short-sleeved top and wide belt, and attached a black woollen skirt to it. She charged only a few francs. Working in a maison de passe,† she said she could afford to be generous to her friends. Pauline talked all the time, even while she was kneeling in front of Ilse with a mouthful of pins, pinning up the hem. Her fiancé

---

*"Old monkey."
†Brothel.

was a carpenter who came from a village outside Aix-en-Provence. As Ilse hemmed the skirt with tiny herringbone stitches and pressed it carefully, she wondered what the villagers would make of Pauline's silk stockings and lace blouses. The girls said that the new dress made Ilse look much older, that it was good enough for a party dress. She scoffed, then, because they were right, dared not wear it. Every day she put on an old hand-me-down skirt and blouse of Renée's that were both much too large.

The soles of her shoes had separated from the uppers so many times that the cobbler could no longer stitch them together. They were like a tramp's shoes, disgraceful shapeless things. The girls clattered noisily along the cobblestones in high wooden platforms. Even with coupons they were very expensive and impossible to walk in. In return for the amber silk, which she had taken a fancy to, La Grande Louise was persuaded to give Ilse her low-heeled black pair, which fitted very well. The clever hands of Pauline transformed the silk into a low-cut evening blouse for the big girl.

Two more weeks passed and still there was no news. Unable to settle to read or think, she paced in her room. It occurred to her that François might visit the brothel at night and see Renée without thinking of her. At eleven o'clock in the evening, when the army boots were coming up the stairs and business would be brisk, she looked through the wardrobe, took out her new dress. Pirouetting slowly in front of the glass in her room, she saw that the girls had been right. Her breasts were prominent when she pulled the belt tight. She had a waist, now, and hips. Though she was still thin, she looked like a woman. She pulled up her hair and caught a sudden oblique view of her mother. She undid her two plaits and brushed her hair hard. It crinkled up across her shoulders, but nothing could be done about that. Red hair was a terrible curse. She gazed at herself critically in the glass and found herself wondering whether some lipstick would improve her appearance. Well, she had none. She pinched her cheeks, to draw a little blood into them. That way, she did not look quite so deathly pale. With a sudden inspiration, she took out her box of treasures and pinned her mother's brooch to the dress, a talisman to protect her. She drew back the bolt, then pulled the door to behind her.

The noise was the first thing, the surge of music and voices as a door opened and a man clattered down the stairs, brushing past her. She went up slowly. The bar was dense with smoke and noise. Pauline came out arm in arm with a soldier who was fondling her breasts and neck, a very young man.

"Are you going to stay all night, my chéri?" she kept repeating to him. She made big round eyes at Ilse as they went on up the stairs. The young man nodded. Halfway up the stairs he stopped, fumbled in his pocket and got a wallet out, then dropped it. Pauline picked it up and started counting his money. There was a picture in it, Ilse saw: a girl, probably his sweetheart. He had not had as much to drink as some of the others. Providing the men were not belligerent, the girls liked them drunk, for then they were more generous, more likely to want to sleep there and that meant that they paid more. They had to pay in advance. La Petite made them wash first and then charged them extra for using her soap.

Ilse went to the doorway. The bar was very full. German soldiers were sitting on the high stools pulled up to the counter; some were lounging with the girls in groups on the low sofas. One was singing "Lili Marlene" over and over. Some men just sat and drank and looked. They could be persuaded into ordering champagne. It was drink that made Renée most of her money. There were one or two civilians there too in ordinary clothes—"mes petits collabos,"* as La Petite called them. There was no sign of her, nor of François. The girls looked pretty, she thought, in their slips or décolleté dresses with plenty of makeup on. She noticed that La Grande was wearing "her" blouse; the big girl glanced at her, but made no sign.

"Liebst du mich? Liebst du mich?"† one of the drunken soldiers kept saying. Because she knew the girls and understood German it was simultaneously familiar and strange. Paul, the barman, stood with his muscular back turned, his head lowered. Raymond's big brother, "the ox," was not as kind as his little brother, "the calf." She could see his wrinkled forehead, grimacing, in the ornate mirror behind. A crate of wines from the cellar sat on the bar and he was unloading bottles onto ice. Any minute now he would turn back towards the room; if he saw her, the game would be up.

Ilse sped up to the floor with the pink roses: standard price. At night, these floors where the girls worked were all forbidden territory to her. She looked down a narrow corridor with four doors; one was open a

---

*"My little collaborators."
†"Do you love me?"

crack. She heard grunting. It was partitioned inside like a dormitory with four beds separated by walls that did not reach the ceiling. The distant bed was occupied. Ilse took a step forward and peeped warily into the room. The tangled bodies on the bed were all knees and white buttocks. Worried that the man was François, she took one more step, then saw the dark pelt on his back. There was a heavy footfall on the stair; another couple was coming up. She fled up to the next storey where the roses on the paper were yellow, the expensive floor with four separate rooms where some men stayed all night. She saw a toothbrush in a glass on the windowsill; a fire in a grate. The light flickering on the walls made this room look homely. A man came out into the corridor, middle-aged, a moustache, braces on a bare chest, smelling of garlic, holding a bottle. His bald head was shiny and looked as hard as stone. "Hola! Hola!" he kept saying.

The bartender, Paul, almost filled the corridor. Behind him was Renée, hard-eyed and furious, hissing, "Salope!"* Ilse hurried down the stairs with the big woman—so nimble—behind her.

At the next landing, Renée caught onto her arm. "Have you gone mad?"

She shook her off, plunged down the stairs. At her curtain, fumbling to draw it back, she was not quick enough.

Renée slammed and bolted the door behind them. She looked her up and down, took in the slight disorder of cotton stockings crumpled where they fell, the cardboard box with its lid askew. "What the hell were you doing up there, all dressed up?"

She did not know what to say.

"Were you thinking of offering yourself?" Her manner was icy.

She shook her head.

"What would your father say to this?"

Ilse went over to the table, picked up the cards and sat down. With bravado she started to lay out the pack. She could hardly breathe. "Well," she said, "it's a brothel."

Renée came forward and leant over the table. Ilse laid a second layer of cards onto the first. Abruptly, Renée lifted a hand and slapped her on one cheek, a slap so stinging and hard that she fell off the chair. She lay on the floor, winded. Determined not to make a sound, she waited for

*"Dirty bitch!"

the door to close behind Renée. She got up, then, and bolted it from the inside. As soon as she lay in the bed, in her usual position, a great anguish rose up in her. Her cheek pulsated. She swallowed her upset and fury, forcing them down like some solid substance that stuck in the throat but had to be absorbed.

In the morning, without makeup, Renée looked old. In the kitchen doorway, hesitating to go in, Ilse realised that she no longer sang in the mornings. She had disliked the sound of her happiness; now she missed it.

"What did you think you were doing last night?"

"Looking for François."

"Ah," said Renée.

"It's not anything like that," said Ilse. "How could you think that? It's because of Vati."

The corners of Renée's mouth turned down in that way she had, which made her seem proud and cruel when really she was neither. She lit another cigarette. She smoked a lot these days. The silence stretched on, was the length of the ash that grew to a centimetre and a half and slipped off, a worm on the floor.

"François will tell us when he finds Otto. Ilse, sit, what did your father tell you about men?"

Of all the conversations she might have had with her father, this was the least likely.

"Did he tell you anything about growing up?"

"Good girls remain virgins. I know all that. Don't worry, I know about sex. I've learnt a lot from the girls." It was true. Ilse knew what a capote anglaise* was; she had long ago asked what the special jug they douched with was for.

"You poor girl." Renée shook her head. "I suppose it's not a father's job." She took a lump of sugar, dropped it in the bowl and poured coffee. She added milk. The coffee was real and smelt delicious. There was only saccharine in the cafés and cups of café national, with the terrible burnt-grain taste. Even the girls only had a brown mass of stuff, confiture de sucre de raisin.† She held the bowl out. Ilse savoured the taste. "I want you to understand what my girls have in common. They're all naive. A

*French letter.
†Grape sugar.

degree of self-deception is required in a whore. You are too knowing for such work."

"I know nothing," Ilse said. "I haven't been near a school for two years. Not since I was thirteen."

"You are ignorant, of course. Very ignorant. But you are not naive." Ilse found nothing to say. "I'll get some books for you. I should have done that before. You should study more. It's what your father wants for you, a better life than this. Ilse, you have to forgive me. We're stuck with each other, we must get on."

"Forgive you? What for?" She pretended not to understand.

"For falling for your father."

"Oh. That." She was squirming.

"Look, it surprised me too. Do you mind it so very much?"

"Why should I?" Of course she minded.

"Sometimes things happen. That we should even meet—who can explain it?"

"I knew—I mean, I know that he cares for you," Ilse said, loathing herself.

The big woman smiled. "I lost my mother and then you came along, you and your father," she said, lighting another cigarette. "The good Lord sent you to me. Let me be a kind of mother to you, just for this time."

This, as much as anything else that had been said, made her feel sick and angry. Nobody could replace her mother. She would never be a daughter to anyone else. "I'm going to make my first communion soon," said Ilse abruptly. She was desperate to change the subject.

Towards evening, Renée placed a box of books in her room: cheap paperbacks, detective stories with lurid covers, Westerns and love stories. Among them was a Bible with a white leather cover and silver bookmark. Where did she get such things? Nothing was ever delivered to the front door; objects just appeared in the house.

Raymond, sitting in La Petite's room, laughed and swirled the blanket like a conjuror's cape until La Petite made him stop. "I'm your conjuror. Appearing by magic. Have you never wondered how I get here?"

Everyone in Marseilles knew that most houses in the Vieux Port were connected through the cellars. They formed a network of tunnels, a honeycomb of connections smugglers had used for centuries to evade customs. Now they hid black market goods or people.

"So François could come that way?"

"Has to. He's getting too well known around here to risk anything else." Then he clammed up and would say no more.

Her private baptism took place in La Sainte Trinité. Ilse found herself thinking intensely and without pain about her mother. She was very sure that her mother would have approved. Four days later she made her first communion. The priest had arranged for her to receive the body and blood of Christ with four other girls. They were all younger than she was, thirteen to her nearly fifteen, but the same height or even taller. She had invited Renée, who staggered her on the morning of the event by presenting her with a white dress and satin shoes. In these clothes she looked exactly like the other girls. It was Renée, too, who understood the importance of getting a photographer to record the occasion. It was a solemn and beautiful moment. All five girls were photographed on the steps of the church. Ilse was intensely happy that the Church had accepted her. Afterwards one of the fathers of the girls came up to Ilse and shook her hand and congratulated her on the generosity of her aunt. It seemed that she had offered to pay for the incense, which was a great luxury. Wearing her white dress, Ilse and Renée walked back to the brothel hand in hand. She hid away the precious baptism and communion certificates. When the church photograph came, it filled the silver frame. That in itself was a blessing.

There was a smell of spring. The old men who sold stumpy winter logs now offered dense bundles of twigs, which made the fire in Renée's grate flare up brightly. This was the epicormic growth Albert had told her about, the old shoots harvested from the lime trees before the new growth started. He had needed to prune and shape his text in just the same way before more could be grown. Aimlessly, she wandered around town. In Paris, at Saint-Sulpice, a blade of light inched towards the place where the priest would stand to celebrate the resurrection of the Lord. Her feet, following their own devices, circled round the Boulevard Dugommier. New letters kept being chalked on walls. First there had been "V" for Victoire. Then the authorities had started adding on a "P" for Vive Pétain. Madame Dumont tapped the wall outside the bar where "VH" was scrawled in chalk. Beaming, she whispered, "Vive l'honneur.* The BBC said to write it."

*"Long live honour."

The son who worked in the customs house had given her a wonderful radio set made by the American Radio Corporation that picked up every transmission, even those from London. "Come upstairs one evening and listen to Claude Dauphin," she said.

"I will, soon." She had never once heard the famous broadcaster. She decided that she would go next week, on her birthday, which nobody knew about. That would give her something to look forward to.

The day of her birthday, a chill wind blew. She could hardly expect anyone to know that the day was special when she had not told them, but the sameness of things was depressing nevertheless. Heading for Madame Dumont's, she was near the tramlines when someone grabbed her from behind. She buckled and nearly fell. François spun her round the other way, back towards the Vieux Port. She struggled to keep up with his long legs.

"Walk. Put your arm through mine. Hurry."

"What is it?"

"Our great Maréchal Pétain is in town. Every hotel combed through—the police are locking everyone up."

The distinctive outline of two gendarmes appeared on the far side of the quay, turning and starting to walk across in their direction.

"They never come this far."

"Today they will. Every house. Do you have papers on you?"

She shook her head. A second knot of policemen stood over near the transporter bridge.

"Shit," said François. "Quick, this way."

They ducked into the next alleyway. Pulling at her arm, he led her into a nearby bar and out at the back. The barman looked, then turned his head away. François opened the door to the alleyway beyond, left it open. But they did not go that way. There was a second building, a storeroom at the rear. Cursing softly and continually in Polish, he pulled her into it. He switched on the light, looked. There was a narrow alcove, which could be used. Swearing and heaving, he pulled the heavy metal shelves loaded with tins forward to make space.

"Go in there." He pushed Ilse into the corner. Then he turned off the light and squeezed himself next to her. Heaving and shoving, with breath rasping from the huge effort, he pulled the shelf a millimetre or two at a time. Then he paused, pulled it again. It was huge and fully loaded. He heaved again. It rocked, he caught it. Nothing fell. Slowly it scraped along the rest of the way. The alcove once more disappeared; the space was filled. Footsteps passed, then returned. The exit door rattled angrily. A moment later she heard the sound of somebody returning. The storeroom door was flung open; a light was switched on. She dared not breathe. Then somebody switched off the light and closed it. There was shouting in the distance. Somebody else put the light on again. This time, the door was left open. A cold draught eddied by. She understood not to speak or move.

Throughout these noises and commotions, Ilse stood with her cheek resting against his chest, her body jammed tight against his. She felt and heard his breathing gradually calming and the steady beating of his heart as it resumed its normal rhythm. She felt his breath on the top of her head and his whole body touching hers. Breathing as quietly as she could, she absorbed his distinctive scent. This combined the olive smell of his skin with a faint sweatiness and the odour of slightly dirty clothes in a way that was not at all unpleasant. It was a very male smell. She closed her eyes, all the better to feel and remain in this state of extreme happiness. Time passed. The room grew quiet.

It was after midnight when they got back to the house. He opened the door, told her to lock herself in quickly.

"Don't tell Renée I went out, please, I'm not supposed to."

He touched her nose playfully with one finger. "Who d'you think was so worried she sent me in search of you? I'll be back tomorrow. I've had a tip-off. I think your father has been in Gurs all along."

His footsteps echoed down the corridor. Then he was gone. Renée had been scared, and with good cause. The newspapers reported that tens of thousands of refugees and "dangerous elements" had been rounded up, to keep all potential harm out of the way of the Marshal of France. Many had been locked up for good, Renée said, and some of these poor people would never come back. Then she made the sign of the cross. The Lord looked after his own and God in his mercy had returned Ilse safe.

For a long time she could not sleep. For her fifteenth birthday Ilse had received a gift after all, an extraordinary one. Her father was alive, could be saved. François had risked everything to find her. Her life, which had slowed to a standstill, was starting again. She held a pillow against her and, eyes tight shut, concentrated on remembering the smell of him and trying to feel his warm breath on her cheek. She had complete recall of the rough stuff of his jacket, the faint stubbles on his cheek. Her body remembered. He was not like other men, the sort who came to the brothel. He was completely different.

The next day, she knew that François had come the underground way for the hand she shook was icy. "Bonsoir, Mademoiselle." He smiled delightfully, though his teeth were chattering. He sipped a tisane, warming his hands while Renée counted out the huge sum of twenty thousand francs. Ilse waited for Renée to turn away. Then she signalled to François, an imploring pantomime. He did not understand, so she mouthed the words "Take me with you. To Gurs."

Then he understood and winked. "I'm taking Mademoiselle. In case I don't recognise him."

"Good," said Renée.

"We leave at four."

"That's good," said Ilse as calmly as she could. It was almost frightening that they took her at her word. She went through her treasures: the photograph frame, the perfume, the brooch. These she left in the cardboard box on the table, so they would be easy for Renée to find. She imagined herself doing brave and remarkable things. But when morning came, she felt very tired and too young to do anything. She was not sure what she should take. In the end she just put her nightgown into the red leather case. She took soap and all the money she had. When François took off the beret, she saw that his hair, cut very short, was now a bright copper colour, just like hers. Even his eyebrows were red.

"Are you laughing at me, siostrzyszka?"

"What does that mean?" she asked, remembering exactly what it meant.

"You're my little sister now," he said and handed her an envelope. He had got a set of temporary papers for her and sauf-conduits, official-looking documents with many stamps in them. They would not hold up to too much scrutiny, he said, but they would probably do. They were in the name of Laure Benoît. He was Luc Benoît. That he had by chance given her her mother's name was a secret joy.

They could not take a train from Marseilles, where the stations were crawling with police. She stood beside a road going north until suddenly a lorry slowed down and his red head was at the window. The driver took them towards Aix-en-Provence; they would get a train there. He was a fat man, who talked too much. Ilse sat jammed beside the window, with

François in the middle. Something about François made people tell him things.

"Thank God we lost the war," the man said. "Or else we would still be governed by those left-wing fuckers of the Front Populaire. If there's one thing I hate, it's a fucking communist. And a fucking Jew."

Ilse bit her tongue. François just smiled and passed him cigarettes. In return for another ten, the driver agreed to be diverted to the station. At Aix, they waited together on the far end of the platform, companions on a bench. He lit a cigarette, blew a smoke ring, savouring the taste.

"Thank God for Raymond. What a pro. Best smuggler in the business."

"How did you meet him?"

"Through friends. Friends of friends."

"What happened to you, after Chartres?"

"I took the voie de terre."*

"What does that mean?"

"I was demobilised, from the Polish Legion. Then I came to Marseilles."

"What did you really do?"

"Mademoiselle, you are very nosy."

"You can't call me 'Mademoiselle,' " she said with glee. "You have to call your sister 'Laure.' "

They crisscrossed the countryside in small trains. The first night was spent south of Toulouse, in a station waiting room. It was very cold and she wondered at his ability to sleep.

"Do you believe in God, François?"

"Luc," he said. "No. But I'm a Jew, absolutely and forever. Born one and I shall die one. It's inalterable, what you are born."

"Oh," she said. She, of course, was born a nothing. Long ago, her father had said that François was "one of us." Actually, it had never occurred to her that he was Jewish. Now it all made sense. She thought about it.

"Because Vati always says that religion doesn't matter. He doesn't believe in it."

"For a Jew it does. If we abandon our God, then we've lost everything," he said.

*Ground route.

"But you just said you didn't believe in God," she said.

François laughed. "But what is there to say that he doesn't believe in us?"

He stretched out on the wooden seat and fell back asleep at once. She stared at his hands with their long delicate fingers, the crooked fourth finger of his right hand with a bump on it where as a student he must have held the pencil too tightly. His long legs could not fit onto the bench and one foot twitched in the big workingman's boot. She kept glancing back at his face, the curve of his mouth, his eyes in case they suddenly opened. There was something cruel about the red hair that made him look peculiar, the strong colouring against his honeyed skin gave him the air of a made-up man, a beautiful clown.

They spent the second night in a village called Pontacq, beyond Tarbes, to be fresh for the visit to the camp, which lay between Pau and Oloron. It was a scruffy place, straggling houses on scrubland with chickens running wild. There was a bare farmhouse with a couple of tables in the front room that called itself an inn. It had a stinking latrine at the back that half the village seemed to use. The husband was off somewhere, the wife keeping shop. François joked and charmed her into wringing the neck of one of her precious chickens to make them a good supper. They had not eaten that day and the smell of the chicken roasting made her mouth water. She watched François take his plate over to the young woman and sit beside her. Ilse stripped flesh from bone. Her appetite was fading and she wanted to look away from their greasy smiles. The woman bent flirtatiously to light his cigarette, brushed against his arm as she offered another glass of wine. Upstairs, keeping her eyes tight shut and lying with the heavy pillow over her head, she could shut out neither the woman's cries of pleasure nor the heavy rocking noise of the marital bed. The cheap romances Renée had given her described courtships full of misunderstandings and reconciliations, always leading to a kiss and the promise of marriage. Those things only happened in books. Real life was much closer to the brothel.

In the morning, on the last train, she fell heavily asleep and François had to shake her awake as the train drew into a small, pleasant-looking town. This was their destination, Oloron Sainte-Marie. They crossed a narrow bridge, then waited a long time for a bus, which never came. They walked. It had rained heavily here, and the ground was wet and hard going.

"Remember," François said. "Poor Alain is my brother-in-law's brother."

"Poor Alain."

Poor simpleminded Alain loved children but was never usually let out on his own. In the confusion of the times, a simpleminded person could be lost anywhere, could be picked up and would not know where he was or why. This was their excuse, so they could look for Alain through every camp.

The land was an endless flat swamp, cut in two by a dead straight road. The camp stretched into the distance, flanked with thick barriers of rolled barbed wire to keep people both in and out. All was mud, except for the road, which, rising a metre above the plain, was good tarmac with a thick layer of dirt on it. Beyond lay more wire and rows of makeshift barracks. There was not a single tree to be seen, not a blade of grass. Just people and earth like a woodcut of the Day of Judgement she had seen in a museum long ago, in which the flat earth split asunder to reveal hellfires. All the prisoners here were women and some came running over when they saw the two of them toiling along. A sudden buzzing noise grew louder and a small plane came over the camp swooping low. All the women turned to the plane and looked and waved—some even cheered. One woman in the crowd kept on waving after the others had stopped. She kept pace with them, staring at Ilse.

"Hello, my dear!" she kept calling in German. "My dear—do you have makeup? Lipstick? You see—I have a rendezvous with a gentleman." She laughed and pointed up at the sky.

Ilse shook her head. "I don't wear lipstick," she said in French.

"You can just throw it over to me," she said.

"I'm sorry. I don't have any."

"Goodbye," said the woman, turning away and walking off very upright on her high heels, which sank into the mud.

Two hundred metres from the gate, a rough-looking wooden hut served as a bar and shop. François told her to wait outside. She got out the rosary beads the priest from La Sainte Trinité had given her and started to say her catechism. She needed to be patient while they waited for the sergeant François knew to come on duty.

It was some time before François emerged with a man in uniform, a thickset man who looked at Ilse and smiled. "So this is the little nun," he said.

Ilse liked that.

Well-fed and friendly, the sergeant had a direct and open way about him. All the way past the gates and through the maze of barbed wire he chattered on. He was a farmer's son, one of five, born and bred in the Pyrenees. The farmland was poor, he said, it did not have enough work for all the boys of his family. What was a man to do to earn a living? Gurs, he said, was the major holding centre for German prisoners, for politicos and troublemakers generally. Most of the riffraff picked up in Marseilles and along the coast would end up here. The guards worked harder and longer hours than in any camp in France, yet, he said, this work paid so badly. Out of sight of the offices and other guards, he smilingly pocketed a big roll of francs.

The men's part of the camp was a couple of hundred metres on. They went from one block to the next, peering into each barrack. Each section held dozens of crude wooden huts with shallow ditches round them. There were not even windows, just holes where glass should have been, wet places on the mud floor inside where the rain came in. The men sitting or lying here looked stubbly and grey, thin and very dirty. There was no place to put anything, no tables or chairs, just rows of soiled mattresses stuffed with straw directly on the damp floor. Some read, others played cards, many just wandered around. Some men looked up as they passed but most seemed too lethargic even to look. Each place offered another view of hopelessness, of misery.

"What do these poor devils eat?"

"Bread, a loaf each day. Vegetables, mostly chick peas, a little soup. It's difficult, in war, to feed them properly."

"What about heat?"

The sergeant shrugged. There were no stoves. It had been a bitter winter and though it was now April the weather had scarcely improved.

"Can they get extra food, if they have the cash?"

The sergeant looked at him. "You know, Monsieur, anything can be bought."

There was a further section of the camp François pointed to, one set apart and flanked by a double layer of wire. A couple of gaunt figures stood there, looking out.

"Ah, you can't go there. That is the barracks of the undesirables. You know. Political prisoners." He made an unmistakable throat-slitting gesture.

"Can we look?"

He shook his head. "Your relative couldn't possibly be there."

In the next block, a bearded old man in a coat flapping like a scarecrow's jumped up and started grunting and capering around.

The sergeant laughed. "There's one of our crazies. We can't get a word out of him. I don't suppose that's your madman," he said.

"Yes," said Ilse suddenly, gripping François's arm and squeezing it very tight. "That's him."

She stood stock-still. His hair was very long. His face looked so ravaged and desperate, one eye looking past her and the other at some distant place where he had never wanted to go. Albert came forward and seized Ilse, staggering a little, and with the desperate cunning of the newly resurrected swung her round, pressing his beard against her in an insane embrace.

"Otto's not here. Gone, sent away," he whispered. "Get out." His voice was thick and rusty.

"Come on," she said, taking his arm. He smelt bad. He staggered. She began to lead him towards the door. Somebody in the barracks started to shout. A couple of men came running up and seized her arm, too, as if she could take anybody she chose. She saw François's face, alive with intelligence and looking at them.

"It's him," she said again.

Between them, they held him up.

"Say nothing," she said to Albert under her breath.

"The idiot brother," she heard the guard saying.

"Brother-in-law's brother, not in my family line," said François. How clever he was to deny the bloodline. As they came out into the air, François took a lot more money from his pocket and stuffed it in the pocket of the sergeant's uniform, very quickly and deftly. It was done before they rounded the corner into sight of the other guards. "My friend," he said, "this poor fellow is very sick, as you can see. It would be good to get him to the hospital with as few formalities as possible."

With Albert stumbling between them, they walked towards the main gate. They paused twenty metres away and the sergeant went up to the guard at the gate, pointing to them. More money changed hands. In just a moment the guard waved them through. And their luck held: a bus could now be seen heading towards them. Sitting at the very back, Ilse held on to Albert's arm more gently. His eyes closed, he seemed half unconscious. Whispering well below the labouring engine, she told François who this stranger was and that Albert had said her father was not at Gurs. "Renée won't mind the money going on him," she said, hoping that this was true.

At Pontacq, the innkeeper's wife, no longer smiling, had to be paid a good deal to let them stay for an afternoon while they washed Albert and his clothes. They got rid of the beard and most of the lice. Solid food made him retch, but the chicken bones delivered up a thin soup, which he managed to keep down.

Albert saw his deliverance as miraculous, said over and over again that it was the red case she was carrying that had caught his eye. "Your father"—his hands wavering in the air conveyed something big and wholly indescribable—"he's a brave man. Remarkably brave."

There were a great number of things that Ilse wanted to ask, but these words with their horrible implications silenced her. Inside the house, a murmuring discussion went on. The night was clear. She and Albert sat on a rough bench outside the backyard behind the house, where the last scrawny hens were pecking. When she leant her head back against the wall, she could see stars. In Marseilles, even in the middle of the night there was life somewhere. Here, there was not even the sound of a distant car. Here, if a dog barked, the neighbours would know about it.

In a moment François came out. "We can stay the night."

He sat beside them, lit a cigarette. It was very dark, very still, a full moon lit the trees. Inside the house the woman started humming some song.

"So where is Otto?" François asked.

"Deported to Germany," said Albert.

Ilse's blood hammered in her head. She reached for one of François's cigarettes, could not strike a light. He steadied her hand, struck a match, went on holding hers, for comfort, in his warm one. The lit ember of her cigarette wavered in the dark. When she had finished it they sat on, not saying anything. His touch shrank the cosmos to this one point, her hand trembling in his. She heard Albert coughing, stared at something or nothing that might be the outline of the trees or the henhouse.

"Albert, who betrayed you?"

His face, when he turned to her, held such a strained expression. Perhaps he had become deaf or did not understand.

"I mean, in Cassis?"

Then his face changed and he smiled at her, more like the old Albert. "It was good that the house was on a hill. I was standing at an upstairs window and I saw the police coming. They could only be coming to me. I had five minutes to hide my papers. That was my good fortune."

"Good fortune?" she said. "But why?" She thought of the huge effort he had put into fabricating so many sets of papers and always being en règle.

"I hid my book, that was the important thing. A manuscript in German—that would go straight to the Gestapo. They would soon work out who wrote it. Then I thought—leave the papers. Without the papers I could be anyone. But it might be that with them, I am dead. I remembered what your father had said about the pink passport and the green. Otto and his advice, always good advice. It worked, you see, because in the roundup there were many of us. Since I didn't have papers, they pushed me in with a vanload of similar misfits. The ones with papers went in a different lorry, straight to the Gestapo. I played the fool. If nobody recognised me, I thought I might get away with it. One day I saw myself in a piece of mirror and saw I had become the madman. I didn't worry anymore. My old mother wouldn't have known me."

"Then the papers might be there still?" François was interested.

"They might."

"But Albert, who gave you away?"

"Who knows? Perhaps the man in the shop or the landlady. Someone in the village. A Jew up on the hill, with money, is a nice catch. There is always a payment."

The knock on the window startled them all. The woman's face was pale.

François let go of her hand, stood and stretched. "Time to go in," he said.

"We'll be one minute. Albert, Vati had no papers, there was nothing to identify him," said Ilse.

"No."

Albert's name was on a list. That was why, in Paris, her father had protected him. Of course her father was on a list, too.

"Tell me about Vati. You must."

"They put him in the middle section, behind the heavy wire." She nodded. "Where they keep the real tough nuts. The political prisoners. Separate from the others."

"Go on," she said. She was beginning to understand why it had taken so long even to find out that Otto was in Gurs.

"I'd have been there too if they'd realised who I was. At first, I couldn't get near enough to speak to him." The hands appealed for understanding. "Because they thought me mad, I didn't count. In the second week I tried again. He'd seen me. He was waiting. I went as close as I could. I said something idiotic, how are you? I could see how he was. He smiled at me. There was a guard coming into sight. When he saw me at the wire, he raised his rifle, so I started to mumble and play the fool. I thought—well, there will be another moment. Get away quick. But in the morning the place was empty. The Kundt Commission* must have had him on their list. They were all deported back to Germany."

"Are you sure?"

Release and food were exhausting him. His eyes were closing.

"Albert. Don't go to sleep yet. What happens to them when they get to Germany?"

He opened his eyes and then shrugged. "They say the camps there are not as bad as Gurs. Some people want to go back, you know."

His hands lifted and then fell, resigned, between his thighs. His good eye stared at the ground. Ilse felt queasy. He had never fabricated an untruth before. He was very bad at it.

"They knew who he was. They knew."

Albert said nothing.

"Albert. That's why he was with the undesirables?"

"They knew he was German," said Albert.

"But I can't understand it. He knew the rules," she said, "never to say anything. Nobody in the German underground ever says anything." Then she understood. Of course they had tortured him: a man with no papers, a man carrying a gun. They must have hurt him terribly, to make him talk. "All men are des espèces de con,"† she said fiercely.

Albert touched her arm. "Your father—he said something. When I said, How are you? It's all I managed. He said, 'The situation is hopeless, but not serious.' He was smiling."

"Smiling?" She blew her nose. He nodded. His good eye met hers. This was not a lie.

"Let's go and sleep. It's a long journey tomorrow."

*Gestapo agency in unoccupied France.
†Shits.

Albert slept. Ilse sat at the window and looked at the moon. Round and round her head went those improbably gallant words of her father, who knew the rules and broke them, who was so hopelessly brave.

Remotely located in the foothills of the Pyrenees, inland from Port-Vendres, the shepherd's hut was conveniently close to the border with Spain and freedom. Ilse and François took the two wooden stools the hut contained outside, sat with their faces turned to the weak April sun. Though François had insisted that they recover the papers Albert had wedged between the dresser and the kitchen wall in Cassis, the wait for them truly irked him. From Cassis to Marseilles, then along the coast to this little harbour town had to take another day, perhaps two.

"Are you sure it's worth the risk," Ilse asked, "and the delay?"

"No. He could offer a refus de séjour,* if you prefer. I've even met one fine fellow carrying a certified French translation of the *Deutsches Reichs-Register* detailing his deprivation of citizenship. Perhaps they will let Albert over the border to Spain with that, perhaps not. Then he can spend a few years kicking around in a Spanish jail, waiting for the Gestapo to pay a visit. Or he can use an excellent set of papers and from Lisbon get all the way to America. You choose."

His sarcasm pained her. In a moment she tried again. "Have you taken so many people across?"

"Enough. British pilots. A couple of Poles. Any Jew who'll pay enough," he said savagely. She could not fathom what she had done to make him so angry, so restless, so perverse.

Albert was resting. Shaken about on a lorry with no load, just folded sacks that scratched, they had rumbled on country roads through the centre of France for days with little to eat and nowhere to stay, always heading east. Reaching Perpignan at last, it had taken another weary day to get from there to the hut. It was primitive and miles from the nearest shop, let alone the nearest village. Ilse was glad of the rest for Albert, whose legs visibly trembled with the effort of the last steep slope. He would need all his strength for the climb across the mountains to Spain.

"Whoever collects your papers will bring your book, too, Albert. Or shall we abandon it?"

*Refusal of permission to remain in a place, i.e., a document which is invalid.

"You're flirting with me," he said. "I like it. But, ma chère mademoiselle, it's not necessary for anyone to take a risk on my behalf. I don't care about the book. I don't care about the papers. I am happy here, with you."

She could not believe him. "It's my work, too," she said. "You must have your papers, then you can get through Spain and into Portugal."

The main thing was that Albert had hope. That made all the difference. Soon, she too would recover a feeling of hope.

From the high ground behind the hut Ilse recognised the small stocky figure picking his way up the rough path. Raymond carried a suitcase on his head, Moroccan style. She was so happy to see him. They embraced with real warmth. She laughed at him for being so bristly, for he was one of those men who had to shave twice a day, joking that he was a "vrai poilu."*

"Where's François? Those bastards have issued a decree that all border areas must be clear of foreigners within ten days. That was a week ago and it's taken me the best part of three days to get to this godforsaken place."

"He's gone down to the town."

François, restless for days, had business he did not choose to tell her about.

"Did you get them?"

"My little Ilse. Can Raymond fail?"

Raymond opened the suitcase with a flourish: inside was a bundle of papers, which Ilse recognised, and some of Otto's clothes. Renée had sent underclothes for her and a sweater. Albert, proud father, carefully took his manuscript and held it on his knee. Later, Raymond and François talked at length.

Early in the morning, awake with the sun, Ilse saw François going up the side of the hill, leaping from boulder to boulder in impossible jumps which only his long legs could have managed. Presently, he came back down. His whole body expressed restless energy, the longing to be gone. Raymond came and stood beside her.

"He's cross with me," she said.

"Not you. He's angry with the world."

"Why?"

*"Real hairy man"; also World War I term for a French soldier.

"Warsaw, his family, the news is bad. All the Jews have been herded into a ghetto, a tiny crowded place. No food. Now the Germans are using them as forced labour."

"Is that where his little sister is?"

Raymond shrugged. "He didn't mention a sister."

A stranger came up the path: the guide. He and François conferred at length. Albert put on her father's raincoat, which, far too short for him, flapped round the knees. He took off his ruined boots and put on the smart shoes that, in another life, Renée had chosen for her father. Ilse could see from the way he pushed his feet into them and laced them up that they were too small, but he said nothing.

François came back into the hut in a fury. "He won't do it. Not today. Not tomorrow. He doesn't know when. The little bastard says he has to go somewhere. It's not money, we offered plenty. And the weather is perfect—it may not stay so good."

"I'll take him," she said. "Show me the map." But despair filled her at the sight of the brown ridges and green shadings, the little symbols. She could not do it. She could recite the départements of France, but she had not learnt any kind of map reading. She could not imagine how any-one could possibly follow such a shapeless thing. Albert saw the look on her face and took it. His good eye tried to focus on the page.

"Perhaps, if you could get a magnifying glass?"

He held it nearer, then farther away, then with an apologetic, gentle shrug, handed it back. "We will do it in words."

"What are you talking about?" François's tone was sharp.

"She can memorise it. She has total recall. Ilse, how did you cross France?"

Ilse looked away from François and spoke quietly. "My mother taught me my journey. So no matter what happened, I wouldn't panic."

Learning the map in words was easy; the guide told her the journey, repeating each phrase twice, then she said it back to him. François went with them as far as the clearing, to test her prowess.

"Tell me?"

" 'Past the empty stable and then take the path to the left and con-tinue. After four hundred or five hundred yards notice a boulder and then a clearing. Bear right,' " she said.

"Au revoir and good luck!" He shook hands with Albert. Then he leant forward and kissed Ilse on each cheek, twice. How ready he was to let them go. When Raymond embraced her, he put his arms right round her. She kissed his bristly cheeks four times, then he hugged her again, told her to take care. Ilse watched François lope away down the path. He did not look back. He was thinking of his family, of the sufferings of his sister and others in Warsaw. Ilse told herself that this urgency was natural. She was rooted to the spot by the set of his head on his shoulders, by the easy way he swung his pack, by the brilliance of his hair, which the sun turned to coppery fire so that even as he diminished, he was a beacon that the eye could not bear to abandon.

The journey would take five hours if the weather remained fine. It was a beautiful clear day. To one side the hills sloped gently down to the sea. Soon she would begin to feel calmer. She had put the manuscript and Albert's papers in the red case, which already seemed rather heavier than it had when they left. She shifted this from one hand to the other. On her back was a knapsack with her papers, provisions, the clothing Renée had provided. If the Germans caught them, the manuscript would destroy both of them. She had not even bothered to discuss the matter with Albert.

"Don't be angry about François leaving," said Albert.

"I'm not angry," she said and, because she could not help herself, "I don't think he knows that I am a woman."

"He knows you're a woman," said Albert. "Ilse. He knows. It is much safer for a young lady to be taking people about than for him to do it. Two men attract attention. A man and a girl can get away with anything."

Ilse felt her mouth set into a mulish line. High above, as promised, and to the left, lay the mountain crest.

Albert reached out and took her hand in his moist one. "Can you forgive me, my darling girl? For being here instead of your father?"

"There's nothing to forgive," she said. They walked.

"Say something."

"Otto wrote well, didn't he?"

"Yes. He's a man of strong opinions," he said.

"You're a writer," she said. "It's your business to fabricate. But Vati didn't make things up."

"Not 'didn't.' Say 'doesn't.' "

A text floated into Ilse's head, one of her father's that Renée had asked her to translate into French: *The Russian and French revolutions* *produced first the wild hope of freedom and then terror, devouring the people in waves of blood. What we behold here in France is the triumph of Deutschtum*—accomplished in a typically thorough fashion, quietly going forward day by day in an orderly way and expelling the Jews—the capitalists—without a soul protesting. The murders, when they come, will be very quiet and nobody will notice or, if they do, care.*

"He's in Germany now. His homeland. It's all happening quietly," she said. "If nobody protests, if nobody changes anything, then things go on and on, and everything goes horribly wrong. So he was right. People have to be made to care. All the time he was right."

Albert would need a rest soon. The shoes were clearly pinching and the soles were slippery. It was as much as he could do to manage himself. The coat flapped open and seemed to Ilse to hamper him. Her father's coat, so thin, had not protected him from anything. Now Albert wore it. Albert, all along, had thought to save himself and also to save her. But who could save her? Only she could. It was the unalterable character a person had that ordained all that would come to pass and nothing could ever be done to change it. She gave him a drink from the water flask. While he rested, she lay flat on her back, staring into the brilliant, empty sky.

They strained up to the narrow ridge above. From the summit of the mountain they looked down steep cliffs which split the sea, so much so that on one side the Mediterranean had glitter and brilliance, while on the other it seemed calmer and a different shade, the colour of green slate. Turning, they felt the warmth on their faces. It was a good place to rest. There was even a flat boulder to sit on. Raymond had given Ilse two hard-boiled eggs, a pear, dry sheep's cheese and bread. Albert spread a handkerchief he found in his pocket: Renée's fine linen, the folds sharp, never before used. Carefully they laid out the feast. Ilse tried to be slow with her egg.

Above them, vultures circled. Albert saw them first. "I hope they don't know something we don't," he said. "Here it's perfect. This moment. From this point, all is downhill." He lifted up his hands to the sun. "Herr: es ist Zeit. Der Sommer war sehr groß†—lay your shadow on the sundials and loose your winds over the meadows."

---

*Germanness.
†"Lord: it is time. The summer was very great."

"Go on."

"I'll tell you the last bit. Then we'll go back and do it from the beginning.

> "Wer jetzt kein Haus hat, baut sich keines mehr.
> Wer jetzt allein ist, wird es lange bleiben
> wird wachen, lesen, lange Briefe schreiben
> und wird in den Alleen hin und her
> unruhig wandern, wenn die Blätter treiben."*

"Who wrote that?"

"Rilke. A great poet."

"Tell me more."

She listened. Rilke filled a good piece of mountain and brought them nearly to the frontier, where it would be dangerous to speak.

"There may be guards patrolling on the road. French sentries, looking after the border," she told him. Then it was a long, silent walk, with Albert stumbling over stones and exhausted long before they saw the red roofs of Port Bou, the Spanish border station. Ahead was a proper road, with tarmacadam, one that led straight down to safety. She tucked the red case under Albert's arm.

"When you're at the bottom, show them your papers. They'll let you through."

"What do you mean?"

She smiled at him. Dear Albert, still he did not understand. He had a dazed look.

"You're not coming with me?" His voice trembled a little. He had only just realised it. For Ilse, the certainty had been growing for miles. Albert took both her hands. "You know how I remember your father? Talking in the café, telling everyone what to do, knowing everything. You're getting to be just like him. Must we part?" But he knew, of course, as he always knew everything about her.

"Café Tournon. Tuesdays at three o'clock," she said. "When we meet again after the war. That's the place. Don't forget."

---

*"Who has no house will not build one now. / Who is alone will long remain so / will wake, read, write long letters / and wander restless in the avenues as the leaves fall." From "Herbsttag" ("Autumn Day") by Rainer Maria Rilke.

"I will always remember everything about you and for you, Ilse," he said. "Franzosen und Russen gehört das Land.* The sea belongs to the British. But we Germans possess the undisputed mastery of the airy empire of dreams." He was smiling. "My friend Heine wrote that, I think just for you. My dearest, my darling girl," said Albert. His good eye was so full it seemed to be floating, the water spilling out and now running down one side of his cheek. He repeated the phrase. Then he bent and kissed her hand. Carrying the little red case, he trudged away. He looked very old. For a long moment she watched him go. He turned and waved, and she waved back until he was gone.

The way back was a gentle incline and then grew steep. She raced along. She would be back in France by nightfall. It was not good to be out in these remote places too late. Though tired, though alone, she would not remain so. That was why she was not at all afraid. It was her jingle-jangle game, to follow the instructions backwards. She knew her way. She knew what direction the village was, where to catch the bus along the coast. Ilse found that she was singing an old song, a German song. She changed it to the Marseillaise. "Allons, enfants de la patrie— le jour de gloire est arrivé!"† She sang at the top of her voice and, light as a child, floated down the path.

Two months later, early on a brilliant June morning as the fishing boats came in to port with their catch, Ilse stole out of the house. She skipped down to the harbour, trailing a hand over the faceted stones of the Maison Diamantée for luck. Raymond insisted that she was not to wait, not even for five minutes, if he was not there. She was just to walk on by. The anxiety she felt at another delay, another frustration, was instantly assuaged when, from the other side of the tramlines, François was visible. He was the tallest man in the little queue at the base of the bridge waiting to cross the harbour. They took the lift up to the top, walked across. The view was magnificent. François was in great good spirits; she hated it when he frowned. He took her hand and squeezed it. When he let go, the touch always remained.

"Are you sure you want to do this?"

"I have to fight, well, try at least. My father fought."

*"The land belongs to the French and Russians."
†"Let us go, children of the motherland—the day of glory is here!"

She needed to be more active, if only because she could not bear to be left alone with her thoughts.

"Bravo. There are some rules you have to remember. Of course, the first one is easy—if you are picked up by the police, you know nothing."

"Very good," she said, though her heart had skipped a beat. If she was picked up and recognised as a German, she would be sent to Gurs.

"I am your only contact in Marseilles, or anywhere. You know nobody else."

"Very good."

Of course, she already knew Raymond and Paul and Renée and the girls.

"If they take you, and release you, afterwards I will never contact you again. Because you won't be safe. I would walk past you in the street. You would have to promise to do and say nothing, not to know me."

"I see," she said, though she did not.

"Do you promise?"

"I promise. When do I start?"

"You started when you took Albert. You're a veteran. I'll come to you when I need you."

"I'll be on constant alert."

She had succeeded in amusing him. Down on the quayside a woman had a bucket with mimosa in it: he bought her a sprig and, smiling, held it out. How bright the day was, his long shadow stretching out on the cobblestones, his eyes narrowed against the light, holding her there. Already the moment was passing. He moved on ahead. She slowed her pace to a crawl, as if that could slow him down and make him stay. "Remember. If you want to back out, you can," he said.

Ilse shook her head. "You're not scared."

"It's different for me. I'm already dead."

But he was smiling, as brilliantly as before. He was five metres away, then ten, walking fast, hands in his pockets, whistling and never looking back.

In October, the mistral blew. She cycled slowly past the poste restante, decided to go in. There was always the faint hope of something from Toni. But, as usual, there was nothing for Mademoiselle Benoît.

"Where do you go on that bicycle of yours?" Renée asked.

"Nowhere much."

François had obtained it for her; she kept it safe in her room. It was a very good ladies' bike, hardly used at all. The pump was specially hollowed out. In it she carried underground pamphlets and newsletters and the new issue of *Libération*, which she kept concealed under her wardrobe. Nobody stopped girls. Without the bike it was impossible to be a courier.

"Are you all right, Renée?" Ilse put a pan of water on to boil, watched it carefully. The gas went off so often; it was easy to forget that it had been turned on. Every day La Petite scanned the Death by Domestic Gas column in the *Nice-Matin* to check on her friends and relatives along the coast. She turned and looked at Renée, who hardly cooked anymore. She had lost weight, was becoming a shrunken version of herself.

"On vivote. On vivote.* I have something for you. Here." Renée rummaged in a drawer, then held out a lipstick. Ilse twisted it up, signalled thanks with a blown red-applied kiss. It was brand-new. "Made in Germany," said Renée with a lopsided smile.

Ilse decided that she would go to mass the next day after her round to say a prayer for Renée and Otto, and for her mother. She felt particularly guilty about Renée, from whom secrets had necessarily to be kept. She would never approve of her doing this work. For Renée, Ilse remained a child.

Raymond was bemoaning his lack of dollars: they were worth a fortune on the black market. Ilse saw an announcement in the newspaper that refugees with exit visas leaving France could buy five hundred dollars at the official rate of only thirty-two francs to the dollar. That was a fraction of the going rate. She showed her friend her set of perfect German documents. "Couldn't we do something with these?"

"You are a natural. Really. Of course we can." He sucked his teeth and thought about it. "I know somebody who can make a nice set of documents to go with these. An exit visa from France and a fake ticket, good enough to fool a bank. I'll look into it. If the bank doesn't check with Vichy, we can do it. I'll give you the French francs to exchange."

She thought how pleased François would be.

The shop in the north of Marseilles sold Moroccan leather goods.

*"One rubs along."

She walked around the back first, to check that there was a way out. The window displayed purses and briefcases tacked up so long that the colours had faded. A bell jingled as she went in. She picked up one of the coin purses that folded into a square, admired its gold tooling, smelt the distinctive aroma of the souk. A figure in a tight red dress wavered ahead, stepping on high heels through the long lines of light and shade.

"Bonjour, Mademoiselle," said a soft voice. A little man wearing a fez peered out through a beaded curtain.

"I'm Violaine," she said.

He beckoned her into a back room. There was a small suitcase open containing rubber stamps and inkpads. He chose a stamp, wiped it clean, inked it up, stamped a document carefully. "Voilà."

He was holding something up. Ilse examined the document. It was a sauf-conduit to Châtel-Guyon, issued by the Préfecture de Marseilles for Mademoiselle Ilse Lindemann. He showed her a ticket in another envelope. "Give me your documents and I can stamp the visas, Mademoiselle."

All she had to do tomorrow was take the early bus to Châtel-Guyon and join the queue at the bank, and come back in the afternoon. And hope that nobody would stop her. Just the name, Ilse Lindemann, had to prove lucky. She was playing the part of a child going to America on her own, a situation full of pathos. The clerk at the bank thought so, counting out the dollars and placing them in a strong brown envelope for fear the child would lose them.

A chill wind was blowing from the sea but Ilse did not want to go directly to the bar. He would not go along the quay, which was heavily frequented by the police and always had a couple of Défense Passive wardens hanging about; there were usually a couple of German guards near the customs house. He would come via the bridge, if he was coming at all. And so she waited, hoping for an extra moment, a first glimpse of him. All day, she had been tight with foreknowledge of their meeting. He spent time inland, less and less in Marseilles, where too many people might recognise him. Twenty minutes passed. She paid her fifty centimes. A figure darted into sight, a man running across the cobblestones, long-legged, hair concealed under a cap, vaulting onto the platform as it left its moorings. Ilse stared across the shuddering cable that drew them over the waters. From the prickles on her back, she felt his nearness. She was taut with anticipation, thrumming with the rope of steel. Beyond that line of silver in the darkness lay the dark and severe romance of the Château d'If. At the other side, she got off ahead of him and walked with the little crowd. Turning, losing her way in the blackout, she could not hear his footsteps but when she stumbled, she felt his hand touch her sleeve, guiding her to the dark door of the café. François pushed through the curtain and went in; the gap let out its blast of light, heat and smoky air.

Ilse waited just a moment behind the curtain, listening to the noise of the bar, then took a peep. It was not busy. A few faces were familiar, no obvious Germans. There was a small group of men, probably fishermen. Still, anyone could be an indic.* François stood at the bar. He called for something from the middle-aged waiter, who was yawning, polishing the glasses with a meticulous disregard for his customers. Slowly, the waiter took a long glass down from the shelf and poured a bock. François turned with the glass in his hand, scanning the room. A small man at the other end of the bar with his back to her tapped a coin on the counter three times. François put the glass down, took a newspaper out of his pocket, looked at the front page, then lit a cigarette and took three slow puffs. Then he extinguished it and put it carefully back in his pocket. The small man turned: it was Raymond. The signal meant that it was safe, that there were no indics here. He came past Ilse, winking at her. She followed him out and round the side of the building to the kitchen entrance of the café. At the back there was a little room they sometimes used.

In a few moments François came through from the café and kissed her cheeks twice. "How cold you are. Are you all right?"

"Fine." She tipped the dollars from the brown envelope, counted the money into two piles.

He made an appreciative face. "You're a most reliable operative." She tried not to show her pleasure.

"It's the first time my German papers have come in useful," she said. "Raymond. For you," and she slid half to him. He would give her the francs later.

"I'm off. Things to do, customers to see," Raymond said. He slipped out. Perhaps François would leave too. But he pulled off the cap, sat, reached for a bottle of wine that stood on a table in the corner and

*Informer.

poured her a glass. Such gestures came when he was pleased with her. She sipped at it. It was a primeur and pretty rough. She was hungry, but knew that he would not eat for hours yet. She shuddered as the wine went down. Still, it warmed her. She could hear the noise of the café next door.

"You've found somebody to do your hair," she said. It was a rich brown, as were his eyebrows.

"A woman in Aix-en-Provence."

François played with one of the empty glasses, placed it beside another. She found another for him, quietly pushed it across the table. His little pyramid was always the same: three, two and one. She put two more glasses where he could play with them until they were perfectly aligned. Ilse took off the scarf which concealed her too-distinctive hair. She smoothed it down. She was wearing it rolled up in a new style. The wine rose to her head, loosened her tongue. The pyramid of glasses was nearly perfect. He readied the last glass.

"Give me a cigarette," she said. "I'm all out."

"Oh la jeune fille,"* he said. The first in-breath was acrid. Determined not to cough, she blew out the smoke and held on to it carefully. She broke the match into a V shape, laid it on the table. She felt a little dizzy. She had not tasted strong tobacco for weeks.

"There's a first time for everything," he said, with that sidelong look which made the heat rise to her cheeks.

"It's hardly my first."

"What's a schoolgirl doing in a bar, drinking and smoking?"

"I'm not a schoolgirl. Why did you call me a nun, that time?"

He remembered.

"At Gurs? I said I was taking you to a convent—that you were going to become a novice." She did not say how much this strange idea pleased her. "I suppose we should enjoy the paradox," he said.

"What paradox?"

"War as a paradigm of freedom. What should you be doing? Sitting in a schoolroom. Learning Latin verbs. Instead, you're here."

"Eat something," she said. "They might have kept something for you."

He shook his head. "Later."

*"My, my, young lady."

She knew that he went to certain black market restaurants, places where he said he would take her one day. Her head felt very light. "When the war's over, will you go back to art school?"

"Did I tell you that?"

"You never tell anyone anything," she said severely. She longed to know more.

"That's all finished. The yellow star's finished it for me. All summer, what have they done but round us up and send us away. For centuries we have run away. This time, we'll be warriors."

She never liked it when he preached at her.

"Won't you go back to Poland?"

"That depends."

"You can settle in France. I can just see it. François the farmer with some hectares and a few cows."

She could make him smile, sometimes, when he was in the mood.

"Who'd want to be French? They don't give a shit what happens to anyone else. Some of these bastards are saying that the invasion of Russia proves that the Germans are the true allies of France. Anti-Bolsheviks. Unbelievable."

"Come on. They're not all like that."

The sweet moment had already tipped over and was turning into something sour.

"Not all, no. But plenty. How do you think they found all the Jews in the eleventh and twelfth arrondissements? The Paris police were ready with their list. They handed over babies born in France. The Germans hadn't even asked for the children. Did you know that?"

She laid a hand on his arm. "It's all right," she said.

"Wait until we have our country. It will all be different."

"You'll go to Palestine?" It had never occurred to her that he might be a Zionist.

"I'll go wherever I'm sent. I'm going to fight."

"It won't go on forever. The war will end," she said. "There won't be anyone to fight."

"The war against the Jews will never end. How do you think that fascist Jacques Doriot blew up the synagogue in Nice? C'est une couille molle, lui.* He had the help of local people. And the Compagnons, of course. Do you see any protests?"

---

*"He's got no balls."

She shook her head.

"Where are our people who were sent on from Drancy? Nobody knows. There are bad rumours coming along the route. Four young men straight from Berlin. I met them yesterday in Spain. They said Jews are being put on a train, supposedly for Poland. To be resettled in a Jewish zone. I know that from Poland they are sending the Jews east. Blue Pass Aktion, they call it, White Pass, Pink. When they're on the train, they gas them all. Men, women, children, babies—"

"Stop it," she said very sharply. "It's all lies. What's the matter with you? You'll believe anything bad. But anything good—somebody trying to help—you just don't notice."

She got up to go, winding the scarf round her head.

"Don't do that."

"It's the fashion," she said.

"For bleached blondes who can't get bleach. Not for my beautiful girl."

He stood and put his arms round her, pulling her close, for a moment resting his cheek against the top of her head. She was a statue, holding her arms high and awkward, and never daring to clasp him.

"Forgive me. You deserve better. I know, we'll celebrate Chanukah together," he said.

Tenderness disarmed her. She did not know when the holiday was, nor how it was celebrated, but dared not ask. At the door she turned back. "Please don't worry about your little sister. In Warsaw. I know she will be fine."

He looked at her with a very level expression. "My sister died. When she was six."

Tears were springing to her eyes, and she turned to go before he saw them. The door slammed. The wind was building up into a mistral. Ilse shuddered with cold. With François, she could never know what to expect, though anticipation was her greatest defence. With François, there would be no end to the surprises and the concomitant thousand little griefs.

She headed towards the quay. Marseilles had grown so silent. She told herself to be calm, to keep watching at all times. She heard no cars, just the moan of the trolley-car horns and the occasional clatter of wooden-soled feet on the cobbles. Waiting at the base of the transporter bridge, trembling from head to foot, Ilse went over in her head what she had heard from him. If this about the train was true, then what? Her head was blank. She had a vision of Otto, his thin body bent, being pushed onto a train. She tried to wipe it away. If this story was true, then nobody could forestall what was to come.

A fortnight later he was back and threw himself down on her bed, as though he belonged there, though she had never made the offer.

"Mind your dirty shoes," she said, mock severe, then coming to pull them off.

"This is heaven," he said. "Oh, to lie in a proper bed."

He was relaxed and smiling; his feet dangled down over the bed and he stretched back on the pillows and closed his eyes. His pale stubble made the bottom half of his face glint in the lamplight.

"You need a shave," she said, tiptoeing closer to drink in the elegance of his profile unobserved. The corners of his mouth turned up; he was in a very good mood.

"Later. Tell me your news. All the latest from the house," he said.

She considered.

"Pauline has finished her trousseau."

"Poor girl. Now she will have to marry the country bumpkin."

"And the mother-in-law will turn up her nose at her silk stockings and make her wear sabots."

"And milk the goats. And?"

"Renée is talking about buying this house. She says she has to pay her dues."

"Renée pays her dues to everyone. Police, the Germans, any authority. But in her business, the most important one is the emperor of Marseilles," he said.

"Who's that?"

"Carbone. King of the thieves."

"She tried him, to help Otto. But he could do nothing. So perhaps he's not even a prince, not even a knight."

"You little cynic."

Ilse always spoke of her father to François in a very practical way. Such questions kept alive the myth that something could be done while placing him in a separate world, one for which François was responsible and she therefore was not. Whenever her imagination leapt to Otto and what could be happening to him, she suppressed it.

"Read my hand," she said.

"No. You do me first."

"Which one? Future or past?"

"Both."

He held up his hands. She drew up the chair and took the right hand, becoming no wiser, pretending to scrutinise it properly while she absorbed the way his chest rose and fell, the whole relaxed air he had. She turned his warm fingers over, looked at the little creases below the fingers, studied the nails. Every millimetre of him was beautifully made.

"I see—a great success. An award—no, a medal. A prize."

"Aha! At fourteen I was the junior table tennis champion of Warsaw."

"Really?"

"Really."

"What happened?"

"I was unbeatable. Until I was beaten. By a boy two years younger, but six inches taller."

"A monster. Was it your finest moment?"

"No."

"What was?"

"Definitely—this," he said. He was deeply relaxed, his eyes closed, as though at any moment he might go to sleep.

"Right," she said. "I'm looking—I see—ten children."

"Impossible. You're losing your powers. Let me do you. Past or future?"

"Future."

He sat up and took her left hand and studied the palm. She moved to sit beside him, bouncing him a couple of centimetres along the bed. In a wave, she smelt the strong scent of gardenias, which La Petite Louise loved so much. He had spent time in somebody's bed. Of course he had. No wonder he was so relaxed. Ilse opened and then closed her mouth. There was nothing she could say. His beautiful mouth went on smiling at her. She hated him.

"I see much walking, Mademoiselle. Serving your country. High mountains and deep seas. Oh, look at this. A tall dark stranger. Or is that me?"

Ilse snatched her hand back.

"No, because you're a gangster," she heard herself say.

"You're a bandit. You should know. One bandit recognises another."

He toppled back again and crossed his ankles. She closed her eyes in silent, blind rage. A match rasped. She smelt the smell of extreme luxury, an English Player's Navy Cut.

"Want one, little one?"

Rage went away. Her mouth hurt and some sad scratchy place behind her eyes. She leant forward, took the cigarette, inhaling as hard as she could until it overwhelmed every other sensation, every other smell. And then she held out her hand.

"Tell me about that tall dark stranger," she said, and when he bent forward in mock scrutiny of her hand, she stared at his long lashes. He brought his head up suddenly, meeting her gaze unexpectedly. Always, this was a kind of little shock.

"Two strangers. A professor and his wife." He waxed cynical, stressing the first word. "They made a mistake. Stayed too long. They thought they were safe and could leave at any time."

"Why?"

"Lithuanian passports. Very good ones from the consul at Aix, a Frenchman. No longer recognised by Spain. Things change. People are getting stranded."

"What do you want me to do?"

She knew. It was much safer for a girl to take them.

"Something I forgot to give you," he said. "I've been carrying it around for weeks." From his pocket, he drew the photograph of her parents, a little crumpled, and carefully smoothed it out.

This time, because she would be gone for so much longer, she was forced to tell Renée something about what was going on.

"I could kill that great Polish streak of trouble," Renée said. "What right does François have to get a child mixed up in such things? I knew you were up to something. I'm not a fool."

"I won't be long. Just a few days."

She sighed heavily. Eyes cast down, Ilse waited, studying the cracks in the linoleum floor. "Please," she said, "don't treat me like a child."

Renée reached forward and took her hands, held them between hers. "You are a child. You are so much your father's child," she said. "I honour it in you." Her warm hands managed to convey some feeling of entreaty. "Be careful. I don't want to lose you."

"I don't want to lose me either." They both laughed.

"If I was your mother, I wouldn't let you go. I would never, never let you out of my sight," Renée said. Ilse sighed, turning away and wishing she would not come out with sentimental assertions that, being untrue, did nobody any good and somehow demeaned them both.

She met them in a house in Aix-en-Provence behind the Cours Mirabeau in a warren of tiny streets and alleyways. It was uneasily close to the Roy René, a hotel crammed full of German officers. The "professor" was white-haired and eminent-looking. He listened very attentively as Ilse explained that they could get out of France without exit visas. She could take them from the outskirts of Marseilles to somewhere near the Spanish border town of Banyuls. A guide, who knew the route across, would take them on.

"I don't know how to thank you enough," he said. He had a very deep, fruity voice. His French was good, but he would never pass for a native.

"My wife will want to thank you herself. Please wait a moment."

"I don't need thanks—"

He had already gone to the door, was calling "Gretli!" softly. His elegant wife, perhaps thirty years his junior, made Ilse feel like a grubby child. Her lovely legs in high heels brought to mind a Parisienne on the boulevards with her tiny dog.

"Mademoiselle, you are very brave and very kind," she said.

She had the unmistakable twang of a Swiss. When she smiled, her eyes slanted up like those of a cat. Ilse could not stop staring at her perfect features, which were unnaturally even in a face that was just a touch too broad.

Fuelled by gazogène,* the bus wound around the loopy coast roads in a series of shuddering starts, depending on whether the gas was firing or, as generally was the case, not. Fortunately the bus was half empty. The professor's wife was conspicuous in a very elegant tweed suit and matching coat, lined with fur. She held her husband's hand and whispered things. She had some intensely female quality, which was beauty, of course, but not only that. It was some other thing, a mixture of innocence and knowledge. Ilse decided that she was aware of her incongruity beside such a man and gloried in it. It was a kind of provocation.

*Charcoal-fueled gas generator. Engines were adapted as petrol was scarce.

On steep roads, the bus kept breaking down. After the fourth halt it emptied out, leaving Ilse and her passengers on their own.

"The Portuguese have stopped giving transit visas on Chinese, Siamese and Belgian Congo visas. They already have lots of stranded refugees, so be very careful once you're across. Don't be conspicuous."

They could not help being that. She decided not to tell them that one of their people had been picked up on the train to Barcelona; another on the train to Madrid. François had told her, not Raymond, who had a soft spot for her and did not want her to worry.

The professor listened to all these hints attentively. "How old are you?"

"Eighteen."

He blinked faint disbelief. "Where are your parents, my dear?"

"I don't know."

"Are they in France?"

She shrugged. She was supposed to tell them nothing: not where she lived nor how old she was, nothing beyond the name they had been given for her: Marguérite. She felt tempted to talk to him. His eyes were so very intelligent.

The driver raked the ash and cinders out of the cooker on the back of the bus, scraped out the tar and started rebuilding the fire from the stack of charcoal in the trailer the bus towed behind it. It was going to take a long time before the fire got going.

"Were your parents in Paris?"

She shook her head.

"My wife would have liked to stay there. Altogether, she loves to be in France. Alas, Paris has become exactly like Germany, Jews excluded everywhere—" His wife nudged his arm. A passenger was climbing back up onto the bus, stamping his feet to keep warm. The temperature was dropping all the time. Night fell. It took a further hour for the cooker to produce enough power to start the bus. Still, it laboured and strained to get over the hill. The passengers were to follow on foot until they reached a level or downhill stretch. Gretli, walking with delicacy on her high heels, would never get over the mountains with that footwear. Ilse could not imagine how they would cope. She was lagging behind already.

"So your mother, what is she like?"

Even while it gave her a sharp pang, Ilse marvelled that he should pick up the conversation so precisely.

"Brilliant. Brave. I'm not at all like her."

"I can see that," he said, and his smile put her back into another moment, one that belonged rather to Albert.

"And your father?"

"You know," she said, "we're not supposed to speak of the past."

"Then let us talk of the future. You tell me what you will become. That is the important thing, not being, but becoming."

She could not think what to say to this.

"What would you like to be?"

The thought truly worried her.

"I'm on my own," she said. "I don't know."

"So what remains?" He seemed to be saying it to himself.

"I don't think there is anything, I mean, anything to hold on to, not anymore," she said.

"Es bleibt uns vielleicht irgend ein Baum an dem Abhang, daß wir ihn täglich wiedersähen,"* he said. She stopped dead. Now it was as if Albert was standing there beside her.

"Is it Rilke?"

"Oh, you are a wise child."

"Wer jetzt kein Haus hat—" She recited it.

"Wonderful," he said. "Did you learn that at school?"

She shook her head. "A friend taught me those poems. He went the same way you're going. I don't know what happened to him."

"I'm sorry."

"He's fine. We'll hear for sure when he gets to America," she said. She would have liked to hear more of his poem, but his interest in her was waning, his attention turned away, as he waited for his pretty wife to catch up with him. Madame scolded him a little for not waiting and he soothed and stroked her, and Ilse hurried away from her sharpness and from the too-soothing tone in his voice, and went at full pelt to the top of the hill. The professor was not a friend. Friendships like this were an illusion.

Very cold now, they waited for the bus to catch up. When the professor ambled away, his wife came very close to Ilse and spoke in an intimate voice. "Can you give him a message?"

Ilse was puzzled. "Your husband's over there." She pointed out where he was.

---

*"Perhaps we might be left a tree on the slope that we would be able to see every day." Rainer Maria Rilke, "Die Erste Elegie," *Duino Elegies.*

"François. Tell him that it was worth it," the woman said, with her perfect smile. "Tell him I won't forget. I will never forget, those exact words."

Ilse could not find a single word to say.

"Will you remember, my dear girl? It's very important." She smiled again. She was so used to charming everyone that perhaps she did not notice when it did not work. Ilse nodded several times. They heard the bus approaching, labouring up the hill. At the summit, it stopped. The professor returned and they got in, went to the very back row, the three of them occupying the central part. Soon, the few remaining passengers fell into tired huddles of sleep. In the morning, with a bleary look Ilse watched the professor's wife open her eyes and spring immediately into beauty, watched her put on her lipstick and face and, last of all, take a little cut-glass bottle from her bag and spray her wrists and neck with perfume. An intense smell of gardenias wafted across.

The call came three weeks after she had delivered the Swiss couple. It was pitch-black outside the farmhouse, which lay many kilometres from the nearest village. Nevertheless, one of François's cheminots* from Marseilles stood armed at the window, keeping a lookout. Others whom she did not know, from farther down the coast, surrounded the farm. These young men had dark, watchful faces. He did not want her to know about their activities and she did not try to find out. These days, it was almost impossible to have a conversation with him. He was perpetually anguished over the news from Poland, over his own powerlessness to change anything. She was there because they needed a woman. A body to wear a nurse's uniform, that was all she was. She had specifically asked for work that would help the fight, something real that would make a difference to the war.

Ilse slipped quietly into the other room. Through the partly opened door, she could see the young Englishman tip-tapping out his code in Morse, frowning with concentration, one hand steadying the other in the sling. There was a piece of paper in front of him. German troop movements perhaps, or locations of ammunition dumps. It was better not to know. He had broken his right arm, the one he was now using, getting out of a prison in the Dordogne and had made his way south.

*Railwaymen.

They had not managed to find a trustworthy doctor to set it. He winced from time to time as it jarred on the key. She knew that he had to stop soon, or else the Germans would get a fix on the signal. She closed the door very quietly, so nobody would disturb him.

When he opened the door and came out of the room, Ilse went in past him, thinking to help him carry the heavy wireless transmitter. She had nothing; the others were all carrying their Sten guns. She knelt before it, taking care not to sully or tear the nurse's uniform she wore, which was too small. The case needed both hands to shift. Made of steel, it was the size of a small suitcase. She heaved. She could barely lift it off the ground.

"May I?"

The Englishman was standing behind her. He leant over and easily swung the heavy box into the air with his one good hand. Soft brown eyes met hers. He was both tall and broad, with a big, good-humoured face and a very gentle manner that seemed slightly at odds with his robust appearance.

"Comment t'appelles-tu?"*

"Violaine," she said. She already knew that his name was Arnaud. He waited, politely, at the door for her to go out first. They walked across the field.

The night was very clear and cold. She was shivering. They had obtained a nurse's uniform for her, but not the cape to wear over it. The ambulance from the asylum was parked beside a ditch. Three men stood beside it. Two of the men put the Englishman in a straitjacket, rotating him. Who would want to interrogate a madman? It must have hurt when they tightened it round him, pulling the broken arm across his body, but he did not complain. They put a bandage over his head. She steadied him, getting in. One man rode ahead on a bike; two were in the front of the ambulance. It jerked from side to side, seesawing over the ruts and onto the road. They made their way by moonlight. Ilse held on tight. The young man lay very still. They were fortunate. So far there had been no roadblocks to test the subterfuge.

She could see the back of François's head through the glass. He did not once look round. Despair filled her, that he needed her only occasionally for missions such as this; that he did not even like her. He was so

*"What's your name?"

contradictory, first using her, then wanting to minimise the risk. Then her mind leapt on to other familiar worries: that she should have fled to Spain, that she had made a mistake, staying in France. In one sense she had stopped caring about what she actually did, day to day, providing she was of some use. In another sense she never stopped worrying. Stop thinking, she told herself sternly. It was impossible.

There came a low murmuring. "Mademoiselle l'infirmière,"* the young man was saying in a weak voice. He sounded unwell. Working against the motion of the ambulance, Ilse made her way over and knelt beside him, steadying herself against the stretcher. He spoke so quietly that she could not hear.

"What is the matter?"

He whispered something. She put her face down close, to hear better. Up came his head. Utterly taken by surprise, she did not move away. His lips were very soft and warm. It was very odd, to be kissing a man. But it was not unpleasant. She pulled away and looked at him. A wonderful smile spread across his face. He had two deep dimples.

"This medicine is the best one for me, nurse," he said. "But I need much more. I can't put my arms round you, can I?"

She shook her head.

"But you can put your arms round me."

He was looking at her with a very hopeful expression. She put her hands round his head and, holding it still against the jolting, dropped her mouth towards his. Just before her lips touched his, she pulled away. He groaned.

"I don't know how to kiss," she said.

"Let's try."

Their noses bumped painfully. Was he laughing at her? No. She moved her head round a little, concentrated. This was rather better. It was not the excitement of standing next to François; it was another feeling altogether. She came up for air.

"This time, breathe through your nose," he said.

"Oh." The ambulance, jolting over the fields, was slowing down. She felt a sense of urgency.

"And open your mouth a little bit."

"Oh," she said. Their mouths locked together. She could taste him.

*"Nurse."

A jolt ran through her, from her feet upwards, a tight shuddery feeling. She was sinking into him. The ambulance slowed to a walking pace. With reluctance, as the ambulance stopped, she let go. Opening her eyes, she saw that his were still closed. There was a very odd look on his face.

"Did I hurt you?"

He opened his eyes and smiled. The men were coming round to open the doors at the back.

"An arrow to the heart, nurse," he said.

The doors opened, she climbed out. François did not look at her, let alone notice her burning cheeks. There was an hour to the dawn and no time to waste. The men helped Arnaud up and unwound him; they were in a high open place. Arnaud showed them where to put three sticks in the ground as markers for the plane to land. The man on the bike had gone; the cheminot told Ilse to hop back into the ambulance. They were to retreat to a safe distance; if the English pilot saw too many people, he would not land. Ilse was shivering uncontrollably with cold and with excitement.

Arnaud took off his coat and, awkwardly, slung it round her with his good arm. "Don't forget me, Violaine," he said in her ear, then shut the door.

She watched as he walked away across the ground and stood beside one stick with his wireless transmitter on the ground, with his good hand holding up a light for the plane to find; François stood some distance away holding another. She looked from one man to the other. Then the ambulance turned, dipped into a hollow and they were gone.

Dawn came but the plane had not and now would not; it was too dangerous to overfly France by day. Still, the audacity of the English pilots gave everybody hope. Each drop of supplies, each man picked up, each little bit of progress gave their struggle a boost.

Arnaud was smiling at her. "I probably sent the wrong coordinates," he said. "Are you glad, Red?"

"Not at all," she said provocatively. Ilse took off her nurse's cap and let her hair down for him, since he loved red hair so much. They sat on his coat under a tree and smoked her cigarettes. François and the other man had gone away in the ambulance, looking for a new place for him to spend the night. They had perhaps an hour, at best two, to spend together.

"How old are you?"

She countered at once. "You tell me first."

"I'm twenty."

"Me too," she said. How young he was to do such dangerous work. It occurred to her that she did not know anybody her own age.

"You don't look eighteen. How old are you really?"

She whispered in his ear. "Sixteen."

He whistled. It was only a little lie, by four months.

"You look wonderful."

"I am wonderful."

Flirting was nearly as good as kissing.

"I don't know anybody like you, at any age. Why aren't you at school? Why do you do this?"

"Oh, you know," she said. "It was this or the Chantier de la Jeunesse."*

This made him roar with laughter.

"Me too," he said. "I'm a Boy Scout. That's where I learnt Morse."

"Any idiot can do Morse," she said.

"Read this message, then." Very gently, he tapped on her neck.

"The enemy is on horseback and has an arrow," she said. He was somebody you could say anything to. When François returned, she would probably be sent back to Marseilles to hang around and feel that she was going slowly mad; this young man would be taken away and hidden in another place. Feeling regret about this, even while he prac- tised his Morse, very distractingly, told her how much she liked him.

"I'm Jewish," she said. "I'm German. A refugee. That's why I can't go to school." She watched his face closely, waited to see it harden.

He looked merely puzzled. "I don't know anybody Jewish. You don't sound German."

"I don't feel it," she said.

"Does it matter very much to you? Being Jewish?" This was too hard a question.

"It's about being. Not becoming," she said. "Life has to be about becoming."

*A fascist youth organisation.

"I come from a village," he said. "I'm a country boy. Is that bad?"

She did not know. She tickled his nose with a blade of grass.

"So, where did you learn kissing?" she asked.

"From you."

When he laughed, his body shook and he winced with pain.

"Be serious. Teach me something," she said. "A poem."

"I'll whisper it in your ear. Come here."

When he had taught her some very enjoyable things to do with ears, he remembered a poem he had learnt at school.

> "My mistress's eyes are nothing like the sun;
> Coral is far more red than her lips' red;
> If snow be white, why then her breasts are dun;
> If hairs be wires, black wires grow on her head."

He translated it.

She frowned. "Not very gallant."

"It's Shakespeare, the very best. I prefer things that are real. And not fantasy. That's why I like you, very much."

Ilse felt herself blushing again. "I don't want to like you too much."

"Why not?"

"I keep losing people."

"How very careless. You'll find it hard to lose me. I'll be back in Marseilles soon. As soon as I can."

There came the sound of an engine. A farmer's van was chugging down the track. She glimpsed a hat. It had to be François. Arnaud started talking very fast.

"Now, that kissing we did. Very nice, but we can do better." He put his good arm round her and pulled her closer. "I want to hold you—that's it. Put your arms round me. Just so you understand the difference, I'm going to kiss you properly. Hold on tight. This is the real thing," he said. And it was.

TWELVE

Hamburg, December 1941

The moon glinted on dirty snow as Nicolai bicycled round the frozen Binnenalster, singing in his head. This, the smaller of the two lakes, had been completely covered with camouflage netting and cleverly made to disappear. The Lombardsbrücke was also hidden under green gauze fixed to wire netting; a false bridge had been built over on the outer Alster to fool the bombers. He too had his false self. Wearing a uniform, his swing gear concealed in the saddlebag, he understood his city's shams and subterfuges. Nearing Dammtor, air-raid sirens howled. He headed for the biggest bunker, concealing his camera under his sweater, fastening his coat up tight. The Leica presented a particular problem; photography was increasingly frowned upon as anti-German.

Pushing his way in, he stood in a crush of sullen people in damp coats, sweating with the heat of people shoved together in too small a space and all afraid as the thunder of distant bombing rippled over them. He breathed through his mouth to keep out the distinctive stench of sweat and unwashed clothes, as penetrating as bleach or lime. People stank and no wonder, when each month they were issued with one piece of soap the size of a matchbox. A joker next to him, a big fat fellow reeking of beer, kept farting and saying "Beware! Gas alert!" with a moronic laugh. Most faces were bleary, with eyes red-rimmed; people short on vitamins were surviving twelve-hour shifts in a factory with little sleep. But they were surviving: they were lucky. Excellent men like his father were sent away to fight and perhaps to die in Crete and Yugoslavia while career officers like Colonel Oster, who should have been despatched to the Eastern front, sat cosily on their arses in Lübeck.

His father's letters described the ice colours of the sea, foaming up on a beach that was a dark volcanic grey. He was collecting little shells for Sabine, and green pebbles of glass, which the sea polished smooth, then slid up onto the shingle. Climbing a broad track, he had encountered a viper sunning itself, coiled, black and fat and looking exactly like a blood sausage until it raised its wicked head and spat. A brown-skinned boy high on the crag had taken fright at the soldiers, had called to his goats in a broken voice, scurrying them away from the column of men. That boy, he wrote, had reminded him of his son.

Closing his eyes, Nicolai wished himself into that cloudless sky, that pure air. If he had been the boy who herded goats he would not have run away. He would have offered his damp cheese and dry bread to the German officer with the kind face, while the animals bleated and nudged them. He could imagine his father's hands taking out his penknife and adroitly pulling out the blade. But the sun flashed on the sharp steel and nothing could be held in place. Away the imaginary boy went, scrambling and scraping, and Nicolai was back in the dark places.

The all clear sounded around two o'clock. The cold was a punch in the face. Somebody had taken his bike. Rage surged up, that electric impulse when a door was slammed in your face. Furious, he called out, "Who stole a bike belonging to the Hitlerjugend?" He had seen an apathetic queue galvanised to homicidal fury when a butcher shut his doors on them. When the man said he had tried to eke the meat out further by issuing eighty grams when the ration card said a hundred, they nearly lynched him. With clenched fists, Nicolai stared belligerently round. He would have to travel on crowded, infrequent trains, the stench such that people regularly fainted. It wasn't just the bike: it had taken him months to get his outfit together, buying it piece by piece on the black market. Nicolai felt his way to the station on the icy cobblestones, his feet sliding about. Dammtor station was a shapeless dark mass, covered with matting to conceal it from the enemy. If he hadn't known it so well, he would have been hard-pressed to find it. No train would leave for hours. The waiting rooms were locked, the benches too public. He could not afford to be picked up by the Gestapo; he had no good explanation for his presence here. He leant against a dark corner, snatching fitful moments of sleep.

The slamming of doors awoke him some time after three in the morning; a troop train had arrived and there were dark figures on the platform, stretcher-bearers wearing armbands. Wounded men emerged on crutches, others were being carried off. A high-pitched screaming noise erupted. One of the men being put on a stretcher was howling like a dog. "Stop them! They're going to cut my legs off!"

Nicolai leant back into the shadows. The man's face was almost completely black with frostbite. One ear was swaddled in a thick clump of bandage. He started to sob. The stretcher-bearer leant forward and threw a blanket over the man's head. He flailed to get it off. His face came into view again, screaming. The bearer wadded a mass of something white together and shoved it into his mouth; abruptly the noise stopped. The head fell back onto the stretcher. The figures of the damned with their blackened skin flowed past; in minutes they were absorbed into the night and the station was empty. Occasionally Nicolai spoke to the ambulant among the one-armed, or to a one-legged veteran swinging himself past on crutches. He knew their bitter tales. He beat his hands together for warmth, to remind himself that he was alive and well.

Klaus said the ones with frostbite were the lucky ones; inside Russia the poor bastards were dying in their scores of thousands. "We got wine and perfume and stockings from France," he had said. "Even the workers were eating foie gras. Now Mother Russia is chewing up our troops and spitting the bits in our faces. The masses won't stand for it." Admiring Russian fortitude, the grim determination to defend the motherland at any cost, he spoke of the coming Bolshevik revolution as inevitable: Germany's working class craved it. Nicolai was not so sure. Because of Russia the shops had emptied. Because of Russia, the previous month every citizen had received a red printed card with a hole punched in it with their ration cards. This, to be hung on the radio dial, obscured everything but the official channel. It held a sharp reminder that anyone who listened to foreign stations would be mercilessly punished. A week later local Party snoopers called at each house to check the cards were still attached.

"They know how to make you curious," said Klaus, who listened to the BBC and Radio Moscow nightly; he claimed half Germany did. After all, it only took a second to twirl the dial back to the Deutschlandsender. Foreign stations were the source of the new crop of rumours, which sprang up every morning; Magda brought them back from the markets, wishing the potatoes would grow as fast. One of the most improbable turned out to be true: that the Japanese had bombed the American fleet in Honolulu, and that Hitler had declared war on the United States.

When, at last, he was home, he went in at the back cellar door, made his slow ascent of the cellar stair, one step at a time, pausing and listening hard—if Lore was awake, his footfall would bring her out. His mother never woke. One night there would be an air-raid alert in their area and he would not be there: he wondered what his mother would say then. Sometimes Lore told him off, said he should not be out at night and especially not in low jazz dives. Cheeks hectic with a pink flush, the hair tumbling down her back, she was her most beautiful. At other times she was still, a strange yellowy white the colour of candle wax, almost as pale as her nightgown. She slept little; frustration woke her, she said, and worry. Once she dreamt that Ilse had found her way to America and for days reverted obliquely to the topic, wondering if dreams could be portents or messages. Misery lay in her eyes, in a certain way she had of staring at nothing. These moments, when he might perhaps take her hand and sit with her for ten minutes, both yawning, speechless and too tired to sleep, were precious. In the day there was never a moment without Sabine or some intervention. She said that he was her friend. He was, of course, but that was not quite how he saw things.

The Hitler Youth calendar for June showed a Bund deutscher Mädel girl in tight shorts and a white top leaping over the camera with arms stretched out. He kept her in his bedside table. Falling into bed, how often he was that camera. Again and again, the tanned girl leapt over him, her long smooth legs and high breasts so arousing that he could not help himself. She was mixed up somehow with Lore's touch and the whore Klaus told him about, who had helped him to wash himself. The idea of a girl washing him was so exciting that at night he could not stop until, brimming with hot shame, he swore he would never touch himself again.

His father came home on leave from Greece, bursting into Nicolai's room very early with a lens and spider-leg stand for close-up photography. They were unused, in the original box; he had bought them second-hand from Major Handelsmann, his commanding officer and friend.

"You can be a little spy with this and photograph secret documents," he said, winking and at once starting to fit them together. Shaking off sleep, Nicolai observed how adroit his father was. He had forgotten his good looks, his fine figure set off by the smart grey tunic, how when his father laughed, he threw his head right back. When Nicolai got out of bed, they were both astonished to find that he was the taller by a good couple of centimetres. His father, embracing him, could not stop measuring the height difference with rueful delight. There was a grey shimmer on his dark hair. Sabine's present, bought during a stopover in Rome, was a huge doll. She hung about in the doorway, sucked her thumb and was shy. Their father sat Susu on his knee and made it talk, showed Nicolai how its big blue eyes opened and closed, and never once looked at Sabine, who, fascinated, crept closer and closer until suddenly she was on the other knee.

The darkroom was big enough for the two of them to stand side by side, his father saying nothing, merely observing and indicating approval with a friendly squeeze to the elbow. He was to develop the films his father had taken; he watched pictures of little boats, white triangle sails forming in his tray, alongside harbours and fishermen mending their nets.

"What was Greece really like?"

"In the water round the coast there are creatures that really do sing, like the sirens," said the gentle voice, "a kind of walrus, I'm told. I've never seen them."

"I meant the war, Vati."

The elbow squeeze was a little firmer then. "War is too stupid to talk about. It's got to be got through, but time here is too precious to spoil. I don't want any of it stuck in your head."

He would not satisfy any curiosity on anyone's part. He was charming and cheerful and Nicolai rejoiced at his kindness, noticing how he included Lore in everything and talked to her in the most courteous and attentive way. But when his father sat down in the drawing room to listen to the news on the radio, his face could no longer conceal itself, it furrowed into anxious lines.

"I hear rumours, you know, about what's really going on," Nicolai said. "Don't you trust me?"

Then his father rubbed his forehead and his face, smoothed out, took on a momentary, false calm. "Let's talk about happy things," he said.

A wonderful smell of warm gingerbread wafted from the kitchen. A bowl of stuffing stood on the side and a fat goose, when there was no goose to be had anywhere, not even a rabbit. In the oven, chestnuts were roasting, the skins blackened and split. Magda took one out, pinched off the skin to reveal the sweet creamy nut, so hot it would burn his tongue if he wasn't careful. Nicolai stirred the red cabbage, breathing its vinegary sweetness, squashed the soft peppercorns with a fork. He had helped for much of the afternoon, setting the table with the best linen and china for a dozen. Sabine helped, too, filling salt cellars and carefully picking up each scattered grain on the tablecloth with a well-licked finger. A distant cousin of his mother's, an officer who had been on the Eastern front, was one of the first to arrive. Nicolai steered Franzl into the sitting room, thinking that he might interrogate him about Russia. Klaus said the officers always knew more. He was a white-faced young man, smelling of nicotine.

"Why have the troops stalled in Russia if General Guderian is such a genius?"

Franzl looked at him suspiciously. "Even General Guderian cannot advance without fresh troops and supplies."

He poured a glass of whisky from the decanter on the sideboard, emptied it. Whisky, like goose, was not to be had anywhere.

"So we'll advance when we get those, will we?"

"Oh yes. We're unstoppable," he said. "Conquering heroes."

Klaus said that the entire army knew how very badly the Eastern front was going; they talked of the Napoleonic jinx, the impossibility of ever reaching Moscow. Franzl helped himself to another slug, swirling it round the glass and sniffing appreciatively.

Unobtrusively, Nicolai poured himself one; Franzl did not seem to notice or care. The Café König watered its beer, when it had any; when there was none, it served a cocktail named the Hollywood. This potent mixture of raw spirit and red-currant syrup delivered a mighty punch. It was disgusting but people fought to get drunk on it, on anything. As the doorbell rang, he finished his whisky quickly. Guests were being shown into the study, where his mother liked to receive people; he could hear muffled sounds of laughter and chatter. The door opened.

"Franzl! There you are!"

A group of people he did not know surged into the room carrying champagne glasses, his mother the rear guard. Unexpectedly, Wolfgang had brought his Lübeck girlfriend. Clara Kröger was a BdM leader whom he had met at a rally. "A pretty toy," his mother had said of her. "No brains, of course. No money in the family at all."

The ripped snapshot Nicolai had studied of a bare-legged girl in a dirndl holding a wreath of flowers and shielding her eyes from the sun had not done her justice. Clara, golden hair hanging down her back, huge eyes turned worshipfully upon Wolfgang, was seventeen. Perhaps she was a toy. With her rosebud mouth and tilted-up nose, she reminded him of Sabine's porcelain doll. Urged to the piano, she played Schubert and Brahms with rich rippling extravagance. Her mother was a musician and Clara practised for hours every day. A girl with hands that could move with such sureness must have a brain. She played, her eyes half closed, and the whole of her body was involved in the music she made, filling the room, the house, his head with her sound. Wolfgang leant against the piano watching her. He wore his black SS uniform with the death's head insignia; the silver oak leaves sparkled and one long fair hair lay vivid across the dark cloth of his shoulders.

"Darling, you need help with your snapshot," his mother said to Nicolai, shepherding the remaining guests into the drawing room for the picture: it would be a souvenir of happy days. "Tell him what to do, Benno," she said.

"The boy doesn't need my help," his father said proudly. So Nicolai told them all where to stand or sit, though he scarcely knew himself which order was correct or how the picture should look. Everything seemed fluid. Was any arrangement of these bodies more real than any other? The camera clicked silkily. Still, he made them change places twice, for the pleasure of moving them.

"Dinner is served, my ladies and gentlemen," said Magda in a voice cracked with nerves. At the table, Wolfgang proposed a toast to "my beloved godfather," Colonel Oster, generous provider of the goose, wines, butter and eggs, whose duties had not permitted him to join them.

"One fewer to feed," said Franzl, sotto voce, nudging Nicolai, to whom the name brought the usual prickling unease.

"The Colonel!"

Raising his glass, Nicolai saluted the picture he held in his mind's eye very clearly though it was eighteen months ago: the Colonel hot and annoyed, the bonnet of his car up, pacing out the long sweltering wait until a mechanic could be found on a Sunday in a place as remote as Timmendorfer Strand. It hurt him that his father, smiling at his guests, knew nothing of his wife's adultery and must never be told.

Fear of accidental disclosure hung above the table; the simplest glance of father to mother made him uneasy. Wolfgang's conversation was full of potential dangers. What was his half-brother saying so confidentially to Gertie, his mother's closest friend? Nicolai leant forward to make it out. It was only a boast, that Wolf would be swearing his oath of allegiance "in the presence of Himmler himself, though I'm still waiting for my full membership to come through from the SS Race and Settlement Office." He smiled at Nicolai, nodding. "Your turn next, Nico."

Lore slipped into the room.

"We would have been thirteen at table—such bad luck," his mother said. "So I've asked our Fräulein nursemaid to join us."

His father rose to his feet as Nicolai did; none of the other men got up because she was a servant. He hated their rudeness. He noticed, as his father evidently did, how well the borrowed evening dress of his mother's in vivid emerald green suited her creamy skin. The dinner wore on, with exclamations of pleasure at the extravagance: globules of real butter, not ersatz oil, floating in soup made with real chicken, not powder. Soup plates were removed. Flushed with excitement and anxiety, Magda served her goose and red cabbage, her mashed potatoes running with butter. They quietened down for serious eating and Nicolai, who had no appetite for the Colonel's goose, circled the table, pouring the good wines. Franzl, the decanter beside him, continuously replenished his whisky glass. His mother was talking to Gertie about food; Wolfgang discoursed on the purity of his family tree to one of his father's university friends. He passed Lore and his father talking, very intently. She hardly ate; rich food made her ill. The wires of their different conversations crossing and crisscrossing wove an invisible mesh, the framework which kept them all in their places. And he, the puppeteer, mentally shifted them all from foreground to background according to their rightful position and the volume of their talk, and lit them, so the hollows of Lore's face were smoothed away. There could be no danger while his father talked only to her. When he laughed, as he did now, it was so infectious that those sitting near him could not but smile.

"Here's a thing, Benno," said Wolf. "Clara wore her mother's old fur coat today." (How the girl kept her gaze on the table, never meeting anyone's eye.) "And a woman actually spat at her upon the street, called her a whore. Because of the appeal for clothing for our troops in Russia. What effrontery!"

"We have created a culture of blame and denunciation—what do you expect?" said his father. Nicolai craned forward, hoping for a real discussion. But Wolfgang, reaching over to touch Clara's hand, did not reply. He had no doubts. He had just wanted that touch, to bring her into the conversation, to pronounce her name in secret delight. Holding up his wine against the candlelight that intensified Clara's perfection, Nicolai watched the tiny faces of the golden-haired young couple sliding across the ruby surface. They were hollow. They were doomed, because the mystery of absolute belief, like religious fervour, was incomprehensible. If only they could be warned. Everybody should be warned. He drained the glass. He felt certainties expanding warmly inside him, rising to his head, just as the wine did.

"Young man! Tell us the news from the East, young man!" Gertie's voice trilling from the far end of the table was a wire snaking across aimed at Franzl, who looked blankly back. "Franzl!" But still he said nothing. Drink had silenced him; with Nicolai, it had the opposite effect.

"Do you want the real news or the usual lies?" Nicolai heard himself saying.

"The real news, of course."

"Ssh, Nicolai, it's not for you to speak here, but Franzl," said his mother.

"Hilde—" said his father in a warning tone.

"The boy knows nothing."

"If he's old enough to sit with us, then he's old enough to have an opinion."

His mother's face grew pink with a flush of indignation, like a child being admonished unfairly.

"Well, my boy?" His father nodded encouragement. They were all looking at him.

"Go on, Nicolai. Go on. Let the boy speak," said Franzl, slurring his words.

Nicolai took a deep breath. His moment had come, but he was not quite sure what to do with it. "Our troops are exhausted. They're stuck in that godforsaken land and there's no more food because they can't supply them," he said in a low voice. "And they're all freezing to death. They bring them in at night, so nobody knows. You see, it's a great tragedy—"

"Benno—" his mother said.

"Train after train," continued Nicolai a little louder. "Stacked with wounded. The Russians hit back, they mine every metre of land, they leave nothing for our men to eat. They strip every factory to the last nut and bolt. So the further the advance goes, the less there is for our men. The state of them is terrible. You should try going to Dammtor at night. Or Hauptbahnhof—" And then he saw that his father's face wore a stricken look and that he was lifting a hand to cover his eyes.

"Benno, just tell him it's nonsense," called out his mother in a tone which snapped the slender threads that kept him in his seat.

Nicolai sprang up. "It's the truth. Can't you ever listen?"

Wolfgang also rose.

"Leave him, Wolfgang—" His father laid a hand on his half-brother's arm. Blundering out of the room, Nicolai cannoned into the doorway.

"Drunk," he heard his mother pronouncing. "Disgraceful. Completely drunk."

Up the stairs and round he went, two at a time; his head was reeling and he sat on his bed, filled with despair.

A moment later, his father rapped gently on the door frame. "May I come in?"

His father sat on the bed, put an arm round him. Nicolai, who was going to be sixteen in two months' time, fell into his father's arms. "What have they done to you?" his father asked.

It took a moment for Nicolai to recover enough to speak. "Nothing, I don't know what it can mean—that I am so very sad. I suppose it's just the war." He let out a terrible dry noise that wanted to be a sob. "And the wine."

"And the wine." His father patted his back. He was looking at him with such a gentle expression, full of concern. The shadows under his eyes were very dark.

"Doesn't the truth matter, Vati?"

"Always. But even when they are true, certain things don't need to be said," and he squeezed Nicolai's hand. "Sometimes we know things just for ourselves. Bad thoughts and ideas expand into the air and then they choke us."

Released, he lay down; his father covered him up. The blood beat through his head and he felt so giddy.

"I'll stay with you until you feel better."

His father's presence was a pool of calm that was spreading and soothing, that was lapping over his head.

Waking with a thundering headache in the middle of the night, Nicolai got up to have a drink of water and to relieve himself and then, when he felt steadier, crept downstairs. Pushing open the door to the cellar and the last flight of steps, he heard a voice coming from Lore's room, a man's voice. He took another two steps. Silence. He waited. If she heard his footfall on the stone steps she would come out, as she always did. Then he would sit with her and hold her hand. That was the only thing that could make him feel better. He waited. He took two steps up and two down. Nothing happened. She was asleep; perhaps it was the radio he had heard; perhaps he had imagined the voice. Holding tight to the banister, he went back up to bed. In the morning, he had a thick head.

There was no other man in the house. The voice could only be his father's, he thought, and all the way to school he could not stop imagining, with a kind of shameful excitement, that his father, who was the master in their house, might do what he himself so badly wanted to do, might slip into Lore's room and quietly lay his naked self against her white body in that small bed. Would she refuse him? The thought, exciting and worrying in equal measure, would not go away. It was one of those bad thoughts that just grew and grew.

That day as usual they shared a meagre lunch, rations of meat, fat and bread having again been cut. All the food went to the army. Magda was frugal with their provisions; everyone feared a long war. While Sabine and his mother had an afternoon nap, the two men went tramping in the snow along the Elbe, his father slipping in the thin civilian shoes he loved to wear despite the cold; he hated his army boots and had no others. Spare shoes used to be collected by the Winter Relief, latterly the Russian appeal had taken a heavy toll on boots, woollen clothing and furs. The river slid by, a sullen slate colour, and his father often seemed far away and tired, so that Nicolai felt abashed. He wanted to tell him thousands of thoughts but the cold air froze them in his mouth. His thoughts were impure. That sorrow in his father made his own concerns seem unworthy. It had to suffice that their footprints, side by side, left syncopated tracks, that he hummed jazz melodies and his father joined in, that they knew so many things just for themselves without needing to speak them out loud.

Afterwards, sitting in his study, the grey afternoon light made his father look even paler than usual. When he lit a cigarette, he half vanished behind the smoke and his eyelids, downcast, looked like sockets. They were white marble, the irisless eyes of a statue, until he suddenly looked up and straight at him.

"Nico, do you remember us skating together, when you were little?"

"I was jealous, because you could skate backwards and I couldn't."

Slipping in his socks on the polished floor, Nicolai tried to do the movements. Like a bird, his father cocked his head to one side; he was listening to the noises of the house. High above a tiny squeaky voice was Sabine, making Susu talk, then replying in a very bossy manner; the lower tone was Lore. They listened to the little girl's chattering descent for tea.

"If you are as good as gold, Susu, then you can have some of the cake the guests had. A very small piece, but you will have to be very good. Fräulein Lore will decide."

"Nicolai, I'm still skating backwards. And you still can't. Not if last night is anything to go by."

Nicolai felt himself flush. "So I shouldn't have spoken. But you encouraged me."

"I think we were both a bit light-headed." His father sighed. "Nico, be careful. I don't know any way to get through this, you see, other than not being noticed and hoping for some luck. People hear and notice things. The most stupid are the most dangerous."

"So I should shut up and say nothing?"

"When you skate backwards, you can't look down at your feet, or you fall over. You just keep your eyes fixed on a point far away. That's what I do. I used to write about honour and duty in the songs of the troubadours. Well, honour's a luxury we don't have. There'll be a time for it, but not now. We're living the time of dishonour." All the time, his father's mild voice got quieter and quieter. The larder door opened and shut, there was a clatter of plates in the kitchen and a tiny voice was Sabine, pretending to be her doll. His father ground out the cigarette and stood up, smiling. "Come on. We can't let Susu get all the cake."

News came that his father's division was being sent south to rest and refit. In all likelihood they would go back to Greece. His father said that it took a certain army wit to send a scholar of romance languages there.

"Beware the literally minded," he said. "It's the German disease. It's everywhere. And we are above all the masters of detail. Denker und Dichter werden Henker und Richter."* He smiled, but his eyes were sad. "I'm in intelligence. I'm very fortunate. I can spend all my time and energy making sure I don't have to kill anyone." Soon he was gone.

It snowed again and heavily, the world from his window white, the branches of his tree thick-rimmed with it. Roads were impassable, schools closed. Unable to leave the house, he set to work to develop his photographs. So many tasks had to be done by touch. Feeling his way carefully through his small blind world, thoughts hummed into his head and placed themselves into position as gently as the paper he manoeuvred in the frame. He played with his variants, seeing that though he might shift people, they also moved to present the best version of themselves, looking right, then left, adjusting their smiles, inventing themselves anew. A face was supposed to be a reflection of character; everyone believed in the power of faces, even their own.

His mother, dressed in her party smile, stood tight with her certainties, giving nothing away. His father, turning a pleasant face to his son in each shot, was endlessly cheerful. Clara, who usually hid her face, had once looked at the camera and smiled. Nobody could ever know why. Placing Wolfgang to the very right of the group made it easy to crop him, yet without him the picture looked lopsided. Even the camera, the magic box of light, was selective, hiding more than it showed. Nicolai printed up the best group picture, a memento for his mother. But the story lay outside the frame. Lore was not in it; Magda was not there, nor was his father's sorrow. Invisibly permeating each tiny dot was the absence of Colonel Oster against the presence of his father.

*"The thinkers and poets become hangmen and judges."

There were other absences. At night, the wind howled and the branch tapped against the windowpane. He heard the stick of the old man going along the road; he heard dead Ilse, rapping on the windowpane so he would look up, so he could see her waving from her bedroom window. He dared not; he covered his eyes. Faces crowded up against the window. Their mouths opened and closed and made no noise, because they could not be seen or heard except at certain times (between four and five p.m.) and certain places (hardly anywhere now). Lore called them "ghosts." "Did you see any ghosts today?" The yellow stars had appeared in September, marking them out from the rest. Of course he saw them. He had seen a little boy hanging on to the pole at the back of the tram with a big satchel on his back half covering the star, not daring to venture beyond the platform to the safety of inside. When he realised Nicolai was observing him he had simply let go and fallen onto the street, tumbling backwards, a little figure sprawled across the tracks. An old woman shuffling along the pavement shrank back into a stairwell when she saw him turn. Jews were scared shadows of themselves, as sensitive to being seen as a vampire was to daylight, clinging to a fading existence in a parallel world. There were so few now. People never noticed that the Jews were disappearing; if they did, they never mentioned it. They were too busy queuing for a strip of meat, for potatoes and carrots and cigarettes. Any decent person would bow their head when they saw a Jew: for shame, and to spare them the humiliation of being stared at. But a face that was not looked at ceased to exist, not just for others, but for itself.

"Are you sure? None at all?"

"A few. They looked fine."

In the streets he saw everything: that little girls, massed in uniform, smilingly sang: "When Jewish blood flows from the knife, then things will go twice as well" and nobody said a word. She had taught him how to see the gaps between things; before, he had only seen what lay solidly before him.

"Don't you think we should go to Wuppertal and see if there's any news?"

"Who would know?" she said. "Do you imagine Father Salomon will still be there?"

"You mustn't give up hope," said Nicolai.

She did not reply. No news came of Ilse. Lore no longer spoke of

France, though her unspoken questions remained written upon her face. Sometimes hers was the stillness of extreme exhaustion. At other times when her thoughts oppressed her she became hectically busy and sewed half the night, remaking old clothes. She made clothes for Sabine, mended piles of linen for Magda. She read stories to Sabine and taught her French, gabbling away in it. She wanted to teach him, too, but he did not care to learn because these frenzies frightened him. During air raids, she was the calmest of them all. She confided that the bombardments directly overhead were a relief; during them she could not think.

Sabine, who would be five in May, had begun to take notice of the world outside her little self. She cried helpless tears because animals died and because people ate them; she herself was guilty of it. She wept because her friend had a dress that was the wrong shade of red, an angry red, and she only liked the happy kind. She suffered bitterly from the unfairness of her life, that she was born a child yet others came into the world fully grown. She could not be convinced that she would ever grow up or have the powers that they did. When Sabine could not be consoled, Lore took her on her knee and soothed her. The two of them sat by the hour on his father's old rocking chair.

"Hoppe, hoppe, Reiter!

"Wenn er fällt, dann schreit er—Fällt er in den Graben, so fressen ihn die Raben

"Fällt er in den Sumpf—so macht der Reiter PLUMPS!"*

And on the last word down they went—her soft bright curls falling forward until they nearly touched the floor. Up and down, on and on, neither of them able to stop.

---

*Child's game: "Jump, rider, jump! / When he falls, it's a thump / If he falls in the ditch, the ravens eat each stitch / If he falls in the bog, he tumbles like a log."

THIRTEEN

Marseilles, November 1942

The thunder of boots marching on the cobblestones jackknifed Ilse awake. She knew this sound. The French police never ventured into the Vieux Port at night for fear of being ambushed. She could not breathe properly. The boots stopped. Fists pounded on the door. It was five in the morning. The hair on the back of her neck was sticking straight up with terror. The heavy tread on the stairs would be Paul, the barman, coming down. German voices shouted in French that Renée was under arrest. The boots went upstairs. The soldiers trampled through every room. The ceiling shook. Ilse stood, frozen, in her nightgown in the middle of the room. Her teeth were chattering. Faintly, above the noise in the house, she heard hammerings on other doors further along the street.

She was a little girl in Wuppertal standing in the hallway with her eyes tight shut while the Gestapo searched their house on the Landsweg. Men shouted, doors slammed and boots marched on. Her feet were very cold but she was not scared. In a moment, when she opened her eyes, her mother would be standing there, her arms also folded in silent defiance and on her face a look of utter contempt. Mutti had to keep her eyes open because she needed to see everything. There was no knowing what a thief might slip into his pockets while nobody was looking. There was no telling what a wicked man might place among your things to trap you.

"Madame, how did you acquire your furniture and tapestries?"

This German, shouting, spoke very elegant French. Renée's reply was muffled. Ilse opened her eyes. She started breathing through an open mouth, pinching her nose, because otherwise a bad noise would come out. Shock stuck her feet to the floor, closed her ears, made her feel dizzy and sick. She could not make out what Renée was saying. Because she could not still her hands sufficiently, it took a long time to dress. She put on the brown suit Renée had had cut down to fit her. She stood up, unbolted the door, pulled back the curtain, crept down the corridor with the blue roses. When they came for you, you had to be ready.

The kitchen was full of soldiers; head down she went past the sitting room, glimpsing between the blur of field-grey uniforms a streak of pink silk that was Renée's dressing gown. She closed Renée's bedroom door behind her, climbed up on a chair, took the suitcase from the top of her wardrobe and searched for warm underclothes, night things, her new tweed jacket; she chose a black wool dress, rummaged through a dozen pairs of evening shoes for something warmer. She found a pair of bootees, fur-lined. It was always cold in the cells. A bottle of perfume. She found makeup, put it in. There was a warm scarf somewhere, gloves. She remembered her silver hairbrush and mirror, scoured through her handbags for money, not knowing where to look, wishing she knew.

Then Renée came in. "I have five minutes to dress," she said. Her eyes looked dead, she seemed bewildered. "They're taking La Petite too." Ilse made her sit on the bed, took off the dressing gown, helped her to put on underclothes and stockings. She was limp with shock.

"But why?"

"Someone denounced us, for harbouring deserters."

She dressed her warmly, twined the familiar pearls round her neck.

"Quick! Hurry!" An officer appeared at the door.

Ilse knelt on the bed, pretending to fiddle with the clasp of the pearls, whispered in her ear, "Tomorrow. I'll come tomorrow. To get you. It's all a mistake. You must take money, do you have money?"

She nodded. Then Renée stood, seemed mentally to shake herself, let Ilse help her into her coat. She drew on gloves, picked up her handbag.

"Adieu, my lovely one," Renée said. She took Ilse in her arms and put her mouth very close to Ilse's ear. "Raymond will look after you," she whispered.

Then the officer had her by the arm. Renée shook him off, picked up the suitcase. They looked at each other.

"Tomorrow, I will see you tomorrow!" called Ilse, following.

"Au revoir, ma fille." They kept each other in sight to the end. La Petite Louise was waiting in the street. She looked very small, head down, not looking at anyone. Then the soldiers marched the two women away, slamming the door in Ilse's face.

The house fell silent. Ilse put on her thin wool jacket. She put the picture frame in the small case, with the depleted jewellery roll. Everything she possessed could fit on top except, of course, for the bicycle. She went back into Renée's room, began to tidy it up and pulled the counterpane straight so everything looked just as it had before. She opened the cupboard door, put the hangers back, smelt her scent, tidied her shoes, hung her clothes straight.

She sat on the side of her bed and remembered the German soldier who had spent many days in the room at the top. Was he the deserter? His name was Hans and he was a simple soul with a round red face. La Petite had made him coffee, had laughed at the enormous size of his feet and hands; he was not the first they had sheltered. Ilse thought that Renée had given plenty of money to the local gangsters, that she had treated the Germans nicely and that she expected and deserved protection. Misery squeezed a tight knot inside her. Falling to her knees, she prayed with all her strength for Renée to be saved.

Paul led her through Renée's kitchen and to the sitting room. The barman put his massive shoulder to the heavy armoire and shifted it across, screeching along the tiles. The painted plates wobbled on their stands. This, then, was the entrance to the secret cellar. She saw a door with a flush-fitting bolt, which was red with rust but had been oiled, for it moved with ease. Steps led down into the darkness. He handed her a torch and a bottle of water and half a baguette.

"Don't wander about down there, you'll get lost. Just wait."

He closed the door. She listened to the heavy scraping as he shifted the cupboard back into position, shutting her in the dark.

The steps were steep, made of rough stone, the cellar echoed away beyond and beyond. She switched on the torch; it wavered across the walls. As far as she could see, the walls were part stone, great square blocks of it, part bare rock. Crystalline patches on the ceiling glittered in the beam. It stank of damp. The ceiling was high here, low elsewhere where it looked more like a cave. The place stretched out and on into further, darker places; the labyrinth extended under the whole of the vieux quartier. Over to one side, hundreds of crates were piled up. She sat on one of them. She clicked off the torch to conserve the battery. It was so very dark. Her feet were freezing. The chill struck up through the floor and right through the thin soles of her shoes and so from time to time she lifted first one foot, then the other. Soon she climbed higher, lifted both feet onto the crate and sat, hugging her knees, with the suit-case safe beside her. Her thoughts drifted away. A faint scraping sound roused her: rats. When she put the torch on, the rodent scuttlings died away. She used the light to keep the monsters at bay, letting it sweep from side to side.

Time trembled and grew icy, and she woke, knowing her mother's voice was telling her about a journey she could undertake, if only she could make out the words.

"Mutti," she said in her head, "I am forsaken." The timbre and tone of her mother's voice slowly became clearer.

"I am a Jew," her mother said. "Absolutely and forever."

Ilse opened her eyes, very surprised. That was what François had said. She had not been wrong about him, because God believed in the Jews. The land drew the people. It went past the empty stable and took a path to the left. It was the witching hour, phantasms were conjured up out of the blackness in the misty cone of the torchlight. "Mademoiselle l'infirmière," said the warm voice plaintively, "this medicine is the best one for me. You'll find it hard to lose me." But she had. She had lost everyone. Drooping with tiredness, Ilse listened to the voices and clicked and swung her torch mechanically. She had forgotten to give Renée her lipstick. That was why she had gone away looking so white-faced. Renée shook her head, she did not mind. "On vivote," she said, "on vivote." Nothing had been forgotten, nothing was truly lost. That was her text: "He who is alone will long remain so."

"Ilse. Wake up."

"Thank God for Raymond," said François. "What a professional."

She was hoarse-breathed, sleep the ice grains in her eyes.

"Wake up. Come on, wake up. We have to get out of here."

It was not François at all, but Raymond who kept shaking and shaking her. "The Boches are all over the south," he said.

As she stood, her bones cracked. She stumbled behind him through the labyrinth. His torch flickered ahead. "The fucking Germans are everywhere. All over the Vieux Port. House-to-house searches. François said to get you out fast."

"Wait!" Her feet were so cold, she kept tripping. Raymond turned, came back, put his arms round her, tried to warm her.

"You're frozen, my poor girl. How long have you been in this icebox?"

"They took Renée, I must go in the morning to see them."

"To the Gestapo? Are you insane? They'll just take you as well. Come on, follow as close as you can." The torch flickered ahead.

"Will the gangsters get her out? The ones who protect her?"

Raymond snorted. "Fat chance. Carbone and Sabiani are in with the Germans. They all are. The brothels and bars go on. They'll find somebody else to run her place. Traffic in gold and drugs goes on. It's business as usual for these people."

His voice was a mist that streamed over his shoulder to flow around her and tug her on. She was in his slipstream. The ground was slippery with unexpected steps and turns, and places where the rough foundations of ancient houses gave way to solid rock. Her thin soles skidded on the wet uneven places. In a high-ceilinged vault, silver flashed from stalactites that dripped and glittered.

She was awake now. "Why have they come here?"

"To fortify the coast. Because of Algiers."

She had heard on Madame Dumont's radio that the Allies had landed in North Africa. They had drunk marc, to celebrate. She had not realised that this would bring the Germans south. "But Churchill said it was the beginning of the end," she said.

"If we don't get out, it will be."

Small as he was, he threw a long shadow. They came to a narrower place. He swung his torch to the side.

"Look."

She saw a series of holes cut out in the side of the chamber they were passing through. Each seemed to contain a shape or box. "What is it?"

"Catacombs," he said.

Directing the torch at the niche, she saw a skull looking back at her. The rock became stones again and narrowed to a cellar, then a trapdoor shut with a long bolt, which took an age to draw back. She waited, listening to him cursing quietly as he worked the rusty iron back, a millimetre at a time. Beyond were steps going up to a gate. She smelt the salt in the air. It was night as they came up through layers of darkness and a steep incline to the sea. Gravel crunched underfoot. The wind whipped at her jacket. They were somewhere at the other end of the port. Raymond beckoned. Beyond the jetty where the fishing boats lay grinding at one another a dinghy was hidden. He helped her climb in, pushed off, got out oars and started to row. She wanted to put the suitcase somewhere but there was scarcely room for their legs, so she held it on her lap. Her throat was rough and she needed to cough, swallowing incessantly instead to suppress the noise. He rowed with great efficiency, dipping the oars into the dark water without ever making a splash. Something was touching her leg. She felt under the seat. A couple of submachine guns were jammed underneath. The sharp wind made her eyes water. She was aware of the bones of her head, which felt cold and hard.

Somewhere beyond Cassis they landed on a pebbly beach. Lucky, Raymond said, that it was a night with no moon. He pulled the dinghy out of the water, left it in an abandoned boatyard. He had arranged a lift for her in the back of a truck going to Toulon. She climbed up. He told her to hide behind boxes of decomposing turnips but the stench made her giddy. She nearly threw up. When he saw that she was not feeling strong, he said he would go with her.

"You're so kind, Raymond."

Her teeth chattered still. He rubbed her arms and shoulders to warm her. She pinched her nose shut against the disgusting smell and tried to make herself comfortable as the truck swayed over the rough road. Raymond knew how to find François, who had joined the maquis* somewhere north of Aix-en-Provence, up in the country of the Massif de Ste. Baume. He had said that she could not go with him, that she was more useful in Marseilles. She had not seen him for months.

"Are we going to François?"

---

*Name given to wild countryside on the coast, hence to French Resistance members hiding there.

"To Cannes," he said.

"Won't there be Germans there?"

"The Italians are claiming that section of the coast. In return for their magnificent contribution to the German cause. Bunch of fucking cowards."

"I'd better go to François."

"There's nowhere safe now. They're everywhere. Cannes is a resort. Not important strategically. François reckons it will be better for you."

Deeply disappointed, she sat with her legs drawn up, breathing through her mouth and from time to time gulping down the sour flux. They stopped once and she walked for a moment, leaning on his arm, trying to feel less nauseated. Then they went on again along the winding Corniche. Early in the morning they slipped into Cannes. They went into a big noisy bar called the Taverne Royale across from the railway station, full of early-morning labourers drinking brandy. Raymond ordered two cups of café national. The hot drink cleared her head.

"They took Renée for harbouring deserters," she said. "Maybe they'll give her a warning, then let her out."

"Look, Ilse, she may be a small player, but she's well known in the Resistance. Information collection and exchange, a safe house. There's a printing press in the cellar."

"But they don't know that. They didn't find it."

He shrugged, drained his cup, called for a petit marc. "Last night, they picked up dozens of our people, men and women. Fighting men. Someone will squeal. We'll do what we can. You know the rules."

She had never seen him look so bleak.

"There's something you haven't told me," she said.

"They got the Réseau Alliance." That was the name of the network based at Cap d'Antibes, linked to the Free French and to de Gaulle. "They were liaising with the English and sent a boat to take our men to North Africa to join the Allies. General Giraud was fine, he got out by submarine. But the next night a second group of officers was embarking. Couldn't wait to get in the war, right? An informer double-crossed us, we had to change the rendezvous. Had to keep on transmitting. Went on too long. The detector trucks drove right up to the villa."

"All of them?" she asked.

"Every last man."

Raymond led her along and down the Rue Carnot to the sea, and they walked up and down the port until she felt better. He had to be gone soon.

"What am I to do here?"

"Nothing. Keep out of sight. Get a job, if you can."

He gave her a piece of paper with two addresses on it and a book of ration coupons. He brushed away her thanks.

"François will thank you," said Ilse.

This raised a faint smile on Raymond's face.

"If you move, leave your address at one of these. Then we can find you. Take care."

She nodded. They embraced. Then she watched him slide down the alleyways and away, wishing him safe too. Arnaud had links to the Réseau Alliance. Ilse leant against a wall and closed her eyes. She could see the gentle young man holding his broken arm, tip-tapping out his Morse, squinting at a piece of paper covered in letters. It was a double cipher, which meant that the message was safer, but more complicated to send. But nothing could save you if the transmitter signal was picked up, if you went on longer than the maximum of seven minutes. At first she had found herself thinking about the Englishman very often. Recently the memory had begun to seem unreal. She crossed her fingers, like a child, wished Arnaud safe. Perhaps she heard the voices of people because they were dead. This frightened her so much that she began to shake. She moved where she could stand with the wintry sun on her face.

One of the two addresses was a grocery shop just a few streets behind the main shopping street they had crossed, the Rue d'Antibes. The shops were still shuttered. Ilse drifted along the Boulevard de la Croisette, past the Casino and the white stucco balconies and terraces of the Carlton Hotel. She chose a bench and sat with her suitcase on her lap, watching the light breeze ruffling the sea. A loudspeaker woke her. A patrol wagon inched along the Croisette, announcing that Italian troops were about to arrive. The voice appealed to the people to remain calm. People came out onto their balconies to listen. A big man cradling a cup in both hands drained it, went into his flat and returned with a little girl sitting on his shoulder. The child clapped her hands and pointed. From the distance came the sound of a military band. The Italian infantry wore highly polished boots, hats adorned with nodding ornamental plumes. They looked like cadets on a parade ground, not real soldiers at all. They swung their arms in time, not one of them carried a gun. It was a strange kind of an invasion. Ilse felt very calm. When the toy soldiers wheeled away, she made her way back to the grocer's shop. A small man with a big moustache was unlocking the door. He rolled up the shutters, pulled down the blinds to shelter the façade from the morning sun. She went in.

"Bonjour, Monsieur."

His eyes flickered down to the suitcase. A customer came in behind her. The grocer gestured to her to be silent as the woman was served. When the woman had gone out, he led her through the raffia curtain to a door at the back. It was a storeroom lined with shelves stacked with tins and dry goods with a camp bed in the corner. All day, Ilse slept in the smell of sugar and vanilla and bleach, waking fitfully from time to time when the shop bell rang, as it did each time a customer came or went. The shopkeeper had the thick accent of a Marseillais and in the evening fed her a stew of white beans and fish. She offered some of Raymond's ration coupons; he waved them away and would not be thanked. He did not ask what her name was, nor what she was doing.

The red, white and green ensign of Italy hung above the portico of the Hotel Gallia. Perhaps she could get a job looking after children or in a shop. Of course, she was not qualified to do anything. She tired of looking at elegant shop windows, went back past the port and up the slopes of Le Suquet with an eye on the big church. She tried to find a way to it through the small backstreets, thinking to say some prayers there for Arnaud and for the Alliance network. A splash of white in a dingy window caught her eye. A tiny card announced that a seamstress was required with machine experience. She went in. The hall held a counter with a pile of fashion pattern books arranged on it, two chairs and a bell. She rang the bell. The woman who came out from the back had a huge mass of grey hair braided and wound round her head, and very big brown eyes.

"I've come about the job."

The woman looked at her hands, then at her face. "What are your qualifications?"

"I can hem and roll handkerchiefs and embroider a little." Her mother had taught her many different stitches and drawn-thread work, but she could not think what the words were in French.

"You're very young," the woman said.

"Nineteen." Ilse shrugged and smiled up her age as nicely as she could.

The woman went away. In a moment she returned with a piece of white cotton cloth, dressmaker's scissors, a needle and a spool of cotton thread. She walked noiselessly on soft-soled shoes like a young woman. Her hair made her appear older. "We need a machine operator, Mademoiselle," she said, "to operate a Singer sewing machine. With a foot-treadle. But there is some hand work. Show me what you can do."

Ilse sat down. It was quite gloomy. She could see that at the back, the light was bright in the workroom, where the sewing machines whirred. It did not matter. Her eyes were very sharp. She folded a triangle along the selvedge and carefully cut the cloth into a square. First she roll-hemmed one side of the cloth as neatly as she could with tiny, invisible stitches as though the cotton were silk, picking out one thread to attach the hem by so that nothing would show through from the other side. Then she hemmed a second side, making a wide border in cross-stitch as for a coat or dress and pressing the cotton at the fold into a sharp edge with her fingers. She stopped three-quarters of the way across, so part of the raw edge was left. Using the point of the needle as her mother had taught her, she began to count the stitches in a half-centimetre to make a simple drawn-thread border, which would come out parallel with the last selvedge edge.

The points of the scissors were too blunt for this task, but she cut a tiny hole and persevered. Absorbed in the work, she concentrated on pulling out the little threads, one by one, hemming round the square holes in the cloth as she created each one with the tiniest stitches to produce the decorative cutout effect. She forgot where she was and why. When the light clicked on, dazzling her, she realised that the woman must have been watching her for quite some time.

Monsieur Mallemet said that she could stay; she introduced herself as Laure Benoît, grateful that she had these papers at least. In the evenings, he prepared beans and fish in the little room that served as salon, bedroom and kitchen. When he knocked on the floor, she came up. Silently, they ate. She dared to ask if he had a family: he was silent for several minutes, then said that he had never married. After supper he took a book from his collection of literature on the kings and queens of France. This was the signal for her to wash up and leave. On Saturday night he opened a bottle of wine and drank it silently, then opened another. Then he started laughing and chuckling to himself. He told her that his was a fine name, for he sprang from a long line of aristocrats. His family had been betrayed.

"Comment aimez-vous Coh-ennes, Mademoiselle Benoît?* Do you like our lovely town?"

She did not know what to reply. Into her mind floated one of François's jokes:

"What is the definition of an anti-Semite?"

"I don't know."

"A Frenchman who hates Jews more than is absolutely necessary." How deliciously his mouth had curved in laughter on those rare happy moments.

On Sunday, the grocer put on his Sunday best and went to mass. As soon as he marched away, she stripped and washed thoroughly in the sink in the corridor near the storeroom, something she had not liked to do when he was in the house. Later she went to Our Lady of Good Hope, in Le Suquet. She put her prayers in a particular order, for when God was listening she did not want him to think that she favoured any one person over another or that she asked for help only for the Jews. Instead, in alphabetical rotation, moving on to start with a different person each visit, she prayed for Albert, Arnaud, François, Lore, Otto, Renée and Willy, asking that each should be kept safe. Then she made mention of La Petite Louise and Raymond and Madame Dumont. She did not want to neglect anyone. If she said every prayer without a mistake, God would hear her. When her careful catechism in the place of hope was done, she would go out onto the terrace below the bell tower with its lovely view of the harbour and sit on the wall in a kind of dream, thinking of how François had looked when she saw him last, how gaunt and yet so handsome. It was wrong to think so much of him, but she could not stop herself. She closed her eyes and watched him blowing smoke rings of Virginia tobacco, while others smoked eucalyptus leaves. She saw the delicate fingers building a pyramid of glass. He sat with his eyes closed, feet propped up on a bar stool, while Marielle applied hair dye with a little brush which left a dark rim on his caramel skin.

Over several visits to Notre-Dame d'Espérance, she understood more clearly what had come to pass. For eighteen months she had been a member of the underground. That had been her father's kind of life. He had been in the German underground, he had placed the struggle against the Nazis above all other things. She had tried to be brave, like him, but the little she did could never be enough. Her father had not

---

*"How do you like Cohen-Cannes?"

saved himself. He could not be something other than what he was. Now that François had no need for her, she did not have to be her father's daughter. Since nobody wanted her and nobody cared what she did, she could now become her mother's child. All her life she had belonged to her mother, body and soul. That was her rightful place. It was a deep satisfaction to be useful, to be doing work, which her mother had taught her. In this small life she felt close to her.

Each morning as she walked up to the atelier Ilse bought a newspaper. Along the Croisette a dark line hung in the sky for three days, as though the giant painter, bored with the blue, had dipped his thumb in the black and scrawled across his picture. The French had scuttled what remained of their fleet at Toulon. Though the radio maintained silence and the newspaper gave nothing away, everyone knew. It was whispered that some captains had chosen to blow themselves up and go down with their ships rather than surrender them to the Germans. The girls in the atelier, working overtime, described this behaviour as "impeccable." Business was very brisk; every hotel in Cannes was overflowing. Jews were fleeing here from the newly German-occupied zone of France in the thousands and many were well-to-do.

The new German zone had swallowed up the greater part of France and stretched from the other side of Cannes all the way to the Spanish border. Official announcements multiplied: death to those who sheltered refugees illegally. The rewards for denunciation of foreign refugees increased. The word "Juif" was to be stamped on all ID papers of Jews in the zone; Jews were expelled from all départements with frontiers with Spain and Italy, and restricted in their freedom of movement. France was turning into Germany, as Albert had foretold. The newspaper reported these developments in a careful, neutral tone. General Vercelli, commanding the Italian Fourth Army, had chosen to live at the Carlton Hotel. On sunny days, sent to deliver a dress or coat, she found the terrace full of Italian officers in beautiful red uniforms. The women drinking and laughing with them were elegant and bejewelled, with elaborately waved hair. Many wore little fox or sable capes. The Italians were nominally in charge of Cannes; but their masters were also present. Everyone knew that the plainclothes Germans and spies had taken over the Hotel Montfleury, on the lower slopes of the ridge sheltering the town to the north and east.

"Marie-France! Come and show this!" The tall girl got up, smoothed back her unruly chestnut curls and went over to Madame Simone. Beyond the workshop was a large airy showroom for clients. She often modelled a coat or dress. Marie-France Bonnard could walk like a model with all the necessary hauteur; but when dared, she also turned cartwheels, like a naughty but very sexy child.

"Quel châssis magnifique!" said the old concierge every time Marie-France passed. Her tiny waist, full, high bosom and endless legs made every dress look wonderful. Her polished skin had the sheen of excellent health.

Ilse progressed to more complex work, found it deeply satisfying to set in a sleeve or turn a lapel. Mastering the machine, she continued to hand-stitch buttonholes, for her work was considered to be particularly fine. Her place was in the middle of the room where the girls' chatter flowed over her. Marie-France could make Ilse's mouth water with her description of how her elderly mother slow-roasted a pot-au-feu, the pastry she made with almonds and butter. The girls endlessly discussed the taste of real coffee and cream and croissants and jam. Then they planned their wedding dresses and trousseaux, full of the finest silks and fabrics, in every detail. Only eighteen, Marie-France was already engaged to Jean-Baptiste, the best friend of her brother Fernand. She swore undying love for this young man whom she had known all her life. Ilse often thought that if she had been a man, she would have fallen for Marie-France, whose gaiety and good humour were as alluring as her looks.

Squads of Italian soldiers exercised in shorts and vests on the beach. They outdid one another, showing off and being funny. Even doing callisthenics, they managed to flirt. Italian soldiers strolled along the Rue d'Antibes ordering handmade boots; they were battle ready with mandolins and guitars. Though the curfew started at sunset, the soldiers never enforced it in the backstreets. Instead, they stayed in groups in the big avenues, always bunched together. The girls called them "the sheep," though more than one had found a new boyfriend in this occupying army of rams. Ilse was stopped and asked for her papers by a group of young men using this as an excuse to look her up and down, laughing as they gave the most perfunctory glance at the Benoît papers. The second time this happened, one of them held on to her card for a long time and then made her plead with him to return it, enjoying the joke with his friends. That night, though it was late when she got back to the grocery store, for a long time she could not sleep. The camp bed was very uncomfortable and sometimes she began to imagine that the shelves of tins might topple over her and then she felt almost breathless with anxiety.

Early in December, leaving the shop as Monsieur Mallemet rolled up the shutters, Ilse smelt Virginia tobacco. Raymond was standing a few metres away, leaning against the wall, smoking as he waited. She crossed the road; they walked on together. His dark head hung down.

"François was picked up in Marseilles by the Gestapo. Four days ago. He was with Marcel." Ilse looked at her feet. She knew the name. Marcel was one of his most trusted men, "a clear head if you're in trouble," François had said. She had never met him. "Marcel got away."

"That's good."

Ilse laid a careful hand on his arm. His eyes would not meet hers.

"They are still holding François. Four days."

"Was he carrying anything?"

Raymond shrugged, shook his head.

"He knows the rules." It didn't matter what papers he carried. The maquisard with the white-blond hair was famous.

"When his hair grows out, they'll know who he is," she said.

He gave her a sidelong look. He was afraid.

"He's very brave," she said. She was afraid too. François knew everyone. It would please the Gestapo to torture everything out of him. "Renée?"

"Taken to Paris with others known to have worked for the Resistance."

Silently, they climbed through winding cobbled streets until they reached the atelier.

Ilse stopped. "I work here," she said.

"You know the little restaurant, L'Indo-Chine? In the Vieux Port?" Ilse nodded.

"They know me. If you need me, leave word there. Or Snappy's Bar. They know me too. My little Ilse, you'd better think about moving on."

"There's no magic the 'poilu' can do for François?" She tried to smile.

"This time, Raymond fails."

"Thank you, Raymond, for coming to tell me."

She squeezed his hand and they parted without another word. She went in to work. L'Indo-Chine was a hole-in-the-wall place up a back-street that served good food, bowls of rice and meat. She would think about that; she would not take a break, today, from her machine. She was not going to think about François. But every time she paused in the work and lifted the foot and turned the cloth to sew back over the last stitches, every time she stood to pass the work over to the next girl, the dark, sick feeling swept over her.

"What's wrong with you?"

"Nothing."

Marie-France invited Ilse to pop out with her for a cigarette break. Madame Simone did not let them smoke inside, worrying that they would drop burning ash on a fabric or set the place on fire.

"You look awful. Is there anything I can do?"

Ilse shook her head.

"Man trouble, Laure?"

She flushed.

"Well, we all know about still waters." She ground the cigarette out under a high heel. "Tell you what, I'll fit an outfit for you. You could do with something decent to wear."

"You're so kind, but I can't afford the fabric."

"You leave that to me."

Marie-France went away to model something and returned with fabric wangled from Simone; by the time work ended, she had half cut out a chic little skirt and jacket. They sat fitting it after the others had left.

"What a tiny waist, lucky you," the tall girl said. Bent over the stitching, glad of something to do, Ilse admired Marie-France's oval face, her huge brown eyes, the shiny long eyelashes which curled natu-rally, her kindness. "I like you, Laure. You're special. If you ever need anything, come to me."

She waved away her gratitude.

That night, Ilse decided that she would not leave Cannes, where people were kind. François and Raymond knew where to find her here. François would not betray his people. And if he did, then they might as well come and get her too. If he died—well, her mind could not con-template that possibility. If he died, nobody would know how to find her; perhaps she would not exist at all.

On Christmas Eve, Monsieur Mallemet offered her a glass of wine. She sipped it slowly. Silently they ate their fish and beans. "See? We're winning the war," he said, grown unusually prolix, with a hand indicating the lavishness of the stock. The shop was nearly empty, the storeroom stripped nearly as clean. After dinner, she presented him with a waistcoat she had made out of flannel fabric left over from a client's coat, the back lined with a little piece of silk purloined from another client's dress. Amazed, he tried it on. She had measured his grocer's cotton coat carefully and was pleased with the fit. His mouth opened and closed several times and at last he spoke. "Mademoiselle Benoît," he said with feeling, "if I still had the almond paste, I really believe I would give you some."

Ilse smiled. A week earlier Maiffret's, the best pastry cook in Cannes, had obtained permission to sell almond paste, and she had been sent to queue for the grocer's share. Monsieur Mallemet had divided his parcel up similarly, kept the delicacy under the counter, slipping his favoured customers a hundred grams each. She knew his remark was a great compliment.

In January the Germans carried out a census obliging every adult to answer a multiplicity of questions, from date of birth to profession, family, descendants, religion. Without this document, no ration cards could be renewed. Question 16: Are you French by birth? Yes. Question 31: Are you of the Jewish race? No. Ilse lied throughout. The first sinister outcome was that a new form of war work was introduced, the Service du Travail Obligatoire.* Every single man between nineteen and thirty-two would have to work in factories in Germany or go to the Russian front. Thousands of Frenchmen were already prisoners of war in Germany in slave factories; now every remaining Frenchman not doing essential work would be taken. The girls in the atelier could talk of nothing else. They were appalled and frightened. Each had a boyfriend, husband or brother who would have to go.

"My Jean-Baptiste is not going," said Marie-France, running her machine with long violent strokes. "My Fernand will not go. It said on the radio, get out of France. It's our patriotic duty to avoid conscription."

*Obligatory Work Service.

"What will they do?" asked Lucie, who was walking out with an Italian.

"Head for the hills and live rough, join the maquis. They'll fight the dirty bastards. Anything is better than being herded into a train at gunpoint and sent off to face Allied air raids in a German labour camp."

The others agreed. It was the first time in three years that Ilse had heard anyone speak openly about resisting the Germans. François had been right: people would not fight until they were affected personally. She smiled across at her.

Marie-France smiled back, leant over confidingly. "You'll see, the bloody Jews won't have to go," she said. "They'll still be hanging around town, lounging about and gambling and hogging all the good things."

"And providing you lot with work," said Ilse, surprising herself and them, for she rarely said a word.

Marie-France burst out laughing. "Bravo! You're not as meek and mild as you look, my friend," she said.

Towards the middle of January an unknown woman came to the grocery shop while she was at work and left a message that she should go to Marseilles for the January 23rd football match at the Stade Fernand-Bouisson and meet "her friends" at a particular spot on the home side. Perhaps Renée had been released, perhaps François. It was easy to obtain a sauf-conduit from the flirtatious Italian officer at the Préfecture, who stamped everything that was presented to him. Though it was bitterly cold, the sun shone and a crowd of several thousand people had assembled to see Provence play Languedoc. Ilse stood where she was supposed to stand. Nobody came. She took her beret off, loosened her hair. She was easy to recognise. A man pushed past her, turned and asked her several times what the score was. She had no idea. He insisted then on telling her: three goals to two for Provence. Three to two. She stared at him, but could not work out what, if anything, this might mean. Raymond did not turn up. Nobody came. Something must have happened. There was no surprise or disappointment, just a quietening down of the spirit to where it had been before, a numb acceptance.

She stayed until the crowd was nearly dispersed, stamping icy cold feet, studying the torn notices flapping on the outside wall of the stadium. There was a notice stopping all fishing, another stopping all traffic. AVIS: PAR SUITE DE DEUX ATTENTATS GRAVES LE 3 JANVIER CONTRE L'ARMÉE ALLEMANDE . . . TOUTE CIRCULATION EST INTERDITE ENTRE MAR-

SEILLE, SEPTEMES, ALLAUCH, PLAN DE CUQUES, PENNES MIRABEAU . . .* The most recent announced that from January 16th all photography was forbidden and that it was illegal to carry a camera, to draw or paint anywhere near the Vieux Port. LES CONTRAVENTIONS SERONT PUNIES CONFORMÉMENT AUX LOIS DE LA GUERRE.†

She could not leave Marseilles without making any attempt to discover what had become of her friends. She would drop in to the Bella Pizza in the Colline des Accoules and see who was there. It was the girls' favourite restaurant. She took a bus to the centre of town and walked down the Canebière. Though it was getting dark, there were still four hours before the curfew started. How quiet the centre of Marseilles was. Where were all the people? There was hardly anyone in the streets. As she approached it, she saw the whole of the Vieux Port was cordoned off. Heavily armed German troops stood on every street corner. Lights were trained onto walls, glinted on their round helmets. Armoured cars with machine-gun reinforcements stood on the corners of the quays. Ilse backed away. Not running—it was never good to run—she walked towards La Sainte Trinité. Her footsteps echoed. The café was locked and shuttered. She banged on the door. At the second attempt old Madame Dumont stuck her head out of the upstairs window and, amazed to see her, hurried down to let her in.

Thousands of police were on the streets, arresting everyone. It had been going on for two days. They had closed most of the bars, including this one, closed nearly all the brothels, hauled innumerable people away. Madame Dumont crossed herself; automatically, Ilse followed suit. They talked in whispers, though nobody could possibly hear. The rumour was that the Germans were going to go through the Vieux Port, in a mass rafle designed to clear the whole place out. Shivering uncontrollably in Madame Dumont's marital bed, grateful for the simple comfort of another human being, Ilse remembered how in another life, long ago, she had resented sharing a bed with her father. She felt the old woman's hand reaching out and patting her. "Sleep, ma petite," she said. "We are warm tonight. Think of those poor refugees and those poor Jews over there, who have nothing. They had no warning of this." Later in the night, she found the old lady standing over her with a cup of

---

*Notice: Following two serious outrages against the German army on January 3rd, all traffic is forbidden between Marseilles, Septemes, Allauch, . . . etc.

†Breaches will be punished according to the laws of war.

tea. "Don't cry anymore, little one," she said. Ilse had not known that she was.

At six o'clock on Sunday morning, as soon as the curfew was lifted, Ilse hurried back to the Vieux Port. A cordon held back the gawkers who already lined the frontier of the forbidden zone. German soldiers stood impassive. She thought of the girls, of Raymond, that surely right now he was leading them out through the labyrinth beneath their feet. But there might be no reason for the Resistance to save girls from a brothel the Germans used. People were coming out of the quartier in a steady stream and massing on the quayside. They carried suitcases, bundles, babies. Some pushed handcarts. In a little while the German troops withdrew. Trucks disgorged young men in black uniforms and berets, crisscrossed with belts and carrying submachine guns. A line of them drew up, facing the crowd aggressively. "La Milice," said Ilse's neighbour with a nudge. That was the name of the new fascist militia. The crowd muttered its displeasure and the fisherman standing beside her spat on the ground. Ilse could not look away from the faces of these young Frenchmen, who strutted onto the quay, ordering people around, and who carried themselves so arrogantly, cradling weapons the Germans had supplied.

"Look at that poor old woman, dragging the bundle," said an equally old woman beside Ilse. "That darling little girl is crying, can't they see?"

A centre de triage* had been set up on the corner with the Rue des Tamaris; a selection process was taking place. Red Cross ambulances took away the sick and the old. Like clockwork, running back and forth continuously, trams took people away at gunpoint: old and young, white-faced, drawn-looking, stumbling, afraid. The bystanders by degrees fell silent, as if at a funeral. A motherly woman beside her crossed herself continually. A plump young woman passed, face and hair hidden by a scarf, labouring to keep hold of the heavy suitcase she carried in front of her with both hands. Was that La Grande Louise?

Where was Paul, the barman, Pierrette, Pauline, Marielle? Perhaps they had been taken in the first raid.

"Where are they taking them to?"

"La Gare d'Arenc. They're putting them onto cattle trucks."

By five o'clock in the evening the thousands had dwindled to a

---

*Marshalling yard.

trickle. Numb, she crept back to the bar. She telephoned Simone at the atelier in Cannes to tell her she was sick. She dared not try to leave. Her papers would never stand up to German scrutiny. Rising early, Madame Dumont brought home the *Petit Marseillais*, which said that fifteen thousand people had been removed from the Vieux Port in the process of "sanitisation." In the market, people whispered that the trains were so bitterly cold and had taken so long to reach their destination at Fréjus that babies and small children had died in the night.

The morning revealed huge removal vans on the quays. Everything was being stripped out of the houses. Even Boy Scouts had been drafted in, were pushing wheelbarrows piled with mattresses and linen. Some soldier's wife in Germany would inherit the exquisitely embroidered linen Renée's mother had collected for the country house of her dreams. Workers were digging out the copper gas pipes and piling them on the quay. Huge notices announced that the death penalty would be imposed on looters. If that was enforced, the Marseillais wags said, the entire German army would have to be shot.

By nightfall, the quartier had been stripped of everything of value. On the next day, February 1st, teams of soldiers carrying explosives and coils of fuse wire assembled on the ripped-up cobblestones where the tram tracks had been at the base of the Colline des Accoules. Ilse watched with the sombre crowd as the men moved up the steep streets laying charges of dynamite. A bugle call sounded at noon. The first thunderous explosions were set off between the Rues Radeau and Saint-Laurent. Huge clouds of choking dust billowed above the buildings as they collapsed. As each explosion rocked the ground, the bells of the abandoned church of Saint-Laurent tolled as if God himself was mourning.

Very early on Sunday morning, Ilse left the bar, walked to the far side of the fishing harbour and, while it was still dark, climbed up the long winding metal staircase to the top of the pont transbordeur. The near side was barred and closed. She went to the far end and stood where the giddy spiral of the metal stair corkscrewed through the top deck, rising to the tip of the structure, and waited near the little bar-restaurant, now shuttered, for the winter sun to rise. Darkness gave way, in time, to a pale yellow haze. A surreal landscape of rubble lay behind a rim of façade. After five days of explosions, the greater part of the collapsed Vieux Port had been bulldozed into nothingness. A few houses had been spared: the Maison Diamantée was one and the old customs house on the Quai Maréchal Pétain. The Saint-Laurent church still stood. The restaurant L'Indo-Chine was gone, of course, with all the other backstreets, along with Renée's house.

> Wer jetzt kein Haus hat, baut sich keines mehr.
> Wer jetzt allein ist, wird es lange bleiben*

Teeth chattering from the cold, she returned to the Fort Saint-Nicolas end, crept down the giddy stair, heading through the side streets back to La Sainte Trinité. The Catholic world was full of gradations of sins and sinners, penalties and penances. But when people were punished so cruelly, it could not be because of anything that they had done. Sinners and nonsinners suffered alike, she reasoned. It seemed to her that the mercy of God was so infinite that he would not judge them harshly and she should not either. The greater question was why God was testing their faith. Walking past a narrow alleyway, she saw a sign for Snappy's Bar. It came to her at once that this was the place Raymond had mentioned. She turned into the alley.

A young woman with bright red lips was setting up for the day and wiping tables. A couple of men drank coffee. Ilse ordered coffee and observed her. She had a knowing look to her: in a little while, quietly, she asked after Raymond. The young woman nodded. Ilse waited. Twenty minutes later, when the men had gone, the young woman brought her a tisane she had not ordered. Neatly folded under the cup was a slip of paper with an address not too far away. It was a walk of twenty minutes or so. She decided to take the risk. Her luck held: the streets were busy with people going to work and nobody stopped her. It was a gloomy house in a backstreet behind the station, overlooking the railway lines.

She went into a narrow hallway that smelt of cabbage and dirt, rang the ground-floor bell. Nothing happened, but he must have had a spy hole somewhere for a few minutes later Raymond appeared. He drew her up two flights of stairs, unlocked a bare little room. He was unshaven and had a ragged look to him.

---

*"Who has no house will not build one now. / Who is alone will long remain so"—Rilke, "Herbsttag."

She kissed him on both stubbled cheeks. "Thank God. I thought the salauds had got you," she said. "I've been here a week. I got your message, but I didn't know how to find you. Are you all right?"

"I've moved a couple of times. Nobody is all right. François is out." Her heart thundered its joy.

"Someone saw them taking him to the station—he took off his hat. Waved. Our man at the station saw him. He recognised him by the hair."

"Was he very badly beaten?" He said nothing. "He waved?"

"Like this," and Raymond reached up suddenly and made a great, flamboyant gesture with his beret, standing and turning round full circle.

"What's the matter? Was he badly hurt? What is it?"

She felt sick. She had a clear vision of his face purple with blood, the dark hair standing out and between the two the giveaway white halo.

"He wasn't touched. Listen. Marcel ran for it. They didn't stop him. I wasn't sure before. He had the impression they didn't want to take him. That François didn't try to run. Something he heard the officer say. There was a full colonel with them. 'Das ist einer unserer Vertrauensmänner.'* Do you know what that means?"

She nodded.

"He's a clever man, François," said Raymond heavily. "Him and the colonel, that makes two clever men. Of course, he knew everyone in the Vieux Port. Everyone that was."

Ilse watched his eyes slide away from her. She waited for him to say more. These long silences dismayed her.

"If he was a double agent, they'd have let him go before."

"Perhaps. Not a mark on him, though. And now he's out."

"You can believe that of him? Never. François is a fanatical anti-Nazi."

Raymond gathered juices in his mouth and spat on the floor.

"Why are you still at large, then, and me?"

"Because they don't want to pick us up yet," he said. "There's enough to do with the triage of the Vieux Port. Or they're waiting to see who we'll lead them to. Did anyone see you coming here?"

*"That is one of our trusted men."

Ilse shook her head. "You're wrong. He didn't name us. He can't have." Then she saw that Raymond, because he so loved him, would have preferred him dead rather than a traitor.

"He was released," he said. "He's gone away, gone to ground. None of us will have anything to do with him. He knows that. You know the rules. I wanted to warn you. He'll have betrayed you too. You'd better think about moving on and fast."

FOURTEEN

Hamburg, February 1943

The two bombed-out families living with them each had three children. The housing authorities had assigned families to every house in their street, an army of sullen supplicants who made them all uneasy. A tribe of urchins ran about the house. When she understood that they had lost their possessions, Sabine thrust a doll into the arms of each child. They ran off to joust with her darlings, ripping out legs or arms in pitched battles. Discarded, they resurfaced in scarecrow versions of themselves. Encountering a tragic orphan on the stairs, Sabine would hover beside it, not daring to pick it up, frozen by the reproach in those staring glass eyes. Then Nicolai had to rescue her, swinging her up on his shoulders. Only Susu, the Italian baby, remained. She sat on her doll's chair beside Sabine's bed, eyes turned to the window so she, at least, should see nothing of this carnage. His sister could not play with her one immaculate child. Nicolai understood it: Susu's perfection magnified the tribulations of the others.

Sabine felt everything strongly. If she thought another child might be hungry, she would refuse to eat. They conspired and connived, keeping bad news from her, evolving stratagems to ensure nobody would go hungry and she least of all. Having no ration cards, the refugees only received potatoes. Lore slipped them lard, onions, anything she could spare. Unaware of this largesse, his mother complained that these women used their kitchen, cooked in their pots and pans and that the children broke so many plates. Nicolai also could not eat with their pinched faces watching; he avoided them. He and Lore were in the kitchen well before six.

"I'm going to open a jar of jam," she said, "but don't tell the others. I saved it for you and Sabine. And I've got a bit of dripping."

The bread, a tasteless mixture of barley meal and wheat, tasted fine with the dripping. He wolfed it down. The pot of jam was labelled in Magda's sloping hand. With a blink, he could conjure up the pile of sugar, the vast aluminium cooking pots, the hills of damsons, blueberries and raspberries. The treasure of the house was her Rübenkraut* and gherkins and onions and peas, what remained of them, still locked away in the cellar. Her stocks of flour, sugar and coffee were long gone, as was she. Her brother was missing on the Eastern front and poor Magda had returned to the Eifel to run the farm, leaving Lore to run the house. Around that time his father, in what he termed a supreme example of Wehrmacht wit, had been reassigned to a mountain division, the 5th Gebirgsjäger. "Presumably the mountain men need somebody from the flatlands, to give them a sense of proportion," he wrote. His division had now been sent to the Eastern front, to the Leningrad region. Letters came from Volkhov, from Mga, from Kolpino. "We are the fire brigade for the Eighteenth Army," he reported, always cheerful, always resolute. Nicolai tried to believe that he was telling the truth. All through January the grey days, already bleak with cold and hunger, had taken on an apocalyptic intensity as they waited to hear about Russia.

"We salute you, Magda." Nicolai spread the jam as slowly as he could, waited with his mouth watering to bite into the succulent sweetness. "We salute your sausage and mash, your Eintopf, your wonderful cheesecake, your goose with red cabbage and apple sauce." By seven o'clock, the jam was gone, the good mood dissipated, the kitchen crowded. The radio played solemn music alternating with an ominous continuous drum roll. The adults sat dumbly awaiting the detail of the

*Sugar-beet molasses.

disaster. News had been filtering through for months, whispers and rumours of Soviet counter-attacks, of frozen bodies stacked in ten-metre-piles, of enemy action where there should have been none. Now it was upon them. General Paulus's Sixth Army had surrendered at Stalingrad. The nation was told that there would be two days of mourning; shops would close. His mother cried when she heard the news, seizing her daughter and rocking her on her knee. When he looked at her and her shabby clothes in that chair, he felt the faint quiver of that old prewar life almost hurting, like pressing an old bruise faded yellowy green to test its powers.

Grandfather's shipyard had been destroyed three months earlier in a night attack. How heavily his grandmother had leant on her stick as she walked up the Elbchaussee, picking her path through heaps of dirty snow, skidding a little in her rubber overshoes with their slippery soles. Spotting her from his window, he and Sabine had run to meet her at the gate. Wordlessly, she had thrust out a piece of paper. It was very neatly typed. He did not take in what it was at first. There, listed alphabetically, were the names of all the men who had died. Unable to part with it, she carried the paper with her, unfolding and showing it to everyone she met, taking continual stock of the magnitude of the human disaster by the chance reactions of strangers. His mother rose from a sea of daily nuisances and complaints (for Colonel Oster had been seconded to Berlin, where life was still decent) to be dashed on a frightening peak of desolation. Her future security was gone. The war had taken away her men, then the business that had been their whole support. Finally she understood that the life that she knew was over. She feared everything. She cried at any trifle. He had half wished unhappiness upon her; now that it had come, he saw how little it suited her.

Sabine trotted to school beside him, frowning at the world, wondering things out loud. School was a waste of time; they learnt nothing and often his year was despatched to carry out some menial task, winding hose reels or shovelling coal.

"What are you thinking, Nico?"

"Nothing much." He mostly thought about his feet, so cold that he couldn't feel them. They bore sizeable calluses where his father's shoes, two sizes smaller, pinched. Some of the calluses were whitish-yellow, the colour of dead flesh; others, blood-filled, were a sinister purply black. With every step they hurt.

"Nico, why was Mutti crying?"

"Relief, I expect. The war's nearly over," he said, and Sabine clapped her hands for pleasure and, smiling, revealed red-raw dots, raspberry pips trapped between her teeth.

After Stalingrad, air raids increased in frequency. Their house was a paper one, made of parchment and twigs that could flare up in a moment, and Nicolai appointed himself fire watchman for the Elbchaussee. Despite bitter complaints from the women quartered with them, he moved all the furniture from the top storeys, insisting that they all live on the ground floor. He overruled his mother, who wept because now even her sitting room was spoilt. He packed everything she said was valuable into boxes, stacked them high in the cellar. He shovelled their remaining coal as far down into the deeper cellars as it would go. He placed buckets of water ready in the cellar, with lids to keep the water fresh, and took towels from his mother's sparse stock, so they could breathe through them if necessary. It was then a matter of waiting for the inevitable.

They sat side by side on hard chairs in the deep coal cellar listening to the steady drone of planes overhead. At first they came only on clear days; then grey skies and rain proved no protection. If they were not there by seven-thirty, they wouldn't come. Then the RAF extended its working hours. Nicolai listened: the short, sharp sound was a firebomb, which could spray fire as far as eighty metres all around. The crack of an explosive bomb was much greater, a 106-kilo bomb that threw out oil or rags soaked in petrol, or a firebomb which covered houses with petrol and rubber "cow-pats." These were the worst, combining with explosions that tore out doors and windows, letting air in to feed the flames. Fire scared him. In the streets, people battled impossible flames with tiny amounts of water, passing chains of buckets from hand to hand. A neighbour, bombed out, howled inconsolably that she had lost the only photographs she had of her son, killed in action. That was why some carried suitcases everywhere containing their most treasured possessions. For the same reason he had dismantled his darkroom, storing the equipment and chemicals in the deepest corner, sorrowing for the loss of the only place where he was truly himself.

When it quietened down, people dozed. War was perpetual tiredness, the ability to sleep standing up. Nicolai looked at the book he had grabbed from his father's shelves in a rush as the siren sounded, delving for the forbidden second layer. It was a thin volume of poetry by Heinrich Heine. "The whole world will become German," it said. The strong, crisp words sang in his head. He read to Lore in a whisper,

> "Es brannte an allen Ecken zugleich
> Man sah nur Rauch und Flammen!
> Die Kirchentürme loderten auf
> Und stürzten krachend zusammen.*

"Why is Heine banned?" he asked.

"He was baptised, but his parents were Jewish. He wrote the *Lorelei*."

"That's in my songbook," said Sabine. They had not realised that the child was listening to them.

"Ssh, go back to sleep."

"Come here, darling," said Lore; she took Sabine's head on her lap and stroked her. He worried that the sorrows and fears Sabine felt were actually Lore's, that in touching the little girl, she was unknowingly infecting her.

"Will we all burn up?"

"No, Sabine," he said. "He was writing a hundred years ago, in bad times when he had to leave Germany. The big fire burnt half the city but it was long ago."

Sabine murmured. Soon she too slept. Her imagination, daily stretching each puddle into a lake and making of every pebble a mountain, could not encompass anything so big.

February 28th was his seventeenth birthday. His mother gave him a watch of his father's, which he put on with pride. Lore gave him a pair of shoes, real prewar men's hiking boots in brown leather, exactly his size. He was staggered by the generosity of the gift. A complex barter of onions and a sack of potatoes for half a dozen sheets—sheets and linen of any kind being particularly valuable to the bombed-out women—had brought her to the friend of one of them, the young widow of a pilot, a man with the right-sized feet. She shrugged away the difficulties, the trouble she had gone to, what it had cost. Yet, for the moment before he

---

*"Every corner burnt at the same time. / There was nothing to see but smoke and flames. / The church towers flared up / And with a roar collapsed." From *Deutschland, ein Wintermärchen*, by Heinrich Heine.

felt the wonderful ease of them (they were worn in but still newish and with a perfect pair of laces) he wished away the dead man's shoes. Sabine had made him a card. He admired her handwriting—excellent for a child of six who was only just at school. Looking closer, he realised that she had carefully traced over words which Lore had written.

At school that day, he was presented with an official document telling him to report for military training to the Reichsarbeitsdienst.* Fear shuddered through his guts. Manpower was short and for some time boys turning eighteen had been issued with a Notabitur† because the fatherland needed them. It was the turn of the seventeen-year-olds. For years there had been talk of victory; now they were spurred on by threats. Bad as things were, they were told that they would be far worse off if Germany lost. The war would eat them all. Yet he could not regret leaving an institution where there were no books, where old dodderers brought in from retirement could not keep order and did not try to teach. His mission was to assist in the manning of local flak stations, thereby releasing trained men for the front. He was to start by learning to operate a searchlight. Nicolai woke daily with the same sense of disbelief. He had not exactly imagined himself running the shipyard, destined as Wolfgang's inheritance rather than his, but it had always been a source of security. That security was gone. Now his half-brother, who wanted things so badly that he generally got them, was a fully fledged SS officer somewhere in Poland. And he, the recalcitrant schoolboy and reluctant warrior, was to spend his nights picking bombers from the sky. Had his father not told him to keep his eyes fixed on a point far away? Perhaps the gods were mocking them both. He wanted to live. It was the only thought in his head.

Riding into town, the S-Bahn crossed areas of Hamburg that had been destroyed, the tracks so bizarrely untouched that the credulous claimed the Allies did it deliberately. (They intend German citizens to travel, went the grim analysis, so they can see the worst and spread the word.) Everyone in the packed carriage pressed to the windows and stared out, saying nothing. Their silence had a muffled quality, as though they were collectively holding their breath. Perhaps, in these superstitious times, they were. Nothing moved in these places; no living soul could be seen. They saw the wallpapers change on bedroom walls; a

*Reich Work Service.
†Emergency matriculation.

black open shaft plunged down a six-storey house to the cellar. Skeletons of houses held one another up. Only the wind inhabited the desolation, creating restless seizures of dust and dirt. Grains of mortar and rubble dust flew up, eddies and clouds of it powdering over black burnt brick.

He found Klaus waiting at the end of the Feldstraße, close to the Reeperbahn. His uniform made him look older, though the helmet sat crookedly, being too large for his small head. His friend, who loved welding and was good at it, had given up his apprenticeship in the boiler factory to enlist in the Luftwaffe. Now he was a gunner in a flak battalion. He had not been able to stand the prospect of two more years of grinding hard work in a factory with a hard boss and no earnings. He insisted that they visit "his" tower first, the brutal concrete mass of the double flak tower dominating the red-light district. Entering, Nicolai saw that the cavernous spaces in the lower storeys of the flak tower were empty.

"In air raids, we fit thousands in here. Up to twenty thousand, but more always try to get in," and, arms outstretched, Klaus swivelled right, then left, to demonstrate the delights of his kingdom. "When it's jumping, we get as many as thirty or forty thousand, packed in like sardines."

They trudged up the broad flights of concrete stairs heading for the eighth floor, where Klaus and his comrades slept. He banged on the walls as they went.

"Look at that. Isn't that lovely? Three metres of concrete, safe as houses and girls all around. We sneak out and visit them. I'm going to survive this war here. Much safer than sitting in a fleapit factory waiting for a bomb to drop on you. I've got the bloody gun platform right over my head. I'm safer than Hitler."

He kept a bottle of schnapps under his army cot. They drank appreciatively.

"Klaus—what would you think, if I could have done better by you? I mean, got you a decent apprenticeship," ventured Nicolai.

"What, if pigs could fly?"

"My mother's family owns a shipyard. Owned it, that is. It got bombed to hell before Christmas, killed nearly everybody in it. Only the night watchman survived. An old man of seventy-three."

"Is that a joke?"

He shrugged.

Klaus let out a long, low whistle. "You big shit. You really could have got me in. A real apprenticeship."

"Yes, and you could have gone up with the works."

"Poor fellows, I feel for them. To the fallen."

"The fallen."

They had another drink, saluting them. Klaus gave him sidelong glances and he felt ashamed of himself for not telling him earlier. What had silenced him was the same cast of mind that told Nicolai to keep stumm about his own fighting ambitions (nil). He thought of the things his father had said. How much energy and intelligence did it take to avoid killing anyone? Would he have enough?

But Klaus was already draining the little glass and now jumped up laughing, bouncing springily on the soles of his feet, mock-punching at Nicolai. "You saved me. Good for you. We're alive, aren't we?"

Somehow they were both energised by the news. What was death for, if not to make life sweeter?

It was a short walk to the Talstraße, the centre of St. Pauli's black market, where they fortified themselves: the bar, hidden behind layers of blackout curtains, belched smoke and heat towards them. The lighting was harsh on the flushed and hectic faces of drinkers who laughed and talked too loud and did not care what they consumed, as long as it kept coming. They left after one schnapps, heading for the main brothel street, the Herbertstraße. A sign said that entry was forbidden for young people under the age of eighteen, a rule nobody enforced. Numerous young people wandered around in the blackout getting up to mischief. Steel gates with obliquely slanted bars screened the alleyway from casual eyes. Nicolai sauntered through behind Klaus.

The narrow street was so full of sailors, airmen and soldiers in uniform that they obscured the girls. They sat on stools in windows or stood, gazing boldly at the men who ogled them: a redhead in a swimsuit, a Spanish-looking woman in a tight black evening dress fluttering a fan; a girl-next-door type in skirt and blouse and sandals, the skirt pulled up, the girl beckoning. He wondered what they did about maintaining the blackout. Perhaps they pulled the curtains to when the air-raid siren sounded. Ahead of him in a business suit an ordinary-looking man, who could have been anyone's father, walked slowly, goggling at the merchandise.

"You and your camera. You could make some money here, photographing the girls. You've got a proper setup, haven't you?"

"Sort of."

"I could sell plenty, the lads think of nothing else. Look. What about her?"

An older woman, tapping on the window, blew Nicolai a kiss.

"To photograph?"

"For a quickie, idiot. She's not pretty enough to photograph."

When he smiled back, rather uncertainly, she held out both hands with spread fingers.

"Ten Reichsmarks," said Klaus. "Go on, haggle a bit. You'll get her for five."

He examined the lipstick creases around her mouth, the bosom pulled high, one leg with a slightly swollen knee pushed out provocatively. Her hands, with their brown liver spots, were very ugly. Nobody could want her. He shook his head.

"This is my one."

Klaus's voice held a certain pride. "His" girl had fair hair in plaits, wound round her ears, was dressed in a similarly foolish short dirndl and low-cut blouse with full, puffed sleeves. She had a silly face, was a rag doll with rouged cheeks. He felt no desire for her at all. He hovered around while Klaus went in. His friend was back in ten or fifteen minutes, grinning. She had washed him, before and after. They all did. Though he did not want to die without having had a woman, Nicolai had no appetite for a "quickie" with any of them. Abruptly, with a sudden shaft of surprise, almost of dismay, he understood why. It was Clara this girl brought to mind; Clara, that pink-and-white porcelain rosebud whom he sharply, urgently desired.

Head jerking (he must have fallen asleep on a sandbag), he leapt to his feet as sirens wailed and the searchlights sprang up, the blue-white glare of the master light a kilometre away joined by its near satellite, his own 150 cm light, sweeping left to right. Running down the slight slope, Nicolai jumped over the electricity cable winding its snaking path from generator to light, hurrying to take up position with the two other lads. Leaning in to the warm metal, his frozen face connected with the heat of 990-million candlepower. The aim was for the two lights between them to cone the lead RAF plane coming in, the "master of ceremonies," blinding the pilot leading the convoy of bombers to their target. Then the gunners would blast him out of the sky. Their job was to turn the searchlight as fast as possible (some were motorised; not theirs) and catch that first plane in the light. The sergeant shouted instructions; Nicolai and the other human mules heaved and shifted the great drum into its new trajectory.

Seated beside the enormous bowl of the sound locator, fat bum spilling over the tractor seat, the sergeant adjusted the wheels of the trumpet to "hear" the course of the oncoming convoy. He cursed continuously. He was an irritable gnome guiding a milky white beam so solid you could have drunk it. Suddenly they had their moth. The beams, intersecting through fuzzy night air, froze the lead plane; there were only sixty seconds before the target passed into the next zone. All along the Elbe, the sky was split by lights. The guns behind them kept up a continual staccato ack-ack; then the MC was gone. Already, the searchlights one sector on were picking up the lead plane, still intact, holding the tiny black smear in the next piece of sky. Following him came the drone of the bombers. Even over the ceaseless stutter of flak he could hear the distant thump of heavy explosions starting up somewhere near the port. He couldn't stop staring up against the constant flashes of exploding shells, the sky a soup of flying objects, black spots, then their precise white negatives burning on his eyelids.

The all clear sounded around five in the morning. Nicolai liked this dark, this quiet, making his way back through air that stank of cordite, feeling for the potholes and new craters. For twenty pfennigs he had magnesium rubbed on the soles on his boots. The sparks meant that others would see him and avoid tripping over him. Not for him the indignity of collisions, the crude insolence of boys groping any woman in the blackout. Time spent in the darkroom had given him a sixth sense. Sometimes he even walked with his eyes shut, feeling his way and using that sense (a boy on a bicycle about to hit the kerb) to divine where he was. His marker on the way home was the dairy. He could just make out the big bottles glimmering through cracks in the boarded-up window, having long ago been filled with salt, not cream. When he got home he heated himself up a plate of soup, the whitish glue known as blauer Heinrich,* more potato starch than anything else. It was the exact colour of watered-down milk. The spoon slopping the liquid on its way to his mouth told him that his hands were shaking. Events came upon him like

*Blue Henry.

this, in after-reaction. It seemed to him that he shook as much from disbelief as from fear, though there was fear and plenty of it. He rubbed his hands together until he had them under control and finished the soup. If, one day, they did not still, how could he ever become a photographer?

The parks started to green and the air smelt of spring. On Sundays, they filled with Fremdarbeiter,* the shouted greetings of Poles and Frenchmen, of Balkan and Mediterranean types flirting, their women dressed up in very short skirts. Everybody looked askance at such unnatural good spirits. People whispered about the reprisals this "enemy within" would wreak on them, just as soon as they could. Foreign workers set up their own black markets in goods train depots; it was said to be the French who broke into food shops and stole the suitcases poor folk shoved outside burning houses. It was the Poles robbing the old and unwary at train stations; it was foreign women spreading the venereal diseases that put "our men" into military hospitals, the harshest penalties notwithstanding. Nicolai noticed how many German women went with these conscripted foreigners, even in public, in the absence of their husbands. He too admired their joie de vivre. These cheerful people were resistant to the German disease of literal-mindedness, so dangerous that it might kill them all. It spread its tentacles everywhere. Since Rudolf Heß had fled to England, apparently influenced by a clairvoyant, all clairvoyants were banned. Even the future was rationed, the wags said. Entertainments were dangerous: Goebbels banned all clowns, "because he had to be the best." First, foreign singers were not permitted to perform, then the opera was closed. There were no legal entertainments left, apart from sex. People said that even Hitler could not succeed in banning that.

The spring brought good news. His father's division was posted to Italy, to a place called Roccasecca. There, sorrel grew wild in the hills and the vines were bursting into leaf. On his days of leave he went north, searching for the lost villa of Pliny in the hills outside Città di Castello, where dark green lines of cypresses delineated the lie of ancient terrains. His father wrote that certain olive trees, so ancient and gnarled that the bark was much paler than the palest leaves, might indicate where, in Tifernum Tiberinum, the writer had walked on the slopes and

*Foreign workers (often conscripts).

fertile hills. He described the craters the Allied bombs made, uprooting the tallest poplars so that they lay neatly on the path, as though a giant hand had lifted them very delicately and then laid them down to rest. Reading and rereading them, Nicolai learnt these letters by heart.

Spring shone even on lawns that were unwatered and unkempt, the grass growing long among weeds and drooping shrubbery, and between the rows where they had planted carrots and beans. Nicolai noticed in the new light that the house had grown scales, where large patches of paint were flaking from walls. He watched the honeycomb pattern the sun made on the ground as he walked in the shade of long, stretched-out camouflage nets, gashed here and there, thus demonstrating both their fragility and the absurdity of relying on this, or anything, for protection. On a brilliant May morning, off duty and playing hopscotch with his sister in the garden, he heard a sound like a huge swarming cloud of bees, saw a dark cloud to the west that shimmered and made a noise that went on increasing, a deep, penetrating humming that made all the windows not already broken vibrate. Over two hundred bombers in one formation, the sun reflecting off fuselages and whirling propellers, were all glitter and shimmer as they passed over the house. Sabine waved gaily at them.

"You sweet idiot. They're the enemy. Americans."

These enormous four-engined bombers were called Flying Fortresses, a magnificent and terrifying sight. To see so many aircraft in broad daylight confirmed what they all already knew, that the war was lost.

Transferred to work on a flak battery of four 88mm anti-aircraft guns, Nicolai was given the job of staring at the sky to spot the earliest sign of a vapour trail, to hear the first drone of a distant engine. He could have volunteered to train as a gunner, if he wanted to, but he did not. He took care to keep his head down, to say little, to use his energy in avoiding killing anyone. He continued to do menial jobs. By day, the Americans flew overhead, usually B-17s and B-24s in tight formation despite the hellish artillery they were throwing up against them, never wavering, never taking evasive action, wave after wave in a relentless advance. At night, when it was the RAF's shift, his job was to pick up the hot shells the guns spat out every few seconds and carry them to a pile out of the way, to be reused later. He dragged over sledges of ammunition when the off-duty factory workers who were supposed to help did not turn up. An 88 battery needed ten men to operate it, the shells weighed seven or eight kilos each and they were permanently short of staff.

A Russian HiWi* was assigned to them, a big burly fellow, a hard worker who did most of the lifting and helped Nicolai, as he did everyone. Nicolai had the impression that, like him, the man was hiding his intelligence for a reason. On beautiful dawns, as the sun hazed through the smoke, he would straighten up to see the man smiling, revealing slablike yellow teeth. As soon as they had the all clear, the men lit up. The sergeant who never stopped talking always threw a packet of cigarettes over to Iwan, who bowed and clapped his hands together. Then the two of them would have their smoke together and chat away, each telling the other the names of things. Though they had barely a word in common, they both understood work. His name wasn't really Iwan; that was what they called all Russians. He was pathetically grateful for anything; usually the Russians rolled up the fag ends the others threw down.

Iwan took a fancy to Nicolai's watch and endlessly tried it on, right then left wrist, daintily turning his brawny arms this way and that to admire it. If it had not been his father's, Nicolai would have given him the pretty toy.

"Keep away from him," said one of the gunner crew to Nicolai with a nudge. "It's foreigners that sabotage the shells."

"How could he? They're all crated up."

"Not here, idiot. In the munitions factories they do it. They've got thousands of foreign workers. They drill into a shell so the propellant and explosive ignite when it's fired. Blows the barrel up when we load it. Then we all go sky high. If we're lucky, they just rupture it. In which case you get a nice new face and both eardrums blown. Or if you're unlucky . . ." He drew a finger across his throat and grinned broadly, happy to have frightened somebody lowlier than himself.

A week later, when the all clear went and Nicolai looked for his HiWi, he found Iwan lying on his back, staring sightlessly at the dawn. The long anticipated dud shell had gone off in the barrel of the 88 just as the Russian was waiting to feed the next shell into the loading mechanism. He had taken the full blow directly in his chest. The barrel of the gun had stripped open like a banana. His face was untouched. When he heard the news, the garrulous sergeant came over and closed the man's

*HilfsWilliger, i.e., "willing helper"; actually a prisoner of war.

eyes tenderly, then squatted beside the big body, waiting for the stretcher-bearers to come, unable to find a single word to say.

All the time the raids intensified. Though orders were issued forbidding workers to leave the city, thousands fled. In the oppressive heat of July, the smoke and dust were unbearable. His mother decided to take Sabine to the seaside, for health reasons. He hoped that it would cheer her up. His grandmother, growing according to his mother "more wilful by the day," refused to leave Hamburg. He and Lore remained. He was not free to leave his post and she was needed to guard their house against marauding "bomb women"—women bombed out of their own houses who seized and occupied any dwelling they found temporarily empty, stripping it bare. But within a week the families already quartered with them were evacuated to the countryside and the house grew very quiet.

Early on a Sunday morning over seven hundred bombers attacked the city, setting fire to a vast area to the northwest and confusing the radar with a new technique so effective that it negated the anti-aircraft fire. On the way home, jumping over potholes, he saw new, smoking scenes of devastation, the grey cloud clearing like morning mist over the river to reveal the jagged shapes of buildings that, overnight, had turned into fantastical torn-paper versions of themselves. Glittering aluminium foil strips lay everywhere; this was the stuff the bombers had dropped. It looked exactly like the tinsel people hung on Christmas trees. He picked up handfuls and tossed it into the air.

Nicolai and Lore sat on the back steps. It was far too hot to stay inside. The garden was cracking in the unremitting heat, the few remaining lettuces wilting. It had been Sabine's job to water them; she often forgot or, when she remembered, the water had been turned off. Lore, who for months had worked ceaselessly, now had little to do. She sat motionless beside him, the dry skin of her face looking used and thin in the brightness. He slithered down and lay flat on the path, letting the sun pound and dazzle him. He was, as usual, desperately tired.

"What will you do when the war ends, Nicolai?"

"Nothing. Eat. Sleep."

"Study, that's the important thing. Go to university. The only thing you can keep safe is what's in your head."

There was nothing in his head. He hadn't even finished school. Anyway, his school was closed now, they all were. He rolled lazily onto his side, stared at the tiny creatures scurrying along the soil.

"Nicolai, promise me that you will get a good degree and use your brain. You could be a lawyer, if there is any law, if there is any justice in Germany, after the war."

"I'll find Ilse. After the war, that's the first thing I'll do and you'll come with me, to France. You can show me things. I promise I'll learn from you."

"No. Learn from decent people." Her teeth were bared in a horrible grimace of self-disgust. "I'll never see France. I don't know why my useless life has been prolonged."

"Don't say that, Lore, please."

Then she said nothing at all. She always talked like that: in intense bursts, relapsing into long periods of silence. Everybody else was trapped in the detail or told lies. Lies made the world feel safe, otherwise they would all fall down the deep cracks between the words and their meanings. But Lore told the truth. The relentless light revealed the pain that lay, always, just under the surface of her face. Long starved of vitamins, his teeth had started to hurt in just that way, as though they had been bathed in some invisible sugary solution for months that had all at once penetrated the enamel to hit the raw agony of pulp. Her malnutrition was of the soul. She was drifting away from him, or perhaps he was just too tired to tether her, too tired to do anything for anyone.

On his grandmother's seventieth birthday they took the trolley bus into town. It was a while since he had been in the centre. The city wore a depressed aspect, dusty and shabby, with shops, restaurants and department stores all boarded up. Long queues stood in front of every food shop; elsewhere streets seemed empty. Flags and posters hung over many bombed-out sites with the legend: FÜHRER, WIR MARSCHIEREN MIT DIR BIS ZUM ENDSIEG.* Along the Rothenbaumchaussee, piles of rubble smouldered and smoked, for the weather continued abnormally hot, over thirty-two degrees Centigrade by day and not much cooler at night. His grandmother, delighted that he had broadened out and grown so tall, seemed shocked by Lore's appearance.

"All bones and eyes. My dear, you're ill. I shall make you an appointment with my good doctor here," said his grandmother solicitously, but Lore did not reply. It suddenly was obvious to Nicolai, but she would not even consider it. She had a way of shutting her mouth and then smiling that he knew well, which meant that the issue was closed.

*Führer, we are marching with you to final victory.

"At least a cup of tea."

While she bustled around with the samovar, she told them how she had spoken in her "good London English" to Canadian prisoners of war working on a bomb site to see if they were well treated. They had presented her with a packet of strong tea.

"I was delighted. Imagine, every month, a Red Cross package from America with chocolate, tins of cheese and margarine and tea and Nescafé. They can give to us, not the other way round. Not, of course, that we have anything to complain of, nothing," and she patted Lore's hand, lowering her voice, "not like some people. We're going out; I've saved my coupons and it's decided. There's nothing good to eat, not even 'under the table.' Still, it may be our last night together for a long time. We'll make the most of it."

Walking back towards the Alster with the heat striking up from the pavement, he noticed here and there strange paintings resembling alpine landscapes on partly wrecked buildings. People boarded over the apertures or broken windows, brightened them with crudely painted flowers or animals. Outside the town hall, untouched by the latest attack, the Winter Relief "sacrificial column" still stood four storeys high, a plywood monument in the shape of a Greek temple testifying to a million privations. His grandmother nudged him as they passed it. "You'd think a bomb would manage to hit that ugly thing. To think of what we've given to 'those people.' And today I stood in a queue for four hours to exchange a burnt-out hundred-watt bulb for a sixty-watt one. And there are no shoes anywhere. And in my queue it was a real slanging match, between those who had been bombed out three times or four. How do people manage?" She lowered her voice, with a glance at Lore. "Of course, we are being punished for what we did to the Jews." Again, Lore said nothing.

They arrived at a crowded restaurant on the Alster, where the head waiter greeted his grandmother with elaborate compliments and led them to the remaining free table on the terrace. Two old men were singing and playing accordions on a little boat moored at the low stone jetty. His grandmother tapped her fingers to the music. They ordered a roast bird, which someone said was pigeon; at any rate, it was not on the ration cards.

"Do you have caviar? That's not rationed. Like hats. You can have as many of those as you like," she said. "Beluga, naturally, the best."

Nicolai made an effort to smile. The bird, when it came, was very small and rather overcooked. He forced it down with a little of the dry bread. Lore would not eat and kept her coat on, even though it was so very warm. His grandmother talked and talked: she told them about the magical boat rides of her youth and the long summer days when Großpapa, an athletic young man, used to row her under the green canopies of weeping willows along the shore and try to kiss her under every tree. Her forced good cheer was beginning to depress him. He felt himself receding far into the distance. The old woman with her mouth opening and closing shrank to the size of a thumbnail.

"We will survive," his grandmother said. "We survived the last war, we built up a fine business." She had taken the list of victims out of her bag, was touching the worn paper and shuffling it round and round. "Our good German people are enormously resilient."

She spoke far too loudly, perhaps because she was growing deaf, perhaps because other people might be listening. Then he realised that she was not saying these things for their benefit at all. It was her unease that was talking, the worries that ran round her head ceaselessly and the little clichés with which she consoled herself. At last, he felt sorry for her. Taking the piece of paper from her, he slipped it back in her bag.

"We must drink to your health," he said, "to another seventy years, Großmama," and they clinked their glasses together. When the sirens started their wail, there was a general groan and everybody stood to run to the shelters. The nearest one, under the Alsterhaus department store, though big, was already packed. They made their way down the broad stone steps just in time, for the wardens closed the doors and told those behind to go elsewhere.

These planes did not stop. He estimated many hundreds, at least as many as the great bombardment of the other night, wave after wave. The thundering of anti-aircraft artillery was continuous; the walls shook.

"Is that you or not?" said a girl's plaintive voice.

"It's me," said three or four male voices at once. Then there was laughter.

The vaulted cellars smelt very bad. Somebody made the old joke about bran bread being responsible for the foul air, but then there was a general silence. Crushed with so many strangers, nobody spoke. Nicolai perched uncomfortably on one of the buckets of sand, his face running with sweat. His grandmother, who was sitting against the wall in quite a good spot, had her eyes closed. Perhaps she was praying. Then the lights went out, there was the rumble of things falling, dust whirling, the feeling of choking on the hot gritty air. His head felt weird. Perhaps it was the beer they had drunk that made him feel so woozy, as though none of it was happening, yet the bombs were so near that the cellar floor shook all the time.

"We'll be buried alive!" It was a woman's voice, high with hysteria.

"Shh. Keep calm," the warden kept saying. Nicolai's head dropped; the lack of air was getting to him. He started breathing very slowly and regularly through his nose. Please, he said, don't let me die from carbon monoxide poisoning. He could feel the sweat running straight down his face and the back of his neck. There was an enormous bang and the whole place jolted. The air filled with acrid fumes, which stung so much that his eyes squeezed shut. A series of explosions followed, sucking the air out.

A door opened in the blackness. He was scrambling up and out, pulling in deep breaths of air, into the brilliant yellow light. He reached down to help the person behind. He knew this woman; it came to him that her name was Lore. The sky was the colour of sulphur and much brighter than day. The houses across the street were on fire, gigantic flames licking at them. Dark outlines of people at the windows were throwing chairs and tables and mattresses out of windows. They fell, flashing light and then dark, in slow motion through the bright air. Brilliant red and white target bombs fell all around them. They were stained-glass windows, coloured panes giving onto a golden sky and everything was beautiful. He pointed up.

"They call them Christmas trees," he said calmly. "You see, it's because of the shape." He strove to capture the sergeant's precision. "A magnesium flare, on a parachute, falling at a given speed. They illuminate the target area beautifully." He could not hear his voice. The woman Lore was saying something, but he did not know what. He indicated his ears. She pulled at his arm, pointing. People were digging at the stones and dirt with their hands. Then he remembered who he was and knew that his grandmother was under there; part of the cellar had collapsed.

The air was full of dirt, he was gagging on it. He fell to his knees and started frantically to dig. A man was tapping on the wall with a stone. Then he put his ear to it, listening. Another man was digging too; the two of them tore at the bricks with bare hands. A woman was putting bits of cement and stone into a bucket. She did it very slowly and delicately, as though handling porcelain. He observed her while furiously scooping out rubble. His ears suddenly did something peculiar. Noises rushed in, very loud, a whooshing sound and a man's voice right next to him.

"Stand back! It's going up."

The fireman's face was black. Nicolai carried on digging. The fireman pulled at his shoulders and made him stand up.

"They don't answer. They're gone. Everybody out of here!"

"But we can get water on it—cool them down—it's so hot—"

"They're dead. The whole city's on fire—the fire brigades are coming from Bremen and Lübeck and Kiel. It was on the radio." The fireman shook his head. The sweat running down his face made him look as if he were crying. Lore took Nicolai's arm, and they ran through clouds of smoke so hot that his face burnt. There was ash and smoke everywhere, and all the people had black faces. A woman with her clothes on fire, burning bright like a torch, ran past them and he jerked Lore to one side. Phosphorus. One touch and her clothes would ignite. Another woman was screaming, pregnant, huge-bellied and completely naked. A man tore off his clothes, which were burning with jets of flame. They ran back towards the lake, past a woman who was laughing hysterically, her shoulders shaking, her eyes wild. The heat took all his breath away; his skin was burning.

At the water's edge, Lore knelt and took off her coat and plunged it into the water. She put it over the two of them. Long tongues of flame were coming out of the houses. The hot wind blew and the flames suddenly changed direction and leapt out sideways. Still the bombs were falling and the sky was ever brighter. On they went, fast, turning away at the next corner. The fire was coming their way. It was a live creature that leapt hundreds of feet one way and then reared high and saw them and chose the new direction, determined to catch them.

He saw shops, a bank, a clothes shop with an elegant mannequin intact next to a blackened mess open to the sky. Lore pulled him into the shop and they went over the broken glass. She led the way down the stairs to the cellar. He stumbled over glass and brick. Still she pulled him on.

"Quick, Nicolai." At the bottom, a dividing wall had partly collapsed and, stepping over the lowest part of it, they found themselves looking into the vault of the bank. She was pushing him now, through the wall and into a smaller space where there was a circular steel door two metres wide. No people were here, just the two of them and Nicolai thought that it was strange, very strange, that a substantial basement like this was empty when so many people were crammed into other ones just along the road and that she was clever to find it.

"Go, crawl, get into the vault," she said, pushing his arms into the coat and shoving him into the dark space. "I'll close this. Get as far as you can. Then it will pass over you." Then he understood; there was no way, on the smooth inside of the vault, which had no handle, of pulling the door to behind him.

"Not without you."

"It needs my strength to keep the door shut."

He started to rise up against her, but she pushed him back down.

"I can't go on. Don't make me," she said, with such anger, such fierce command that he recoiled.

"I'm staying with you, Lore, don't do this—"

"You will do this for me. You must." He held her hands, to prevent her from pushing him, but her face was so desperate that he could not bear it and at once let go. She saw then that she had won.

She smiled at him and touched his cheek. "Thank you, now go quickly, as far and as fast as you can." Then he was crawling in the dark to the back of the vault with his own breathing echoing loud and the coat, heavy, dragging, but cooling him down. He went round a corner. He went until he could go no farther and huddled, drawing the coat over him. He could hear something, beyond his own rasping intakes of breath. She was talking to someone. She was a distant voice, crooning in the dark.

The door closed. Somehow, she had found the strength to shut it. A great rushing sound and whistling dinned in his ears and then something came up and thumped him.

He lay in blackness listening to the sound of his breath. Nicolai opened his eyes. He saw nothing. He reached out, touched something hard. He was lying on the ground, which was warm. He was not at home. He lay for a long time hoping that Lore would come, though he also knew that she would not. Perhaps she had gone to find water. He was so thirsty. He waited for a time, feeling dizzy and sad. There was something wet on his head. When he came to again, he realised how silent it was. It was all over. He was inside the vault. His head hammered; the air might give out. With an effort he made himself sit up, crawl forward. He felt his way to the front of the vault in the pitch-dark. Now, at last, he felt something that was round and that had to be the big steel door, which he put his shoulder to, wrenching it. Then he flopped onto his back and kicked at it as hard as he could, his strong boots shoving, for it did not move at first, he was trapped. Terror gave him strength for the thing formed a faint grey rim, which turned into daylight. He came out into the cellar where he had left her, gasping for breath.

The black thing he was looking at—that was not her. Lore was wearing a blue dress. The little mummified doll had nothing on at all. She was very small, smaller than him, the size of a child. Her dress had had flowers on it, blue flowers on a pale background. Vergißmeinnicht. She had told him once that this was her favourite flower. Nicolai sat for a long time and looked at this funny person with no clothes on. The legs and arms were shrunken, and the wizened little face was a brown monkey's face. Lore had a very pale face. He laid the still-damp coat over her. There was something in the pocket, which had to be saved. The overwhelming smell of hot bricks and cement made him feel sick. The sky had entered the building or, rather, there was no building left, just a pile of smouldering rubble. He climbed an incline of loose bricks and pieces of metal into the street. A chain of women were passing buckets from one to another. An old man covered with fine white ash seized his shoulder and shook him.

"Genieße den Krieg. Der Friede wird fürchterlich sein."*

He was grinning, teeth white in a black face.

So many buildings were reduced to ruins and there were no place-names or signs. He wandered slowly along, trying to work out where he was going. The heat came off the ground in nauseating waves. In an open space, people were lying on the ground, others passing had terrible burns on their faces. Farther on he was surprised to see a whole pile of wood stacked up, which surely would have burnt up straight away. Looking closer, he saw it wasn't wood but bodies. He carried on. The church had lost its steeple, just as the poet had predicted. An army truck was giving people water. He stood near it for a while, for he had no cup

---

*"Enjoy the war. Peace will be appalling."

to drink with and no energy to ask. A man noticed him and took a cup, offering a drink. He realised that he was very hungry and thirsty.

"You all right, pal? What about your head?"

When Nicolai touched it, it was extremely painful. His hand came away wet and sticky.

"Better get it seen to."

"I need to get to my unit," he said. "They're in the cellar over there."

"I see," said the man.

"I'll be off then. Thanks for the water." He walked along. The man shouted something about his head. Nicolai knew that the river would lead him home. His body ached, but he knew not to stop, for if he sat down he might never stand up again. He plodded along the Elbchaussee to their turning.

Though their neighbour's house was rubble, theirs appeared intact. Close up, he saw that a bomb had collapsed part of it. The front door remained firmly closed (Lore had the key), while Wolfgang's bedroom was gone and Sabine's, on the floor above. The wallpaper looked fresh and clean, though, and his brother's shelf of trophies stood intact, blinking in the sun. The stair went up one half-landing and cantilevered into a void. He walked around to the side and climbed over the bricks into the dining room, went into the hall and down to the cellar. The stone steps held firm. The cupboards stood at a crazy angle off the wall and many jars had slipped down and broken, but he found a jar of peas intact and another with carrots. It took a long time to get the lid off, but he managed. Thirstily, he drank the sweet liquid. He lay in Lore's little room with the green window, smashed long ago. In the little piece of mirror his face was black all over. Then for a long time he came to himself and went in flashes of light and dark.

Rats were everywhere, big fat brown ones kept popping up all the time. They could reach the food from the broken jars that lay beneath the cellar floor, though he could not. In any case, he did not like to stand, because it made him giddy and sick. Long ago, water came out of the taps. The flies, fat iridescent green ones, liked it here. Hamburg belonged to the animals. The flies, first of all, were the lords of creation. They sat on the splinters of glass in the hot sun and they shone, just as the glass did. The sound of the flies humming was the first thing that he heard in the morning. They rustled and hummed all day long. He was a little boy who shinned down trees, because the stairs were gone. He was a child who liked trains and who would unpack his train set and place it in the centre of his room and watch it grow to the periphery until there was no room for anything else. Meanwhile he lay still so his head would not hurt and watched the rats run wild from the garden into the house and out. They were his friends, they and the child. He kept the photograph from the pocket of Lore's coat propped up near him. The child looked back at him with her wise and charming face. He had a wonderful image of her mother, which he would go up and look for in a minute; he was sure he would manage to climb the tree up to his room, when he was not so tired. He liked the dark. In the dark, he felt that he was truly himself. He sank into it and with soft fingers felt through his small blind world. On the day when his mother came quietly stepping down over debris she screamed because of the rats. That woke him up. Then, stumbling to the bed, she cried.

When he woke up properly, he was lying in a white room, on a white sheet, spread on an army mattress, a metal bedstead. His head was bandaged and a young girl was looking at him, very pretty and noticeably pregnant.

"Don't move," she said.

In a moment he remembered who she was.

"Wolf?"

She shook her head. "Don't speak," she said.

So he lay perfectly still and looked at her.

Clara's parents had been killed in the big raid on Lübeck and she had come to live with them. Wolfgang had wanted to marry Clara, who had written to tell him that they were expecting a baby, but he had not come back. There was no news of him at all. Sabine came to the military hospital, hopped from one foot to the other and told him things. They were going to be evacuated and live on a farm. She had every reason to hope that there might be lambs. Certainly, there would be chickens to feed and pigs, whose backs she could tickle with a stick.

His mother sat beside his bed and tried to control her tears. She wept for him, for her mother and Wolfgang and for all the miseries crowding upon them. He wanted to tell her not to cry, for it quite destroyed her small remaining beauty, but he did not have the strength to talk. Even when she heard that his injuries and his youth exempted him from further service, she cried. It was good news, Sabine said, clapping her hands together; she and Clara were so happy that he was to go with them. Nicolai said nothing. Just looking at these three, his women-folk, took up all the strength he had. He needed to husband his energy to fight the daemons that came at night. Sometimes they were huge-bellied women, burning like torches, with his grandmother's face; some-times little men with black faces who spoke in Lore's voice and said such wicked things.

The station apart, the centre of Hamburg was unrecognisable. The sweetish stench was bodies decaying under the ruins; the silence, where he remembered screams, was eerie. On the day they finally took the train east on the first leg of the journey to a rural billet near Schwerin, it fell to the man of the family to push through the lines at the station to get something to eat for the journey, to brandish his mother's MUKI* cards in the faces of the grumblers. The train was a special one, crowded both with evacuees with their suitcases and those with empty rucksacks going out of the city to "hamster," to barter cash or belongings for food. He fought for a seat for Clara and then for one for his mother, who took Sabine on her knee. Sabine soon left to go to Clara, for she was totally fascinated by her. He could understand that. She was white and pink and gold and long-lashed, succulent as a peach.

Nicolai stood in the corridor, endlessly buffeted by those making their way up and down the crowded train, looking out at the black sea of rubble that had been their city. People talked in hushed voices of the disaster, claiming that the firestorms had consumed anything from twenty to fifty thousand people. An old man spoke in a quivering voice of Sodom and Gomorrah. Everything had been swept away; loved ones had died, some bodies would lie forever where they had fallen. Yet the train rocked from side to side, and people swayed and knocked against one another and apologised and ate whatever they had with them and breathed garlic and belched, just as though none of it had happened. He carried with him a few Reichsmarks, the green leather book of his father's sketches, the photograph of the child he had never met and the package of photographs snatched from his demolished room. Head pressed against the glass, staring out, he knew only that he was with the wrong people and that he was going to the wrong place.

*Mutter und Kinder—mothers and children.

FIFTEEN

Cannes, August 1943

Ilse pulled on a cotton blouse and skirt, tiptoed past Marie-France, who in this heat slept naked, a Mediterranean Venus with silky, sprawled limbs. She went past Maman Bonnard's bedroom, through the parlour with the pull-down bed Fernand used to sleep on, before he left for the maquis in January. That very week Marie-France had offered her a home, masking her kindness with a shrug. "Our flat needs three people," she had said. "Besides, I'll need company with Jean-Baptiste gone." Leaving the Bonnards' address with Monsieur Mallemet, Ilse had moved the next day. She wheeled Marie-France's bike from the hallway into the brilliant light and inspected the tyres. Early as it was, the heat was searing. She hoped the tyres would last. A used one in reasonable condition cost five cartons of cigarettes and she had no spares. She cycled down and across the Rue Meynadier. Approaching the Mairie, air-raid sirens wailed their screech. Traffic stopped and the streets cleared. In the nearest shelter, people sweated, listening to the flat concussion of anti-aircraft fire somewhere to the east.

"Americans," said one girl. "Probably Cap d'Antibes."

They smiled at one another. Everyone had hope these days. When the all clear sounded at last, Ilse stepped out into the beautiful day. In the atelier they were packed like sardines and at home, grateful though she was to be there, she was always with the two women. Every train and tram was crammed full, the town crowded with refugees and soldiers. To be alone and freewheel along the coast was an exquisite luxury.

The road towards Antibes was extremely steep in places. There was almost no traffic. Pedalling blithely on, she absorbed the blinding dazzle of the sun on the greenhouses where vegetables grew and marvelled at the extreme beauty of the coast. Her white skin burnt much too easily. By eleven o'clock, Ilse had to stop and rest. Up ahead was a villa with a magnificent view. All along the coast, workers were constructing a wall to repel an Allied invasion from the sea. The beaches bristled with anti-personnel mines and barbed wire; now they were building blockhouses and setting booby traps. Observers would be making precise notes on any obstacle that might stop landing craft from coming in. Yet others would be risking their lives, relaying that information in Morse to the Allies.

Nearer the villa a group of men were turning cement mixers. She pedalled the last few yards and stopped under the shade of a tall pine tree, unclipping her water bottle. The villa was aptly named Bellevue. Her legs shook from the exertion. The water was warm. She took a big swig and let it gurgle down her throat. This villa was being bricked up, turned into a blockhouse.

"Mademoiselle!"

One of the workers from the Organisation Todt,* sweating in thick winter trousers with no shirt, had seen her. He put down his shovel and sauntered a few steps in her direction. "Trop chaud pour travailler, Mademoiselle!"† he said in an accent she knew at once was Polish. It was not too hot to flirt, however. She wore no brassiere under the thin cotton blouse; evidently, he noticed. He was very muscular, smooth-skinned and deeply tanned from the work outdoors, with wonderful blue eyes.

"J'ai beaucoup soif,"‡ he said.

---

*German organization employing forced labour.
†"Too hot to work, Miss!"
‡"I have big thirst."

She held out the bottle towards him.

"Je remercie, Mademoiselle."* He came closer, took a very modest drink. He spoke very quietly. "Can you help me, Mademoiselle? And my friend, he's an Armenian? And there's another, Hungarian? We want to fight in the maquis."

Why had he picked her? His eyes, which were very clear, looked at her with an almost defiant expression. Over his shoulder Ilse saw a second man, his friend. They were all being watched by an armed guard cradling a machine gun. He came round the side of the house and started walking towards them. She backed off. The Pole returned the bottle and stepped back a pace.

"Merci, Mademoiselle!"

He stood, just watching her. Ilse got back on the bicycle and set off. The macadam was so hot that the tar was melting, it pulled at the tyres as she coasted downhill. Things were blurring. The day of pleasure was spoilt. It was too late, she no longer knew anybody, she could do nothing for anyone. She was perfectly useless. She could not stop thinking about the Pole, how he smiled and that the blue of his eyes was the exact same colour as François's and that she would not help him and he knew it.

Lucie, the seamstress with an Italian soldier boyfriend, sobbed, her head leaning on her machine. Her face was blotchy and wretched, her eyes so puffy that she could scarcely see. She was pregnant. Desperate that her man would be sent away, she worried equally about what her mother would do when she found out. Marie-France knelt beside her. "It's good if Italy makes peace. Then he won't be killed."

Her waist was thickening. From certain angles it was obvious. Ilse wondered if her mother already knew.

"But what if they're all sent home, what if he doesn't come back?" Her voice rose, quavering. "Then what becomes of me?"

"For God's sake," said Marie-France, "we've all had no word in seven months. At least you know where he is." Lucie, overwrought, burst into tears.

Simone put her head in at the door. "Will somebody take her home?"

Marie-France rose. "Come on, don't cry. I'll walk with you."

*"I thank, Miss."

Fernand and Jean-Baptiste were somewhere in the hills. The Italians—heavily defeated in Sicily and Messina—could not possibly carry on. At the beginning of September, Montgomery's Eighth Army landed on mainland Italy. The tide of war was turning towards the Allies. Ilse asked herself what would happen when the Italians went. In an emergency, a person needed cash. She took the silver photograph frame out, twisted the two tiny clasps. She kept her money there, on top of the fifty-dollar note which still held the tiny blue flower. She counted the worn bills twice. She had only two hundred and fifty francs, plus what was in her purse. She had given half her dollars to François long ago. The remainder, eked out over time, had bought such necessities as shoes and a coat, enabling her to keep her mother's flower brooch and one gold chain. She gave Maman Bonnard most of her earnings for her keep. She had wasted money on cotton, for dresses; the woollen dress for Madame Dumont at Christmas had been very expensive, then there had been Marie-France's nineteenth birthday. She touched her mother's face and wondered: What would her mother do? What would her father do?

They were woken by wild rifle fire. Children were shooting off rifles they had found dumped in rubbish heaps. The Italians had surrendered to the Allies and Marshal Badoglio had signed the armistice. The radio broadcast the news and General Eisenhower himself announced it. At once a wild celebration broke out, with Italian soldiers embracing girls in the street, taking off and throwing away their uniforms. There was music and dancing all along the roads that led from the Croisette. By dawn the next day the Italians were gone. A swastika appeared on the Hotel Excelsior and on all public buildings: the Wehrmacht had arrived. The Germans set to work shooting any of their former allies that they could find, those who had not had the sense to flee. A thousand Germans arrived in Cannes by train, some SS troops and some in plain clothes. News spread instantly that these civilians were members of the Gestapo.

The German troops patrolled in couples. Unlike the Italians who had herded together on the main boulevards, the Germans went down every street and alleyway. The night was silent but for the tramp of their boots. At dusk, despite the heat, the girls closed all the shutters and stuffed twists of newspaper into them, and then shut the windows tight and drew the curtains across. It was airless in these tiny rooms as Ilse and Marie-France set about preparing supper for the three of them. They were fortunate. They had potatoes and onions to eat. They had one another.

Ilse woke in a sweat of anxiety, dreaming that she had been stopped with incriminating posters hidden in the bicycle pump. It took a little time for her to breathe more easily. Those days were gone. If she was picked up by the SS, her papers would not be sufficient: each ID had to be backed by a full set of papers, a French birth certificate, the parents' marriage certificate, certificate of baptism and so on. For some time now she had held on to the idea that being called Laure was a kind of protection in itself, as if her mother was watching over her. She lay and worried about the papers. She should have kept her dollars and spent them on a better set. There had been a time of bad dreams when nightly her father haunted her; now her dreams were all to do with her own mistakes.

On Monday Lucie did not come to work. The next day she did not turn up either. Finishing their shift early, Ilse and Marie-France set off to see her. As they got near, they saw that the area near her home was cordoned off, the street blocked with a barricade; Vichy police stood outside every hostel and pension, and German troops with them. A soldier, seeing them, made a threatening gesture with his gun.

"They're taking the Jews," said Marie-France, tugging at her arm for her to come away.

They walked back. Ilse could not speak. It certainly never occurred to her friend that "Laure" was German, or part Jewish. Why should it? Uncle Willy in Morocco was a Frenchman, obviously. And when she talked about her Uncle Albert, he was French, too, and when she talked about her parents she said she was an orphan and, beneath the covers, crossed her fingers and toes and later whispered a special prayer, so that this catastrophe should not come true.

Marie-France went to hunt for cigarettes. Well before the curfew she returned to her mother's flat, running up to the small back room the two of them shared with a face as pale as death.

"What happened?"

She sat on the bed, fumbling for a cigarette, daring only to whisper. "I met her neighbour. They took Lucie. She was beaten, her neighbour said. Anyone who resisted was beaten—they took children too."

Ilse took her friend's hand; she felt sick.

"The neighbour said—she had an Italian soldier in her place. A deserter. Another neighbour told them he was there. The Germans took him out and shot him."

Ilse nodded.

"They're going through the hospitals, churches, nursery schools. They don't bother to look at papers with the men, the woman said. Just tell them to drop their trousers. And if a man has had—you know—the operation for another reason, they take him anyway."

Now that it had come she felt completely calm. She wondered if the neighbour who had told Marie-France the news was actually the one who had denounced Lucie's boyfriend. What people did no longer surprised her; there was jealousy and hatred everywhere.

"They'll go through the whole town. Can you believe it?"

Yes, she could believe it. She looked at her friend's brown velvet eyes, which were brimming with tears, and thought how much she liked her.

Marie-France stubbed out her cigarette with resolution. "I'm going to go and see her mother. She's in a bad state, very bad."

Later, as they tried to sleep, they heard a staccato outburst of gunfire in the next street, which went on and on. In the morning the girls went to work arm in arm, hugging each other tight, walking on broken glass. German soldiers, spotting a chink of light in the laundress's window, had fired at it, peppering the room and all in it until they succeeded in putting out the lightbulb. The shop front was destroyed. There was no sign of the laundress or her husband.

Ilse kept her head down. When a German came your way, the wise course was to get right off the pavement and into the street. It was only a matter of time before her ID was checked by somebody. Germans were suspicious by nature. She darkened her eyebrows with a piece of burnt cork. She went back to wearing a turban tightly wrapped over her hair. Without the headgear, she was too noticeable. The Gestapo sent spies in private cars to patrol the streets, arresting anyone who looked Jewish, taking them off with their families. Anyone denounced as being Jewish was arrested. Anyone who protested was arrested. At the atelier, Simone whispered the horrible story that, when babies being taken away cried, they silenced them by smashing their skulls against the nearest wall. There were rewards. Rumour had it that the Milice could get as much as five thousand francs per Jew. Rumour had it that two Catholic nurses had been deported because one was named Esther and the other Rachelle.

Ilse and Marie-France came home one evening to find a young man in the hallway wearing a trench coat with a green fedora pulled low. The

Gestapo wore such coats, so did the Vichy security police. The man stood very erect, had a military look to him. With a quick glance at each other, the girls went past.

The man reached out and touched Ilse's arm. "You. Come, Mademoiselle. Quickly."

Marie-France froze on the stairs.

Ilse felt nothing, not even surprise. "You go on up," she told Marie-France, terrified that she might say or do something rash.

"Hurry up, Mademoiselle. You can take a suitcase. Five minutes."

Ilse went upstairs to the room, packed mechanically as she had so often packed, quickly throwing her things together. Marie-France came in a moment later with a small bag: there was a tin of tuna in olive oil and another tin of sardines, a bottle of wine. Ilse's head was flashing with quick thoughts. The roof? No. There was no way out of the house that could avoid the front stair. She would not run. If she disappeared, they would take the others as hostages. She closed the case, knelt on it, clicked it shut.

"I'll be back, don't worry," Ilse said.

They embraced. Marie-France, very white-faced, hugged her tightly.

"They've made a mistake. I'll see you in the morning." Ilse put on her jacket; it was the only warm thing she had. She walked slowly down the stairs into the fading light, the case in her hand.

They walked round the corner. Her feet kept moving. Would she run? There was a moment to run, a moment to save oneself. She transferred the case to the other hand; the man's face flickered as he noticed the movement. She saw that there was something in his hand, in his pocket, the grip of a pistol. A black Citroën was parked at the kerb, the kind the SS used. Ilse slowed when she saw it. The man motioned to her to carry on, to hurry up, took her suitcase. He went up to the car and opened the back door. She got in, twisted round, the boot slammed shut. Her papers were in it. The driver, in the black uniform of the Milice, started the engine. The other man got in at the front, pulling the hat down low over his face. He had a sharp jawline, clean cut like a cartoon character. Gunning the engine, the driver pulled away.

Everything slowed down, was unreal. Ilse sat looking out at the streets of Cannes as so many pale faces had looked out of cars like these, at people on the streets like these people, crossing, walking, blurred figures who chose to look away. The glimpse of a child's face, crossing the street, clutching Maman's hand. Even the child knew to look away from the devil car. Inside, behind the glass, she was already in hell.

On the main boulevards they passed police, German troops, a cluster of officers, shades of grey on grey and the flash of Heine's eagle. The car went faster. It was dusk. She kept one hand on the door handle, loosely but ready, thought all the time about jumping, soon, not now, not here, where the soldiers were, nearer to Petit-Clos, where she knew every backstreet. She sat forward, ready, her feet clenched, her mouth concentrating. The Vichy man took the pistol out of his pocket, held it in his hand, also in readiness. He turned and looked at her steadily. She looked away. Better to be shot than tortured. She stared at the streets, the corners, the places to hide. But they were turning and she had not done it, they were accelerating, they were going away from Montfleury. They picked up more speed. With a hot flash of despair, she knew that she was not brave enough to jump from a car moving this fast.

She flickered a glance at the Vichy officer; he was looking at her in the mirror. He smiled. She looked away, then back.

"Violaine, perhaps you know my name. I'm Marcel," he said. It took some seconds for her to understand what this meant. This was Marcel, who had a clear head, who had been taken with François but had run and got away. Time passed. She allowed her hand merely to rest upon the handle. It was going to be all right. Time slowed down to its usual pace. She took a breath, leant back against the seat. Her head was thundering. She was so hot. She took the jacket off. The acrid smell was her sweat. Her jaw hurt; she had been clenching it so hard, grinding her teeth together. They headed out of town.

"Where are we going?"

"I'll tell you later."

In due course they would let her know what they needed her for. Nobody stopped them. Who would dare? In fifteen minutes they were out of Cannes and heading into the hills. Marcel knew the back routes, touching the driver's arm to say now this way, now that. It was dark; the car was very fast. Arranging herself in the back of the car, Ilse flicked off her shoes and stretched out her legs. It was years since she had travelled in such comfort. She was flooded with relief, a strange metallic taste in her mouth. She woke and drowsed, looked at the dark and slept again.

They were in a wild place. The car was bumping slowly up a rutted track. Marcel walked ahead, to light the way. The beam of light from his torch swept from side to side in a neat arc. Then he switched it off again. It was a clear night, moonlit. The car went as far as it could. She saw that he was looking at the ground, worried about wrecking the suspension. They got out. The driver went somewhere, came back with sacks. He started covering the car. When he was done, they shook hands: he was called Gaston. She had still not seen his face properly. Marcel carried her suitcase. The ground was rough under her feet; she kept to the centre of the cart tracks, walking on the mound. After about fifteen minutes, she made out the farmhouse, nestling snugly in a dip in the hill.

Gaston led the way inside, then disappeared upstairs to change out of the black uniform. "Round here I'll get shot in this," he said.

Marcel put down her case, took off the hat and coat, lit candles. He was straight-backed, with dark hair and eyes and a serious expression. She looked round the room. The blackout curtains hung to the floor. The flagstones were neatly swept. A large table was flanked by a dozen chairs. There was no sign of any military presence.

"Do you want a drink?"

Ilse nodded.

Marcel found glasses and a pitcher of water. The water was tepid but good. "I was worried that you'd run away."

"I wasn't brave enough. It was a fantastic trick to pull off."

"It's the authenticity of fear we need, to make it work. But you were so cool. Quite wonderful," he said. Ilse thought how wrong he was.

Gaston returned in normal clothes. "Are you too tired to go on?" His voice sounded different, louder, as if it had been strangled by the Milice uniform.

"I'm fine," she said.

They probably wanted her for her German; Marcel presumably knew that it was her mother tongue. The two men nodded at each other.

"You stay here," said Marcel to Gaston.

The ground was rough, hard going in espadrilles. Bonfires flickered. The land was scrubby, there were huge boulders which she stumbled against. The drone of an engine passed some way overhead.

Marcel stopped, listened hard. "A Halifax," he said.

Ahead was a group of men. She could hear some of them talking Polish; it gave her the familiar pang. She smelt the donkeys before she saw them. A pair stood in harness at a farm cart. The drop had been successful. The metal containers were some two metres long and immensely heavy. It took four men to lift them; they had carrying handles. Ilse watched them being manhandled onto the cart. There were five such containers, an enormous load. They put the first ones on the cart. The donkeys shifted their feet, flattened their ears, were shoved forward. The cart wheels turned with difficulty. The cart edged on, then stuck. Men stood at either side, supporting it on the rough track. A man started to swear softly, in French and then in Polish. The hair on the back of Ilse's neck stood up. They were very close, her shoe dislodged a stone which spun away.

"Who is it?"

A torch flashed in her face, she flinched, the torch went off.

"Violaine," said François. The bonfire glinted on white teeth, as he smiled. There was a glimpse of his pale hair. Then the men were kicking the fires out, covering the scorch marks with scrubby bush. The cart was pushed loose where it had stuck fast. The donkeys were shoved onwards; the men talked softly, cursing when the canisters threatened to come loose from their moorings. It grew very dark, clouds covered the moon. All the way back to the farmhouse, François held her fast, his arm round her waist. She was stumbling and slipping and had lost her bearings. She stumbled, so he would hold her tighter.

The unloading had to be done before dawn. A dozen men worked flat out. They cracked the canisters open on the stone-flagged floor and unpacked them. The arms were taken away; three of the men went to dig a pit somewhere outside for these and for the explosives. The detonators went in a row of empty milk churns. There was real coffee, socks, armbands in patriotic red, white and blue. One parcel contained blankets, another full British battledress.

"I wonder when we'll be using these."

From time to time he smiled at her. The men called him Raoul. He was the leader, telling them what to do in a mixture of Polish and French.

The fourth canister revealed a real treasure: the wireless set he wanted, packaged neatly in a brown suitcase. "Marcel will be happy," he said. "He's the one who loves taking risks. He did a good job, fetching you, didn't he?"

She smiled. The men went outside. She woke when François threw a canister of Player's Navy Cut onto her lap. "Very precious. We wrap them up well and put them in the donkey dung, nobody goes in that stink," he said. "Don't look so shocked."

She shook her head. Was she shocked?

"You're exhausted," he said. There was a tender note in his voice. He took her upstairs; they passed the farmer's bedroom with its huge old-fashioned bed. There was a second bedroom. She could sleep there. Ilse sat on the bed. A cockerel was crowing somewhere outside.

"Why did you send for me?"

"To make sure you were safe."

Of all the possible reasons, this one had not occurred to her.

She slept deeply. Waking in the late part of the morning, she went to look for him. There was a woman cooking whom she greeted, who seemed unsurprised to see her. The men were in the fields. François was out there, digging, in an old blue workman's overall and shirt. In a little while he stopped and fumbled for a cigarette, threw one across to her. Navy Cut, the best, and very strong. She blew a smoke ring into the beautiful day.

"Bravo, ma petite," he said, laughing at her.

"François the farmer," she said. They looked at each other. He must see, now, how different she was. His hair was almost white. She had forgotten how it grew and the way his eyes smiled. In a little while, she had to look away.

"Didn't I tell you that that was what you'd end up doing?"

"These villages support us. So we support them. Dig potatoes. Help with the harvest. The land is very poor. We live off it—no ration cards. From time to time we steal some."

When he went back to digging, she could look at him properly. He was being so kind and everything was simple; something about him was different. Perhaps it was to do with the betrayal. She pushed the bad thought away.

"You like it, don't you?"

"It's good to labour," he said. "It's good not to think."

For supper, madame offered white bean soup, coarse farm bread and onions, which Ilse sliced as neatly as she could while François washed himself outside at the well in the yard. The three of them sat to eat.

"Madame—for you." From behind his back, François magicked a tin of coffee beans, real ones, and held them out. The farmer's wife was dumbfounded.

"Will you make us some?"

"On va se régaler,"* she said.

The old-fashioned grinder whirred; the aroma was magnificent. The three of them drank the coffee in silent enjoyment. François played with the empty glasses, three, two and one, until the pyramid was perfectly aligned. The day had gone fast. She knew the rules, understood not to talk too much to madame, not to ask anything about where she was or why. She helped wash the dishes, standing by her side. By eight o'clock madame was yawning, her head lolling. She wondered where the farmer was.

"Where will mademoiselle sleep?"

"She can have my bed."

His was the second bedroom, his bed the one she had already slept in. She washed in the basin set on a little stand near the window with the blackout curtain open onto the warm night and a breeze flowing in. She brushed her hair several times and put on her nightgown. She drew the curtain, lit the candle, sat on the bed and waited. Softly, François knocked on the door. He sat on the bed, pulled off the heavy boots. Then he stood, looking at her. "Excuse me," he said politely.

"Oh."

Ilse turned her back, hoped she was not blushing. Anyway, it was almost too dark to see. The rustling sound was him undressing. Then he came round to her side of the bed and blew out the candle. She waited. He went back to his side of the room and sat down on the bed, which creaked heavily.

"So many Poles," she said. "You must feel at home."

It was an exceptionally stupid thing to say, even for her.

"From the mines, there are thousands of them near here. A big Polish community."

"Oh."

"Lie down, Ilse," he said. "There's plenty of room for two if we make ourselves small."

Stiffly, Ilse lay down, turned onto her side. When he lay down, the bed creaked again. She told herself to breathe. He pulled up the cover, lying with his arms crossed behind his head, and sighed heavily. The sigh turned into a yawn.

"Good night, ma petite. Sleep well."

"François, what happened to the farmer?"

*"We'll have a real treat."

"Poor man. Taken as a hostage. Nobody knows."

His breathing deepened.

Ilse lay wide awake, becoming angry.

"Am I to stay here?"

"Hmmh? No."

"Then what do you want of me?"

"This isn't safe. I've arranged a place for you. High in the hills." His voice was slurred with tiredness.

"Far away, is that it?"

She knew that she sounded cross.

"It won't be for long. Don't worry, Ilse. The Allies are in Europe. We'll take Italy. We'll win the war," he said.

She did not trust herself to speak. He was going to sleep. She coughed, twice.

"What's the matter?"

"Nothing," she said in a tight voice.

"Don't you trust me to do the best for you?"

"With my life," she said.

"Then what do you want of me?" He reached out, patted her on the shoulder. Ilse found nothing to reply. This question, the one he would never answer, went round and round her head.

François slept. She edged as close as she dared and smelt the smell of him on the nightshirt, the sweet fragrance of his skin, faintly olive-smelling with its little edge of coffee, of cigarettes. He had been up half the night, she told herself, he had laboured in the fields all day. It was only natural that he was tired. He did not want to touch her. It never occurred to him. She did not dare to touch him. She could not stop thinking about the woman in Pontacq, whom he had taken in the night. In due course, anger gave way to the weary, familiar feelings.

The faint noise was the sound of a man screaming silently in his sleep, the bed rocking violently.

"It's all right, it's all right." She reached out, tried to calm him. He struggled wildly, the muffled noise rising until, with a huge effort, he sat upright in bed and let out a real scream. Sweat was pouring off him. His shirt was sodden.

"Please, please—don't—"

"I'm sorry. I'm sorry."

He lay back, his chest heaving.

"Was I screaming?"

"Yes."

"I can't be in a town. Not while this is going on. I have to stay in the country, where no one can hear me."

"Take off the shirt," she said. He was shivering with cold. He threw it off. She told him to lie down and warm himself under the covers. Eventually he stopped trembling.

"You can tell me," she said. "Maybe that will stop the nightmares. If somebody else knows."

For a long time she listened to his quiet breathing. She was almost asleep when she heard his faint whisper.

"You see, Ilse, it was bad luck. A resistant decided to squeal and they took him for a ride round Marseilles and he saw me almost immediately. Marcel ran. He got away all right, but of course they kept me." His voice was weary. "We had very good papers. I wanted to try and bluff it through. Once you run, they know. Marcel was right and I was wrong. I had several months to think about it."

"How many months?"

"Long enough. The time went slowly. I used to get news. You know, the FFI* would cycle past the prison, call out the news from the BBC bulletins. For all the prisoners inside. To give us hope."

There was a long silence.

"Shall I light the candle?"

"No. I'd prefer not." His voice was very even. She knew that tone.

There was a long silence. In that darkness, she felt that she had never been so close to another human being. He exhaled, a long soft sound.

"They brought in a child. A little girl. Jewish, of course, there were so many there. A little German Jewish girl. Pretty, dark hair, a little girl maybe ten years old. Her parents were in the building. How did he know, to choose a little girl?"

He was a quiet voice in the silence of the night.

"The German officer. He knew a nursery rhyme, he said. Do you know what happened to little suck-a-thumb? She knew the rhyme, she said it, to please him. Then he cut off a finger. The sound, the click. I hear the click. And she didn't cry for a second—she didn't cry for a

*Forces Françaises de l'Intérieur.

moment—not to begin with. A click. You see, when the bone is cut through. Snap. It's the click that wakes me, in the night."

Ilse swallowed.

"It didn't matter to him, what he did to her, because he wanted the information. And I was to watch—so much blood, Ilse, I have never seen so much blood. I see it when I close my eyes."

She waited, trying so very hard not to let the words go into her head.

"Then he held up her hand and said, Shall I start on the other one? You know the rhyme, of *Struwwelpeter*? Are you familiar with the works of Heinrich Hoffmann? He is quite a connoisseur of little children who are naughty. You can save the other hand, if you want. Her parents are musicians. There is, of course, a famous concerto for one hand."

His voice went on and on in the darkness until the little girl died. Then he fell silent. Ilse breathed in and out until she thought she could control her voice.

"Cigarette," she said.

"Let me find a match," said François with the weary gentleness she remembered. He got out of bed, felt for the cigarettes, lit one for both of them. Then he turned, lit the candle that was stuck in an alcove in the wall. In the light of that sudden flame she saw his back. It was a mass of scars, from the neck down and around the sides and down to the buttocks. She touched it. His body shuddered away from her hand. He turned. In places, his back had the angry red of a fresh wound.

"François, what did they do to you?"

Hers was the high, thin voice of a child. She took a deep breath, steadied herself.

"Nothing," he said. "I am alive. You see, they left my face alone. They are monsters of the most subtle kind. When you see me coming, I look fine. So when you see me coming, if you know me, it is best to run away. That's the rule. Those who know you avoid you. You have probably betrayed them. Because the torturers are right behind—infinitely wise, knowing exactly how to destroy a human, body and soul."

"But it must hurt, the digging—the work—"

"Pain is good for me. So I won't forget."

Then she was quiet. They smoked in silence. Gradually, the tension went out of him. "Sometimes, if someone holds my head," he said humbly, "sometimes I can sleep." She knelt and held his head with her hands cupped round it. When at last his breathing deepened into sleep, she held herself together and was very still, for fear of waking him. While she held his head, he seemed to have peace.

In order not to think about *Struwwelpeter*, Ilse thought about the art student with the white-blond hair who got on a train to Paris and joined the heroic Polish Legion and who drew so beautifully in the dust. He relaxed and slept more deeply. She could look as much as she chose. She prayed to her God for a moment's rest for him. Many broke under torture. Most did. Marcel trusted him, evidently, for in reconnecting with a man returned from hell he had broken the most inflexible rule of them all. She knew so many things about François with absolute certainty. She was certain that he had given nothing away.

She kept one hand resting on his head, for reassurance. Gently, fearful of waking him, she let the other hover above the latticework of scars which covered his back and upper arms, so that there was no whole skin left, red weals piled on one another, a contour map of her world with places where the blood oozed freshly, where the crust was broken anew. Every slight movement had to hurt him. Perhaps he sensed the hand. Perhaps she was hurting him even now. The light flickered as he turned, groaning very faintly. She held her breath, took his head back between her two hands. The candlelight laid its golden rim on his beautiful untouched profile.

In the morning she came down the stairs.

Whistling cheerfully, dominating the farmhouse with his presence, François held up a clutch of eggs. "We've been given a present. The hens have laid."

Hey presto, there was another little miracle he whisked from behind his back. "And madame has presented us with a little butter she has made."

She watched as the long fingers of the artist carefully cracked the eggs, one by one, into the ancient black skillet. They slithered in the pan. Her thoughts slid away from what lay beneath the shirt.

As the dish was put before her, she tried to smile at him. He smiled back. The dark angel was gone. Ilse lowered her head and started to eat the eggs, slowly. She had not eaten anything so rich for a long time. It was important not to wolf them all down at once. Things went on, they went on and on. The fact that François could not be healed or helped did not change the way that she loved him.

When she had eaten, he said it was time. She picked up her suitcase.

Gaston, once more in the black uniform, had brought the car as far as it could go. Some of the men had returned.

Ilse saw Marcel rolling a heavy milk churn along the ground and went over to him. "I didn't thank you," she said.

When he smiled, as now, his solemn face lit up and he was suddenly charming. "You and I will meet again. One day, when the war is over. I am certain of it. You can thank me then," he said.

François walked with her to the car. "Have you heard of the military academy at Saumur?"

"Yes," she said, though she had not.

"Marcel was there. He was a cadet when the Germans invaded. They had been taught the finest codes of honour. Nobody had ever told them that a French soldier could run away. And so these boys of sixteen saw it as their duty to fight."

Ilse waited. She did not think she could stand to hear another sad story.

"These children raised the flag and held a bridge against the German advance for a whole day. While the rest of France collapsed. And the good folk of Saumur stoned them, from behind, so they should surrender faster and spare the town. Marcel is the best man I have."

She nodded. They had reached the car. Lightly, he kissed her on both cheeks.

"Where am I going?"

"A beautiful place."

She nodded again and tried to smile. She got in. The car bumped away down the track. François was waving. When she could no longer see him, Ilse grew calmer. Of course she knew what he wanted of her. She had always known it. She was the child whom he was going to save.

SIXTEEN

Pic de Baudon Mountains, December 1943

Standing in the sacristy, brushing the rim of mud from the hem of the spare soutane so it would look decent for Sunday, Ilse heard old Totain talking to Père Lemusier. "It is a national tragedy for France. Look what they are sending here. An army of Jews, blacks and communists." Totain was deaf. He had lost half his teeth and made a whistling noise when he spoke. Some counter-expostulations came from the curé, but the old man was not finished. "They are bombing us, mon Père," he cried. "Us. Not Germany. They are bombing our cities. Our towns." He was small, ruddy-faced, over eighty and full of opinions. Many of the village were red; not Totain.

Ilse finished the soutane, started chiselling away the thick clumps of mud that clung to his shoes. So bent by arthritis that he could scarcely walk, the curé nevertheless visited his flock daily. She dug with the blunt knife, levering off the heavy mass at a snail's pace, careful not to remove the soles at the same time. Patiently, her employer expounded the strange facts of war. She ducked out of sight when Totain passed; she would see him soon enough at mass. She knew the Latin by heart. Much could be deduced from the solemn tone of it and from the grammar, which was a little like German, and the words, which were a little like French. The words were fascinating. It was harder to like the people.

Violent winds swept through this tiny hamlet. Père Lemusier said this remote village would be beautiful in the summer; he spoke of bees and honey and fields of herbs. It was safe here; François had sent her here for that reason. The watchdogs knew everyone; there was an out-house with a corrugated-iron roof she was to go to, if strangers came to the village, if the dogs barked. She had been dropped near a farmhouse and the farmer had offered the barn to sleep in, in return for working in the fields. Within days, the priest had heard about her and come slowly hobbling up the steep slope to ask if she would work for him. Yet his tiny stone house, leaning up against the church for protection, barely had room for him. She was especially grateful now that winter was here, because the cardboard soles of her shoes soaked up the water and then froze, and she was very susceptible to chilblains. The hot red itching which made any shoes a torment was her particular affliction. She was very fortunate. In the towns, where they had no fresh vegetables, epi-demics of boils and carbuncles were breaking out.

When she had cleared up the supper dishes, Ilse chopped dried herbs, breathing in the sweet smell. In spring and summer, Père Lemusier collected wild rosemary, sage and basil, verbena, savory and wild thyme, and dried them. The herbs supplemented his income and gave flavour to the simplest meals. On winter evenings he laboured to sew his little sachets, the tiny needle held in fingers gnarled like tree roots. With perseverance and time, those fingers taught her, anything could be accomplished.

The curé went to bed early; Ilse slept in the kitchen. Often she woke, remembering the words of François, railing at her inability to for-get them, to marvel at the silence. In this quiet place, with nobody to talk to, a person who kept very still might in time hear the voice of God. The curé heard it, even if she could not. She wanted to ask God why she was cursed, why she had always to live without those whose affection and company she so greatly craved. As she made her confession, week by week, her mind grew calmer. She had been angry and hateful to her father and they had quarrelled; she had not loved him. She had told lies. She had felt rage against her mother for abandoning her. She had been unkind and jealous of Renée, impatient and cruel. In the calm dark of the confessional she laid these burdens down.

That bitter winter there were only deaths, no births. In the mountains, Père Lemusier said, death came closer when the light was low. Twice he was called out to the dying in the middle of the night and the next afternoon she found him, lying quietly on a pew with fingers interlaced, sleeping as peacefully as a child. Ilse, too restless and too young to sleep so much, sat up late. Her fingers were so cold that sometimes she pricked them and did not realise it until tiny spots of blood bloomed and browned the fine muslin. Then she stuck the needle through the work and, closing her eyes, thought about the pink dawn over Meknès and what Toni would be doing that day, and pictured her high heels moving through the souk. When the wind made the door rattle and the candles guttered so low that she could not see, she would crouch over the dying embers of the fire and call up the heat of Morocco, and wonder about the future. She felt certain that Toni would live, though she was not sure of any of the others. Perhaps knowing how to survive was a defining characteristic of the Poles, like their courage and their recklessness. Always, her wilful thoughts crept back to François. She possessed almost nothing, but still she held on to that empire of dreams that Albert had spoken of. This told her that, though she might feel that her soul had become French, her bones would remain German forever.

Word got around that she was a seamstress. She did sewing work for the village in return for vegetables and wine.

Père Lemusier shook his head. "You waste your time. With your intelligence you could easily learn Latin and Greek."

The remark astounded her. "I've had no education."

"Life has educated you," he said. "You have a good brain. Don't let it rust."

He gave her a Latin grammar book for schoolboys. Years ago, when the village still had children, he had taught them. She puzzled over the texts, extracts from Cicero and Caesar and Pliny and Livy, working out what the words meant. Later, he started her on Greek. It took her a long time to learn the letters, but when she had, she found it satisfying to decode. Now that it had something to study and to occupy it, her mind found some ease. She reflected a good deal on what the curé said. Perhaps she was intelligent, after all. It was true that she liked books more than she liked most people. She knew hardly anything about herself. She seemed to have grown up on her own, without having had those conversations which told a person things about herself. The smallest comment fell deeply inside her to be turned over and considered. If her mother lived, if her father lived, she might still discover who she really was.

Young men carrying arms appeared on remote country roads wearing berets and tricolor brassards, members of the FFI. The sight of them made Ilse restless. She, who could have been useful to them, swept floors and darned shirts. She could not live in this paralysis forever. But François, who had got her into the war, had also removed her from it, and she could not oppose his will.

The harvest had been half ruined by the early onset of a bitter winter cold and spring brought no relief. Those who grew shallots, tomatoes, aubergines and courgettes to sell down on the coast in the big markets of Monte Carlo and Beausoleil and who were relied upon also to supply the maquis were in despair. In May the first American air force Liberators droned overhead. June was another month of heavy clouds, driving rain, leaden skies. When the extraordinary news came that the Allies had landed in Normandy, it rippled through the village. Totain, drunk on homemade brandy, charged up to the church carrying a bottle of firewater for the curé. In August the weather changed. The village lay under sultry heat. News came through the farmers' markets that the Germans were withdrawing from France. She itched to be with her friends, to see Marie-France, to find François. Everything that mattered was happening without her.

That Sunday, one of the villagers presented them with a leveret he had snared to celebrate. Ilse skinned the lanky creature, jointed it, sprinkled the tender flesh with leaves of sage and thyme and roasted it. She served it that night with potatoes, a salad made from tomatoes and fresh basil with the good olive oil, a second salad of wild sorrel she had gathered. They feasted. As a child, she could never have eaten hare. The war had given them the ability to stomach anything. They drank a bottle of wine, savouring it, and then opened a second, for luck. They took their chairs out to the little patch before the door and looked at the stars. She grew steadily more tipsy and odd thoughts kept coming and strange questions.

"I read those Roman emperors and the wars of the Greeks. It's all about gods and kings and warriors and battles. Nobody tells you what happened to the children," she said.

"History is written by the winners."

"All those children who die before they grow up, they're not recorded anywhere," she persisted.

"They're baptised, they go straight to the arms of God."

"What about the Jews? They're not baptised."

She waited. The moon was very high and pale, and shone clear on his face. He said nothing. So she stood up and went in and set about scraping the dishes and washing them and rinsing them, and he was quiet for so long that she thought he had probably gone to sleep and that she would wake him and help him up to bed. When she touched his arm, she saw he was not asleep at all.

"The people here are very ignorant. They don't even know that Jesus was a Jew. We see the Jews being taken away and we make the sign of the cross and are glad, that they have not come for us. All the early Christians were Jews. I can't tell you how God will account for it. You are right. Nobody will tell the story of the children. In the Great War, terrible and cruel as it was, men fought other men on battlefields. Now we bomb cities and kill innocents." The curé stood and, easing himself as straight as he could, he stretched out his arms in the pale light. "Before I became a priest, I was a soldier. They gave me a medal for killing people in the last war. I became a priest because of what I had seen and done. I still have the medal, the Croix de Guerre. That is my terrible sin of pride, that I kept it."

"Before I became a Catholic, I was a Jew," she said. "Well, half a Jew."

By his lack of surprise, she saw that he must have always known. That was why he had sought her out. She should have realised that he was the chief resistant in the village, that he was the contact François knew of.

"People can be more than one thing," he said. "Perhaps that will save us, in the end."

It was the longest speech he had ever made.

Perhaps it was because she had completed the final part of her confession that she felt so free. In the morning, Ilse pulled her suitcase out from under the canvas bed and inspected her valuables. She had some francs still, inside the silver frame. She took out the fifty-dollar note and turned it over. It was her talisman, too precious to be changed into bread or meat. Her mother's fingers had placed it there for a reason. She wondered what its purpose was.

"You are taking away all the youth of the village," said the curé sadly. She gave him the address of the Bonnards in Cannes and a shirt she had made for him and had been saving for his birthday. Père Lemusier blessed her. He had filled a flour sack full of red onions, courgettes and tomatoes; this he pressed upon her together with a bottle of olive oil. She walked away backwards, waving. Braced against his stick, he waved back. As he dwindled to a black comma against the sky, she saw again what daily life obscured, that God had chosen this tall man to bend down towards the earth. Perhaps it was because of that sin of pride. Without complaint, he bore it.

Ilse took the precaution of getting off the bus before Cannes in case roadblocks were still operating, but there was no Gestapo checkpoint in the suburbs. When air-raid sirens sounded, she sheltered with two old women in the cellar of an empty factory that once made packing cases out of cardboard. They listened to the Allies bombarding the coast and the heavy German guns on Mont Agel booming their response. When the all clear sounded, she waited for a bus down to the Croisette. Nothing came. Eventually she walked down. The suitcase and bag grew heavy. Walls in town were plastered with notices warning that the cur-few was lifted only for a few hours, until eight p.m. A German soldier on guard waved her on with a menacing gesture of his gun. It gave her pause, that the Germans were still a presence in Cannes. She needed to find shelter fast. But there was nobody in the quartier where Marie-France and her mother lived; the entire street was boarded up and empty. An old woman carrying a cat in a basket told her that the inhabi-tants had been evacuated to the empty houses in the La Californie dis-trict at the other end of town.

With burning feet, Ilse plodded up the steep winding street, the largest of those that went from the shops up to the elegant quartier of La Californie, the wind coming in off the sea giving little relief from the heat. Halfway up, the Boulevard Montfleury cut across the district. Squinting up, she could see the Col St. Antoine; below lay the sea. Above these handsome villas but screened from sight by the trees, a huge blockhouse dominated the wooded ridge. Lying two hundred metres above sea level, the big naval guns were a major target. It was an un-scrupulous choice to move civilians in here, knowing the Allies would not spare the blockhouse for this reason. People were bustling around in the short time left before the curfew. She felt extremely tired and dispir-ited, that she had left her place of safety for this; that the Germans had not left after all. She put her suitcase and bag down and sat on a wall, dropped her head into her hands, stared at the ground. When she had rested she would ask somebody if there was a place where she could go for the night.

A pair of dusty feet came up and stopped right in front of her, feet in preposterously high-heeled wooden-soled shoes. "I've seen that dress somewhere before." The familiar voice was full of suppressed laughter.

Ilse leapt up. Marie-France embraced her warmly, drew her along the street. "Maman said she had seen a girl looking exactly like you. And I said, 'Well, did you ask if it was Laure?' 'I didn't think to,' says she, 'I just thought it couldn't be.' Isn't she the limit? So I said, 'Well, then I'd better go and see.' " She embraced her again. "I'm so happy it's you."

"Did you think I was dead?"

"A man came and told us you were safe—good-looking, young, very nice."

"Blond with blue eyes?"

"No. Very dark. A chic type." It had to be Marcel. Marie-France linked her arm to hers, drew her closer. "It made me so happy, when he came, to see the quality of the people in the maquis. Because of Fernand and Jean-Baptiste."

"That person you saw—he's not maquis—don't say that."

"I won't tell anyone anything, don't you worry."

Her dark eyes shone with excitement. Ilse saw how invigorated she was by the idea that "Laure" had gone to the maquis and returned, as though that guaranteed the safe return of her men. She said nothing, not wanting to disillusion her. The penalty for leaving the maquis was death; contact with families was frowned upon. For some reason Marcel had broken a rule, out of sheer decency. He had a mind of his own; that was why François prized him so.

Along with their downstairs neighbours and her mother's sister-in-law, Aunt Annie, the Bonnard family occupied an ugly pink villa, partly sheltered by the ridge. Fortunately it had a very deep cellar where they could shelter during air raids. "Concrete." Marie-France rapped a wall. "We've not had one clear night without a raid up here." She told Ilse to leave her suitcase down there. They set to, making a ratatouille of her vegetables while the gas was still on. It was only an hour before the first siren sounded. The Allies were shooting up minefields, attacking the batteries along the coast and aiming at German targets all over Cannes.

"Wehrmacht engineers filled the Carlton's cellars with dynamite.

They'll blow it up in one huge blast when the Allies come." She shrugged. "But the Germans still eat and drink there."

At one of the first bombardments, seemingly directly overhead, Marie-France's mother soiled herself from terror. Stiff with fear, she lay on the stinking mattress with a pillow over her head. She seemed to Ilse to have aged considerably in the past year. They cleaned her up as best they could, but could not make her happy again. From time to time she wept. Eventually she slept; Aunt Annie and the elderly neighbours did too. It was the one small benefit of age. Ilse and Marie-France sat with their heads together, went on whispering as the earth thundered and shook. In spite of everything, the pleasure of being with her was intense. Friendship was precious, it was worth the bombs. In snatches, they too slept. The day passed in the cellar; another night of raids succeeded it; the authorities stopped bothering to turn on the sirens. Spooning up the last taste of good mountain food, trying not to eat too fast, Ilse remembered the intense silence of village nights as if they had been experienced in centuries past. They had very little water and the electricity was cut. Succeeding waves of Allied aircraft attacked the coast, point by point. Back thundered the Nazi coastal batteries on Mont Agel with ear-splitting explosions. The earth shook all day with the thunder.

The old neighbour crawled over to Ilse, pointing a finger at her. "You see?" he said, his hand shaking with rage or perhaps just old age. "The Allies are ten times worse than the Boche."

They rationed the candles and for long periods sat silently in the pitch-blackness. Exaltation, the certainty that this must be the end, gave way to hunger and thirst and misery. The ground near them rocked and shuddered with extremely near hits.

When the bombardment stopped, they came like moles blinking into the light and the strong, green smell of mashed undergrowth and pine. The tarmac, ripped up by the blasts, was still hot. Bundles of clothes lay here and there: people who had been caught in the open or pieces of those who had been blasted into it. The ball was an old woman's head, a mush of festering grey with flies on it; the rest of the body nowhere to be seen. White bones stuck out of a severed leg. As the stench reached her, Ilse retched, dry-throated, behind a bush. She had nothing to bring up but bile.

Down the hill, a truck was giving out cups of water. Civilian casualties were heavy everywhere. Nice had also been attacked, and Marseilles.

The business of collecting, identifying and burying bodies had already begun. Ilse watched a man slowly picking his way through the burnt-out cars and pieces of shrapnel, bending over and looking at each body as though he were a connoisseur and then carrying on. On this beautiful evening he might have been a typical inhabitant of Cannes out for his daily stroll. He told them that somebody down the road had a functioning radio. Ilse and Marie-France went from house to house until they found it. There was insurrection in Paris. They heard a brief report on Soviet successes, another on the Allies' advances in Normandy but not a word of the Riviera.

"Paris has been mined," said Aunt Annie with finger-wagging authority. "You'll see. Hitler will never surrender it, except in ruins."

"A tragedy for the nation," said Maman Bonnard tearfully. She treated her sister-in-law as an absolute authority.

"The Allies are going to land tomorrow, August fifteenth. Napoleon's birthday. It's all planned." Annie was very certain.

"Ssh. You're ridiculous," said Marie-France.

The siren began to wail. The shelling started up and went on. It was another day before they knew that in one respect at least Aunt Annie had been right. The Allies had indeed landed, not at Cannes, which was so well defended, but elsewhere along the coast. The radio reported that German troops were falling back everywhere. But the shooting and shelling went on.

"Wait," said Marie-France. "Wait. They're gone except when the population comes out to celebrate. Then they'll shoot us all."

But the next time they came up into the still suffocating heat, Allied warships were anchored offshore. A French warship was shelling the German positions at Grasse. The huge black pillar of smoke that never stopped rising into the sky to the east marked the fuel dump at Antibes; it had received a direct hit. It burnt for days. A week later the guns fell silent. Overnight the FFI took both the blockhouse above them and the other main one at the extreme point of the Croisette. The old man spoke of la gloire and Marie-France winked at Ilse behind his back.

"Do you believe it?"

Neither of them believed anything.

The girls cleared the cellar out; dragged their possessions into the garden where the branches of the torn pine trees hung down, tired and sad-armed. Then, too weary to do more, they sat on ground littered with broken tiles and pieces of stucco, shredded mimosa and jacaranda, letting the sun warm their backs. The silence was eerie. The fighting had swept over them and gone elsewhere. Later that afternoon the sound of batteries bombarding targets started up and, like a film, they saw the response of the warships lying offshore in little white puffs of smoke. They heard the thump of bombs, the noise of exploding anti-aircraft shells, the odd salvo of artillery somewhere on the Esterel, all muffled like a storm carrying on beyond the next hill.

Marie-France went off on the scrounge, came back with a jug of water and two bottles of wine. A bomb had smashed open a house further up the hill and people were taking wine from the cellar there, which was very well stocked. Filling glasses, they saluted the warships on the water. When it was her turn to drink, Maman's hand shook so much that most of her wine spilt. Venturing into town later, they found the shops shuttered and closed. Toiling back, they saw an open staff car race in from the direction of La Napoule. It was a funny drab colour with a white star painted on the bonnet and unfamiliar markings. It screeched to a standstill. The Americans had stopped to look at a map. The light was fading. They were discussing something, gesticulating; one of them got out a torch and held it over the map. Marie-France nudged Ilse and stepped boldly closer. One of the young men was very blond and somehow golden in the light. He smiled at them, folding the map and saluting with one finger to his cap as they accelerated away with a sudden jerk. The car abruptly changed direction; the torch, resting on the front ledge, rolled over and toppled out. Marie-France picked it up. It was a big heavy one and very good quality. She turned it on and off, on and off. For a year, nobody had seen a battery that worked.

They climbed silently back up the slope with their spoils of war. The light of the torch went ahead, a beacon against the dark. Ilse was reflecting on how strong their accents were; she had not understood one single word the soldiers had said. Her friend looked very thoughtful. "You know, we've just seen the future," said Marie-France as they turned into the Boulevard Montfleury.

Camped out in the garden, the two girls were woken at four in the morning by the pipe in the kitchen first hammering, then coughing up a mixture of air and brackish water. It sputtered and spat brown gobbets. After ten minutes, the small basin contained a thin layer of rusty silt. The bathroom upstairs was smashed.

"That's it," said Marie-France. "I'm going to have a bath. I'm desperate for a wash. I'm filthy."

Ilse looked at her. "Where?" After all these days of semi-imprisonment, her skin was crawling with dirt.

"Somewhere. I'll find something. Well? Are you coming?"

"Of course I'm coming."

They took the torch and, using it as little as they dared, carefully felt their way down the hill. The night was velvety still. The fountains near the post office were gushing. Stripping to their underwear, Ilse and Marie-France waded into the shallows. Lacking soap, they beat at the clothes with their hands to get the dirt out, rinsing their frocks and spreading them on the dolphins' heads to dry. Then they washed themselves and their underwear, putting it on again in case someone came. Floating luxuriously in the wide stone basin, faces upturned to the sun climbing in the sky, they were still splashing and giggling when the air-raid siren sounded.

"Forget it," said Marie-France. But the sound went on and on. The fifteen-minute signal was the sign for the Resistance to rise up.

In spite of the heat, Ilse was covered in goose pimples. She scrambled out of the fountain and started to dress. "It's started," she said. She clutched at Marie-France. "They'll be bringing out their hidden weapons," said Ilse. "I don't have anything."

They looked at each other: two girls with their clothes clinging to them. Marie-France brandished the torch. Then they both burst out laughing.

Fifteen minutes later a unit of men passed, carrying weapons with armbands sporting the tricolor. Other men passed, walking fast, in a disciplined way. The streets began to fill with people. A small group of disarmed German infantrymen marched through, their French guards jubilant. One of them shouted that the Germans had left. Only a few Polish soldiers were still in Cannes and these too had surrendered. Now women and children also started coming out onto the streets. Rumours circulated: the surrender was true. It was false. The German armour and artillery had all been removed; no, they were waiting in the hills and would return. Then the news that the Germans had all left before dawn was confirmed on the radio. With every rumour or surmise, emotions tore through the gathering crowd like electricity, sparking every way, rippling into outbreaks of cheers.

People were heading for the Palais de Justice. By eight o'clock on the cloudless perfect morning of August 24th, the broad expanse of the Boulevard Carnot was jammed with men, women and children. It was extremely hot, with none of the humidity or haze of previous days. The two girls threaded their way over to the shade of the plane trees. Ilse embraced and was embraced by weeping and laughing strangers, whose cheeks were damp with tears or sweat, who were unshaven, lipstick smeared, who smelt of garlic or dirt, of perfume and ersatz tobacco. She hugged these strangers and was alive; underneath each unknown face was a real person being cracked open, as she was, each prickly conker splitting at last to show its kernel of polished goodness. People started bringing out banners in red, white and blue: sheets torn up, material that had been hoarded and cut up in secret. They swarmed up trees and soon banners hung the length of the long, dead-straight boulevard as far as the eye could see. Men with tricolor armbands and weapons stood on every corner. A small thin man climbed the steps of the courthouse and stood at the top, very upright in his white shirt and FFI armband. News sang through the crowd: it was Commandant Jean-Marie, the leader of the Resistance for the area. He held up his arms and the whole crowd quieted down. He announced that the German occupying army was gone. The Resistance had liberated Cannes. A tumult of noise broke out. The crowd started roaring out the "Marseillaise," Ilse and Marie-France with them; the day of glory had arrived. Tears ran down her friend's face.

Half an hour later news shot through the crowd that German tanks were on their way from the direction of Grasse. In a panic the crowd melted away, a group of resistants remaining defiantly on the steps of the courts.

"Let them come," said Marie-France. "I'm not running." She sat on the steps and Ilse sat beside her with the sun pouring throbbing heat onto them. She waited, staring down at the tiny golden hairs on her white arms, at the marks of strangers' shoes on her dusty espadrilles, holding the torch between her knees. It was a false alarm. Some hours later, marching in single file, a long line of American infantry from the Seventh Army filtered into town. A young man with a dog-tired face threw out packs of Lucky Strike cigarettes. Marie-France caught one. Leading them all was a small boy on a bike waving an American flag.

They left La Californie and returned home, half carrying Maman down the steep hill. The flat was extremely dusty but untouched by bomb damage. They sat her down in the parlour and went to get pails of water from the fountains at the bottom of the hill.

Maman kept asking when Fernand would return, when Jean-Baptiste would be back. Scrubbing floors which ran with filthy water, the two girls on hands and knees looked at each other. Ilse said nothing.

"Very soon, Maman," said Marie-France. "Don't you worry."

Tired out from the cleaning, they went to bed early. While Marie-France settled her mother, Ilse opened the Lucky Strikes and sniffed at the Virginia tobacco. They were going to ration them, to make them last. Marie-France combed and put up her mass of brown curls, much too hot to have hanging down, and for the hundredth time Ilse admired the beautiful sweep of her neck and jaw. Distant noises of rejoicing flared up and down. Silently, they smoked a cigarette each, filling the tiny room with the delicious aroma. This smell and taste marked the beginning of a better time, a better world that she would start to comprehend when she stopped being so tired. Ilse was nearly asleep when Marie-France lit another one. The light flared through her eyelids, illuminating the veins, mapping a different world.

"When I think how I made him wait and how important it was for him to have a good job I can hardly believe I'm the same person," she said casually. "I'm twenty-one soon. If Jean-Baptiste wants, we can get married right away."

"Good idea," said Ilse. She held her breath, then exhaled. She wanted to whisper that it was bad luck to think ahead. She wanted to say that Marie-France should never count on anything.

"And we can have a little reception, maybe at my aunt's. Or perhaps in a restaurant. I wonder if I can get some coupons from someone to make a dress—you'll be my bridesmaid."

"Don't—" said Ilse.

"Don't what?"

"I'm not called Laure," she said, blurting it out. The truth of it was, she only wanted to stop her from jinxing all her hopes. "My real name's Ilse. I'm Jewish. Well, I used to be but I'm baptised now." She did not quite dare say that she was also German. She waited in great anxiety for the response.

Marie-France said nothing. In a moment the tip of the cigarette glowed bright. The rich smell of the smoke wafted over. "Well. I don't see what difference any of that makes. You can still be a bridesmaid," she said.

Two days later the atelier reopened. As Simone put it, war or no war, a girl still had to earn a living. Women in the neighbourhood noticed them taking down the blackout curtains and cleaning the windows, and came in. Everyone wanted new dresses, now that there was something to dress up for. The girls unpicked anything usable, collected coupons and scoured the town for fabric. Evidently, they would be able to sell everything that they could make. They had the radio on all day in the workroom and from time to time, when there was important news, the machines fell idle and everyone listened. General de Gaulle marched at the head of a victory parade across a Paris hung with flags, which the war had apparently left virtually intact. The girls listened to a brass band, crowds cheering, the victory parade passing down the Champs de Mars. With eyes closed, Ilse remembered Paris. When the commentator described the Foreign Legionnaires in the parade she sat up, thrilled. She had not even known that the Legion was in France. When they turned the radio off a buzz of conversation erupted. None of the girls had ever been to Paris.

"That's where I'm going on my honeymoon," said Marie-France.

They were all making plans. Ilse said nothing.

"You need a boyfriend," said Marie-France on the way home.

"I do know somebody—" She stopped. She had never said as much before. The word "boyfriend" hardly applied to François, though perhaps it might to Arnaud, if he was still alive.

Marie-France looked quizzical. "You introduce me. I'll tell you if he's the right kind."

"What's the right kind?"

"The marrying kind. You haven't got a clue about anything, you poor innocent. You leave it to me. I'll frighten him away."

"I might not want to get married," Ilse said.

"And work all your life for Simone? No thanks."

"Well, there are other things to do."

"Such as?"

"There are other types of work."

"A factory? No. Long hours, anyway you're not strong enough. Shop work is boring. And don't tell me you're going to enjoy being something really dumb." Marie-France ticked away her future on her fingers, one by one.

"People find better jobs, you know."

"Such as?"

"Writing—and being a secretary for somebody—you know." Her voice trailed away.

"Writing?" She made a mock curtsy. "Oh, là là. Can you type?"

Ilse shook her head.

"Who's going to employ you then?"

Ilse looked at her. She said nothing.

"A husband, my dear. That's what you need."

Ilse turned and left her right there, on the pavement. She marched round the streets for two hours, drank a marc in one café and a coffee in another and returned late. Even after she and her friend made up, the heavy feeling did not go away.

She lay on her bed, frowning and smoking one of the precious cigarettes that, alongside the rush of real tobacco, gave a painful but necessary taste of François. Through the thin wall, she could hear Maman clattering around the kitchen and dropping things and muttering to herself, while Marie-France did the actual clearing up. Her own mother had qualified as a lawyer, though Hitler had not allowed women to practise. Her father was an educated man who had owned property and a business, though both had been taken away. Children learnt by watching adults move through the world, always assuming that one day these things would happen to them. She had always believed that she would be as they were. That was idiotic. Everything they had had was gone. None of the things that had happened to them had been good. She herself was nothing and had nothing. She had no education or qualifications, just the skill of her hands. There could be no return to that lost world. Yet she had not realised until now how distant it truly was. She was amazed at herself for having had such expectations. What was to become of her? She had no idea. Wrong though it was, she felt very depressed. If she could go to Marseilles, she thought, she might feel better. For down the coast, the war went on. The 148th Division of the Wehrmacht was mounting a fierce defence of Marseilles and Toulon, and François, who wanted and needed to fight, might be there.

In Cannes, the FFI rounded up a huge hall full of Miliciens and collabos. They knocked the hell out of them, then paraded them through the streets to be jeered at. Women who had slept with the Germans were being shaved and put on stands in the marketplace and marched through the streets with swastikas painted on their foreheads. Ilse felt such pity when she passed them. One young whore had a little girl, perhaps five or six years old, who stood at the side of the street with her bare legs streaked with dirt and looked at her mother with a crumpled face. The face of the whore, herself barely more than a child, was puffy and tragic. Ilse did not turn away, as many women did, including Marie-France, who said that they deserved what they were getting. She looked carefully at every girl, in case one of them turned out to be La Petite Louise or Pauline or La Grande, who had wanted no fewer than six children. Ilse looked and then turned away quickly and hoped that they understood that she was not being curious or mean. People did not understand what it meant to be a prostitute. These were not clever girls: they were not wicked at all. It was the fault of the men, who had wanted and taken them. They had been taken in by the times, as so many others had. The haunted look in their eyes made her feel ill. Renée had understood it very well: a degree of self-deception was required in a whore. But Renée's was another of those lost lives that Ilse could never recover.

News came all the time, too much of it. The Legion was in Paris but nothing was said about the liberation of Marseilles. Thousands of people were on the move, trying to get back to their old lives and homes. The newspaper reported that a young man discovered burying his Milice uniform in the garden had been shot on the spot. Public executions went on. Ilse began to avoid the detailed local news. Then she stopped reading the newspapers at all: the radio told her all she wanted to know. A giant hand-painted poster appeared on a wall near the atelier. IL Y A DEUX CHOSES ÉTERNELLES: LA FRANCE ET NOTRE FIDÉLITÉ.* Marie-France said that the hypocrisy of it made her feel sick.

Returning from work, Ilse saw that the streets were suddenly full of FFI men, thousands of them back from the hills. She ran all the way home, rushed up the stairs and burst into the room.

Marie-France was lying flat on the bed. "What's the matter?" She lifted her face. She looked stricken.

"Fernand?"

The head flopped down again. "He's with Maman. It's Jean-Baptiste," she said.

Seven months earlier Marie-France's fiancé had been caught by the Germans in a village and shot out of hand somewhere against a wall.

*There are two eternal things: France and our faith.

They had shot a dozen village men too, at random, to teach them not to help the maquis. Jean-Baptiste had been buried somewhere in those bleak hills, where he had lived for a year. The grave was not even marked and they would never find it. Her brother had brought the news.

Fernand, sitting with his mother—once more in tears—awkwardly turned his beret in his hands. Head down, he shook hands with Ilse, muttered that he had to go. He had things he had to do. He, who had had to wait so long to bring the bad news, could not bear to spend a moment longer with them. He said he would return, sidled out and was gone almost immediately. Ilse saw how the old place, the old ties, even their faces constrained him.

Marie-France lay facedown for a week. She had known Jean-Baptiste all her life; she could not absorb the fact that he could disappear out of the world. She did not cry or complain; she simply did not move. Ilse tried to comfort her and when she could not, she went out and walked. Bad news made her restless, but had the opposite effect upon her friend. On one of these walks she saw half a dozen men sporting the kepi and sash of the Foreign Legion strolling along the Rue d'Antibes. Ilse went up to the nearest one. "Excuse me, Monsieur—where can I find the headquarters of the Legion?"

"Mers el-Kébir. That's where the Legion is, safe and sitting on its fat arse," the Legionnaire said.

She did not understand.

"Most of the Legion chose Vichy, Mademoiselle, to their eternal shame," another Legionnaire said. This one looked at her more nicely. "Only the treizième demi-brigade is here, Mademoiselle. We're with the French commandos."

"The treizième DBLE? You don't know a Willy Lindemann?"

Suddenly the men were laughing.

"You wouldn't perhaps know where he is?"

"Willy? Where did we leave Willy?"

"Where do you think?" the other said. "Hotel Carlton. Only the best for our Willy."

At full pelt, she sped along the Rue d'Antibes. She turned abruptly onto the Croisette; panting, she raced up the steps to the terrace. She stopped and looked. The terrace was half full. She shaded her eyes against the sun. A man in the uniform of the French Foreign Legion was sitting at a table on his own. The sun lit up reddish-gold hair. Urgently, she threaded her way through, pushing a little against tables, jostling people to get closer.

"Willy? Willy!"

He looked to see who was calling. It took him a moment to see, to understand. Then he was on his feet and she was in his arms and then at arm's length again, as he looked at her, then back in his arms. "I never imagined it—" he said.

"Nor me." That was exactly how it felt.

"Sit down, little mouse. Or are you going somewhere?"

She laughed at the idea. Shyly, she stole glances at him. This was a sadder version of Willy; the smiling eyes had more crinkles around them, he was thinner. He jumped up and signalled to a waiter. He seemed smaller than she remembered and a good deal older.

"You haven't changed at all," she said.

"And you are wonderfully different. Listen to you. Look at you. Impeccable French. Altogether a little Frenchwoman and a woman. Like Lore at seventeen—the image—"

"I'm eighteen now."

They spoke at once, were silent together, then both laughed. She explained that she lived in Cannes, that she had found work here as a seamstress. When the waiter came, he ordered champagne, a whole extravagant bottle of it.

"Well, we must celebrate. Every time you can in life, celebrate."

He was amused when she took one of his cigarettes—he had a whole carton of Lucky Strike there on the table—and lit up like a real hardened smoker. The tobacco was strong. The sun on their faces was as strange as the blue sky and the palm trees and the crisp, delicious cold bubbling up of the wine in her nose. None of it was real.

"There is something I heard. You must be strong." When her uncle smiled, his mouth curled up and pleasure crinkled his face. But he did not smile. "It's about your mother."

The people he knew in Hamburg had written to him in Meknès; Marie the maid had sent on his letters. Half Hamburg had been destroyed in raid after raid. The flames had leapt higher than the houses. Fifty-eight churches, including the Michaeliskirche, had burnt down. Thirty thousand civilians had died. Most of them had died instantly, he said, not burnt at all but suffocated by a great hot wind that simply sucked the air out of their lungs. She said nothing. She just watched his mouth and the way his hands held the cigarette and waved it about a little, and the way he never looked away, even when the news was very bad, even when it was news no person should have to bear in any place. The chatter of the crowd on the terrace went indifferently on.

"She had a nursemaid's job in Hamburg," he said. "She found it through friends of mine, good people, the Riemke family. I am sure your mother was happy there."

"I remember," she said. "I was in Meknès, with you, when she went to get the job."

Ilse thought of the big house her mother had described in that one brief letter, set in an avenue lined with trees and with the wonderful view of the river; it should have been safe, but had not been. There had been children in that house, but she would never know anything about them. The white flash of jealousy she felt was instantly subsumed as the hot wind carried them all away.

Ilse tilted back her head and stared without blinking at the way the light filtered through the green of the palms and blurred the edges of the leaves until they were shining silver. In a little while the palm trees steadied themselves. Whatever she had expected and hoped, it was not this.

"Mutti had a plan," Ilse said. Her voice was very flat and very far away. "I mean, she was planning for me to go back to Germany. With proper papers. I chose not to. Vati thought it was too dangerous."

"He was right. It was," said Willy.

"She was so certain that they would win."

She was gulping a little, swallowing air.

"So were most people. Ilse, people can decide things meaning well, from the best of reasons and sometimes they are wrong. When I sent her to Hamburg, I thought it was safer in a big city and easier to find work. It wasn't safe. And I let Toni send you back to France. That was wrong, too."

"Why did you let it happen? Was it because of money?"

Her flat voice went on asking things the old Ilse would never have asked.

Willy sighed and lit another cigarette. "Not money, no. I don't know. I knew that I had to rejoin the Legion. I had to fight the Nazis, or at least try. And then you would be on your own with Toni. Because I couldn't ever make Toni do anything she didn't want to do. And I suppose I didn't want to give her an excuse."

"An excuse for what?"

He looked down at his hands. "For leaving me. She was so necessary to me, but she went her own way. I didn't think that she would look after you properly, she was so sure she could not—you know Toni and her certainties. She seemed so certain that you should be with your parents. My darling girl, there is much to blame me for."

Ilse thought that she did blame him, but it was all too long ago. For a time, neither of them found anything to say.

"Did she leave you?"

"I don't know. Probably. I know she's not in Meknès now. I heard that she's in Casablanca."

"I'm so sorry."

He brushed that aside. "Your mother wrote a letter which travelled half round Africa before it reached me in Eritrea. In 1941, but written earlier. She was frantic, that you were missing in France. She blamed herself, she wanted me to try and find you. I couldn't leave the Legion—I wrote and told her that."

"So she knew that she had made a mistake," said Ilse very calmly, glimpsing the dark abyss of her mother's despair and pushing it away from her at once.

"Where is Otto?"

"Vati got caught. He was deported back to Germany. Nearly two and a half years ago. What do you think happens to the people in those camps?" Willy was looking at his glass. "Willy, could he still be alive?"

Then his eyes dropped. He could not meet her eyes because it was too much to bear. With a jolt, she understood that her father was dead and Willy knew it. A cold tremor ran from her head right to the soles of her feet.

"Tell me," she said in a tight voice.

"I don't know. There were stories in the American newspapers about camps. We'll see when we get into Germany. The world will see," he said. "Every German battalion has a movie operator, did you know that? Wherever they go, they take miles and miles of film. On the Russian front, everywhere. No matter how bad it is. In Sicily, we caught a battalion and found the film and showed it. Everyone will be made to watch it, when it's all over."

Willy had faith, still, in the goodness of people. Ilse took her hand back and lifted the glass. The prickling drink seemed to go straight to the ice-cold place where her heart was.

"Where have you been? When did you arrive in France?"

He had landed on August 16th at Cavalaire-sur-Mer, proud to be one of the first Legionnaires to touch the soil of France. His war, he said, had been fine. There had been action here and there, in Eritrea, in Italy at a place called Monte Cassino. She nodded. The main thing was that he was here and safe. The Legion was going after the retreating Nineteenth Army into Germany. First, they wanted to liberate Marseilles and in particular Fort Saint-Nicolas, where their recruits were traditionally tested and screened. It was a matter of honour. They would be moving on almost immediately. It was a precise conversation and every word was crisp and unreal. Delicately, he looked at her and then away again, as though the weight of his eyes was too much as, indeed, at times it was. When he took her hand he squeezed it and very gently she then let go.

"You know," she said, smiling as much as she could, "I've been here before. I came to the Carlton to deliver clothes. For the atelier. They always told me to go by the back door. This is the first time I've sat on the terrace."

He took a long pull at the cigarette and looked at her. "Perhaps you have a friend I could invite to dinner here? Several friends?" It had always been one of his gifts, knowing how to say the one thing that made everything all right.

When they parted, Ilse walked until her feet hurt. It was good to substitute a real ache for the deep sorrow that she could not talk about, not to anyone. There had been many friends: Albert and François and Renée and Madame Dumont, who had probably died in Marseilles, because that was what happened to people when you loved them. She had Marie-France. She went home and harassed and cajoled her until she got out of bed.

The three of them had dinner that night at the Carlton. Marie-France, famously late for everything, had to be urged at each stage of dressing to get ready at all. At the hotel, she ate and drank and danced and flirted herself into a semblance of happiness and then from that into something closer to the real thing. Ilse knew that her friend, who was making an enormous effort to appear normal, must seem very hard and uncaring to Willy. It was Ilse's fault, because she had not found a way to tell her friend that her parents were dead. Marie-France believed that she had long been orphaned. She could not resurrect and kill them in one sentence. She turned and turned the words in her head, but it was hard to explain to anyone who had not known them what lives her parents had lived; yet more impossible to explain how they had died. Telling people things never did anybody any good. Willy smiled at her and Marie-France drank champagne and grew giggly and Ilse, with so many things in her head, smiled back and was silent and went on feeling as though it was all happening to somebody else.

They only had two days and one of them was already over. Willy got hold of a jeep and petrol. Early the next morning they drove along the coast.

"I want you to see the most beautiful town on the Riviera," he said. "I always said to Toni, 'If one of us dies, I shall go and live in Nice.' "

They walked along the Promenade des Anglais and looked at the beach.

"There is a decent Germany," said Willy. "People like us."

"Life must go on," she said in her new, calm voice. "Even in Germany."

He pressed her arm. "I mean it, little cynic. There is the Germany of good people, of Goethe's *Faust* and of Bach and Beethoven. When this is over, that Germany will return."

Ilse knew that the Germany of Heinrich Hoffmann, of *Struwwelpeter*, would prevail. "Will you ever return?" He shook his head. "Me neither. I'm never going back," she said. She had nobody to return to.

"Of course not. You're coming to Meknès," he said. "You're coming to me."

In the lobby of the Hotel Negresco the doorman saluted Willy, resplendent in his uniform. They walked along the red carpet to the restaurant and settled at a table with a brilliantly white cloth. Ilse sat in the sunlight shafting in from the huge window onto the Baie des Anges. While Willy read the menu and considered what delicacy they should sample, she saw herself entering the little white room with the small bed and the sun slanting across the floor. Turning, she found herself reflected in the mirror on the wardrobe door, grown large.

"You're too old for school. Time you found a decent job," said the familiar voice. Toni swam into the image and stood, perfect as ever, red lips smiling but shaking her knowing head as their eyes met in mutual recognition of the impossibility of that return, of any return, for either of them.

That evening, Willy went foraging. He carried boxes of K rations up the stairs to the Bonnards' flat. These included white sugar and two huge boxes of Lucky Strike cigarettes, and tins of the Nescafé the Americans preferred to coffee beans. She found chewing gum and a powder to disinfect water and Mars bars, which were mostly chocolate, and dozens of tins of beef and ham. He had liberated four bottles of bourbon and four pairs of men's army boots, really strong ones, which she could trade for something. When they said their farewells, she clung to him like a little girl. They would not lose each other now, he said, stroking her hair. The Legion would liberate Fort Saint-Nicolas in Marseilles and she should leave a message there, or in the barracks near the seafront in Nice, care of the treizième DBLE.

Within weeks, the skies turned grey and the temperature dropped abruptly. It rained. The sudden bad weather jolted people to their senses. The public roistering finished. The Germans had burnt many stocks of food. The Allies were still at war and the Germans were resisting strongly in Holland and elsewhere. On the Eastern front, Warsaw had risen against the Germans, on the assumption that the huge Russian forces encamped outside the city would come to their aid. Warsaw was burning; the Poles could smell the smoke from fifteen kilometres away. The Russian army remained stationary. They waited as the Germans obliterated the freedom fighters and then, in reprisal, the city centre, reducing it to rubble, building by building, street by street. She prayed that François was not there. The French forces, Willy with them, were sweeping across France. In the middle of November they were involved in the battles for Belfort and Mulhouse, then the defence of Strasbourg. Next came Colmar. It looked as though Willy and the treizième DBLE would be among the first combatants to go into Germany. It was not to be expected that he would find time to write.

France had no rolling stock to transport food. No petrol could be had and so many bridges had been blown that it was in any case impossible to drive anywhere. People were stuck where they were. Nobody could buy anything worth having. In the atelier, they had used up every scrap of fabric and now remade old clothes.

Trailing home with a bag of onions she had snapped up in the market, Ilse found François standing in the street outside their flat. The shock was so great that she dropped the bag. He had gone to the mountains to see her. Père Lemusier had given him the address she had left there, of Marie-France in Cannes. He had a jittery look. Perhaps he would not even have gone as far as climbing the stairs up to the second floor, had she not happened to come home at that time.

"I'm going away. I had to say goodbye," he said.

She took him past the parlour, where Maman sat and muttered to herself all day, through to the kitchen. While she chopped onions to fry with potatoes, François smoked and watched and made her clumsy. He said that he missed the Polish miners from the maquis. They were his friends. She understood from his manner of speaking that she was not a friend; she was probably a duty. The onion juice stung her hands and eyes. She peeled potatoes and kept her face turned away.

"Are you going back to Poland?"

"I tried, but there was no transport. I'm going into Germany with the Polish Brigade."

"What's the news from Warsaw?"

"They're all gone. The Russians sat and watched the Germans massacre them. The Americans and the British left them to it. The Jews have all been liquidated and the patriots. The students, my friends, anyone who might have survived—they're all dead." These were the flat cadences of a person with no hope.

"I'm sorry," he said. "I didn't mean to upset you."

"Onions," she said, unable to help herself.

"But what is it, my poor little siostrzyszka?"

Any sympathy undid her. Gradually, she recovered herself.

"I felt upset because of my parents," she managed at last. "It's because they're both dead." Then she stood awkwardly, red-nosed and hideous in front of a spitting frying pan, loathing herself for finding this excuse, this misuse of the truth, this double betrayal of self.

Marie-France took her to one side. "Who is this fellow? One of those people from the maquis?" Evidently she did not like the look of him.

"He has nowhere to stay in Cannes." She shrugged.

"I suppose he can sleep on Fernand's bed, if you like."

Obviously it never entered her head that he might be the boyfriend. Ilse made up the pull-down bed in the sitting room. Exhausted, they went to bed early.

In the early hours Ilse crept into the sitting room and sat and listened to his breathing. Behind the shutters and curtains the room was pitch-black. Her teeth chattered with cold, but she was afraid to go back, even for a blanket, in case she woke him. He was afraid of his dreams; she was afraid of everything. She turned the request over in her head. François, please take me with you. Why? What would she say then? In her head she prepared the impossible shameful words: she loved him. She wanted to be with him. Even in the dark, her face burnt at the idea of saying it. She prepared another statement: she wanted to be a Jew. Did she?

He could not know that she had taken the Catholic faith. She had never told him, any more than she had told him that her mother was a Protestant. For him, she was a Jew, as her father was. She did not know whether a person could stop being one. The Nazis did not think so. Her head was burning, her feet like ice. In their different ways her parents had both been so difficult. If either of them had told her about their religion, then she could have been what they were. But neither had let her in. They had not needed faith, but she did. What they had in common was stubbornness. That was her inheritance. She would have to hold to what she was now.

He was so quiet. She strained to hear. Perhaps he was awake and knew she was there. She opened her mouth but she could not force a word out. Surely, she thought, surely he knew.

"Are you awake, siostrzyszka?" How soft his voice was. She must have dozed off on the sofa.

"Mm," she said.

"It calms me, being with you."

"Good."

"Will you hold my head?"

The moment had come. She moved towards him, knelt at the side of the pull-down bed and took his head in her hands, preparing to say the words.

"When I was eleven I used to tease her," he said. "By the time I was thirteen I knew she was dying. I used to run home from school, worried that she would not be there. She had red hair like yours. Such big eyes. A child doesn't always know what is happening, but Polinka knew. I tried to make every minute matter. I used to draw funny pictures, to make her laugh. But by the end she was too tired and it was cruel, the exertion was too much for her. Everybody tiptoed around and she hated that. She wanted as much energy around as she could get. Told me to go down to the yard and stand on my hands and turn cartwheels, so she could watch. They lifted her to the window. That pale face, laughing."

"What was wrong with her?"

"Tuberculosis and blood sickness. They sent her to the mountains, but nothing could be done."

His head was warm between her hands, his breathing relaxed. "Thank you, siostrzyszka."

The faint grey of day glimmered under the curtains. She happened to have red hair; that was all. He knew to drain all the magic out of their connection. A man did not want to marry his beloved sister. She went over it, over and over. Fiercely she told herself that, like Polinka, the child he had saved would live on in his head forever.

She made him some of the Nescafé. She had almost got used to the taste. They sat opposite each other at the table and he drank the stuff with little grimaces.

"What a Frenchman," she said. "Only real coffee for you."

He was quiet; she had succeeded in calming him. The shape of him against the kitchen cupboard was something to remember always, the way he sat, upright, never lounging as he used to, because the hard back of the chair would hurt.

After he had gone she walked through Cannes sightlessly. As soon as she heard that the road down into the north of Marseilles was open for civilian traffic, Ilse asked for a couple of days' holiday. She told Marie-France that she needed to find out what had happened to Madame Dumont. This was correct but not accurate. Her true unhappiness lay in Marseilles and she wanted to immerse herself in it. Very early one morning, she took the first bus north out of Cannes. The coast roads were not yet open in places; the route circuitous. She stared out at the rain.

The bus came in through La Capelette, a part of town Ilse hardly knew and so it took her a while to get her bearings and see that the Rue de Rome, packed with American trucks, actually ran parallel to the Boulevard Dugommier. She had brought several sachets of the curé's herbs with her and she made a stew and flavoured it carefully and then soup, from the bones. Madame Dumont exclaimed several times what a good cook she was.

While the old lady rested, she walked behind the few houses at the rim, which the Nazis had preserved, up across the rubble of the Vieux Port to the Maison Diamantée. The air, like the ground, was grey. She made her way across to where she thought the brothel might have been. She wanted to say prayers for her father and mother, and for Renée, but the ground was uneven and hurt her feet through the thin soles of her shoes and the wind whipped at her. Instead, she went back to the Maison Diamantée and leant against the walls for shelter, looking out over the harbour. It was full of boats. One after another the troopships and boats steamed in, packed full of provisions that went straight out again on the long line of trucks carrying everything away to the army.

In Snappy's Bar, she left a message for Raymond, who left word the next day that he would meet her on the quay. He turned up half an hour late. They embraced, laughing, and he bought her a drink. He had had a few glasses already. He was flush from black market business. The Marseillais being as they were, it was possible to abstract one of the American trucks if you paid enough. He complained about the expense of persuading an American driver to go AWOL, especially when you did not know what lay inside the sealed boxes. Still, the risk was worth taking and business was good.

"We'll drink to the real heroes of the liberation," he said, winking. "The cheminots who blew up so many railway lines. It was the genius of Arnaud. He sat down and planned it all. And I am proud to say that I played my small part."

"Where is Arnaud?" He shrugged. "Is he alive?"

Raymond did not know; his stubby hands waved in the air. Ilse wondered what his real name was and whether she would ever find out. Barely six months had passed, and already the young heroes of the maquis seemed part of a great romanticised past.

"How is Paul? Does he know what happened to Madame Renée? And the girls?"

Raymond pulled an expressive face. "Paul is all right. The girls who came back are still in business. They deported so many, the ones who were let out from Fréjus, they filtered back within days," he said. "You know, everything they had was stolen. And they had almost nothing. By us, by the French. What salauds, eh? Poor Renée. Not one of the ones sent to Paris came back—not yet," he said, seeing her expression.

"They do come back. Raymond, I saw François with the maquis, and afterwards," she said, suddenly bold. "He told them nothing. I know that. They hurt him very badly. I saw the scars. He's gone into Germany, to fight the Germans."

"Sure."

"Don't you believe me?" Raymond sighed and sucked his teeth. "I know he's on the right side," she said. Even as her words came out, Ilse wished them unsaid. She wished she had not mentioned him at all.

"Sure he is. His own," and he drained his glass and put it down very firmly. "He'd better not come back to Marseilles."

Soon Ilse got up to go. Head down, she scurried along the waterfront, to say a prayer for Renée in Saint-Ferréol.

On the last of her days off, the weather was better and Ilse went down to the harbour and took the boat across to the Château d'If. It was a whim, just to see if the dark romance the guidebook had promised still existed somewhere. But when the boat docked and the few soldier sightseers left, she could not bring herself to get off. The book had recommended the spectacular view from the old chapel, but she did not care to see anything picturesque. She stared at the horizon where Africa was and felt tremulously sorry for herself. After a while she noticed someone watching her. Also leaning on the railing of the boat was a man in British battledress. Tall and gaunt, he seemed the shadow of a much bigger man. She thought of Arnaud. Though this man was much older, she detected a small likeness. It was something to do with the easy way he stood there and the curve of his mouth.

"Don't you like castles? Or is something wrong with it?"

He spoke French like Tommies did, full of slang, but with rigorous grammar underneath. He had been taught it long ago, he said. His manner was gentle. She asked, Was he with the RAF? No. He had soft hazel eyes, a long face, dark hair, had come straight off a ship. From? Hong Kong. Ilse knew nothing about Hong Kong.

"Was the war bad there?"

"No worse than anywhere, I expect."

She went back to staring at the sea.

He spoke slowly in English. "Do you speak English?"

"A little."

In Meknès, other girls had struggled with English, but she had managed to learn a few phrases. Maths had been a very different matter. In maths, as in most subjects, her ignorance was as wide as this vast ocean.

"Mam'selle, excuse me." He was still looking at her. "What are you doing here?" He waved a general hand at the scenery. He was easy to understand, not like the Americans, but Ilse could not think what to reply. It was too complicated. Her intention was to make herself thoroughly miserable, but she could not tell him that. She did not know how to be unhappy in English. The thought brought a smile. He smiled back. The smile improved him.

She reflected. "I do like to be beside the seaside," she announced.

He laughed so much that he coughed violently. He recovered quite soon, but she dared not try her English again.

He was to report to a convalescent home along the coast in Cannes, on the fringes of La Californie. Did she by any chance know where that was? She explained that she lived in Cannes and was going back there the next day. She told him about the bus station and what way to go to find it and when the bus was going. Once he got to Cannes, she said, everyone would know where La Californie was. At the quayside, she said goodbye and walked away, feeling better for having made someone happy, even if it was just for a moment.

Leaving Madame Dumont at breakfast, neither of them caring for long goodbyes, Ilse was at the bus station early. The bus for Aix was half full when the Englishman got on, carrying his kitbag. She nodded and looked away. He sat a few rows behind her. Glancing round, she saw that he was immersed in a book. It made him laugh softly from time to time. At Aix-en-Provence they spoke briefly. Further along the road at lunchtime it seemed rude not to accept a glass of beer. He jingled coins in his pocket, said he was feeling rich. He said his name was Thomas Halladay. He would not have to fight again; apparently his condition, whatever it was, meant that he was being invalided out.

"Don't you want to go straight home, to England?"

He shrugged. "They don't send us back in poor condition. Don't want to frighten people too much."

"It's good, isn't it, not to have to fight?"

"Ah," he said. "Anyway, I'm too old."

She was too polite to ask.

"Thirty-three." He grimaced. She thought that he looked older. "An old man to you."

She could not deny it. Then she thought that Willy had to be well over forty. By the time they were on the last of many buses, rattling down from the hills into Cannes, it seemed ungenerous not to help him find the place.

"You didn't tell me your name," he said as they walked from the bus station.

"Ilse," and she paused. Without thinking, she had used her real name for the first time. "But some people call me Laure."

"Fair enough. I'm Thomas, but my friends call me Tom."

She thought perhaps he was laughing at her, but he wasn't.

He held out his hand. It was warm. "How do you do?" he said in English and was amused by her puzzled look. "You say the same thing back. I know, it doesn't make sense."

"How do you do?" she replied.

The convalescent home had been set up in a huge Belle Epoque house. It was dinnertime. Through a glass door, she saw rows of men sitting at long tables. All the heads turned as they entered. A pleasant woman greeted them, took them to a little office.

"Don't leave me here," he whispered, while the woman was finding his name on her list. When he smiled, she understood that it was a joke.

"Come back and have tea, whenever you like," she said to Ilse. "There's a café here and we need visitors. The men really appreciate it."

"This man really would."

Walking to the gate, Ilse passed tall windows lit up with the curtains drawn back and saw Tom joining the crowd, indistinguishable from the uniformed mass.

Three weeks later, not long before Christmas, Ilse came in to find Marie-France dressed in new high heels and applying lipstick.

"What happened?"

"I've been thinking," she said. "I can't be unhappy all the time. I'm going to marry a British conqueror in uniform. Or an American. So. Where can I meet someone?" She brushed her hair vigorously, turned and held it up in a different, more sophisticated style, the glossy curls piled high on her head. "What do you think?" The style suited her.

"I know just the place," said Ilse.

At the convalescent home, silent men sat in rows in the garden with their faces turned to the wintry sun. She looked at their RAF wings glinting. Tom jumped to his feet and came to greet them. "I'd given up hope," he said. He seemed so pleased to see her that Ilse felt herself blushing. She introduced Marie-France.

"I shall talk to some of the others," she announced, moving on. Excitement visibly fluttered along the row as she sauntered by in her high heels.

"It's good of you to come," said Tom. "Not to mention bringing Rita Hayworth along." She noticed that his eyes had a twinkle to them.

"Who's that?"

He laughed. "A film star."

"Mm," she said. Neither of them could take their eyes off Marie-France, working her way down the row, for all the world like a cattle merchant looking at hooves and teeth. Of course, no man could resist such glamour.

"Really," she said, "I came because it's good for my English. I have only a little English."

"I'll teach you," he said. "Come and have tea. It's cold out here."

Tea was served in the cafeteria, and cakes. They fell easily into conversation. Tom lent her his book, by someone called Aldous Huxley, a writer he described as both very funny and very serious.

"Very good for your English," he said. Again, she had the impression he was laughing at her, but he smiled so nicely that that hardly seemed possible.

Marie-France appeared in the doorway and waved.

"My friend says we have to go."

"Oh dear," he said. "She's done already. Will you come again?"

She rose. "Of course. I have to return your book, don't I?"

"Read fast," he said.

Marie-France linked her arm through Ilse's as they left. "I don't like these British men. I'd prefer an American. Better looking. Not so sick."

The book he had lent her was called *Crome Yellow*. With her smattering of English, this book was impossible. It was written in a style of such complexity that she looked up twenty-one words in the first three paragraphs and, reading the page again, felt no wiser as to what it actually meant.

On Christmas Eve, Marie-France announced that she was going to a nightclub frequented by the military. Ilse went with her. After all, she had five words of English to each one of Marie-France's. She took a whisky bottle and filled it with cold tea. It was a trick from the brothel.

"We'll have this when the barman fills the men's glasses."

Marie-France marvelled at her. The place was packed with soldiers. The band was good and all the girls were dancing; hardly anyone in the place was over twenty-five. The waiter ushered them to a table close to the dance floor. Right away, a man asked Marie-France to dance. With a wink to Ilse, she rose. She danced beautifully.

Ilse looked from face to face, trying to choose the right man for Marie-France from all those who were watching her. A young man suddenly appeared and asked her to dance; Ilse said she did not intend to. She had noticed a tall blond American staring at Marie-France; as if prompted, he stepped forward and cut in. He danced elegantly and they looked good together. Ilse smoked and watched them. Somebody waved. She ignored him; then saw that it was Tom. As the dance ended, he started to make his way to their table. Marie-France was making no move to sit down but stayed where she was, talking to the tall blond man who still held her loosely in his arms. "I've been watching you. You're even more of a dark horse than I thought."

She liked the expression. The music started up, so she did not have to say anything. She noticed how Tom drank his whisky, throwing it back and placing the glass on the table with exaggerated precision. All the RAF men drank like fish.

He leant over, spoke near her ear. "Will you dance with me?"

She shook her head. When she saw how disappointed he looked, she stood. He held her carefully and respectfully, as though she were very fragile. Drink made him more, not less, gentle. She closed her eyes, remembered how she had felt in François's arms, waited. With Tom, she felt a sort of ease at moving, at being held by a man. When she opened her eyes again he was looking at her intently. The song ended. She would not dance with him again. Instead, they sat together and she drank the cold tea and they watched the American sergeant teaching Marie-France to jitterbug.

"You're not like your friend," he said. "You take your time."

She pretended not to know what he meant.

They were very late home. Annie, who had sat with Maman, grumbled. Marie-France got into bed. They smoked a last companionable cigarette.

"Do you like your American?"

"Gene? He's nice. Yes. I like lots of people."

"No you don't," said Ilse. "What do you really think?"

"Attach yourself to someone who climbs and he'll take you with him." She inhaled deeply. She had a new pack, courtesy of the sergeant. "He's going to take me out on Friday."

"You can't fool me, you know."

"What do you mean by that?"

"You're not a vine that climbs and has no feelings."

Marie-France exhaled. "I dream sometimes about the baby I would have had with Jean-Baptiste. He'll never be born. Then I wake up crying. I don't want to feel like that my whole life."

Ilse could not imagine a baby. Instead, she thought with longing about the book she would have typed for Albert.

"I really so much wish I'd had a book with someone I know," she burst out.

Marie-France laughed until she got hiccups.

Gene, stationed in the quartermaster's office, could get a pass in the evenings and as often as he could, he took Marie-France dancing. If he could get an afternoon off and the atelier was closed, they went sightseeing along the coast. It began to look like a courtship.

"He's mad about me," she said. "Sex mad, too. Hands everywhere."

Ilse could understand that.

"But do you really, really like him?"

"Of course I do."

On these too-quiet afternoons Ilse took to calling at the cafeteria of the convalescent home. She always found people there to chat to. It was not romance, she told Marie-France. It was to learn English, which would always be useful. Tom, who was generally reading, put his book down at once when she appeared, was always pleased to see her. She got very little further in understanding the book, though a story in it about a dwarf named Hercules and his anguish at producing a monstrous, but normal, son upset her. While quite unlike what she knew of Albert's work, it had the same brutal but beautiful candour.

"What are you thinking about?" he asked.

"Nothing." She thought of something. "What did you do in Hong Kong?"

"I was in a prisoner of war camp," he said. "Until one day I decided to leave."

"The camps here were terrible," she said. "Filthy, people were starving. Awful."

"They weren't too good there either."

She pushed the bad memories away.

"Tom, what did you do before the war?"

"Ah. I went to Hong Kong to make my fortune," he said.

"And did you?"

He shook his head. "I'm afraid not. I buried one there. I'll have to go back and find it one day." She had learnt to smile at his jokes.

In civilian life, Tom had worked in a bank. He had a good head for figures, he said. She could see that he was an intelligent, pleasant person, if a little on the quiet side.

"Will you take tea?" She brandished the pot.

"Sugar and milk, please. Say when."

RAF tea was premixed with sugar. It tasted much too sweet.

"Do you know why?"

Ilse thought. "Because tea taken on its own attracts ants," she said.

He laughed helplessly for a long time. "You sound like something out of a Noël Coward play. How old are you?"

"Eighteen."

"That's awful," he said. "I could be your father."

She said nothing. She could not speak about her parents. The thought that she would never see her mother's face again brought the familiar wave of undiluted helplessness and grief. She had suppressed her pain for so long; now she was training herself never to think about them at all.

One teatime Tom did not turn up. She went up to the ward, found him in bed, shaking with hot sweats. It was malaria.

"I'm all right," he said. "I just need bed and quinine."

The condition was brought on by the winter, he said, and the bitter cold.

"What can you do to cure it?"

"Nothing. It's just a hangover from the East. It'll go."

His whole body jittered helplessly on the bed and yet he smiled at her, his teeth knocking together. His hazel eyes had lost their shine, but they still looked at her with the same intensity. She noticed for the first time what long eyelashes he had. In profile, he was actually quite attractive; he had an elegant nose and a very high forehead. She decided that his was the face of an intellectual.

He recovered slowly; he put on a little weight. He taught her many words, swearwords and then more serious ones. It turned out that they were both orphans. He had been married, but his wife had died in Hong Kong. She wanted to ask about his wife, but he deflected the question easily.

"So what was Hong Kong like? I mean, in the war."

"Oh, you know. The usual. A spot of bother."

That was his humour, the quiet understatement and then a sideways conspiratorial glance, to see if she had got it. With other people he spoke differently. He seemed to see her as a special friend. He did not want to talk about the past and neither did she. Instead, they talked about the future. Tom dreaded the return home. French prisoners of war were returning; the newspapers were full of pictures of receptions at station platforms, of the brave soldiers kissing wives and sweethearts. He found these pictures amusing.

"It won't be like that in England," he said. "We have too many heroes."

How sad, she thought, that when he went home there would be nobody to meet him. But then he, like her, was the sort who stood apart.

An exchange was organised by the Red Cross: German civilians for French deportees. Those who had worked in Germany as farm labourers came home fat, with good-quality clothes. They were surprised at how badly those who had stayed in France had fared. The first walking skeletons returned, women who had been in the camp of Mauthausen. Again, she had a vision, quickly suppressed, of the river of human misery that flowed through Gurs. The skeletal women were whisked away. Nobody wanted to hear those depressing stories. Nobody wanted to see pictures like that in the newspapers. Nothing was sure. When the war ended, she thought, she would go through the camps and look for Otto herself. But the thought of returning to Germany made her sick with anxiety.

"Tom, do you think any of those in the German camps will survive?"

He did not answer.

"Tom?"

He seemed far away. He could not talk about the camps any more than she could. Then she saw that to open this discussion at all, he had to be told who she really was. It should have been easier to disclose her secret, but it was not. It grew harder each time.

"You do know," she said, then paused and chose slightly different words. "You should know—I'm German. A refugee from the Nazis. And I'm half Jewish. Nobody knows here. Not even Marie-France really understands."

His eyes came back to her. "You're full of surprises."

"Do you mind?"

"Why should I mind? I don't mind who you are," he said. "None of us are what we thought we were, are we? We've all had to become something else. The main thing is that whatever you are, it doesn't stop you seeing me."

Incredibly, that was all it meant to him. Perhaps all Englishmen were this tolerant. She stared at her feet, absorbing this. Glancing up, she caught him staring at her in that intent way he had. On the boat that day, as the others went off to tour the Château d'If, he had stood at the railing watching her with just this look. It was a very flattering look. She thought about it. It was as though she had something he wanted badly.

"Tom? That day you docked in Europe, in Marseilles. You were supposed to go straight to La Californie, weren't you?"

He kept on giving her that look.

"But you didn't."

He produced his most charming smile. "I went sightseeing. And I met someone," he said.

Gene had nowhere private to take Marie-France. Sometimes, Ilse found them grappling on her friend's bed in their little room, intense struggles from which Marie-France emerged energised and pink-cheeked. She refused to go to a hotel: nice girls did not do that. Maman was always in the way, or Ilse was. Marie-France made certain of that. "If I fall—and there's no certainty of it—it won't be before Germany does," she said.

The Ardennes offensive terrified everyone with its unexpectedness and accuracy. Hitler chose the precise place where the Germans had reached France last time and where they had defeated the French so unexpectedly. This was where François might die and Willy. Ilse felt ill at the thought.

Tom scoffed at her fears. "We'll defeat them. This is their last attempt."

Such certainty began to be reassuring. Then the news started getting better all the time. The Allies, racing to get across the Rhine, forded it on March 7th. Inside Germany, soldiers were surrendering in vast numbers. Eventually the Russians and the Americans met. Everything was easing. With good air force contacts, a person could hop just about anywhere they wanted to in France. Gene announced that he was going to take Marie-France to Paris because she had never been there. That, said Marie-France drily, was not the real reason. She asked Simone for a holiday. Gene cadged them a lift in a plane. They would be there from Sunday to Wednesday. Jubilant, he came to collect her, bearing a bag of first-rate provisions for the stay-at-homes.

Marie-France returned with cheeks as pink as ever. Ilse had never seen her more full of life and mischief. Proudly, she showed off three tiny splinters of diamond on her finger. Admiring the ring, Ilse liked better the confiding way Marie-France leant against Gene without ever letting go of his hand. Maman cried when she understood the good news.

"Did you find the café?"

"Café Tournon, Tuesday afternoon, two o'clock. The big round table. We had the hot chocolate. We sat for two hours but nobody came. We were there, weren't we, Gene?"

"Sure. You know my fiancée, she's on time everywhere."

They all laughed, knowing Marie-France. Ilse wanted to say that the rendezvous was for three o'clock, but then she thought that it could not matter. Albert was never late. Sitting for two hours, they could not possibly have missed a very tall, unusually ugly but attractive man with a squint so noticeable you just could not look away. So she merely thanked her.

When they were alone, Marie-France told her what had happened. They had wandered through Paris, lovers in every respect but the crucial one. Gene had spent several intensely frustrating nuits blanches in bed with a naked but still chaste Marie-France. Ilse started to ask her friend if she was absolutely sure about him.

"Don't start," said Marie-France. "You can see that I'm very, very happy."

So she desisted.

On Sunday she went to the convalescent home. Tom said how much he had missed not seeing her that week. She laughed and smiled and was cheerful. There was nothing to do but be cheerful. He noticed what good spirits she was in and complimented her. She thought about how much older Tom was. He had certainty about things. He seemed to be right all the time. People like François were not safe. With François, it had never been possible to anticipate anything, though anticipation was her greatest defence. With someone like François there would be an endless procession of surprises, most of which would be unwelcome.

Tom gave her an easier book by a writer he admired called

Rosamond Lehmann. The book, about a girl growing up, was full of intimate feelings between men and women with a constant note of sadness, of loneliness, that she recognised in herself and that carried on resonating in her. Tom enjoyed her surprise, that this should be his taste. He had scribbled a bit, he said. She, with her quick intelligence, should try. Alone, she wondered how he had divined the ambition she kept secret, almost from herself. The author obviously was German and probably Jewish.

The next time she saw him she ventured the question. "Is she German?"

"Oh no, English," said Tom.

"Are you sure?"

"As English as me."

She understood, finally, how different his England must be, where a person wrote such things and did not have to hide her surname and yet could still be English.

That evening Ilse opened the back of the photograph frame, took out the fifty-dollar note and presented it to a stunned Marie-France, insisting that she use the money to buy fabric for her wedding dress. The girls made a collection to buy her shoes. Marie-France persuaded Simone to let her have a length of the most beautiful oyster satin that Simone's sister-in-law had squirrelled away. They cut and fitted it in the atelier and Ilse did all the embroidery, hand-scalloping the hem. As soon as the war was over, as soon as Gene was demobilised, as soon as the wedding happened, Marie-France would be gone. All the time she sewed she kept asking herself what she was going to do. The next time Ilse had a couple of days off she suggested to Tom that they might spend the time together.

"What do you want to do?"

Life, she said, ought to contain more celebrations. She would surprise him. On the train to Marseilles, she asked him where he was from. Perhaps he was a country boy, from a village. She had never thought to enquire before. No, he said. He was from a small industrial town in the northwest of England called Birkenhead. It was very near Liverpool, which was a great seaport. She nodded politely. It would be just like Marseilles.

On a bright spring day, she led him down the steps from the Gare St. Charles, along the Boulevard Dugommier and down the Canebière to the seafront. It took a while to find the perfect restaurant with an awning and a view of the sea. She insisted that she must do the ordering.

"What's this all about?"

"We are going to try a very special dish only made in Marseilles," she said.

These plates were almost too hot to touch, the reddish-browny liquid seemed an odd colour and the rascasse slightly sour. Her mother had imagined something lighter and creamier. Still, Ilse quite liked the taste of bouillabaisse.

Tom managed a couple of spoonfuls, then put his spoon down. "Very nice," he said. He was frowning.

"What is it?"

"It's all bits," he said. "I mean, with all this ocean—just look at that water out there—you'd think you could go to a restaurant and get a decent piece of fish."

It was uncanny. This, of all possible comments, deeply moved her.

"You're right," she said. "Tom, tell me, what would you like to have?"

"Lobster," he said. "We're celebrating, aren't we? I'm hoping you'll tell me what and why. So let's go mad."

Ilse did something very strange and unexpected, which she had never seen anyone do. She laughed uncontrollably and at the same time she cried. Tears flowed down her cheeks. She could not speak for several minutes. He patted her on the back, offered his handkerchief. Then he took her hand in his two warm hands and would not let her have it back. As speech returned, she tried for several helpless moments to say that nothing was wrong. With one thing and another, she never did manage to explain.

Acknowledgements

This book was championed by Charles Walker of PFD, London. Robin Desser of Alfred A. Knopf, in New York, and Courtney Hodell of Fourth Estate, in London, edited it with great skill. My mother kindly gave her advice, as did Dennis McKay. My husband was, as always, a source of inspiration and endless support. I thank them all.